THE SECRET BILLIONAIRE

THE BALTIMORE BOYS
BOOK 4

SAMANTHA SKYE

ISBN 978-0-6457144-7-0 (ebook)

ISBN 978-0-6457144-8-7 (Paperback)

ISBN 978-0-6459897-8-6 (Alternative Paperback)

Cover Design: Angela Haddon

Editor: Nice Girl Naughty Edits

Proofreading: Kimberly Dawn

❀ Created with Vellum

CONTENT WARNING

1

KATIE TAYLOR

Is this real? I must be dreaming. I pinch the skin on my inner forearm just to be sure.

"You have the bathroom right through here. Two large bedrooms and one with its own bathroom in here. The *walls are soundproof, by the way...*" Brian, my new building super and winner of friendliest person I have ever met award, murmurs to me, his eyebrows wiggling in a way that makes it hard not to laugh.

"There is a full kitchen and living room, and· this island counter is fantastic for dinner parties." He continues, and I try to remain serious, looking like I am used to this type of environment. Though I'm sure my awe is evident all over my face.

"Do you live on-site?" I ask, proud of myself for showing an interest. I usually keep to myself. It is safer that way. But I made a pact that when I moved, I would start fresh. A new Katie would be reborn. No one knows me here. I can be whoever I want to be.

"Ahh, I wish, babe," he says, flopping on the sofa like

this is his apartment. Is it unprofessional? I dare say yes, but I kind of like him already, so I sit on the armchair and take his tour as it comes.

"So, you know Doctor Wakeford?" My shoulders stiffen at the question. I'm not in the habit of sharing my life with outsiders. But I take a breath and step into the *new* me.

"Yes. We worked together," I tell him honestly, my smile soft. That wasn't so hard. Opening up a little at a time will hopefully make it easier. I touch my cell that sits in my pocket, eager to send a text to Dr. Wakeford, letting her know I have arrived and that her apartment is amazing.

My chest feels heavy, knowing that she did all this for me. A letter of recommendation. An apartment to live in for a year. All because she could see the ER in our busy Philadelphia hospital was not where I could shine my brightest. She wanted to give me a lift to try something she thought I would excel at. *Who does that?* She has literally been my guardian angel, and I don't think I will ever be able to repay her. Not only for the apartment and career development opportunity, but for getting me out of Philly. She, of all people, knows what it is like when you are running from something. And unbeknownst to her, she has helped me run a little farther.

"Nice to have friends in high places. Keep her on your good side. All my friends are raving bitches half the time, but I love them nonetheless. Isn't this view ah-mazing?" He jumps up from where he sits, continuing his tour as I try, once again, to keep from gaping at my surroundings. This is, without a doubt, the nicest place I have ever been in. Not just lived in, but actually *stepped into*. Fancy is not my life, and this apartment is *Fancy* with a capital *F*. To be honest, if my former boss, Dr. Wakeford, had told me this was how luxurious her apartment was, I wouldn't have taken her up on the offer of letting me stay here. I am too scared to even sit on the sofa.

"It's a beautiful apartment. How long have you worked here?" I ask, standing and walking to the window, positioning myself next to him. My eyes flick down, noticing the window locks and my shoulders automatically lower a little.

"Oh, a few years now. I love this building. I get to use the facilities, and the owner is great. Most of the tenants are nice. *Although...*" he says, leaning closer to me, his voice lowering. "The old guy in 2B can be a bit of a pain in the ass sometimes. You didn't hear that from me." He gives me a knowing smile, and I nod in understanding. I like that he seems to trust me.

"So, you moved here from Philly?" he asks as he spins around and heads toward the kitchen. The stiffness in my neck comes back, and I roll my shoulders to ease the ever-present tension.

I took the bus from Philly this morning, and although the trip was fine, finding my way from the bus depot downtown to this luxurious apartment on the waterside at Harbor East proved more challenging. Getting turned around multiple times and having to ask a stranger for directions did absolutely nothing to ease my anxiety. I clear my throat, feeling out of step again as I prepare to share more about myself.

"Yep. I needed a change of scenery... I wanted something new," I tell him the truth. *Well, most of it.*

"I know all about that, honey. Bad breakup? Crazy boss? I lived in New York for years after a damaged heart had me sprinting here with my tail between my legs. So, I know all about fresh starts. You have come to the right place. Baltimore just feels good... Plus, I'm here, and I already know we are going to be best friends in no time." He looks back out the floor-to-ceiling windows at the amazing view, missing my brows hitting my hairline.

"We are?" I have never had a best friend before. Not in the way most girls do. I never could.

"Absolutely. I can already tell. Your pink hair and tattoos are really my vibe. You give off this don't-fuck-with-me energy, but you are a softie underneath it all." My chest warms at that assessment, just as his cell phone chimes. "Hmmm, I need to run, the old guy in 2B has an issue. *What did I tell you...*" He taps my shoulder playfully, rolling his eyes. His tone and expression have a laugh bubbling up my throat.

"Well, I like your vibe as well," I say, trying not to sound too awkward. How the hell does anyone make friends when you are an adult? I even had trouble as a kid, so my skills in this area are sadly lacking.

"Good. We need to do a movie night soon. This TV in here is huge. Here are the keys. As you know, there is no payment required. There is a welcome basket from the building owner on the kitchen counter for you as well." Pausing for a second, his lips purse, like he might be forgetting something. "Oh! And here's my card. Program my cell number into your phone so we can text later." He hands over his business card, stopping his quick last glance around the space to look back at me.

"Keys, program your number into my cell, and welcome basket. Got it," I say quickly, trying to tamp down the nervous energy strumming through my body. I feel like I have won the lottery. A new friend and a new apartment on day one. This is not like me at all.

"Do you have any other bags downstairs? We have this really old doorman working today, and my nails aren't really the kind that can lift heavy suitcases, if you know what I mean?" Brian asks, flashing his very well-manicured fingers in my direction. I have never had a manicure, but now I really, really want one.

"No. That's it," I say with a smile, my eyes flicking to my bag near the front door. The only dirty thing in this entire apartment, further highlighting the differences between me and my new living standard. *Is it sad that it alone carries my entire life at this point?*

"Seriously, when I left New York, I literally had the clothes on my back and that was it. Don't worry, babe. I see a shopping trip in our future." Giving me a wink, the tension yet again leaves my shoulders as my body starts to fill with more confidence. I might as well start acting like I deserve this level of luxury. I am going to be living here for the next twelve months.

"Okay then, I will let you get settled. I am downstairs most days at the concierge desk, so don't hesitate to let me know if you need anything, and... welcome to Baltimore!" he says, throwing his arms out wide like a game show host, showcasing the amazing view just outside the large wall of windows. His smile stretches a little wider before he gives me a nod and then walks out the door, closing it firmly behind him.

I blow out a breath and check the lock on the door, ensuring it works and it is securely locked. Then I tentatively sit on the edge of the sofa, taking it all in. A fully furnished, city high-rise apartment that screams high end, with every amenity I could possibly need and then some. In my entire twenty-four years on this earth, I have never seen such opulence.

With everything I need and more, it is a simple move in and move out kind of place. Somewhat similar to my life. But you can tell it is unlived in. While aesthetically stunning, it has that smell about it. It is a mix of cleaning products and emptiness. A smell I know too well.

My eyes rest on an art print on the wall. It is of the heart. An old-school doctor's drawing of sorts. Maybe something you would ordinarily see in a vintage textbook for an anatomy class. It is stunning. It highlights all the different parts of the organ, all of which I know by name. I have always been fascinated with the heart. The muscle that does so much work, gives so much life and love, yet it's so easy to break.

Baltimore Hospital is known as one of the best for cardiology and is now my new place of employment starting Monday. I may not be able to mend a broken heart like a heart surgeon can, but as one of the best ward nurses around, I am highly skilled and ready for a challenge.

I stand and walk over to the large stainless-steel refrigerator, pulling open the double doors. The lights are bright, the interior stark white, each shelf empty. My stomach grumbles at just the thought of food, the chocolate bar I had on the bus doing nothing to appease my hunger. I need to find a nearby grocery store, preferably a cheap one.

Closing the refrigerator, I walk back to the windows. The water's calm and peaceful, especially from this high up. There are fancy boats docked in the jetty and a few people walking along the boardwalk.

Plunk, plunk, plunk...

What is that? My body jolts, and my fight-or-flight kicks in immediately. On edge, I spin around from the amazing view, my eyes darting from side to side. Now that I have heard it, I can't unhear it. A slow, almost silent thumping. Soothing yet totally annoying at the same time, just like the second hand on a wall clock. As I look around, I'm half expecting the noise to jump out at me.

Plunk, plunk, plunk.

I tentatively walk around the apartment, my head snapping from left to right, looking for clues as to what it might be. I didn't hear it earlier when Brian was here, although he was talking almost nonstop, so there was no way this would have stood out. Following the noise to the kitchen, I open cupboards, check out the refrigerator again, and then open the dishwasher.

Plunk, plunk, plunk.

Frustration starts to dig into me until I spot it. The kitchen sink. The tap drips in a constant rhythm. I turn the tap tighter, hoping to cease the noise, but it is already tight. Hopefully, I somehow fixed it. But just as I slowly pull my hand away, the drips keep coming.

"Shit," I say to no one other than myself. My eyes flick

across the counter, which is bare, except for the nice basket left from the building. I could ring Brian, but I don't want to be that annoying person who finds something wrong with their apartment on the first day. We got off to a good start. Finding a kitchen cloth in the cupboard, I place it at the bottom of the sink, something to block the drip of water against the stainless steel. Silence greets me.

My eyes flick around the apartment once more. The quietness now is almost deafening, so I put on music, which always gives me the strength I need to get through my to-do lists. I make quick work of unpacking my bag, then settle in with a small box of artisan cookies I found in the welcome basket. Ease and excitement fill me at my first night in a new city.

2

EDWARD LANGFORD

I f only my mother could see me now. Jeans and a workman's shirt. Boots and tools. A far cry from the suit-wearing Baltimore billionaire poster boy I am portrayed as being in the public eye.

"How did this break again?" I ask as I drill into the cupboard, wondering how the older gentleman in 2b was able to break it again.

"These things are not made as good as they used to be," the man grumbles from beside me where he positioned himself the moment I arrived, directing me where to drill and how to fix the cupboard he broke. I am sure he will start to tell me all about how he had to walk to work in the snow because he had no fancy car back in his day, or how he had to handwrite letters instead of email or text messages because cell phones were not yet invented when he was young.

"They sure aren't, sir," I reply through gritted teeth as I test the door. It now moves perfectly and closes snugly. There is no question that it broke under stress. These things are European, and they don't break so easily. Our whole building is made of high-quality fittings and fixtures, everything of the highest standard. From our staff to our amenities to our fit-out and our location. This building is one of the best in the entire city. And it's mine.

My eyes flick to the tenant, who now moves across the kitchen as I pack up my tools, and I see him lean against the cupboard door that is open on the other side of the space. The penny drops.

"Maybe don't lean on the door like that. They may be tough, but I don't think that they're made to hold our weight," I offer, hoping I don't offend, but seriously, this old guy should know better.

"Oh," is all he says as he waves me off before closing the door and moving around to wipe down the counter.

As I clean up the mess I made and start packing my tools away, I huff a small laugh. My parents paid thousands of dollars in private school fees and sent me to one of the top universities in the country, and while I did graduate with a degree in International Relations, I prefer to work with my hands over my brain whenever I can.

"Don't forget to tell the super that this is the third time this thing has broken. If it breaks again, I will have to contact the building owner to complain."

"I will be sure to let him know." I nod and smile tightly, keeping my head low so he doesn't get a good look at me. Not that he would expect a Langford to be fixing his cupboard, but my poor disguise hides very little.

"Tell him I know Edward Langford personally. I have his number, and I will call him if the maintenance you provide is not professionally done." He continues with his light threat, pointing a finger at me. I bite the inside of my cheek to prevent the laugh from slipping as I pull my cap down on my head. He doesn't know me, nor does he have my number. I don't give my number to anyone. My brothers and my assistant, but that's about it.

Privacy for us Langford brothers is paramount. Our lives are played out so publicly most of the time that anything we can scurry away for ourselves, we do. I am happiest when we are just hanging out, or on the golf course, away from prying eyes. Because that's where I get to just be me. That's maybe why I enjoy secretly working with tools on the weekends. Teaching myself a trade. It allows me to just be, without the weight of Baltimore society on my shoulders, along with the heaped expectations from my mother.

Here I am known as simply Eddie, the maintenance man. Not Edward Langford, owner of this building and half of Baltimore. The only person in this building who knows who I am is Brian, the super, who tends to work the concierge desk. Everyone else either doesn't say anything or doesn't expect a billionaire to be mending broken cupboards and faulty doors in their free time.

"All fixed. Don't hesitate to call the desk downstairs if you need anything else." I grab my tools, and he walks me out. After a quick handshake and a short ride in the elevator, I meet Brian downstairs just as he is getting off a call.

"Hi, bossman," he says, and I roll my eyes at him.

"How many times do I need to tell you, just call me Eddie." We play this game almost every weekend. I know he only does it to get a rise out of me. He is playing with fire half the time, but he is full of energy and great to have on the front desk. Plus, I would be lying if I said he wasn't one of my best employees. He is also fully aware who pays his salary and gives him a healthy bonus every year, so he kisses my ass at every opportunity.

"Oh, stop being such a grump," he says, flapping a hand at me. "There is a new tenant in 10A."

"10A?" I ask, confused. That is the Wakeford apartment. It's been vacant for years. Ever since old Dr. Wakeford died in New York. Whispers say it was mafia related. His daughter Catherine now owns the apartment.

"Yeah. Katie Taylor. A young woman. Beautiful, actually. A little quiet, but she is now my best friend, just so you know." He says it like he's laying down the law that she is not to be messed with. Not that I mingle with tenants. I see them occasionally when I need to fix something in their apartments, but that is rare. I usually mill around, tinkering with the common areas or offices.

"Best friend, huh?" My eyebrows rise with a smirk. Brian collects best friends like someone does stamps. There is always a new one. But he seems serious about this tenant, so I pretend to conspire with him.

"Yes. The bestest one of all," he says quietly, like he doesn't want anyone else to know. For some reason, it has piqued my interest. He is a good judge of character. That is one of the reasons he is so good at his job. He picks up things before they come to light. "Catherine Wakeford called last week. Asked me to get the apartment ready. Must be a friend of hers, I am guessing." I shrug. Not that it matters. Catherine

Wakeford owns that apartment. She can come and go as she pleases. Catherine can offer that apartment to anyone she likes, as long as they reside within the building regulations.

"It is nice to have someone in it since it has been vacant for so long," I murmur. All apartments need life in them; otherwise, they become a little stale. Plus, as the owner of the building, I like to see it at full capacity and in high demand.

"She just called, actually. She is having trouble with the kitchen sink. Says the tap won't stop dripping. I told her that the devastatingly handsome building maintenance man would be up within the hour," he says, fluttering his eyelashes at me in jest.

"Please tell me you didn't," I moan. I wouldn't put it past him to say something like that, but it is not the level of professional demeanor I want in this building.

"No, bossman, I didn't. I just like to see you squirm." I roll my eyes at him again, and he just smiles wider.

"I'll go up and take a look at it." Grabbing my tools, I ignore his satisfied smile, taking the elevator back up. The Wakeford apartment is one of the best in the building. But the fit-out is similar to the rest of the apartments, and like all our apartments here, the tapware is from Europe. There also shouldn't be any issue with the plumbing, since this building is still considered new. Maybe, like 2B, the new woman broke something herself. I am deep in thought about the project ahead of me when I step to the door and knock.

"Eddie. Building Maintenance," I say in a baritone voice that doesn't get old. A small grin dances on my face at me being incognito. I hear the lock unclasp before the door opens, and I look up.

My eyebrows shoot to my hairline at the sight before me.

This is not what I was expecting.

"Good. You're here," she pants, which does little to stop my dick from growing in my jeans as I take her in. She is wet. Dripping in water. Brian was right, she is beautiful. Beyond, really.

The first thing I notice are her tattoos, then her long pink hair, currently plastered against her face and down her shoulders. But I pay little attention to that, because her white t-shirt is completely see-through, clinging to her body in a way that should be illegal. I swallow roughly at her black lace bra, fitting around her perky...

"Hey, eyes up here, *Eddie!*" she snaps at me, and I shake my head. *Fuck, that was a slimebag move. I was basically gawking.* I clear my throat and make a concerted effort to look at her forehead so my gaze doesn't drop again.

"What's the problem? With the plumbing... I mean, the water... err, what is the problem with the sink?" I ask, my voice hoarse as I stumble over my words. Fuck, you would think I have never seen a pair of tits before. *Pull it together, Eddie.*

"Tap explosion. Water is everywhere!" she wails as she struts back into her apartment, leaving the door open for me. My feet won't move as I take in her ass. Her jeans are wet as well, the denim stuck to her figure like...

"*Eddie!*" she yells, and I rush in after her, stopping short as I see the mess that has her stressing.

"Shit!" I mutter as I drop my tools on the kitchen counter, whipping off my hat and diving under the sink. I soon become drenched, but I am not bothered. The cold shower is exactly what I need right now as I try to get my mind off the pink-haired beauty and on the task at hand. Water splashes on my back as I get to work. Tapping, tightening, trying all the things I know to stop the spray of water until I hit the jackpot. I spot a loose valve at the back, and by the look of it, it must have been like this for years, especially since this apartment hasn't been used in a while. I tighten the valve as best I can with my hands, slowing the spray of water so it remains a small gush. I still need to tighten it off completely, so I rush to my toolbox and grab some tools to do the rest of the job. As I do, I see her out of the corner of my eye, leaning against the kitchen counter, watching me. Even from my peripheral, she is fucking gorgeous.

"What's your name?" I ask, trying to make conversation while averting my eyes. My voice barks out, though, startling us both, and I wonder where the fuck my charm has gone. My brothers would be pissing themselves laughing at me if they could see me this frazzled.

"Katie Taylor. I'm a friend of Catherine Wakeford's," she says, seemingly a little more relaxed now that the water is not spraying everywhere.

"Just move in?" But I already know the answer. I still don't look at her as I sort through my toolbox. My heart is thumping harder in my chest. *What is wrong with me?*

"Yesterday. The tap was dripping last night, but I thought it would stop," she says, bringing my thoughts back to the task at hand. I place the tools I need on the kitchen floor, but my wet shirt sits heavy on my body. So before I maneuver back under the sink, I level the playing field. I reach to the back of my neck and pull my now soaked shirt from my frame, slapping it on the kitchen counter, then get back to work to close off this water flow entirely. And while I am not sure, I *think* I heard a small gasp of approval fall from her lips.

3

KATIE

I like to think that I have my own sense of style. I go through life at the beat of my own drum, not paying any attention to anyone else. But it is at this moment that I realize I am like every other red-blooded woman in this world. I feel my cheeks heat and my heart race as I watch him peel his wet shirt off his spectacular body, right here in front of me. He is confident, and why wouldn't he be with a body like that. It is sculpted. Tight. While I forget to breathe, he completely ignores me. He is hands down one of the best-looking men I have ever met.

I watch him slide to his knees and dive straight into the cupboard under the sink again, showing me that he is not only strong but also agile. He works with speed at closing off the water flow, and I step to the side and monitor him closely as his large arm muscles contract and pulse with his movements. My eyes may have lingered over his tight ass and thick thighs while his head was buried earlier. But now, as I watch his bare back, muscles clenching and bulging, I forget my own name.

"What did you do?" he asks, sitting back on his heels. The small gush of water has now stopped, and I get a full glimpse of his now naked torso. Water droplets trail down his strong chest, my eyes following them, watching them glide over his skin. "Hey, eyes up here, Pinkie," he says, throwing my earlier words back at me as my eyes flick to his face like I'm in trouble.

I hear him suck in a breath as our eyes connect, my own breath catching in my chest at the same time. He has the clearest eyes I have ever seen, the kind you could easily get lost in. We stare at each other before he gives me a sly smirk, and I feel my cheeks heat even more.

"I didn't do anything." I cross my arms over my chest, recalling what he just asked, my defenses up as I ignore his cute nickname. I haven't had a nickname before. Not one used positively anyway. I straighten my spine. One, because it wasn't my fault. I just tried to tighten the tap some more, since the dripping was still constant and highly annoying. At my touch, it flew off, coating me in so much water, I won't need to shower today. And two, because I have no money to pay for any of this, so I will deny any involvement until my last dying breath.

"What? So the tap just flew off the sink?" he asks sarcastically as he stands and takes a step toward me. My heart thuds harder as I take in his height for the first time. I feel like I look up forever until I meet his eyes that currently dance with humor. I tried not to pay a lot of attention to him when I flung open the door. I just wanted to be saved from the Niagara Falls happening in the kitchen. But not only is he broad with thick arms, a chiseled torso and back, but he is also really tall. In comparison to me, that is not hard. At five foot two inches, everyone is taller than me. As he places his tools on the kitchen counter, I notice the curves of his biceps that show me that he either works out or does a lot of heavy lifting in his maintenance job. Probably both. It's incredibly sexy.

"Yes. As a matter of fact, it did. It nearly hit me in the face. It could have broken my nose!" My hands find my hips as the lie spills from my lips. The tap hit the floor straightaway, not coming anywhere near my face. As Eddie and I stand here in my kitchen, we both look around and take in the mess. Water is *everywhere.*

"I am sure it wasn't that dramatic," he says, looking at me intensely.

"Are you suggesting I am being dramatic?" I ask, narrowing my eyes. I can hear my tone rise, and I know I sound batshit crazy. This is not like me at all. But I feel on edge. I am in a new place, already seemingly causing problems, and there is a smoking hot half-naked man standing right in front of me. I have no idea what I am doing. This is not normal. Not for me anyway.

He chuckles then, clearly joking, and I sigh to myself. I really need to loosen up.

"Relax, I'm just teasing you. I am sure a tap falling off and water spurting everywhere is not something anyone wants to combat when they first move in," he says, his tone kind as he leans against the sink like he is a model from a jeans commercial.

"Sorry, it's been a big few days," I admit, remorseful for taking out my stress on him. Yet another man who appears to be super nice and friendly.

"No need to apologize. Moving is hectic, I get it. I was just enjoying your sass, but it's nice to see you have a sweeter side too." I notice his eyes shimmering as his smirk turns into a smile that shows me his teeth, and I grab on to the kitchen counter before I melt into a puddle. Is he flirting with me? *This is new.*

I clear my throat, swallowing roughly. Day one, I get a new best friend, and day two, I nearly swoon onto the floor? "That's me, sweet and sour rolled into one." Before I can stop it, my mouth is rambling. "Look, I... I have just moved here on my own, and I have been here for less than twenty-four hours. The tap exploded, water is everywhere, and in an apartment that I don't even own. And now, I have a half-naked man standing in front of me, who looks like he is cut from stone or something. I need a little bit of grace at the moment." Biting my lip, I shut myself up, seeing him eyeing me curiously.

"Yeah, well, if it helps, my mind is not exactly on the job either." His eyes flicker down my body and back to my eyes, and a shiver runs through me at his perusal. My knees suddenly feel weak in the best way.

We look at each other in silence. I'm not sure what is happening exactly, but there is a current in the air that started the minute I opened the door, one that feels like it has just zinged around the room. My gaze lowers to his waist without my permission. I can't help myself as I zone in on his torso muscles, then follow a small trail of hair leading straight to his jeans. My eyes are magnetized to his body or something. I can't look away.

"Do you have a mop?" I see him swallow again, as he is clearly trying to put us back on solid ground. Rubbing his head, he surveys the damage. His hair is a little long, as it flops across his forehead, curling at the back of his neck in a way that gives him a boyish appearance.

"No. I don't have anything," I say, looking around the room again, trying to get my bearings, my shoulders slumping as reality kicks in. I have no idea how to clean this up. I have no cleaning products, no money to go out and buy them. At best, I can probably mop it up with a few bath towels, but I prefer to do that without an audience. "Let me get us a towel. At least we can dry ourselves." I feel bad for snapping at him earlier, so I am trying to not be a total pain. Eddie looks at me, his eyes searching mine like he is trying to figure me out.

"Thanks, that would be nice," he says, giving me a smile that I swear melts my underwear clean off my body, then pulls out his cell to make a call.

It is then I look down at my appearance. My hair is wet, and I feel it stuck to the sides of my face. My clothes are damp. I was so busy checking out his wet torso, I didn't realize that I had a whole wet t-shirt contest going on right now. No wonder his eyes were glued to my chest earlier. Self-conscious thoughts start to rise, so I turn quickly and head to the bathroom, grabbing two clean towels, and head back out to offer him one.

"Cleaning team will be here soon. They can mop up and ensure there is no water damage," he mumbles as he turns back around and grabs the towel I offer. *Shit, I didn't even think about water damage.*

"It's fine. I can clean it up somehow," I say in a rush, not used to people doing things for me.

"You just said you don't have a mop?" His brow

furrows as he looks back up at me. What is it about him? Holy hell, every time his eyes meet mine, I feel like I'm about ready to combust.

"I don't, but I can do it myself. I don't need help," I say, my shoulders stiffening again. It's so natural for me to do everything on my own. It's how I'm most comfortable.

"Hmmm, stubborn too. Well, I'll be back at some point. I need to replace the tap," he says, pushing past the comment about me too quickly for me to reply. I watch as he rubs his bare chest, my mouth watering a little.

"How long will that take?" I jut out my hip as I try to get a handle on these new feelings swirling in my body. I don't know why I asked, because I start work tomorrow, and my shifts will be so long I won't even use this sink when I get home. My bed will call me almost instantly, I am sure.

"It is German made, so I am not sure if we have any in stock. Could be a couple of days, a week, tops," he offers, sounding a bit nervous. *Of course it is German made.*

"What am I meant to do until then?" I ask, my eyebrows rising, almost demanding he give me the answer.

"I will need to get a plumber in to check over everything tomorrow. Water flow to the other wet areas in the apartment should be fine. Just no using this sink."

"I won't be home. I start work tomorrow." I know I am being difficult, but there is no way I can miss my first shift. I need this job. I step away from the counter, remembering I spotted some paper towels in the top cupboard when I put the small bag of food items away this morning. That thought sits heavy in my stomach, because now I also remember that I only have thirty-five dollars left in my bank account until payday. I feel my anxiety start to swirl.

"What do you do for work?" he asks, stepping forward, the two of us now using the towels to mop up some of the water puddling on the kitchen counter.

"I'm a nurse. I start at the hospital tomorrow in the cardio wing. I can't leave on my first day to get here to babysit a plumber, all because the owner of this building doesn't provide taps in good working order," I smart, not able to help it. I am tired, wet, hungry, frustrated, and really, really don't want to get lumped with a maintenance bill in this place.

"The building owner is actually a nice guy," he grits out, and clearly, I hit a nerve. His jaw is tight, his hands a little white-knuckled as they move around the countertop. Perhaps they are friends, although I find it hard to see how a maintenance man, no doubt on minimum wage, could be friends with a gazillionaire or whomever owns this obscenely elegant building.

"I can be here early before you leave for work and stay while he checks it out. We can see if we can have something sorted by the time your shift finishes," he offers, and I sigh. I don't want to leave my apartment in his care. I feel like it is my personal space, not for his eyes. Not without me here, anyway. I also don't like depending on people. History shows they always let me down. But... I know he is doing me a favor. This guy doesn't even have to be here to help me mop up the mess. But he is, and I know the only way to get this fixed is to give Eddie access to my apartment. Rock, meet hard place.

"I don't know..." I say, looking at him, wondering if I can trust him, which is a stupid thought. I already know that I shouldn't be trusting anyone. Let alone a man I just met.

"I get it. You just moved here solo, so you are obviously independent. It takes a lot of guts to move on your own, where you don't know many people. But I will let you know that I have had a full police check and security clearance to work here, and your apartment will be safe with me." He smiles, and damn, he really is too pretty for his own good.

Now that the stress of the situation has settled, he seems like a genuinely good guy. He is working on a weekend, so he is obviously dedicated to his job and has a strong work ethic. Or he needs the paycheck just as much as I do. Besides, I have nothing of value here for him to steal, and the apartment isn't even mine... so it doesn't really matter.

"Fine. Okay. Um... thank you," I mutter my appreciation and offer him a small smile. I haven't had anyone be this nice to me ever. And for no reason. For a situation like this, it's working out perfectly. And to my surprise, I feel a strange sense of ease.

But with the life I have lived, I know nothing is ever perfect. So I reserve my judgment on my current good luck and push any happiness down. I can't go thinking my life is changing. My past will always catch up to me.

4

EDDIE

I should be on my way to the office, in my suit, rushing to get through the morning of meetings I had scheduled. But my plans flew out the window yesterday when the pink-haired assassin flashed her wet t-shirt and her sparkling blues my way. Now, as I carry two coffees to her apartment, I look at my reflection in the elevator and see myself in my jeans, casual shirt, cap, and boots again, something that never happens during business hours.

To say that yesterday took me by surprise is an understatement. Brian said she was beautiful. I should have been prepared when I first saw her, but I wasn't. She is like no one I have ever seen before. Beautiful, for sure. Sexy as fuck. Spiky, but also soft. A wonderful contradiction and one I want to know more about.

There is an extra spring in my step this morning. One I haven't felt for a very long time. I feel good. Light on my feet. Excited. I try to tamper it down, though. It is a new day, and maybe my memories are hazy.

Maybe I imagined the heat, the connection between us. How when our eyes actually connected, I felt my heart stop beating. Her eyes are so fucking blue, I could sink into them. Coupled with her pink hair, they pop, vibrant like the waters of the Mediterranean. It is pretty rare to have something so instant. That crackle of tension. That desire to learn more. It hasn't really happened to me before, and I am a little shook about it.

As the elevator opens, I strut to her door and am about to knock when it opens. It is like my mind short-circuits. I am not even sure how it is possible, but she is even more beautiful than I remember. I swallow hard, then clear my throat as I try to pull myself together.

"Morning, *Pinkie*," I tease, offering a warm smile and holding out a coffee to her. My grin is so wide it almost hurts my face. I am fucking happy with what I see. Dressed ready for work, her hair in a messy bun on top of her head. Her face is free of any makeup, but she is absolutely breathtaking.

"Morning," she says warily, looking at my outstretched offering, then to me and back again like she is confused.

"Coffee?" I ask, suddenly feeling a little nervous that she may not accept the simple gesture. I rushed to get these before she left this morning, knowing she had a long workday ahead of her. Her hesitation has me even more intrigued. I have never offered to watch someone's apartment for maintenance. Usually, this would be Brian's job, but there was no way I was giving away another chance to see her. Even if it is just for a few minutes.

"You brought me coffee?" she asks, surprise in her tone, her eyebrows rising. *Has no one done a good deed for this woman before?*

"Yep. Figured you might need the caffeine hit for your first day on the job." I shrug, acting nonchalant, yet hoping she takes it, wanting to put a smile on her face. Standing at her door, looking at me with a small amount of trepidation, further cements to me that she is obviously fiercely independent.

"Thank you," she says, grabbing the cup, albeit hesitantly, her smile small but still there.

"I didn't know how you take it, so I only added a little sweetener."

"How do I know you haven't poisoned it?" she murmurs, looking at me over the top of the cup. Her lips curve a bit, and I start to feel hot as my smile mimics hers.

"Only one way to find out." I enjoy seeing the way her blues sparkle, this playful teasing new for me. Her gaze hooks on to mine as she lifts the cup to her mouth and takes a sip, almost in a challenge. Eyes closing, she hums, the sound vibrating around my body.

"Perfect." Opening her eyes, they instantly connect with mine. "I need to go. I have to walk, and my cell tells me that it will take half an hour. You will lock up when you finish?" she asks, grabbing a small backpack as she looks at me expectantly. *She walks to the hospital?*

"No problem. Your apartment is safe with me." I am a man of my word. "Good luck on your first day," I offer, sipping my coffee, trying to act unaffected while my heart thumps hard in my chest. I watch her move effortlessly around me, her small frame making me clench my fist so

I don't do something stupid like reach out and run my hand down her side, tracing her curves.

"Thanks. And thanks for the coffee!" she says sweetly, and I watch her go, clearly nervous as she takes a few deep breaths and gets into the elevator. Glancing at me once more, flashing me a small smile, I don't miss the pink tint to her cheeks as she keeps her eyes on me before the elevator doors close on the visual.

I sigh as I walk into her apartment. You wouldn't even know there was a leak yesterday. The cleaning crew came and fixed it all. Brian had them air it out, and right now, as the morning sun streams in from the large windows overlooking the water, it's immaculate. As I take in the apartment, I realize she hasn't added anything yet. There are no personal touches, no photos, no knickknacks. The only thing I notice is the soft smell of her perfume as it lingers in the air. A sweet floral scent, and it's sexy as hell.

"Morning, boss," the plumber says from behind me, startling me. "This the sink?" he asks, walking straight into the kitchen, getting to work.

"Morning. Yeah, that's the one. I stopped the water flow yesterday, but there is a bigger issue, I think." He looks underneath, testing, tapping, and mumbling to himself.

"Sorry to say it, but this tapware will all need replacing." My brow crumples.

"Okay, we have them in stock, right?" He is the plumber I use across all my properties, so I know he is honest. I have a whole trade team stationed across Baltimore that runs all my property maintenance in this building and in my many others. Some of them have taught me a thing or two over the years.

"Not this one. We will have to order it in," he says, closing the cupboard and looking over the sink.

"Can we put a rush on it? Even if we need to pay a rush fee, let's get it done ASAP." I don't want Pinkie having to wait for this.

"Sure, I will get it ordered today and let you know when it will be in. At best, it will be a couple of days. Good job on the patch up too. It is solid. No more leaks, as long as no one touches the sink." I appreciate his comment. I am not qualified in any trade, but I enjoy tinkering.

"Hey, bossman," Brian says from the front door I left open. I can't see his face from the large basket covering him—the one I asked him to put together this morning. I may have gone a little overboard, but I spotted her empty cupboards yesterday when we tried to mop up the water. She obviously hasn't had time to go food shopping yet.

"Come in, Brian," I tell him, as the plumber nods and leaves us to it.

I need to be across town. I have a meeting with my brother Tennyson about a new building he developed that I now have to manage as part of our growing portfolio. While Tennyson has always been good at his job, he has now exploded into a stratosphere on his own. He and Willow make a good team, and he is building new complexes all around the country, and even in other global markets. It makes my job more demanding as I run the family real estate holdings, managing the buildings he develops, such as this one, as well as others across

Baltimore and elsewhere. The more he develops, the more I have to manage.

"Do you think it is big enough?" Brian asks sarcastically as he places the large basket on the kitchen counter. "You sure are offering her a lot, but I must say, given she is my new best friend, it is totally worth it. Told you she was special..." he teases, and I don't miss the way he is fishing for information.

"It is just nice to offer something for her unsettled first twenty-four hours here," I mumble, pretending to check the emails on my cell as my eyes flick up to the hamper. Chocolates, artisan biscuits, olives, pesto, nuts, cheeses, and a whole assortment of other things. I will admit, my mind is still in a jumble from her.

"Can you do a final check and then lock up? She won't be back until later, but make sure everything is all okay," I ask him before I shake his hand and strut out of her apartment. A new nervous energy makes my steps quick and my heart thud. Racing to the building office downstairs, I quickly change back into my suit, ready for the corporate workday. I look at myself in the mirror, sharp in my standard uniform of a tailored suit, black shoes, and now slick hair, in complete contrast to my messy, unshaven appearance of yesterday and my casual look of only moments ago. Katie has no idea who I am. Which is great, because I get to see the real her.

She is in total contrast to the usual women I meet who know me as Edward Langford, the last billionaire bachelor in Baltimore. They flirt, play seductress, gloss their lips and pout, flutter their lashes, all in the hopes they look appetizing enough for me to choose them. But they don't. I've never been more attracted to a woman than I am now. Pink hair, a small scattering of tattoos, and a body tiny enough for me to grab and throw onto my bed and...

My cell phone shrills in my hand, breaking me from my thoughts. I clear my throat and pause for a moment, not only to get my bearings, because apparently, I have turned into a daydreaming asshole, but also because my mother's name lights up the screen, reminding me yet again why I can't meet a nice woman. After what my brothers went through, it will be a cold day in hell before I have a woman in my life for Mom to get near.

"Hey, Mom," I say, taking a big breath, steeling myself for this conversation.

"Where are you?" she demands. No *Hi, sweetheart, how are you? What are you up to today?* falls from her lips. Not once has she ever asked how I am. Not in my adult years, anyway. No kind, soft words a mom is meant to use. The soft mannerisms, caring nature. The nurturing side of a female I crave. None of that comes from Diane Langford. Ever.

"I am checking on some maintenance at the building in Harborside, about to go into the office," I tell her, as I'm walking across the lobby to get back in my waiting town car.

"Edward. You are meant to be meeting me for brunch. I am waiting." I imagine her gritting her teeth behind her public smile as I pace out of the building foyer and to my car. I totally forgot about brunch. Now my anxiety swirls in my stomach.

"Sorry, Mom, I completely forgot," is all I get out before her wrath takes over.

"Forgot?! How can you forget? That stupid girl you have as an assistant is obviously not doing her job very well. I will wait five more minutes, Edward, and not a minute longer," she hisses in a whisper before the line goes dead. I wonder for a minute what would happen if I just left her there. But I am not that kind of a person. I am the only son left who speaks with her and the only one who meets her for brunch, and even then, it is only monthly. Having her in my life any more than that would be too much.

I have no idea what made my mother into the horrible, angry woman she is. But she has been this way for years. My father's death amplified it, but her nastiness has always been there. It wasn't until us boys were adults ourselves that we really saw what she's capable of. As the youngest, it is something that took me a lot longer to understand. I focused on school, then went backpacking, so I spent little time around her. It is why I enjoyed my gap year in Asia so much. My mother was horrified I went backpacking instead of getting straight to work in the family business after college, but it was by far the most fun I have ever had.

My brothers took most of the brunt over the years. But I feel it now. The weight of her. The negativity. The lack of love and emotion other than anger and spite. She hates most women who are around us. My three brothers have found their life partners and not one of them spends any time with her. The relationship you think a woman would have with her mother-in-law is not one any of them have with her.

"To the office, sir?" my driver, Tony, asks as I get to the car. I stand on the sidewalk and suck in another deep breath of the clean, crisp air, hearing the water lapping at the boardwalk. There are some beautiful yachts docked today, bobbing up and down calmly. I envision how great it would be to get on one of them and slowly sail around the warm waters of the Caribbean, away from my mother and everyone else.

"The Charleston restaurant, please, Tony." I get into the back seat, and as he drives, I text Tennyson, canceling our meeting, then speak to my assistant to reshuffle some things.

"Shall I wait, sir?" Tony asks as the car pulls up outside the restaurant, and I step out, buttoning my suit jacket. He rushes out of the car to my door.

"Probably a good idea. We both know how this is going to go," I murmur to him, slapping him on the arm in thanks as I strut into the fancy restaurant my mother has chosen. As I walk inside, the low hum of conversation hits my ears, soft music from a live piano playing in the corner. I ignore the looks I get, the room full of mostly women, all wearing designer clothes, their hair perfectly coiffed and nails freshly manicured. I see my mother across the room, a few women chatting to her, all of whom look up as I approach.

"Good morning," I say, my smile as fake as their lips. I lean over to peck my mother on the cheek. A standard public greeting that always has my shoulders up near my ears.

"Edward, *so glad* you could make it," she says with a smile, sitting in her chair like the Queen of England. Only the two of us know how barbed her words are. I smile politely at the nearby women as they take their leave, and I sit opposite my mother, wondering if I should bother ordering.

"Sir?" The waiter offers me a menu and pours a glass of water. My eyes flick to meet Mother's, her stare drilling into me. We both remain silent until the waiter leaves.

"I don't like waiting, Edward. What had you so consumed this morning that you forgot about your own mother?"

"Just some maintenance needing oversight at the Harborside building." I offer her just enough and nothing more.

She scoffs at me like I am utterly ridiculous. As the youngest, I am used to people not taking me seriously. I fly under the radar, for the most part, even though I am a successful businessman in my own right. After my time backpacking, I came home to help my older brother Harrison with his campaign for governor. Once he won, I slotted right into managing the family business real estate portfolio, simply because there was no other box that I fit in. I have spent the last few years focused on that job, and I have provided year on year growth. I am not merely born from money, but I make it. A lot of it.

"Maintenance? Really, Edward? Have you no shame," she seethes, and I swear I see smoke coming from her ears.

"Shame?" I tilt my head in question, knowing what is

about to come. My chest tightens, and I clench my fists under the table.

"It is about time you stopped playing around like Bob the Builder and focused on your future. You don't think I know about you working on the weekends, fixing things and cleaning up. Seriously, Edward, what in the world would possess you to do that? To look after people like that. It is beneath you. It is not what we do," she says, taking a sip of her wine, her glass nearly empty. I can tell by the smell of her breath that it isn't her first one. As suspected, she waves her hand at the nearby waitress, who walks over and tops her up, the bottle now two-thirds empty.

"What future are you talking about?" I ask her once the waitress has gone, and I am relieved that all the tables surrounding us are empty. No one needs to overhear this conversation.

"You need to stop using your free time playing around in this pretend life of being a maintenance man and start spending your weekends finding yourself a respectable wife. You are a goddamn Langford. You need to start acting like it. You are nearly thirty; you can't be single forever. The other three may have totally thrown my feelings in my face with their chosen partners, but you, Edward, *you* need to choose wisely."

I would like to think she is saying this because she cares. That she cares about my heart, my feelings, and what's best for me. But she doesn't. No doubt, she has some young socialite in mind for me. Someone whose family is just as wealthy as our own, so her place in society can be further cemented. I can already see the wheels in her head turning at the thought while my jaw hurts from clenching it so hard. This is the last thing that I want. I don't want a socialite wife, and I don't want my mom meddling in my affairs. I thought she might have learned from my brothers that it never ends well.

"Mom, I am entirely capable of making my own life decisions." It's the same thing I tell her every month. While I don't elaborate with her, I do want the whole deal. Wife, kids, the large house behind the white picket fence. My older brother Ben has that, and I am very jealous. But I haven't met anyone in Baltimore who seems genuine and likes me for me and not my money, connections, and name.

"I will give you a month. If you haven't found anyone by then, I will be finding someone for you. It is not leeway I gave to the other boys, so appreciate the small amount of grace I am giving you," she tells me, as if what she says is gospel, and I sigh. She is so deluded. The fact that she thinks I would even entertain a woman she suggests is not only amusing, but infuriating.

"Leeway or not, your meddling ways have done nothing but damage the family. I think you are the one who needs to focus on your charity work and giving back to society. Leave me to find my own wife. I don't need your help," I say, and she sits in shock. Nervous energy runs through my body, and I play with the napkin on the table, waiting for her wrath. Her eyes thin, clearly not liking me talking back to her, something I rarely do. But I know that I am on her hit list. I am her only blood relative who even sits at the same table as her these days, and to be honest, I am not even sure why I do. Maybe because

I feel sorry for her. Because if I wasn't here, then she would have no one.

"One month," she confirms quietly, disregarding me, and I see her rub her chest. Where her heart would be if she had one.

"So, how is the charity gala coming along?" I ask, steering the conversation away from me, seeing if we can have a normal conversation.

"What gala are you referring to?" she asks as she takes another sip. I wonder if she does this a lot. If getting day drunk is a common occurrence for her. By the look of how she is drinking the chardonnay like water, my guess is that it is.

"Whatever one is coming up," I press, throwing my hand in the air, having no idea what, if any, gala is on the calendar, but she is always organizing something. Either in our name or in her honor.

"Oh, Edward." She sighs like this conversation pains her, sculling her wine and ordering another bottle. So I decide to order brunch. I might as well eat while I am here.

5

KATIE

I hold on to the nurses' station, because if I don't, I think I am going to fall over.

"He's tough, isn't he?" Shelley, the nursing unit manager, says from where she sits in front of the computer, updating patient files.

"Tough? He is so disrespectful. He checks everything I do three times before he seems satisfied. He is always looking over my shoulder, constantly disagreeing with everything I say. I may be only a nurse in his eyes, but I am still a professional, with experience in ER and trauma. I know what I am doing," I huff out, probably too harshly on my first day, but I can't help it. I hate being treated like I don't know what I am doing. I sigh away my frustrations to Shelley, grateful to have a friendly ear and someone to talk to at work. I met her when I arrived this morning, and she has been checking on me all day.

"I worked for him when I first arrived here too. It's like a rite of passage. Everyone hates him and moves to a different doctor after three months. But the hospital never questions why he has such poor staff retention. Clearly, it is not an HR priority." She quirks a brow, shaking her head.

"I have one more round to make, and then my shift is over," I say, willing my feet to keep up. I wasn't ready for the pain they would endure. Dr. Wilson had me walking from one end of the ward to the other. Grabbing stupid things from clipboards and pens to bandages he didn't need, and even a coffee for him. He berated me every chance he got. In front of other staff, in front of patients, and even in front of the cleaning crew. I didn't miss their empathic looks or the way they quickly scurried out of his way every time he came near them. That should've been the first red flag. The fact that he worked me into the ground without giving me a five-minute break should have been the second. Dr. Wilson is an asshole—I would know; I am a magnet for them.

"Here. Have some candy. It will give you the last bit of energy you need before you crash," Shelley says, passing a glass bowl of bright jelly beans, and I grab a few pink ones. Throwing them in my mouth, I try to ignore the fact that the pink color reminds me of my new nickname and the sexy maintenance man at my building.

I wasn't sure what to think this morning when Eddie showed up at my door with a coffee for me. His sexy smirk and his deep brown eyes were almost my undoing the minute I opened the door to him. I haven't really had many positive interactions with guys. While I don't know him well enough yet to judge, I am usually good at understanding people quickly, a skill I have acquired at work, and I feel at ease in his presence. But it makes me nervous. I never let anyone get too close. *Never.*

I roll my ankles to try to help the pain in my feet from being on them for eight hours straight. I crack my neck to clear my thoughts and snap myself out of this stupid daze I am in. I have seen the man twice. He is there for work. Nothing more, nothing less.

"Shelley, do you know if they are looking for volunteers in the neonatal ward?" I ask her. It is something that I used to do in Philly, and something that is important to me. It has been on my mind for the past few days since I got here.

"Sure, they always are, and from a qualified nurse, I think they would jump at the chance. Just speak to Tracey, the head nurse over there. She will still be there if you want to go after your rounds. Tell her I sent you," she offers, and I am grateful. I file that piece of information away and push off the desk.

"Thanks, Shelley. You have brightened my day," I say with a smile, taking a look at the chart in front of me and getting back to work, finishing my rounds so I can go home and finally rest.

Pure exhaustion nips at my feet as I trek the last few steps into the apartment building. I can honestly say that I underestimated my need for stamina. This walk home almost kills me. I am sure I have blisters covering my heels and toes.

"Hey, 10A!" Brian almost shouts with glee from his front desk, the warm welcome startling. I am so used to keeping my head down and being invisible that I am unprepared for the acknowledgement. But I give him a small smile. He has been nice so far, and I get the feeling that he is genuine, and a total extrovert. As I walk inside, the lobby lights reflect off the polished marble, the whole area looking alive, and dare I say, almost like home.

"Hi, Brian." I smile, giving him a wider grin, and the last amount of energy I have. I am in my scrubs, my flimsy backpack flung over my shoulder, and feel like I am operating with less than one percent battery.

"Big day, honey?" he asks, looking concerned.

"The biggest. How did the plumber go today?" I ask as I walk over to his desk to chat.

"As suspected, I believe a part needs to be ordered. Eddie supervised and everything is all clean and tidy for you," he says, his smile wide. "We need to organize our shopping trip. I know those scrubs are required, but seriously, girl, blue is your color!" I feel the stress from the day melt away already. He is like my own personal cheer squad.

"A shopping trip would be great, but not this week, I am exhausted already," I muster, my grin small but there. I would like to go shopping with Brian. I have a feeling it would be so much fun, and I have never had a big shopping day before. I have only ever seen them in movies, where friends go to a mall and walk out with bags and bags of goodies. But while my pay is okay at this new hospital, and I don't have to pay for rent, the little money I do have left over after bills, I am trying to save. There is always a rainy day in my future, and this time, I want to be prepared. Spending money on new clothes and handbags, although it sounds fun, is not something I can justify in my life at the moment. I am going to have to put him off for as long as I can before I fake some other excuse. The whole thing makes me feel queasy.

"We will plan it in a few weeks. Let you get settled first. Plus, the season will change soon so we can get a heap of bargains!" he says, almost jumping in excitement that is almost contagious.

"Why do I get the feeling that shopping is one of your favorite activities?" I tease.

"Because it is. Now get your butt upstairs and get some sleep. You look like the devil sucked the life out of you today." He couldn't be more right.

"Love you too," I say sarcastically as I step away and walk toward the elevator.

"*Oh my God*—you love me already? I am going out tomorrow to buy us a necklace. You know the one with the broken heart. I will wear one half and you wear the other!" I laugh, even though I know he is serious.

"See you tomorrow!" I shout to him with a smile as I step into the elevator and watch the numbers as it climbs to my level.

Opening the door to my apartment, the first thing I feel is relief. Relief that it looks just how I left it and relieved to be home. I fling my bag against the wall, kick off my shoes, and let my feet sink into the thick carpet. My eyes then catch the enormous basket on the kitchen counter.

"*What the*?" I murmur and walk over.

The basket is from the building owners again, apologizing for the faulty tapware. It is massive. Full to the brim of food and snacks. My stomach rumbles just at the sight. I see another box of those yummy cookies and know I will devour the entire box for dinner tonight. There is also wine, chocolate, some Mediterranean olives, breads, and dips. This could feed me for a week, and although I have a cupboard full of packet noodles, I almost cry with joy at the selection of food now available to me. If I ration it out just right, I think this will see me through to payday. I nearly cry.

I know all this is because of Eddie. He must have told them about the water issue. My thoughts from earlier start circling my brain again. No one has ever done a nice thing for me, not without expecting something in return, and I don't like feeling as though I am in debt to him. I already feel like I owe him after he brought me a coffee this morning. I know that he got it from a fancy shop too, because I walked past it on the way to work this morning, the logo on the window matching the one on the cup in my hand.

As I open the basket, my mind continues to drift to his half-naked frame yesterday. I remember it vividly because I have never seen a body like it. Strong. Fit. Clean without tattoos. Too perfect. Shaking my head, I brush those ridiculous thoughts aside. I can't go daydreaming about a random maintenance man.

I don't date anyone, and I am also not really wired to do anything casual. A few one-night stands are more than enough for me. The feeling of being discarded afterward brings back childhood memories of never being wanted. Hence why I have been perpetually single for years. Of course, like most young women, I've always dreamed of a beautiful married life, with kids, and maybe a dog, laughing every day with a man who loves me more than life itself. But I am a realist. I know they are just dreams. And my life has taught me that dreams don't come true for a girl like me. Dreams can be dangerous. You get attached to people, and they constantly let you down. I can't go thinking my life is anything other than what I have now, and already, that is more than I ever imagined.

I pull out the cookie box from the basket and take it to the sofa to eat away these rising feelings. Sighing, I think about my day, wondering how I am going to get through another twelve-hour shift tomorrow. But the bright side is that I met Tracey and am now a volunteer in the neonatal ward, the one area that really makes me feel at ease.

Since I had already provided reference checks for the hospital, it was easy for Tracey to allocate me a few hours per week. Working with babies is not new for me. I was a cuddler at the previous hospital I worked at, and I am glad to have the opportunity to do it again.

I tilt my head side to side and roll my shoulders, hearing my bones creak before I mold my body into the soft sofa. My feet ache, so I throw another cookie in my mouth and lift them up off the floor, but as I do, my foot spasms.

"Argghhhh," I scream out to my empty apartment as the cramp overtakes my foot, like an invisible zombie is twisting it in all different directions, yet it is almost frozen. I pause. Too scared to move. I have had cramps before, they are nothing new. Obviously, I have been on my feet for too long today. Looking down at them, they are red, the toes a little swollen. I have no idea how many steps I did today, but my feet are feeling every single one of them.

I gingerly place it down so I can stretch it out. Pulling on my toes, I push past the initial pain and lean into the stretch, slowly releasing my breath. My body relaxes as the muscles flex out and the cramp disappears. I slump back, wondering how my body can feel like it is eighty today.

I need a bath, then bed. I already know tomorrow is going to be even worse. But at least I get delicious cookies, and tomorrow, I can cuddle a baby.

6

EDDIE

"Thanks, Miranda," I murmur as my assistant positions a steaming cup of coffee on my desk in front of me. I appreciate her. She runs my schedule and keeps things moving, but my eyes don't leave the contract in front of me. It's for a new development we just completed in Singapore, and I just need to sign this off before my team can start filling it with tenants.

"Do you need anythi—" Miranda starts but doesn't get to finish her question before my mother stalks in the door.

"Seriously, does no one work in this place? No one was at reception, and clearly, you are not at your desk," my mother says, giving Miranda the evil eye. My assistant looks like she has seen a ghost, my mother's mere presence enough to scare most people.

"Thanks, Miranda," I grit out my frustrations, ready to climb the walls at my mother's sudden appearance. I throw my pen on the desk and lean back in my chair, looking at my mom as she takes a seat opposite me with a grin on her face, looking all too pleased with herself.

"You heard. Close the door on your way out," my mother berates her.

"Mom. Enough!" I bark at her as Miranda stalks out of my office. Mom sits up straight, shocked at my tone. This is the first time in a long time she has been here, and the way she walks in like she owns the place makes me unsettled. She has something planned. I can already feel it.

"So, Edward, I have a list for you," she says, grabbing a piece of paper from her handbag and passing it across my desk to me. She is smug, and I don't like it.

"What kind of list?" I ask having no idea what she is talking about. I only saw her at brunch last week and she didn't say anything about stopping by. I'd remember because I would have made sure to be unavailable had she mentioned it.

"A list of single females in Baltimore who are worthy to have our last name," she says, cuffing her hands together on her lap, sitting forward in her seat, obviously looking for praise that she isn't going to find. I take the paper from her, and without looking at it, I leave it on my desk.

"Mom, I don't—" I start, the tension in my neck already building.

"Edward. I gave you a month. A week has already gone by. I just want you to look at the potential list of women I have put together and see if anyone catches your eye."

"I can already tell you, none of them do." I know

everyone in Baltimore. Or at least, I know the types. Everyone here knows us. They know our name, our financial situation. My brother is the fucking governor. Our faces come up regularly in the Society News, on social media, fucking everywhere. The women in this city already know everything about me, which means they will be interested in me for who they *think I am*, not who I really am. There is no one suitable in this city for me, and I am one hundred percent confident that whatever names she has on this paper are most certainly not the woman for me.

"But you haven't even looked at the list!" She waves her hands before her, not able to accept I am not doing what she is asking.

"I am not ready to settle down," I lie, but she doesn't believe it either.

"You need to find someone," she pushes, her shoulders now tightening. I am waiting for her outburst. She is normally not so quiet.

"No. I. Don't." I punch out the words as I grip on to my desk, and I see her straighten even more as she rubs her upper arm. "Are you cold?" I ask because it is an odd move. It is unseasonably warm in Baltimore today.

"No. I think I hurt my arm playing tennis the other week. Stop changing the subject. Look. At. The. List." She points to the piece of paper that still remains on my desk.

"You play tennis?" I ask, my brow crinkling. I cannot imagine Mom playing any sport. She doesn't like to perspire. Says it is unladylike.

"Concentrate on this, Edward. You need a wife," she

demands, her cheeks reddening in anger, her eyes piercing mine.

"Mom, seriously, I need to work. I don't have time for this." I am getting agitated. The late afternoon sun streams in through my floor-to-ceiling windows, the amber glow illuminating the city below. I sigh. I was hoping to get this contract signed off before I went home, but now that is going to be a difficult task.

"Edward. You need to look at this list!" Her voice rises another octave.

"No. What I need to do is get this contract signed; otherwise, the whole deal will crumble, and we will lose close to ten million within a matter of minutes if I miss the deadline," I growl. My eyes narrow at her. I have never been this vocal with her, ever. I usually let her get away with most things, but organizing a wife for me is a step too far.

"Fine. I will leave it here and come back and talk to you about it another time." She purses her lips, not happy about it, but realizes that it is us boys who keep her finances healthy. I'm sure she doesn't want to jeopardize that for herself. I do need to get this contract done, but it isn't due for a while. I may have exaggerated that small detail. I watch her stand, smooth down her skirt, and walk straight out the door, leaving it wide open without a care in the world and without another word.

"Jesus," I murmur to myself, rubbing my head. She frustrates me beyond words. I clench my fists as I look at the paper that sits on the edge of my desk before I lean over and grab it. I don't bother looking at it before I rip it in half, then in half again. Over and over until there are tiny bits of white paper like confetti now sprinkled on my desk.

"Sir?" Miranda asks from the doorway. "Your five o'clock just canceled." Thank God. I feel like someone is watching out for me.

"Thanks. I need to go. You pack up and have an early day as well. After that debacle, I think we both need it," I offer with an apologetic smile, which she graciously returns, and I watch as she packs up her desk and leaves.

I try to finish the contract but have lost all focus. My teeth continue to grind, my shoulders on fire with how tense they are. What in the world is she even thinking? Why would she think that setting me up with some society princess is what I want? With the rest of the office starting to clear out, I shut down my computer and grab my jacket.

I need to go and hit something.

The ride to the Harborside building frustrates me even further as peak-hour traffic has Tony snaking around the streets. By the time I get to the foyer, I am more on edge than I have been for a long while.

"Brian. Any maintenance?" I blurt out, stalking to the back office and grabbing the jeans, cap, and shirt I keep here. He cocks a brow at me and is about to say something sassy but thinks better of it. *Smart man.*

"Actually, yes, there is. The older man in 2B broke his cupboard again and wants it fixed before he gets home from his weekend in Florida," Brian says, looking at me with a worried expression. "Did something happen, boss-man?" he asks tentatively, eyeing me with suspicion.

"My mother happened," I mutter. I know he heard

me, and I shouldn't speak outside of the family, but she has a reputation, and everyone is aware of it. I make quick work of getting changed and grab my tool belt. Taking my frustrations out on 2B cabinetry is just what I need.

Leaving Brian at the desk, looking at me with a furrowed brow, I stalk to the elevator and take it to 2B. I do a loud courtesy knock, just in case anyone is home, but there is no answer, so they must be in Florida as Brian mentioned.

I walk straight to their kitchen and see the offending cupboard. It hangs from the bottom, the top hinge completely off. A frustrated growl breaks from my chest because I know he was leaning on it again. I wonder if the old guy actually realizes he is breaking all these cupboards on his own.

I dump my tools and get to work, attempting to pry the bent hinge off the timber door, trying to get it loose. The way it is hanging off the door, it is out of shape, making it hard to remove.

"C'mon, you stupid fucker..." I grumble to myself, my frustration heightened as I put all my strength into flicking it off the timber so I can reattach a new one. I take a deep breath and push with all my might. The hinge comes loose, flying through the air, along with the screws. But that isn't all. A piece of wood snaps off, just as my body falls forward from the force, and the sharp wood pierces my shoulder. The pain is instant.

"Son of a bitch," I yell, throwing the cupboard door onto the floor as I lean against the kitchen counter.

"Don't look at it, don't look at it, don't look at it," I repeat to myself, forcing my eyes closed while trying to slow my breaths. I have never been able to stomach the sight of blood. Ever since I was a kid. I have done my best over the years to try to get past it, but for the most part, I just look away. Already feeling nauseous, I put down my tools and make my way out of the apartment and to the elevator. I feel dizzy, and my legs start to feel like jelly as I feel the warm wet liquid coat my fingers. The distinct metallic smell rises up my nostrils as I bang on the elevator button, willing it to hurry up. I need to make it back to the foyer and to Brian before I hit the floor. I am sure he will be able to slap some sense into me. Maybe he can send a warning letter to 2B as well, because if I ever have to go back there and fix a cupboard door again, it will be too soon.

7

KATIE

I walk into the foyer, my legs still tender, but not as sore as they were last week. I give Brian a smile and a wave as I cross the lobby, seeing him on the phone and not wanting to interrupt. Being greeted by his smiling face every evening when I get home has become a nice little part of my life that helps me feel connected. Like, in some weird way, someone is looking out for me. I make my way to the elevators, where I wait, seeing the numbers on the side coming down to ground. The days at the hospital are still long, but now my mind and body are growing more used to the demanding hours. As the elevator doors open, I go to walk in, but Eddie falls out.

"Eddie!" I call out, seeing the state of him. He is pale and barely walking. As soon as I spot a little blood on his shirt at his upper chest, I go into nurse mode. Instantly, I'm looking around, searching for the culprit of his injuries, ensuring no danger is nearby. "What happened?" I ask quickly, trying to remain calm. He leans on me, nearly crumbling me in the process.

"Hey, Pinkie," he murmurs, his hand flinging around my waist, his head resting on my shoulder. His warm breath skirts down my neck, making my heart race and my body feel electric. I wrap my arms around his waist, trying to take his weight, which is futile as I stagger under the pressure.

"Brian!" I yell to get his attention, and I watch as his eyes widen as the two of us stumble toward the concierge desk. Brian runs over to us, grabbing Eddie on his other side and taking most of his weight. Eddie is barely lucid, his feet stumbling over each other like he is drunk. He can't even walk straight as the three of us stagger behind the concierge desk into a large office, one that is just as luxurious as every other thing in this place. My guess is he doesn't like the sight of blood because there is not enough of it on his clothes for him to be feeling faint due to blood loss.

"I'm bleeding," Eddie whispers, his eyes going wide as he looks at his hand. Blood coats his fingers as he takes a seat in a large armchair, and I stand in front of him, assessing.

"Don't look at it," I say quickly, wiping the blood away with a tissue before pulling his hand from in front of his face and holding on to it. His hand is bigger than mine, and he wraps my fingers in his, the connection sending goosebumps up my arms. "Look at me. Don't look at anything else. Just look at me." I soften my tone, my initial concern starting to leave my body now that I can see the gash is not too bad. I give his hand a squeeze of support.

"I'm fine," he mumbles, trying to sit up straighter, still paler than I'd like him to be.

"You don't look fine. What happened?" I ask, grabbing his shirt and undoing some buttons. His hand falls to the side before he lifts it and grabs me. I am standing right in between his legs, and he grabs my thigh, his hand so big it wraps almost completely around my muscle. Flames lick my legs, my skin tingles, and my heart thumps as I swallow roughly, trying to calm my traitorous body. I am trying to assess him, but the reaction I'm experiencing is something entirely new. I have never felt this way with a patient. I have never felt this way with *anybody*. His thumb strums then, slowly, hesitantly, across the side of my thigh and goosebumps scatter over my skin once again. My eyes flick to his, where I see evident heat in his stare, before he clears his throat, and his eyes lose focus as he answers me.

"I had a fight with a cupboard," he says, barely audible. It is common for people to feel woozy if they don't like the sight of blood, and I suspect Eddie is one of these people. I roll my lips because he looks so innocent and cute right now.

"So, the cupboard won, I'm guessing?" I ask, undoing the last button to pull the shirt from his frame.

"Unfortunately." He huffs a laugh, his smirk small but there. I relax a little, knowing he isn't in pain and can laugh at himself. He sits forward slightly and pulls his shirt off his arms, flinging it on the ground nearby. I should be prepared for what I see, but I am not. I lick my lips and my breathing quickens. I saw him shirtless only a week or so ago and that image has been on my mind every day since. But now, touching his skin, looking at him closely, I am struggling to remain professional.

"What did the cupboard do to you?" I ask as I look at the wound. A small cut, something a few butterfly clips will fix. Brian rushes in and delivers me a full medical kit, which is extremely impressive, before he is called to go out the front, leaving Eddie and me to it.

"Not the cupboard. My mother," he murmurs as he leans back, his head resting on the back of the large armchair, his eyes locked on me.

"Your mother?" I prompt, confused, watching him, wondering if he hit his head as well. He could be concussed. He takes a few deep breaths before he continues.

"Yeah, she is trying to set me up with a wife." My eyes flick to meet his, and his brows furrows slightly. The look he gives me almost melts my underwear clear off my body. He is angry, his jaw sharp and tight, his eyes alight, and without thinking, I run my hand down his jaw, wanting him to relax. I softly cup my hand around his face, and he tilts it upward to me before I come to my senses and remove my touch. *What the hell am I doing?* Clearing my throat, I get busy digging into the medical kit for supplies as I refocus on the small talk.

"And you don't want one?" I ask, raising my eyebrow in question as my fingers press on the wound with a bandage I found, trying to stop the small trickle of blood.

"I want to choose my own," he says with a growl. Obviously, his mother is a handful. I can't imagine it at all, having not ever met my own mother.

"That makes sense. Now, I just need to wash the

wound, and then I will dress it. You will be right as rain in no time," I say, trying to focus on the work I have to do and not the feeling of his skin under my touch. He is warm, his skin smooth, the light scattering of hair across his contoured chest making my mouth water. He is too perfect for his own good. I am sure he has a myriad of women falling at his feet. His mother is probably wanting to set him up, so she doesn't have to see them all melt around him. I shake my head, getting back on track, and squirt some saline across the wound and wipe it a little. The bleeding has almost stopped.

"You okay?" I ask him, the two of us having a quiet moment.

"Hmmmm," is all he responds with. I can feel his face right in front of mine, my eyes zoned in on the wound I am nursing. I can smell his aftershave. A woodsy cologne, it is masculine, as is the broad expanse of his chest. Every inch of him screams protector, even though I am the one helping him.

"Am I hurting you?" I ask again to be sure. I am trying to be gentle as I stick him back together.

"No." His one-word reply is too quick, which concerns me. I look at him, and his eyes are closed again.

"Open your eyes," I demand, and as our eyes connect, I see his pupils dilate. His face looks white as a ghost again, and I know that he is going to faint.

"Eddie!" I yell, loud enough to grab Brian's attention, and I hold on to Eddie as he slumps forward, his face planting right on my chest. "Shit." He is heavy. Thank God Brian is nearby, because I would have no hope in moving him on my own.

"Sorry, I should have mentioned that he faints at the sight of blood," Brian says as he rushes in, and we both get him onto the floor on his back. I lift his legs up onto the chair he just vacated. "Will he be okay? Should I call an ambulance?"

"He should be fine. He is breathing fine, just a little woozy is my guess," I say to Brian as I position Eddie on his side into the recovery position.

"Damn, man is a baby when it comes to blood," Brian sasses before the bell dings at the front desk, and he leaves me to deal with Eddie.

"Eddie. Eddie," I say, lightly tapping his cheek to rouse him. Watching his chest rise and fall and feeling his breath on my cheek, I lean in to ensure his breathing is consistent. "Come on, come back to me."

"Pinkie?" he says roughly, his eyes remaining closed. "Pinkie from 10A." I laugh, and I hear Brian huff a laugh too, as he stands next to me, passing me the cold pack and shaking his head.

"Yeah, Pinkie is here," I say, grabbing his hand and giving it a squeeze. This man is turning me into mush. His limbs are a little cold, so I rub his hands in my own, trying to warm them up a bit. Brian steps away again, back to his desk outside.

"What happened?" he asks, still half-dazed but coming around.

"You fainted," I tell him, looking down at this massive man who lies completely still on the floor next to me.

"I'm too tough to faint," he says, giving me a smirk, and I laugh at his attempt at humor.

"No, apparently not." I can't help but smile, relief rushing through me that he really is okay.

"Just don't make me look at blood." Sitting up a little, he tries to get his bearings.

"Just look at me," I offer as I help him to stand and get him back in the armchair.

"That is not a hardship." I swallow at his confession. His grip on me is tight, and I don't let go either. The need to comfort him is strong. Once he is settled back into his seat, I finish washing his small wound and place some butterfly patches on. It may be a little sore, but he shouldn't have any other issues.

"There you are, as good as new. Just keep it dry for a few days," I offer, my fingers mindlessly brushing the bandages. "As long as you don't pull it again, it should heal just fine."

"Thanks." He sits up straighter and runs his hand through his hair, staring at me as he starts to get a bit more color to his cheeks.

"So your mother?" My eyebrows rise in question, wanting to learn more about him, but also trying to get my mind off the fact that he is still half-naked and my hands were just all over his body. I'm not usually one for chatting too much. I do enough of it at work, and that exhausts me to the point that I prefer a quieter life at home. But Eddie has me thinking and feeling a whole range of things I ordinarily don't, and I *want* to talk to him. Be with him. Get to know him.

I sit in the spare chair next to him, keeping us close. His leg leans out a little, and our knees touch, The old me would sit up straighter and create space. Pull my knee away and make myself small. But I don't. I leave it there, touching his, as he shifts his arm to rest on the back of my chair, opening up to me, my body instantly relaxing back into him.

"Yeah, believe me when I tell you she is not a woman that you ever want to meet," he says, and I scoff.

"She made you, so she can't be all bad," I say, giving him a small smile, and I can feel my cheeks heat at my statement. He looks at me and smiles. His mouth is not the only thing that reacts, as his eyes glisten in glee as well. I feel almost giddy. What is it about this man that has me feeling things I never have before? Shit, I need to pull it together. Who knew all it would take is for a bare chest to be right in front of me to have me start acting like a flirtatious schoolgirl hanging off the most popular guy at school.

"When I have kids, I am going to be a much better parent," he says, rolling his neck and taking a deep breath.

"How many kids do you want?" I find myself asking.

"A bunch of them. You?" His eyes search mine, and I swallow, not believing I am having this kind of conversation. Our conversation feels normal. Not hurried, not forced. That is why I am probably not running out of the office back to the safety of my apartment. I feel almost content. *Dare I say, happy?*

"Maybe one day," I offer with a shrug, not wanting to tell him that having children is something I yearn for. I never had that family life, and I want to create it for myself.

"You're home late?" he observes, changing the topic.

"You keeping tabs on me?" I tease, looking up at him, pleased to see his eyes now focused and his familiar sexy smirk is back in place.

"I thought your shift finished at seven?" I smile at the fact that he remembered. It is sweet. No one ever cared where I was before. Ever.

"It does. I volunteer," I tell him. It's nice that he is showing an interest.

"Volunteer? So, you not only look after sick people during your working hours, patch up dying maintenance men, but you do it in your own time as well?"

"Well, we both know you are not dying, Eddie." I roll my eyes at his exaggeration, a laugh bubbling in my chest. "I volunteer in the hospital neonatal ward. I am a cuddler," I say, not able to stop the smile on my face. Seriously, if they had a paid position, I would want it.

"A what?" he questions, clearly intrigued.

"A cuddler. There are babies born addicted to narcotics that need constant handling. So that's what I do." My stomach feels like lead as I think about it. I often wonder if I ever had a cuddler. I want to believe that I did.

"Wait. What?" he says, sitting back, looking at me in disbelief. "You're actually telling me that babies that are born to mothers who have drug dependencies come out addicted, and as part of their treatment, they need cuddles?" The look of shock on his face would be humorous if we were discussing any other topic.

"Yes. It takes weeks and months for the babies to get it out of their system. Cold turkey is hard for adults, but excruciating for babies. There is an army of volunteers like me who take a few hours each week to sit with them and cuddle them. Keep them safe and calm where possible." It isn't something that people really think about or concern themselves with. Usually, the cuddling program is so underfunded that it simply flies under the radar.

"Wow. I had no idea." The look on his face is one of awe. "So, with week one down, how do you like Baltimore?" he asks me, and I take a moment to think about it. He sits near me, still half-naked, our arms brushing against each other. It feels nice. I wonder what it would be like to lay my head on his shoulder and lean into him.

"I haven't seen much of it, but so far, I like it." I don't miss the glee in his eyes.

"Is cardiology somewhere you want to be long term? Along with the cuddling, I mean?" he asks, smiling.

"I think so. What's not to love about the heart?" I joke, and he smiles, his eyes dancing in delight. "What about you?"

"Me what?"

"Have you always worked in building maintenance?" I ask, looking up at him with interest.

"Yeah. After college, I went backpacking for a little bit and then kind of fell into it. I bet you have some good stories from what you have seen in hospitals," he offers, changing the conversation quickly back to me.

"Oh, there are plenty. One time, a patient got really angry, and he threw a bedpan at me. But he didn't realize it was full and the whole contents sloshed all over him instead." I roll my lips, laughing.

"That is disgusting," he says, mock horror on his face.

"It really was, especially since I had to clean it up and

bathe him too." I wipe the tear that falls from my eye, laughing at the memory.

"Then, the mafia men who came in, they were the scariest. I remember one time when I first started in the ER with Dr. Wakeford in Philly, I was so new I had no idea what I was doing. They were rough and battered and bruised... But turns out, they are actually really nice guys!" I say, smiling, remembering the first time I met Carter Grange. Eddie looks at me for a moment, only blinking, before continuing.

"When I was backpacking in Asia, I remember one night I went to the local market to grab some food, and I tried a local delicacy that made me so sick I was in the hospital for days," he says, and my eyes widen.

"Oh no, what did you eat?" I ask, wincing. Food poisoning is the worst.

"Goat testicles." I sit in shock as we both look at each other before we totally lose it. I laugh so hard, my eyes are watering again, and that makes him laugh even harder.

"Goat balls?! You ate goat balls?" I clarify through my laughter.

"Well, in my defense, I didn't know they were goat balls when I was eating them. I just thought it was chicken. I guess it wasn't cooked properly, because I had to be strapped to an IV drip for two days." He leans forward, his thumb connecting with my cheek, and he swipes a stray tear that was falling. The minute his thumb grazes my skin, the world stops. I forget how to breathe, and his eyes look right into mine, the temperature in the room increasing.

"Sorry, you just had a tear..."

"It's okay," I whisper, seemingly forgetting how to talk as he brushes his thumb across my cheek a few more times. It would be so easy just to lean in, maybe touch my lips to his. But I can't, so I lean back a little, my cheek feeling cold as his hand drops away.

"So where is your family? Are they still in Philly?" he asks, and my body stiffens. It is an innocent question, but he doesn't need to know. It is not worth bringing up.

"I grew up in Boston," I offer, leaving it at that. I don't want to get into it. Not here, not now. There is no point. I can't go thinking that these feelings I am having whenever I am around Eddie are worthwhile. Nothing good lasts in my life. My history has taught me that, and it is a history that is not worth repeating. "I should go."

"I didn't mean to pry," he says, sitting forward as I stand, and I feel my nails dig into my palms. Because, really, I don't want to leave him.

"It's fine. It's just getting late, and the day is catching up with me." It's only an excuse, but as I say it, I yawn, my body agreeing. I gather my things, having been sitting here with him for the better part of an hour. I want to stay. I want to curl up on his lap and never leave. But... I can't get attached. Everyone I attach myself to leaves. My parents, the one boy I thought was my forever. He is the one that hurts the most. I thought we would be together through thick and thin. Turns out, he was the worst thing to ever happen to me.

"Take it easy on that arm, okay?" I offer him a small smile as I start to step back to the door.

"Yes, ma'am," he says, giving me a mock salute as he

grins at me. It is contagious. As hard as I try to tamp it down, the feeling of happiness is too overwhelming and my own wide smile beams.

"See you around," I offer with a wave.

"See you around, Pinkie." He winks, and I almost trip as I walk backward through the door.

What the hell is happening to me?

8

EDDIE

It has been almost a week since I last saw her in her scrubs after work, patching me up, and every day I have been here, in my maintenance uniform, hanging around Brian like a bad smell, hoping to run into her again. I will admit, while I was delirious and probably looked like an idiot fainting at the sight of my wound, I didn't mind her hands on me and wouldn't mind feeling them again.

Katie Taylor, the pink-haired, tattooed pocket rocket from 10A, intrigues me. Her eyes are haunting, yet captivating. She has a quick wit, and is obviously well educated, since she is a nurse. Independent, since she is living on her own, at what I think is her early twenties, especially in a new city. I also noticed she didn't have a ring on her finger as my body thrummed under her touch.

I should have asked for her number. That is what a normal guy would do. But no. I am a billionaire hiding in civilian clothing. Prancing around this complex like I fucking know what I am doing when, in reality, this woman has thrown me, and now I feel almost out of control. I could go and knock on her door, but it is her home, and I don't want to invade her personal space without her permission. So, like a pathetic idiot, my plan is to hang around here in the lobby until I run into her, to see if these feelings I have are reciprocated and, if so, maybe ask her for a date.

"You back again, bossman?" Brian says, watching me walk toward him after getting changed out of my suit.

"You never know what might need fixing," I offer, ignoring his nickname for me and looking through my toolbox, trying to act inconspicuous while my eyes flick to the building entrance. I am never here during the week. Monday through Friday is strictly Edward Langford's time. But this week, Eddie, the maintenance man, has been in full effect. I even got a jump start on a few minor projects I had been putting off.

"Well, she hasn't arrived back from work yet, so you might be in luck tonight," he says, a sly grin on his face. He clearly knows what I am up to.

"I have no idea what you are talking about, Brian." I shake my head at being caught.

"No, bossman, I am sure you don't." He grabs some paperwork and starts logging his work into the computer.

I know her shift finishes at seven, but now that she is also volunteering, she gets home at all different hours. A cuddler. I have never even heard of that before. I am not ashamed to say that I looked into it this week, and the statistics around the number of babies born in Maryland with opiates, alcohol, narcotics, or other drugs in their systems is frightening.

It is dark outside, and I don't like the fact that she walks home from the hospital at night. Baltimore is not overly dangerous, but it is a city, with lots of different characters. Personal safety is something that you have to watch wherever you are, and Baltimore is no different. I walk toward the front glass doors, looking at my own town car and driver waiting outside, and a thought comes to me.

I am about to turn around and head back to Brian, when the doors open, and she rushes in, looking panicked.

"Oh, hey, Eddie," she says, seemingly out of breath, striding straight up to me, but glancing back out the doors to the night sky. Her expression is full of worry.

"What's wrong?" I ask, my senses now on high alert as I stalk toward her, the two of us now only inches apart.

"Oh... um... nothing," she says, waving me off, her independence any other time admirable, but now as she looks so uncertain, I don't believe a word she is saying. I stand in front of her and watch her body shake a little as she pants, regulating her breaths. I grab her hand and hold it in mine by our sides, trying to get her to slow her breathing. It seems to work for a moment, but she is still frightened.

"Pinkie?" I growl, giving her hand a squeeze. Letting her know that I'm here. She swallows but won't meet my eyes.

"I'm fine. It's fine, really," she says quickly, looking around the reception area like a ghost is about to jump out at any moment. "I'm... I'm totally fine." Stepping away from me a little, my eyes narrow, not believing her for one second. I step toward her, closing the gap she created, and grab her chin, angling her face to look at me.

"I get it. You are fine. You said it three times. But I don't believe you. Tell me what happened?" I ask her, my eyes searching hers, and I feel her soft warm breath touch my skin as I take in the fear in her eyes.

"I just thought someone was following me. It is stupid, really. It isn't that late. The streetlights only just came on." Her words roll out into each other, she is talking so fast, making excuses.

"Brian. Security cameras," I bark out to him, my eyes not leaving hers.

"Already on it." I can hear him on the phone and tapping into the computer. We have state-of-the-art security in this place, cameras around the entire building.

"No, no, it is probably just me. It's been a long day. I'm just seeing things," she blurts out, clearly still a little frazzled, her stubbornness shining through. I grab her face in both hands, preventing her from moving, and her eyes widen as I remain close to her, not leaving her for a moment.

"It is building protocol. Now I am going to take your hand, and together we are going to walk to the elevator and go up to your apartment. Brian, your new best friend over there, is going to look over the cameras and tell us if he sees anything. You are safe with me." She remains quiet but wide-eyed as her head nods in my hands.

"Okay," she whispers as my eyes flick down to her lips briefly before I lower my hold on her. I can't remove my hands from her body as they skim her shoulders, and I hear her take a deep breath before I run them down her arms and entwine my fingers with hers.

"Let's go," I say as we walk toward the elevators. I don't let go of her, and I also don't miss the fact that her hand is shaking in mine. She is scared, I can feel it. She saw someone or something happened, but for whatever reason, she is not being honest about it.

We stand quietly, and I rub my thumb across the back of her hand as we wait for the elevator. Both of us look over our shoulder toward the front glass doors like someone will suddenly appear. But the doors remain closed, only showing the lights reflecting from the lobby. Brian looks at me, concerned, and I give him a silent nod to take care of things down here while I take care of her. The elevator opens, and we walk in, remaining silent until the doors close and we are in the small, private space.

"Are you alright?" I ask, turning to her, even though I know she isn't. She takes another deep breath, trying to calm herself.

"I'm okay," she says quietly, nodding, not meeting my eye.

"That's different than fine, so it's progress. You're safe here. In this building. No one can get up these elevators without a pass, and no one can get into your apartment without the key," I reiterate to her, wanting her to know that no one can harm her here. No one will harm her if I am here. "Brian sits at the desk all day, and security is watching all night."

"I know. Thank you," she says, her grip on my hand tightening.

The elevator opens at her floor, and I walk her to her door and drop her hand, feeling cold without it.

"Thanks, Eddie," she says, looking weary now that the rush of adrenaline has worn off. I watch her hands shake as she takes out her keys.

"Here, let me." Taking her keys, I open her door. Then I push it wide, getting her inside.

I grab her bag from her shoulder and place it near the wall, then move around her apartment, turning on the lights for her.

"I'm okay," she whispers, like she is trying to convince herself, and I look at her. She most certainly isn't okay. I can physically see her making herself small. That is not what this woman should be doing. She is vibrant, smart, sassy. She needs to hold her head high and be illuminated for the world to see. Not cowering into herself.

"I know. I'm just going to triple-check all the locks for you, so you know everything is secure," I say as I walk around, unlocking and relocking the windows while I clench my jaw. I pull the curtains closed and fist the material tightly, having a sudden urge to hurt anyone who scares her like this. My shoulders are high as I walk to the front door and do the same, making sure the lock is working well. I feel a headache coming, I'm so tense. I don't like seeing her vulnerable like this. It isn't like her at all.

"Everything is all working fine. Once Brian leaves for the night, security monitors the desk downstairs. No one gets in here. It is manned twenty-four seven." I watch as she takes another deep breath, seemingly more at ease.

"Thank you," she says, offering me a small smile.

"You want me to make you a hot drink? I'm pretty sure the hot chocolate from the basket is probably the most amazing hot chocolate you have ever had," I offer, my grin now overtaking my face. Her stance softens, her grin reflecting mine.

"That would be nice. Ohh... I never thanked you for the baskets, by the way." I raise an eyebrow at that. She doesn't know I own the building and personally organized those for her.

"For the baskets?" I ask quizzically.

"Well, I know you must have spoken to the building owners or organized it all yourself. I appreciate it. What I've tried so far has been delicious," she says, a small smile on her face, one that looks a hell of a lot better than the fear that was there moments ago.

"I'm just going to change real quick." I don't hesitate as I move into the kitchen and get busy while she is taking a moment. The tapware is now all fixed, thanks to my plumbing team, and the sink is sparkling clean. I look over the baskets and notice the artisan cookies are gone from both baskets, so I make a mental note to get her some more. She clearly likes them. As I search in the cupboards for the mugs, I open almost every one to find them still empty except for a few pieces of cutlery and dishes. One cupboard has a small amount of food, like packet ramen, but otherwise, there is nothing here. Likewise, when I open the refrigerator to grab the milk. Aside from milk, a few apples, and some cheese from the baskets, it is empty. I frown, looking at everything so barren. Her job keeps her so busy, it doesn't surprise me.

"Smells good." She gives me a small grin as she walks back out from the bedroom, and I almost stumble. She is in jeans and a soft white knit sweater, bare feet, her pink hair brushed out and long around her shoulders, flowing down her back. This woman could wear a cardboard box and look sexy as hell, but right now, with her hair down, just in denim, she is fucking beautiful.

"Take a seat, I'll bring them over," I say, my voice a little hoarse as I try to shake off my immediate reaction. I grab the two hot cups and make my way over to the sofa where she sits.

"Baltimore is usually a pretty safe city. But the building has a town car. I will have Brian book it for you every morning and every night to get you to and from work." The idea came to me earlier. I will give her Tony and my car. At least that way I know she will be safe. Although now that I am thinking about it, it is something we could offer to the building as an added value. I will bring it to the table with my brothers at our next operations meeting. A building of this caliber certainly needs to continue to up its game and a town car and driver to take tenants wherever they need to go sounds like a good idea. It could give us a competitive advantage. However, giving her my car and driver is something I will implement immediately. Clearing my throat, I roll my shoulders. The number of lies I am now telling her is growing by the day.

"Won't the other tenants need it too?" she asks as I

pass her the cup and watch her take a sip of the hot chocolate, listening to her sweet murmurs of approval.

"No. There aren't many here in this building who need a driver. They mostly have their own cars parked downstairs. The parking garage is always full." She puts her cup down and tangles her hands together, still shaking slightly.

My instincts kick in almost automatically as my hand shoots out and covers both of hers. Her eyes flick to me before she turns her hand and cups mine, entwining our fingers. She takes another deep breath, and her shoulders lower as she relaxes some more. She talks a tough talk, strong and independent, but right now, she is like a small scared little bird. I don't like how this dulls her shine.

"How's your shoulder?" she asks me, and if changing the conversation helps her, then I am all for it.

"Healing fine. See," I say, pulling open my shirt a little, and I see her eyes flick to the thin dark-pink line that is almost all healed.

"Have you always fainted at the sight of blood?" she asks, her nose scrunching, making her look so fucking cute.

"Always. I remember when I was a kid and my brother pushed me off my bike. I landed on my knee, saw the blood, wailed for my oldest brother, then fainted right there in the driveway," I say, taking a sip, smiling to myself at the memory.

"So you have two brothers?" she asks.

I swallow. I should just tell her who I am, but now is not the time. It would be good to see if she actually likes me for just being me, and not the name and money that comes with me. But I am also a little worried about what she will think.

But I need to tell her who I am because I want to kiss her. I want to feel her under my hands, want to wrap my arms around her and tuck her in tight. But tonight is not the night. Whatever happened scared her, and she needs time.

"Three. All older," I say, telling her the truth about everything, except for exactly who I am. "My father died a few years ago. My mother is still around, though. As you know," I add, opening up a little more. "My dad would have liked you." A small smile dances on my lips as I think about my father. A serious businessman who was always busy, but when he spent time with me, he was present and one hundred percent focused on me.

"Why's that?" she asks, looking at me inquisitively.

"I can just tell that you both have the same type of personality," I say, swallowing. When I went backpacking, my father was very supportive. I spent a lot of time volunteering in the local villages over there. I know my brothers think all I did was sit on the beach, bed women, and drink cocktails, but that was far from reality. Only my dad knew what I did. I would call him every week without fail. And every week after our conversation, the charity I was volunteering at would get a big donation. He never said anything and neither did I, but between my dad and me, that year we built a new school, supplied an entire library with books and supplies, and funded a maternal health support service for a small Cambodian community that I personally still fund to this day. Reliving the memories is good for my soul. My life now is too polished for anything that fun anymore. Remembering where I am, I clear my throat. "What about you? Siblings?"

"No. No blood siblings," she says on a sigh. It is an odd way to answer a question, but I let her be. I don't want to dig, and she offers nothing more.

"Are you hungry? Want me to fix you something? Or I can order something in?" I ask her, knowing she came straight from work and probably hasn't eaten. I have no idea how to cook packet ramen, but the pizza shop down the road does an excellent pepperoni pizza that makes my mouth water just at the thought.

"I've kinda lost my appetite." She is looking more tired now, so I finish my cup of hot chocolate.

"I should go. Let you rest," I say, standing, grabbing her empty cup and mine, taking them to the sink and rinsing them, the new tapware now working a treat.

"Make sure you call Brian if you need anything. Just dial nine." She stands and meets me in the kitchen. "If you need security at all, dial four. They have someone there twenty-four seven."

"I'm sure I will be fine." I almost believe her.

"Here," I say, grabbing a pen and paper from the side desk. I scribble my name and number. "If you need anything or just want to chat." Giving her the paper with my number feels weird. I don't ever give out my number, but with her, I am coming to realize, I do everything a little differently.

"I'll be okay." She comes to stand next to me. I can feel her body heat, and I watch her look up at me, her long hair falling like waves down her back, my fingers twitching to touch her. I feel her then, as she grabs my hand and squeezes it before she lifts on her toes and kisses my cheek. Her movements are slow. Deliberate. Her lips soft, they barely touch my skin, yet the warmth that spreads through me is instant. My hand moves immediately as it lightly wraps around her lower back, holding her for a moment.

"Thank you," she murmurs, keeping her face close, her eyes calling to mine.

"You're welcome," I murmur, my heart nearly thumping out of my chest. I strum my nose against her cheek, liking the feel of her close to me. All I would need to do is move my head a little and put my lips on hers.

"I appreciate everything you have done," she whispers, pulling away and lowering back to her feet, and I fight the urge I have to scoop her up as my hand moves up her body. I cup her face, looking at her seriously for a moment.

"Call me. For anything." I try to cement the words into her, wanting her to call me the minute she needs something. Reluctantly, I release my hold on her, and she slips her hand into mine as we walk to the door. I am not keen to leave her, but I have to. I can't stay here all night and watch her sleep. Besides, I wasn't lying earlier. She is safe here. No one can reach her when she is in this apartment.

"Good night," she says quietly as she leans lazily against the open door, the shock of the last few moments now wearing off us both.

"Good night." I stand there, watching her until the door closes and I hear it lock. I still, taking in some deep breaths as my heart races. Now I want her even more. Being close to her like that has lit a fire in me, and now I crave her. Knowing that she is locked in and safe, I strut back to the elevator and make my way to the ground floor. As I stalk out of the elevator and back into the lobby, Brian looks up.

"She alright, bossman?" he asks, his tone now serious, his concern evident on his face. It appears that the beauty with pink hair from 10A has him wrapped around her finger as well.

"She is locked in. Safe. What did you find?" I ask, looking over his shoulder at the computer screen.

"Nothing. It is dark, the images a little grainy. If she was followed, then we didn't pick up anything. I have security on alert, and they are looking around outside, but so far, nothing."

"Keep security on it over the next few days. I will have Tony here every morning to take her to work, and he will drop her back here every night," I say, and he nods.

"Ohhh, can we take Tony to the shops next weekend? There is a new clothing store that has opened down-town," he asks cheekily.

"If she needs to go anywhere, Tony will take her," I grit out, never wanting her to be walking the streets alone again.

"That is mighty nice of you, bossman," Brian says, a small sly grin on his face.

"Yeah, well, I told her it was the building car. I trust you to keep that and my real identity a secret, please." I feel bad asking him this when they are becoming friends. But I just need a little more time to get to know her. The real her. The woman who kissed my cheek because she wanted to, not because she wants my money or name.

"I'm not condoning it, but I will not mention it." I can tell he's not happy about it, but it won't be for long. Then maybe I can send them both shopping with my card, and I can spoil her on my dime. I smile, thinking of the possibility of that being in my future, already knowing she is the kind of girl who needs spoiling, and I am the man to do it.

"Where are you taking her shopping?" I ask, now wanting to know what she might be doing in her spare time.

"Just downtown. Although she works so much, I think we might find it hard to organize the time."

"She does work long hours... Keep on eye on her for me when I'm not here. Let me know if there are any other security issues."

"You got it, bossman." He nods in agreement, and I strut to the office and close the door. I'm angry that she was scared. And I'm frustrated at myself for the secret I am keeping from her. She is the first woman in a long fucking time who has held my interest, and already there are two obstacles in my path. I need to tell her who I am. The question that rolls around in my mind, though, is, will she like the real me?

9

KATIE

It took two weeks. I was gone for just two weeks, and he found me. I didn't need to see his face to know that he was following me. I felt him. I always feel him. There were only a handful of people who knew I was moving to Baltimore, and as I mentally run through the checklist, I have no idea who would have told him. But like with everything my foster brother Steve does, he probably found out illegally.

I hardly slept last night. I stared at the ceiling for most of the night, weighing up my options. I could catch the Greyhound out of Baltimore and straight to a new city. Start working at a new hospital, perhaps even change my name. But I am sick of running. Sick of working so hard at being somewhere new, for it all just to be taken away by Steve. Then I think of what I have already in Baltimore. After a few weeks, I have a good job, secure housing, and a great friend in Shelley and Brian. Eddie...

Eddie. His protective instincts had my emotions scattered. It was uncharted waters for me, but it wasn't hard to navigate because he is like a beacon, making me feel settled just in his presence. I have never had a man take care of me like that. Never had a man make me a warm drink, check my locks, ensure I was safe. No one has cared for my safety before. *No one.*

His hands on my body made my skin tingle and my heart race. Then I kissed him. It was only on the cheek, but I felt like I was floating. His large warm hands encased my waist, and I had to ensure I didn't totally fall into him. I shouldn't want him, but I do. He doesn't need to get caught up in my drama, but I am finding it harder and harder to push him away. I don't want to. I want to dive right in, kiss him more, touch him, feel him. That is what any normal girl would do with a man like Eddie. His strong arms, his boyish charm, his sexy as sin smirks. But it would be selfish of me to have any of that. The constant fear I live in is not something I want him dragged into.

He gave me his number, which is now stored in my phone, right next to Brian's. It is not lost on me that I now have two people I would consider friends, and that is almost more than I have had before.

I was grateful to have the car drive me to work this morning. It felt entirely out of place. The car is yet another luxury that has now been placed in my life. Leather seats, a hot coffee just how I like it waiting for me in the morning, along with bottled water, the whole nine yards. Tony, the driver, is super nice and even opened the door for me. Now I know how those celebrities feel, not lifting a finger for themselves. It will take a while to get used to it, but my safety has to come first. So, I will swallow my pride and be driven to and from work in a flashy town car, all so I don't come to harm or worse. This is now my self-preservation. Tony and a town car.

As I slip out of the warm soft leather seats and say good night to Tony, I make my way back inside my luxurious compound. No longer can I have thoughts of walking around the water, watching the night fall or going out for a late-night junk food snack. Instead, I now have to be holed up in my new apartment. Thank God it has a nice view, or I am sure I would go crazy.

"Hey, bestie. How you feeling today?" Brian greets, giving me his warm smile, which automatically makes my shoulders lower and allows me to take a breath. *I'm home.*

"Much better," I say, smiling, my body almost on autopilot of exhaustion at this point.

"Hmmm. I don't believe you. You know we have a full gym, swimming pool, and sauna on the top floor that is open twenty-four hours for all residents. You may not feel like it today, but any time you want to relax or swim, just use your key to access the elevator. If you want to go when it is a little quieter, I highly recommend a nighttime swim," he offers with a knowing nod and smile.

"A pool?" I ask in disbelief.

"Yes, it is the best in Baltimore."

"And a sauna?" I ask again, just to be sure. Brian winks at me.

"Yes, all on the top floor, open to residents, only I did sneak in my mom once for Mother's Day."

"Of course, you did," I pretend to scold him but fail miserably, my smile automatic when he is around. This place really keeps on giving. I love the water. Swimming is something I enjoy when I can. Now that I have my own pool, that may be more often than before.

"Hey, there is a new shop that opened over in downtown. We should get your new driver to take us over in a few weeks," Brian says, looking at me expectantly.

"Sure. But my roster at work is crazy at the moment. I am not sure when I will get a day that doesn't require me to sleep instead," I say honestly, because I may not want to spend money on clothes, but likewise, my days are long and the time I do have off I will need to rest.

"I understand that, but don't forget you need to take care of yourself too. Sometimes a little shopping with a good friend can also do wonders for your soul." I smile at that. "Besides, I am sure it won't be long before you have a date or something. A woman as pretty as you will be on every straight man's radar very soon," he adds, and my eyebrows rise.

"Yeah, I don't think so. Do you see what I look like right now?" I say to him, spreading out my arms. My work clothes are well worn and wrinkled, my hair falling from its high bun. I am pretty sure I have mascara rubbed under my eye, and my lips are chapped, the hospital air conditioning doing nothing to help my skin hydration.

"Well, there is a maintenance man around here who looks at you like I look at my morning coffee," Brian smarts, raising a brow.

I shouldn't ask, but I want to know. "What look is that?"

"Like he wants to devour you whole and do it every day for the rest of his life." Brian is quick as he watches for my reaction. I try to school it, but my damn cheeks heat and give me away.

"Uh... I am not really looking for love, so you can put your matchmaking skills away for now," I say, trying to get off the topic.

"You are gorgeous. He would be a dumbass if he didn't find you attractive." Brian shuffles some papers on his desk, and I huff a laugh.

"Aw, thank you, Brian. You are great for my ego," I say with a guarded smile.

"Oh, stop. You are a strong, independent woman. I knew that the minute we met. Now get your fabulous self upstairs and try to relax. All this taking care of everyone else must get tiring." I am starting to understand his sass comes from a place of love.

"Thanks, Brian," I say, moving toward the elevators, already feeling a little lighter. As I unlock my apartment door, I fight the yawn that breaks through. I am too tired to swim tonight, but I might go up and check it out. If nothing else, it gives me another space to sit in while I am trying to stay inside and away from danger.

Pushing through my front door, the instant feeling of calmness soothes my weary soul. I take my time tonight in de-stressing from the day. Moving a little slowly, showering and changing before I hit the kitchen, trying to work out which packet of noodles I will make up tonight.

I stop short as I see a box on the kitchen counter, hiding almost out of sight. I didn't see it when I came in earlier. Grabbing it, my eyes widen as I see it is my favorite box of cookies. A smile forms as I read the small note stuck to it.

These are clearly your favorite. Hope you don't mind I dropped them off. They remind me of you—sweet, delicate, and pack a punch. - Eddie

My smile is immediate, and my heart stutters a little. I feel like a grinning fool. *Maybe Brian was right just a minute ago.* My stomach gurgles, reminding me that I do need to eat something today, since lunch consisted of candy lovingly supplied by Shelley again. Putting the cookies down, I open the cupboard to grab some noodles and balk.

I open the next cupboard and the next, almost in a state of shock. I move quickly to the refrigerator and pull the door open and just stare.

The colors that now shine out from my kitchen are like nothing I have ever seen before. My cupboards and refrigerator are now crammed with so much food it is almost a crime. Everything you can imagine, from fresh fruit and vegetables, bagels, cheeses, meats, chicken, ice cream, sweet treats, more cookies. I feel overwhelmed. I gasp for air, can barely breathe, as my eyes water and my hands shake.

Eddie.

Warmth spreads as I continue to look at everything. Taking it all in. He has even supplied cleaning products and new kitchen towels. My stomach drops. He must have seen my empty cupboards last night. I am embarrassed as well as grateful. I don't like feeling like a charity case, yet he doesn't know that I can't afford food. It is a kind gesture, but I'm not sure how I feel about it. On the one hand, I want to sing from the rooftops and jump in his arms. On the other hand, I am scared to touch anything, worried that it was an error or mistake.

I close the cupboards and refrigerator and grab my cell. I need to speak with him.

"Hey, Pinkie." His voice floats out after only two rings, and butterflies swarm my belly.

"Did you fill my cupboards?" I ask nervously, my face scrunched. I didn't even say hello or ask about his day. It is not my most eloquent greeting, but I am nervous and frazzled now.

"Yes. I realized when I made the hot chocolates that you haven't had time to go food shopping properly since you've been here, and, well, you did stop me from dying a slow and painful death the other day..." He trails off. I don't correct him. I found a small food store not far from the apartment that I could visit easily, but their prices were astronomical. So, I bought a few things and had plans to ration them out for the week.

"You were not dying, Eddie!" I say, laughing. My tiredness from earlier dissipates as my laughter dies down.

"Regardless, I had some time, and I wanted to surprise you. You work hard, you volunteer... I want to look after you for a change," he says, just like it is a fact and that is the way it is going to be.

"Thank you, Eddie, but it is too much," I say, starting to protest.

"No. It isn't. I know how busy nurses are at the hospital. You probably don't even get a chance to buy lunch. Now you have everything you need at home." I can hear him moving around.

"Have you eaten?" I ask and immediately cringe. It is well past seven. Of course, he would have.

"No, you offering to feed me now?" I can hear his smirk through the phone.

"Well, if you are nearby, I could put something together for us," I say, holding my breath. God, why is this so difficult? My heart is pounding.

"I'm just upstairs in the pool at Harborside," he says, leaving me surprised.

"Brian just told me about that. Why don't I prepare something and come up and get you when it is ready? I want to check out the facilities anyway. I haven't been up there yet," I offer, opening the refrigerator again and mentally working out what I can cook.

"Sounds great. I'm famished and was really hoping to see you today. After last night, I wanted to check in. Make sure you are okay." I sigh. He's so thoughtful.

"Give me half an hour, and I will be up," I tell him, offering him no other explanation for last night, preferring to think ahead to my future now, not the darkness that is my past.

"Great, see you then." I cut the call so I can get to work, pulling out all the fresh ingredients to make a chicken stir-fry. I am craving fresh vegetables after weeks of not having any. Chopping and dicing everything and putting it all together takes me twenty minutes, and by the time it is ready, the apartment smells like a Thai restaurant, my mouth already watering. I leave it all warming as I run and take the elevator up.

I'm feeling nervous and catch myself in the reflection before I start to panic and brush my hair out with my fingers. Rolling my eyes at myself, I take another deep breath. This isn't a date. It's a thank-you. I just need to erase the images I have of kissing him and the feel of his hands on my body. The desire swirling in my tummy for him has become intense.

But... this is the new me, right? And if the opportunity opens up with Eddie, shouldn't I take it?

10

EDDIE

After I got off the call, I had to swim laps to get out my nervous energy. Just the sound of her voice has my body humming. Shit, even seeing her name come up on my cell phone did weird things to my chest. Now as I sit and try to relax in the sauna, my body is coated in sweat, and I have no idea of the time.

I wasn't sure what she would think coming home to all the food I bought. But I have a feeling she often puts herself last, and working like she does, she has no time to go out and shop for herself. Plus, she is in a new place and probably doesn't know the best places in Baltimore yet. I simply asked my team to order exactly what they get me every week, and I had Brian place it in her apartment. It was easy for me, and by the sounds of it, it meant the world to her.

I crack my neck before sitting up, grabbing my towel and pushing open the door. The cool air hits me immediately, my brain refocusing before I nearly stumble when I come face-to-face with my pink delight.

"There you are," she says quickly, taking half a step back, almost startled. Her eyes are wide as they trail my body. In nothing but black swim trunks, my body is on full display, and my lips curve as I watch her take me in. I clench my stomach a little, showing her what I am made of, and I can't stop my hand as I reach out for her and instantly pull her to me.

"I'm right here," I murmur as I lean toward her. I hear her small intake of breath as I lower my face to her cheek, brushing my cheek against hers before placing my lips on her skin, right near her mouth. My heart is thumping out of my chest. It isn't enough, but I am trying to go slow.

"Hi..." Her voice is almost airy now, as I feel her body turn liquid in my arms.

"Hi," I say, grinning like a loved-up fool, but I can't help it.

"So, is this where you hide out?" she asks, her eyes leaving mine for a moment to take a look around the facilities.

"The best pool in Baltimore," I say, stepping back, conscious of my wet body as I put her hand in mine. "Let me show you around." Throwing the towel around my waist, I pull her along. There is no one here, so I can be myself. That is one of the reasons I swim here so often. The guests in the building are all older. The few who swim do so in the morning, not at dinnertime, so it is always empty.

"Swimming pool, relaxation area, sun deck, infrared sauna, Swedish sauna, female and male restrooms, and there is a heated spa through there, and a gym through that way." I give her the tour quickly, knowing we don't have a lot of time.

"Wow, this is amazing," she says in awe, taking it all in.

"Mmmm, it is," I murmur, staring right at her. She moves her head to look at me, her eyes reflecting the lights from the pool, the motion from the water dancing in her eyes. "Let me just have a quick shower. Why don't you look around, then take a seat in a cabana. That one over there looks right up into the night sky. It is amazing." I point out my favorite spot to her because I know she will love it, before I squeeze her hand and make a quick dash to shower. While I like her eyes on me, I prefer not to be a sweating mess around her.

As I step out from the restroom area after my shower, my cell rings. No sooner do I answer, my brother Tennyson is chewing my ear off.

"I haven't seen you in a week. Where have you been?" he asks me accusingly. It is true, all my brothers and I share an office, but I have been hanging around Harborside so much that I haven't seen much of them.

"I've been busy," I say, my mind not on this conversation as I look around the room to find the pink hair that is usually so easy for me to find.

"Doing what?" my brother Ben barks. Clearly, they are together and I am on speakerphone. Great. I look at my watch. They are probably having a whiskey in the office and debriefing something.

"Just at Harborside. There is a bit going on," I murmur, not really lying to them, but not being totally honest. But they can tell. They are my brothers; they always know when something is up.

"What's going on over there?" Ben asks again. It is the lawyer in him. I can't get anything past him, not one inch.

"Just a new tenant," I say quickly, hoping they skip past this piece of information.

"New tenant? What, causing you trouble?" Tennyson asks, and I grin.

"Yeah, you could say that." I smile down the phone.

"Shit, it's a girl, isn't it?" Ben asks immediately. I knew I couldn't get this past him.

"Yeah, it's a girl. Just met her, taking things as they come."

"Wow, she must be something. It has been months since you have been out with anyone. I was starting to think you were losing your game," Tennyson half jokes.

"I have not lost my game," I scoff. My brothers are assholes, but I love them.

"Nice work, bro. How is my best friend Brian doing?" Tennyson asks, and I balk.

"What do you mean, best friend?"

"He gave me a fantastic recommendation for a new client for Willow, so I had cupcakes from Willow delivered to him the other day. His favorite is chocolate, just so you know," Tennyson tells me, and I shouldn't be surprised that Brian is friends with my brothers. My scheming staff member probably has a black book full of names and numbers. He is a born networker, and I wonder if I should be utilizing his skills in other areas of the business aside from the front desk at Harborside.

"He gave me a fantastic recommendation for a spa that I sent Emily to the other day," Ben acknowledges.

Brian has wormed his way into my family pretty easily, it seems.

"Yeah, well, get your own Brian and leave mine alone." I start walking again toward the cabanas where I left her earlier. I look around and spot her lying back on the sun bed in the cabana I told her about. She is gazing up, straight through the glass ceiling, looking at the Baltimore night sky.

"I need to run. See you at golf," I say, hanging up on their voices and pocketing my phone, my eyes and mind now on only one thing.

"Beautiful, isn't it?" I say without looking. I come here a lot. I love my place, my apartment, my residential building, but I spend a lot of time here as well. It is almost like a home away from home.

"This is so pretty," she says, turning her head to look at me.

I take a seat, then lie down next to her. "It is a great place to come and think. On really clear nights, the stars sparkle like they are now. During thunderstorms, you get an excellent night show, and in summer, the sunsets are breathtaking." My hand reaches out for hers, our fingers interlocking together by our sides.

"It is very relaxing," she says, grinning at me.

"About last night..." I say, not able to forget about it easily. She was spooked, and I want her to know she is safe with me.

"Oh, it's okay. Like I said, I am sure I was overreacting..." She scoffs at herself, but I know it is an excuse. I can tell by the look in her eye.

"I want you to know that the building security looked

around but couldn't see anyone either outside or on the cameras. But they will be implementing nightly building surveillance for the next few weeks, on the hour, just to ensure no one is lingering around," I offer her, hoping it gives her some peace.

"I don't want anyone to go to any trouble because of me." Her brow crumples in a way that makes me want to flatten it again with my fingers. So, I do. I reach out and gently stroke her forehead with the back of my hand, before trailing it down her cheek. Her skin is soft, delicate. I feel her rapid hot breaths on my skin as she looks at me intensely.

"No one is getting in here. Whether you saw someone or not, you felt unsafe; I know you did. So I have asked the building to take every precaution to ensure all our tenants remain safe," I tell her, swallowing roughly as her big blue eyes lock on mine.

"Thank you, Eddie. I feel like I need to keep saying thank you for everything that you are doing for me. I am not sure I will ever be able to repay you." Now it is my turn to frown.

"I don't want anything in return." I don't want her thinking she owes me. She doesn't owe me anything. I keep my hand on her cheek, my thumb brushing against her soft skin.

"Nothing?" she asks me, her free hand grabbing my wrist with the lightest of touches, keeping my hand on her as she moves her body toward me more, our torsos now only inches apart. I don't miss the look she gives me. Her lips dance upward, her voice filled with innuendo.

"I have no expectations," I say, wanting to make it clear.

"So... I should kiss you because I want to, right?" she teases again, and I cough out a laugh.

"Do you?" I really fucking hope she says she does.

"Yes. Desperately," she whispers softly, and I cup her face fully and pull her to me. My lips brush hers, and I immediately feel centered. Almost anchored to her as her lips part and our tongues tangle. Her hands run up my arms and settle at the back of my neck, pulling me closer, my body itching to be closer to her too.

I run a hand down her body, feeling her small curves, getting familiar with her shape, and loving every minute of it. We kiss slowly and deliberately for what feels like forever, and even then, I am not ready to come back up for air.

"Oh my God!" she says, panicked, pulling away quickly and jumping to her feet.

"What?" I jump up too, looking around for the threat.

"I left dinner to warm. It might be nearly ruined!" she cries out, and I let go of the breath I was holding and chuckle. She races out, and I grab my things, following her back downstairs to her apartment for dinner. I keep her hand firmly in mine, her body next to me, my thoughts only on her.

11

KATIE

After rushing back here to find dinner still perfect, we now sit around the table, both full to the brim.

"Where did you learn to cook like that?" he asks, stretching his body. He had two servings of the chicken stir-fry I made, clearly enjoying it. I smile at him while I wonder what to tell him. Do I tell him the truth, that I learned all my cooking skills from a foster family who forced me to cook for everyone in the house, then left me the scraps to eat? Or from the professional chef who took me under his wing for the two weeks I was staying with the well-to-do family who wouldn't let me sit on the white sofa?

"YouTube, those videos are fantastic," I say, sipping the wine we poured, hiding behind the glass.

"Hmmmm, I will have to start watching some. Build up my repertoire," he says with a wink, causing me to smile again. "So, you are feeling okay now? After yesterday?" he asks for the second time tonight. It must keep playing on his mind, as it is mine. Steve showing up is nothing new; I just had really hoped that he forgot about me. Perhaps moved on, found someone else to occupy his time. The move to Baltimore was supposed to make it harder for him to get to me. Obviously, that didn't work.

"Yeah, I'm fine. Just a little scared. I'm not used to the new neighborhood," I say with another smile as I stand to clear the table. "Thank you again for organizing the driver. After the week I have had, it has been so good just to slip into that car and get back here. Strange thing, though..." I say with a small grin on my face, one that makes him smile wide back. I do wonder how he has all these connections. It could be that they are all part of the same building, but I am starting to think there is more to Eddie than meets the eye.

"What's that?" he asks, tilting his head a little as he starts to help clear the table.

"The driver, Tony, turns up every morning with my exact coffee order. The exact same one you got for me on my first day of work. Do you know anything about that?" I ask, smiling, already knowing the answer. I wait for his reaction to see if there is anything that may tell me more about the man Eddie is.

"Tony is a pretty smart guy. I am sure he had good intel from a trusted source," Eddie says, almost laughing, doing a terrible job of acting clueless.

"He also seems to refer to you as his superior, rather than his colleague. Why is that?" I press.

"Well, everyone who works here just wants the best

for the tenants, so we work as a group. Maybe he acts that way because I organized the car for you instead of Brian?" Eddie says, shrugging, not appearing to be hiding anything, so I let it go. My sixth sense is a little off tonight, it seems. "You know, you are tough, Katie."

"Oh, why do you say that?" I ask, wondering what his assessment of me is.

"Any other woman I know who had a fright like that would probably stay inside for weeks. Too scared to face the world again for a while. But not you. You went straight back to work, and I am sure if I let you, you would probably have declined the driver and car. Strong as well as stubborn," he teases me, his eyes sparkling.

"I guess I am just not like any of the women you usually meet."

"No, you are not. Much more beautiful." His voice lowers slightly, and it leaves me breathless as he dashes back to the dinner table to collect the remaining dishes for the dishwasher as I get a hot sink of water going to scrub the pots and pans.

"Do you compliment all the women who make dinner for you?" I ask playfully, but I am fishing. This man is so perfect, I am sure he has had a lot of women.

"You are the only one, so how am I doing?" When he stops next to me, I look up at him in slight shock.

"No one has cooked you dinner before?" The words come out before I can stop them.

"Not like this. I usually go out," he says with a shrug. "Oh, you have something on your nose..."

I dry my hands quicky to brush my nose. "Did I get

it?" I ask, scrunching my nose, feeling borderline embarrassed.

"No, here, let me." He brings his hand up and covers my nose in soap suds from the sink.

"Eddie!" I say in shock before I bark out a laugh as soapy water sits on my face.

"You look cute all sudsy, Pinkie," he says, too busy laughing at me to notice where my hands are.

"Oh, really?" I ask just before I scoop up a lot of the suds and put them on top of his head. He now looks like the King of Soaptown, his sudsy crown high and flexible.

"Now it is game on," he warns before he turns on the tap and shoots me with a short spurt of water. I scream in laughter as the spray hits me before he loses his grip, the rest splashing on him. He turns off the tap, the two of us in fits of laughter.

"I think I have soap up my nose," I say with a giggle. This is by far the most innocent fun I have had in a long time. I feel relaxed. Safe. I can let my guard down with him and be secure in the fact that it will be okay.

"You light up a room when you smile." He gives me the compliment as he grabs a kitchen towel and wipes my face for me. His touch is soft, his large hands gentle, as I stand still, hardly breathing. He is close, we are almost chest to chest, and I look up at him as he cleans my face. "Back to beautiful again," he murmurs, staring down at me as one of his hands scoops around my middle so effortlessly, it is like it was always meant to be there. He holds my body in place right next to his as our breaths mingle between us. I feel his fingers as they caress my lower back, and he watches me, waiting for me to make the next move.

"I like being in your arms..." I say quietly, almost scared to say the words out loud, feeling vulnerable but wanting to be with him as the space between us grows smaller.

"Good, because I like having my hands on your body." His other hand wraps around my waist, now firmly holding me to him. My breathing is rapid, my breasts pushing against his chest, and I run my hands up his arms, wanting to feel him too. I feel the ridges of his arm muscles before I rest my hands at the back of his neck, almost on my tiptoes as I try and get closer to him.

My eyes search his, and he leans forward, putting his forehead against mine.

"You look like you are wearing a crown," I whisper, my eyes not leaving his. My heart thumps a million beats a minute, my body hot all over.

"Well, permission to kiss thy lady, then?" he murmurs seductively as he lowers his mouth even more, his nose skirting across my cheek, almost toying with me, waiting for me to say yes.

"Permission granted," I say on a breath, and he wastes no time leaning in and taking my lips for the second time tonight. He is soft at first, almost playful, exploring, and I can feel us both smiling against each other, enjoying this moment. His hand moves from my back, running around my waist, his fingers touching my bare flesh at the top of my jeans, goosebumps covering my skin. His hand is warm as it circles my waist again, this time under my top. The skin-on-skin contact makes my body feel like liquid as I lean into him. Lost in his embrace, in his kiss, feeling warm, safe, comforted. I am not without nerves. *Am I doing the right thing?* I have no idea. But it feels right. He feels right.

Our tongues dance as we taste each other, wanting yet not rushed. It is sensual as we feel our way. I sink my fingers into the back of his head, tangling them in the curls he has there, and he moans in my mouth. His hand travels up my back, his palm flattened against my body like he wants to feel as much of me as possible before cradling my head in his hand. Keeping me close, wanting me just as much as I want him. He pulls back slightly, a whimper leaving my mouth, missing his touch already.

"I've never met anyone quite like you before, Pinkie. Fuck, I could kiss you all night and still not get enough." His voice is slightly hoarse as his eyes search mine, moving his head to brush my nose with his. He hasn't let me go, our bodies are still smashed together, my breasts pushing against his chest, my feet still on tiptoes to reach him.

"The feeling is mutual. I have never met anyone like you either..." The words float from my mouth to him, and I see the minute they hit. His eyes widen slightly, his hand clenching around my waist.

"You make me feel alive," he whispers, his warm breath coating my jaw, before he peppers small kisses on my skin. "I touch you, and I feel sparks. Just talking to you energizes me. I really, really need to keep my hands to myself; otherwise... I am not sure how I can handle being in your orbit and not wanting to be with you more and more." His admission coats me in warmth as he releases me, albeit hesitantly. I feel cold without his hands on me. It is on the tip of my tongue to call him back to me. I want to be in his orbit. I want to feel his touch. But the words don't leave my lips, and I watch him swallow and step toward the sink as he clears his throat. As if his words made him feel a little vulnerable too.

12

EDDIE

I scrub the pot like my life depends on it, because if I don't, I am going to push her against the kitchen counter, strip her naked, and fuck her each way till Tuesday. I wasn't lying when I said she lights up the room. The moment she smiles, she is bright, and then she laughs, and it is like she powers all of the city with the amount of light that comes from her. She is like pure happiness in a bottle. I am not sure what I like better, her independent borderline stubbornness that comes with a side of sass. Or this soft, gentle, feminine energy she gives me when we are alone.

I leave the poor dish to the side and start on the other one as she turns on the dishwasher that is now full.

"Here, let me decrown you," she says from the side, her smile wide, mine instantly now as well. One look is all it takes to have me spiraling down the rabbit hole that is Katie Taylor.

"I am still your king, though, right?" I say in jest, trying to get myself centered. With any other woman, I would be pushing toward the bedroom, stripping our clothes off us as we go. But a quick fuck, Katie is not. All we have done is kiss, yet I already know that when we make it to the bedroom, I won't be leaving. How could any man leave a woman such as her? It would be a crime.

"The only one," she says, and I look at her. I really look at her, taking in her eyes, her smile. Her words hit me in the chest. She means them. I can tell by her tone. I squat a little so she can reach the top of my head, and she removes the suds and wipes my hair. We then work in comfortable silence as I finish the dishes and she packs away everything else.

"I can finish off the dishes. You can relax," she says, coming to take over, but I don't release them. Besides, there's only a few left.

"I'm happy to help. And you made dinner, so it's the least I can do." I watch her lips thin. She doesn't like receiving help much. Just like that first morning of her new job when I got her a coffee, she is unsure about it. Not timid. No, Katie is not timid, but more so unsure about letting others in.

"Thank you for the help," she says as we both now stand in the clean kitchen and I set the last dish aside. The place where I first met her. "Let's take a seat. I want to check your shoulder," she says before turning and walking to the sofa. I follow her willingly, not wanting to leave, needing more time with her.

"How does it feel after your swim?" she asks, already in nurse mode, again taking care of another. My heart thuds as I unbutton my shirt to give her access. I only need to unbutton two or three buttons, and she sits up next to me and pulls one side over to get a clear view of my almost healed gash.

"It's fine. It pulled a little, and I know you said not to get it wet. I think I wrapped it pretty well, so it stayed mostly dry," I murmur, her face now close to mine again, her eyes firmly on my chest. I can smell her beautiful floral scent, and my hand moves on its own as I lift it from the sofa and cup it around her hip.

"Is it itchy or throbbing?" she asks, and I almost moan because my chest isn't throbbing, but my dick certainly now is.

"No. It feels good. I must have had an excellent nurse to stitch me back together." My head falls back on the sofa so I can look at her easily. Her fingers softly trace the area, sending sparks across my skin, and I fight to hold in the growl that wants to rumble from my chest.

"I hear she is one of the best," she jokes, giving me a sweet smile.

"Her hands on my body are like magic," I say, and her eyes flick to mine. She pauses, just looking at me. Like she is unsure of what the next move should be, so I help her make the decision.

"Come here." My hands grab her hips, and I pull her body toward mine. She half sits, half leans on my lap, and I smash my lips onto hers, moaning in her mouth. Even though it has only been a short while since I last kissed her, it feels like a lifetime. Her hands flatten against my chest, and she runs them across my body, feeling me, finding her way over my hard ridges before she skirts them up my shoulders, scooping my neck, and then delving into my hair.

"Your hair is so soft," she says in between kisses, my fingers flexing on her hips, pulling her closer. I want to pick her up and have her straddle me. I want to feel her hot core on mine. I want to strip her of her clothes, lay her perfect naked body down right here on the sofa and taste every inch of her.

Her hand lowers again, down my chest, over my pecs and my abs before resting on my belt. This woman is killing me.

"Eddie..." she murmurs, my name on her lips almost a moan, and my heart hammers as I take her lips again, with more purpose.

She opens a little more, my tongue slipping to meet hers with rigor, and it is electric. I run my hands up her back, spreading my palms, wanting to hold her and keep her close and touch as much of her as possible. Our kiss turns more serious, our tongues tangling. This is the best damn kiss of my entire fucking life.

Fuck, I need to get out of here before I lose control. I want to take my time with her. I don't want to rush things, but I am so close to coming in my pants just by kissing and touching her, I am not sure how I can rein myself in for much longer. Like the universe is listening to me, my phone rings in my pocket.

"Shit," I say, startled. We pull apart a little, my forehead touching hers as we pant.

"It's okay, get it," she says, moving off me, and I suck in a breath as I grab my cell, not yet sure if I want to throw it against the wall for the interruption or bow down in thanks for ensuring I slow down. I look at the number and see that it is my man in Singapore. No doubt he has some questions on the new property, and I know this is something that can't wait. The thought of my real life comes into my mind, and I clench my jaw. I feel guilty wanting more with Pinkie when she doesn't even know the real me.

"Everything okay?" she asks, her eyes looking hesitant, and I feel like more of an asshole for putting that look on her face.

"Fine. But I need to go. There is a work issue on the back of the property I need to go check out," I lie through my teeth and feel like shit for it.

"Of course. It's getting late anyway," she says, offering me a small smile that doesn't quite meet her eyes. Before she gets up from the sofa, I grab her face and bring her back to me, kissing her again quickly. "I don't want to go, but, baby, if I don't leave now, then it is going to get harder and harder for me to pull myself away from you tonight." She may not know my full name, what I do for work, or my bank balance, but she is fucking getting all of me right now.

"You're right. Plus, I need to start work early in the morning," she says, almost sighing in disappointment, and I can't help but smile. I have no idea what is happening between us, but it is something new for me. I am delving into the unknown, and I have no fear and no desire to get away like I normally do. I just want to jump right in. As Eddie, as Edward Langford, however she will take me.

13

KATIE

"You're all done. You should go home," Shelley says, looking over the roster. It is almost time for shift change, when I can take my weary body home and rest for the night before coming back and doing it all again. I have just enough energy to try out the pool and sauna. After seeing it with Eddie, I have been dreaming about it since. Along with our make-out session.

Our dinner together was so fun. We spent the night eating and talking, laughing and kissing. We get along well and have the same sense of humor. Our night was a mix of lighthearted conversation about everything, such as hospital horror stories, what foods we like, and places in the world we would like to see. Then we had moments of scorching hot desire, his hands, his lips, his sexy smirks. He had to peel himself away from me in order to be a gentleman and kiss me good night. I like that he is vocal about his attraction to me. The way he wants to spend time together and get to know me. It's refreshing.

"My feet are killing me," I say, having worked too hard this week already. The days are long, but I am now in the swing of things. I have settled in, I know the ward, Shelley, and a few other nurses. It is feeling more comfortable, more welcoming.

"Excuse me?" a feminine voice says, and I look up to see a stunning brunette at the nurses' desk.

"Yes, how can we help you?" Shelley asks, her professional demeanor in place. I look at the woman who appears a little apprehensive. Her hair is long and glossy, her clothes simple. She's beautiful without a scrap of makeup on, even though most of it is hiding behind thick Coke-bottle glasses.

"I was hoping to see Dr. Colin Wilson?" She looks between us, pushing her glasses up her nose from where they slipped. She looks familiar, yet I know that I have never met her before. Appearing nervous, carrying a thick file, I assume she must be a patient.

"I'm sorry, he is in surgery all afternoon. Here are his office details. You are best to call and make an appointment with his team directly," Shelley says, passing over his business card.

"Thank you. I appreciate it. Have a good day," she says before turning and walking out the door.

"She was pretty," I murmur, watching as she retreats out the door.

"There are lots of pretty girls around here. Let me take those files. I will mark them off for you. You go. Take off early, you deserve it. Besides, we have a new group of volunteers starting with us next week, so your days might just start to get a little longer," she says, smiling, and I don't hesitate. You rarely get off early as a nurse, as there is always something to do. The next shift has already started, so they have enough bodies to manage the workload, and me leaving ten minutes early is not going to harm anyone.

"Thanks, Shelley, I owe you." Giving her a smile, I head to the nurses' lounge and grab my backpack. Throwing it over my shoulder, I text Tony to let him know I am ready early, and I make my way outside to the front of the hospital to wait for him. It is just about dusk, the air getting colder as I step outside and walk over to the side of the entrance, away from the hustle and bustle of people coming and going. I take a deep breath and relax, de-stressing from my day, glad to have some fresh air on my face.

"Well, well, well, Baltimore is looking *good on you*," *his* voice says from behind me, and I hold my breath. My body starts to tremble the minute his voice hits my ears. I feel the fear crawl up my spine, and I swallow as my eyes dart around, looking for Tony. My cell vibrates, and I look at it quickly. Tony is five minutes away. *Shit*.

"What's wrong, *Kitty Cat*? Don't have a warm welcome for your brother these days?" Steve asks as he steps around in front of me, positioning himself right in my line of sight. I notice a woman standing just behind him. I don't know her. She is young. Bleach-blond hair with dark regrowth that looks like it hasn't been washed in weeks. Her eyes thin as she takes me in. She looks just as unkempt as Steve, and I wonder if it is his latest flame of the month. They probably met each other on the streets.

That's where most of his friendship group is from these days.

I swallow, my eyes moving back to him as he stands confidently in front of me. He is not my brother. A true brother wouldn't do what Steve did to me. He looks worse than the last time I saw him merely a month or so ago. His hair is a little longer at the back, the dark circles under his eyes more apparent. He has a new tattoo that I see crawling up his neck. I can't make out the words entirely, nor do I want to. I'm scared, but I try not to show it. I know nothing I say or do will make this any easier for me.

"I need money," he says, his eyes boring into me.

"I don't have any money," I grit out at him. This is what he does. He follows me. He intimidates me. He threatens me until I give in. I think about the measly amount of money in my bank account. I was finally paid, but by the time I organized some food, paid a little off my college debt, and put some away for bills, I was back to merely a few dollars in my account. I am now even more grateful to Eddie for stocking my cupboards.

"Now, now. Working at a big hotshot hospital like this, I know you are lying," he says, his eyes leaving mine for a moment to take in the hospital behind me. His girlfriend huffs in mock laughter, staring at me like I am the bad guy in all this. Who knows what he has told her. He is good at spinning lies. He gets away with everything. "I need cash, and I need it today," he reiterates. I wonder how he got here without any money. Probably hitched a ride or snuck onto the train for free.

"I don't have any money," I repeat, my teeth grinding.

I hate him. I hate him with every fiber of my body. To think I used to look up to him. Admire him.

"Well, I have seen where you are living. So, someone, somewhere has money, so best you get it," he sneers, taking a step closer, right into my personal space. I bite the inside of my cheek, trying to keep my mouth shut. But I can't stop the words as they fly out of my mouth.

"Why? So you can shoot it up your arms or snort it up your nose?" I say, anger being the emotion that wins in this moment. Drugs have always been a part of his life. Ever since I met him as a teen in a foster home we shared. Now they rule him. He is not the same boy I first met. "You need to leave me alone, Steve. Even if I had money, I wouldn't give any to you." I am so tired of this being my life.

The past few weeks in Baltimore have been so different for me. It has given me a glimpse of another life. Of a life that could be mine if I work hard enough. It has been the light to an otherwise very dark history, and I want it. Badly. My body shakes, my heart races. I'm no longer able to calm myself around him. The instant reaction I have when he comes near me is suffocating. I carry a lot of trauma from my life, but he amplifies it. Despite my colorful past, he is the one that spikes the fear in me.

"Oh, you are such a pathetic little sister. We both know you are trash. The fact that you got a job here surprises me. How many times did you open your legs to get it?" he asks, and his words almost make me vomit as his girlfriend looks at me with one eyebrow raised in question.

"Did you let the rich old doctors fuck you? Did they

shove their filthy fat cocks inside you? Did you let them, or did they just take you? You won't let me fuck you, but you let them, didn't you?"

"Steve, you need to leave," I grit out as I look around, smelling alcohol on his breath. With the busy entry behind some bushes to the left of me, I am not in anyone's line of sight. *Stupid!*

"Maybe you got on your knees; maybe this sassy little mouth of yours sucked them off? Is that how you got this job? Because we both know they don't hire trash. Especially trash as slutty as you. But, fuck, I bet you give really good head. I wouldn't mind your lips on me, Kitty Cat," he threatens as he cups his groin, and I feel my nails biting into my palms at my sides.

"We both know I could ruin your career. All I would need to do is show everyone that rather entertaining video I have of you, and you would lose everything." He knows how to get me to do what he wants. That video haunts me every waking hour.

"Miss Taylor." Tony steps up, forcing Steve and me to look at him. He is a big man, much bigger than Steve, and I watch Steve taking him in as he immediately retreats. I have never had anyone step in for me. Steve doesn't know what it is like for anyone to have my back. I've always been alone. "Everything alright here?" Tony asks me, and I swallow.

"Everything is fine, big man. Isn't that right, Kitty Cat?" Steve says from the side, where he continues to step backward. I can no longer see his girlfriend, as she obviously left the scene pretty quickly.

"Thanks, Tony. Everything is fine," I say, my voice

shaking, and Tony doesn't look like he believes me. I look back at Steve, but he is already gone. Slipped back into the night like the ghost that he is.

"Let's go," Tony says, walking me to the car, opening the back door for me to slip inside. I take a few moments of peace to stare at the roof of the car, willing the tears not to fall.

I need to get out of this situation. I need to put a stop to Steve and his constant threats for money. Because if I don't, then there is no future for me.

I might as well be dead.

14

EDDIE

I push my body through the water, feeling my lungs burn and my muscles move. I wasn't lying to Katie when I told her I swim here often. It is where I come to relax. The Harborside building has the best swimming pool in the entire city. I come here at least a few nights a week just to unwind. While my mind usually continues to race, the movement expels the energy running through my body enough for me to sleep.

As my freestyle glides through the water, I think about the week. We had a new building opening in Singapore. The tenants we have moving in are all loving it, and my team, who I have on the ground there, are managing it well. Then I think about my mother. I haven't heard from her since she stalked into my office. Her thinly veiled threat is still filtering in my mind, though. There is no way I am even going to go on a date with a woman she chooses, let alone entertain one as a wife. The thought runs through me, making my arms pump even faster. I think I hear a door slam, but I am too focused on my strokes, so I pay little attention.

Then my mind moves on to Katie. I have stayed away from her this week. Not to be an asshole, as we have still either spoken or texted every day. But the guilt of not telling her who I really am is starting to eat at me. That, coupled with the fact that I just want to see her all the time and get to know her more, has those two feelings colliding like a ship in the stormy seas, ebbing and flowing, just waiting for it to sink. The outcome of my little secret I already know is not going to be great. That thought sits in the pit of my stomach.

But she is who I have been thinking about the most. She is something. Last I saw her, I wanted to completely devour her, strip her naked, and make her mine. But I really don't want to fuck this up.

Also, getting involved with someone is not ideal, considering my mother's history. While I may want that perfect family dream, I know what my mother is capable of, and I do not want that for me or my partner of choice. I swore to myself I would stay single, at least for a few more years. It's been easy up until now.

I pop up at the end of the pool and grab on to the side, heaving in some air as I look at my watch.

"Training for the Olympics?" a voice asks from beside me, and I nearly jump out of my skin.

"Shit!" I gasp, looking up and around wildly until I find the source of the statement. Pink hair, a black swimsuit, and a scattering of intricate tattoos up her arms.

"Katie?" I pant out, taking off my goggles, wondering if I am dreaming. I have thought of her and her wet t-shirt for weeks, but looking at her now, I get a whole other vision. Her pink hair is coiled on top of her head, and she sits on the edge of the pool with her feet dangling in.

"Sorry... I didn't... mean to... scare you..." she starts to say, but she is giggling at me so hard, she can't even get her words out. Her hand covers her chest like she is now finding it difficult to breathe. She is stunning.

"I think you shaved a few years off my life," I joke, relieved and pleased as I grab on to the side of the pool near where she sits.

"You're a pro. Such a great swimmer," she says, her laughter now subsiding.

"I normally don't see anyone else here," I say with a stupid grin. Any thought I had earlier of pushing her from my mind has now died. I need my lips on hers again.

"How was work today?" I ask as I tread water in front of her. It is night outside, so the large windows give us an amazing view of the sparkling lights of Baltimore, while the low lights inside glow from behind her, illuminating her like a fucking angel sent from heaven.

"Ahhhh." She cringes as she slips slowly off the side and lowers herself into the water. Her body moves fluidly, slinking down from the edge, right in front of me. She goes all the way under before she bobs up again. "It is good, but I am a hundred percent positive that my boss hates me." Treading water along with me, we stay close to one another.

"Why do you say that?" I question, not sure how anyone could hate this beautiful woman.

"He is near retirement and has worked in the field of cardiology for years. While he is well respected in the industry, he doesn't go easy on me. Nurses usually don't get a lot of respect from our doctors. The older they are, the less respect we get, and my boss is ancient," she explains.

"So it was a tough week, huh?" I say, trying to keep my eyes on her face and not her amazing tits as they float on top of the water, her bathing suit barely containing them.

"Each day keeps getting better and better. The nursing staff are great, and I have made friends with the nursing unit manager, Shelley. It's just the doctor…"

"What's the doctor's name?" I ask, because chances are I will know him. Maybe I can put in a word.

"Dr. Colin Wilson. Old guy. Been there for decades." I swallow. I know Dr. Wilson. All too well, unfortunately.

"Could you move to another doctor?" Dr. Wilson is the last person Katie needs to know. He is friends with my mother, so I don't trust him as far as I can throw him.

"Maybe in time. At the moment, I need to see out at least three months with him before I can request a change. This water is so nice. No wonder you come here," she says, laying her head back and taking a few breaths. This woman is killing me and doesn't even know it.

"It's the best in Baltimore," I say with a big grin. I do love this building.

"I like how they let you use all the facilities. I don't know too many buildings that would let their mainte-nance team indulge like this. You must have a good boss," she says, and my stomach feels like lead. I should tell her. This is the perfect opportunity to come clean. Tell her who I am and that this building and swimming pool are actually mine.

"Yeah, well, full disclosure..." I start before she interrupts me.

"Ouch. Ouch. Owww," she squeals, contorting in the water.

"What's wrong?" I ask, panic rising as I see her face scrunch up in pain as her head bobs dangerously close to the water line.

"Cramp. In. My. Foot," she pants out, holding her breath.

"Here." Wrapping my arm around her waist, I lift her a little, swimming us both to shallow waters. Secretly loving having her in my arms again.

"Oww, oww, oww," she continues, and I smile, knowing a cramp in itself isn't dangerous, and she looks cute with her scrunched-up face.

"Here, sit." I find the pool step and place her down. "Give me your foot." I need to stretch it out. That is the only relief for foot cramps.

"I've got it." She tries to maneuver to grab her foot, independent and stubborn even now, but the steps on the pool are not overly wide so she slips off and goes straight under.

"Shit," I murmur, grabbing her by the waist again and hauling her back up as she coughs and splutters.

"Give me your foot, Katie," I almost demand as I run my hands down her legs a little to reach her foot. The action is intimate, and I think we both stop breathing as her eyes connect with mine. I grit my teeth as I reach her foot, and her eyes wince again as I pull her toes back. Her hands rush and grip on to my shoulders so she doesn't go back under the water, digging into my muscles. Her touch is electric, and I watch her beautiful face pinch before I see the instant relief and we both take a breath.

"We need to stop meeting like this," I murmur, my smirk on full display. I can see her breathing hitch as her breasts move up and down, creating little waves around us.

"In the building?" she whispers.

"No. Us being half-naked. If it happens again, I am not sure I can be a gentleman about it," I grit out, barely being a gentleman now as it is.

"Maybe I don't want you to be a gentleman..." The words fall from her lips like dripping syrup. A heavy, sticky, delicious fucking syrup that nearly has me sucking her lips then trailing mine down her amazing body then and there. "I've missed you this week," she adds quietly, looking up at me through her lashes, and my heart starts pumping blood around my body at a rapid pace. She looks a little vulnerable, her breathing shallow. I watch her swallow, following the movement of her slender neck, itching to put my mouth on her.

"Good, because I have missed you too," I say before my lips crash into hers. I am needy, fucking famished for this woman as my hands circle around her small waist and I pull her to me. Her mouth opens, our tongues colliding as her hands run up my shoulders and wrap around my neck. *Fuck, she feels good in my arms.*

Her fingers thread into my hair at the nape of my neck, pulling my head closer, telling me she wants me as badly as I want her. My hands move then, running up and down her back, touching as much of her as I can before cupping her ass and squeezing her in my palms. She has a fantastic ass. Her legs part then, and she wraps them around my waist. I stand in the water, our bodies submerged with her hooked on to me. I groan in her mouth at the feeling of her center now touching mine. There is no hiding how I feel. I am fucking hard and ready.

"Eddie." I nearly come on the spot at her moaning my name. The way she says it, in almost a whimper, God, what I would give to have this woman say my name like that over and over. My mouth peppers her jaw with kisses, sucking and licking her skin, and I don't miss the way her hips grind on me. Fuck, this feels amazing.

"Pinkie, unless you want me to fuck you right here in this pool, we better stop. You are so fucking beautiful and feel so good in my arms that this is driving me insane," I growl as I pull back and look at her, acutely aware that the cameras in here are seen by not only Brian but my entire security team. They are all bound by confidentiality, but the last thing I need is for a sex tape to go viral. That's about all that keeps me reined in.

She laughs then. Her head falls back and laughter echoes around the pool, and I look at her, mesmerized. A sly grin forms on my lips. If we were anywhere else, I wouldn't hesitate.

"Let me guess, you would have to clean the pool too, right?" she says, her blues sparkling, and my stomach drops. I should tell her. Right here, right now. No lies between us. Because if this is going how I plan it to go, she is going to be a screaming, moaning, naked mess underneath me very soon.

"I might outsource that job," I lie quickly behind the wide smile I give her, the truth now combating with my hard cock. The latter currently wins the silent argument. My grin remains as I start to move. I keep her wrapped around me and step up the pool stairs and out of the water.

"Where are we going?" she asks, hanging on to me, in no hurry to get down. Her fingers are still playing with my hair at the back of my neck, and I swear I feel the light touch all the way in my toes. I was going to get a haircut this week, but now you couldn't pay me to make the appointment.

"Your place," I say with full confidence. This is happening. I walk us to where our things are as her lips find mine again.

"Fuck, you are beautiful," I growl into her mouth, and she lifts her body a few inches, almost climbing me more. I have no idea how I have the self-control not to lay her down on this bench and fuck her right here, but I do. I keep one hand wrapped around her ass, because I can't stop touching it as the other comes to cup her face. Pulling back, I touch my forehead to hers. Her panting chest makes it evident that she is just as needy as me. "There are cameras everywhere, Pinkie, and I sure as hell don't want anyone watching when I strip this bathing suit from your fucking fantastic body. I don't share. I want you all to myself. No one else gets to see you but me." I must say something right, because she bites her bottom lip and Miss Sassy comes back.

"But I haven't even done my laps!" she mocks, looking at the pool, and I place her on her feet, our torsos touching. Putting my hand to her chin, I lift her face to meet mine.

"There is plenty of exercise in your future. I will get your heart rate up, don't worry," I say in a deep voice laced with innuendo and give her a wink.

"Well, I think it might be true what they say..." she whispers, her eyes still hooked on mine as she bends down and grabs her things.

"What's that?" I ask as I wrap my towel around my waist, hiding my growing obsession with her, and throw on a t-shirt.

"You boys with the tools are good with your hands," she says, just as mine skirt around her hips again, running up her back. I keep it trailing all the way to her neck and cradle her head in my hand. Leaning forward, I drag my nose up her jaw and her cheek before I whisper in her ear.

"If you are a good girl, maybe I can show you exactly what my hands are capable of." I feel her nipples pebble against my chest as we stand silent for a moment, my hand still around the back of her neck. At this point, I am not sure I am capable of taking my hands off her body.

She takes a big breath and leans back a little to look up at me. I lift my other hand and cup her face, her head relaxing in my hold. We are an inch apart. My eyes flick to her parted lips, plump and almost begging me to kiss them. The heat builds between us, and if anyone were to walk in right now, it would look extremely intimate. Yet neither of us appear too keen on leaving. Her hands relax on my shoulders, one moving down, touching my skin softly as it travels from my shoulder to my bicep. Her fingers skirt around my fresh scar as she looks at it.

"Just tell me one thing, Eddie." This woman could ask me for the world right now and I would give it.

"Sure, Pinkie, what's that?" I ask, my smile still wide as her big blue eyes look up at me like I am her world right now.

"Can I trust you?" she asks, looking at me like whatever we do now totally hinges on the answer I give. She appears a little unsure, and I don't blame her. I feel like I have a fucking red flag hovering over my head and she can see it. But regardless of my identity, she can trust me. She one hundred percent can.

"There's one thing I do need to tell you," I say. Now is the time. Like a Band-Aid, I will just rip it off and get it over with. I have thought over the past week how I will say it and what words I will use.

"Are you secretly married?" she half jokes as she pulls away a little, startling me from my preplanned thoughts a little.

"No, not married." I laugh nervously.

"Girlfriend?" she presses, tilting her head at me.

"No, single and very much interested," I say, reinstating my desire for her, my grip on her tightening. Her body relaxes back into me then.

"Well, then nothing else matters. I just want you and you want me. It can be that simple." Lifting onto her tiptoes, she kisses me again.

But just like with the rest of my life, nothing is ever that simple.

15

KATIE

I need this. I need him. I don't usually come on to men so strong. In fact, I don't usually come on to men at all. Maybe it is the fear of rejection or the fact that any other man I have been with has disregarded me like I am trash. Maybe it is the fact that being with me is dangerous, for both of us. But Eddie had me from the moment we met, and every moment since, and after my run-in with Steve, all I want to do is forget. I want to feel wanted, alive, give in to this lust. I want to throw myself at him and have him catch me. He is the light I need after living in darkness for so long. I feel like I'm drowning, and Eddie is the only one who can save me right now.

I need to feel. I want to live, and I haven't been living, just merely surviving. I don't know when it happened, but Eddie makes me come alive. He sparks something inside.

He pulls me into the elevator, and as soon as the door closes, he pushes me against the wall.

"You're sure about this, Pinkie?" he asks, his hands

gripping my waist as his nose nudges my jaw. A shiver of excitement rushes through me. I don't think I have ever been as sure of anything else in my life. Not for a very long time.

"I'm more than sure," I say, my lips moving upward into a smile before they connect with his.

He is an incredible kisser. He kisses me like nothing else matters. Like I am the only person in the world for him. Like I am his one focus. I know he wants this too, because he puts everything into his kiss. His hands are firm, and I like the way they fit around my waist. His tall frame totally consumes me, and I like how I feel protected.

"What are you doing to me?" he moans, his lips trailing down my neck. *To him? It is more like what is he doing to me! I have never been like this.*

His hands remain on me as the elevator doors open, and we stumble out on my floor. I open my apartment door, and we fall through a second later, Eddie kicking it closed behind him.

"Last chance," he warns, and I giggle. I never giggle, but this man has me giggling like a schoolgirl. It feels good. *Is this what I have been missing?*

"I'm all in, pretty boy," I say, slinking away from him teasingly. I forget all my insecurities when I am with him. Whether we are talking and just hanging out or lustful like now. I feel almost like a new woman; that is the effect Eddie has on me. And I want to feel like this all the time.

"Pretty boy?" he asks, his head tilting with a cute-ass smirk on his face.

"Mm-hmm. You are pretty to look at. Very easy on the

eyes." Leaning against the kitchen counter, I watch as he walks toward me with a smile that has my thighs clenching.

"Well, keep your eyes on me, Pinkie." His hand reaches for the straps of my swimwear, pulling both off my shoulders. Nerves dance in my stomach, and my nipples peak as the cool air touches them. Once my arms are free, he continues dragging the swimsuit off my body, down my legs, and letting it fall to the floor. My eyes remain on his, and I watch as he looks at me. His eyes travel my body, my blood heating under his gaze. I have seen lust before. I am not immune to a man's attention, but this is different. He looks at me adoringly, like I am his most prized possession. And I want to be.

"Later, I want you to tell me all about these pretty tattoos, but right now..." He groans, his eyes flicking to meet mine. They are half-lidded, his sexy smirk returning as I watch him fall to his knees. My lips part on a gasp. On his knees, his face is right in front of me. He leans forward and kisses my hip bone, his nose trailing around my middle.

"Eddie?" I say softly, his touch so delicate, I'm trembling for more. I have never been touched like this before.

"Relax. Lean back," he whispers, and so I lean back a little on the kitchen counter. My elbows hold me up on the cold surface as his hands run up the back of my legs. The curtains to the apartment are wide open. I see the glittering lights of the yachts in the harbor below, like magical stars sparkling quietly in the distance.

His hand smooths up to my knee, and he lifts my leg,

putting it over his shoulder. He handles me like I will break. My breathing is rapid, and I feel his warm breath on my center as he slowly moves closer. Butterflies flutter like a storm deep in my core, a feeling I have never really had before him, and I look up to the ceiling as he peppers kisses on my inner thigh.

"You're wet for me," he murmurs as his thumb brushes against my center, and my body shivers expectantly.

"You're teasing me," I moan as I bite my lip. I look down at him, and he gives me a wicked smile.

"Just taking my time." Our eyes remain locked as he leans forward and puts his mouth on me. I whimper at the contact, my head falling back again as his eyes close and he groans.

"So good…" I hear him say as his hands glide back up my legs and grip my ass. He puts his mouth on me again, his lips sucking a little before his tongue slides in, circling my clit and lapping my core.

"Oh my," I breathe, my legs shaking from how good this feels, and he's barely begun.

"Mmmmm," I hear him rumble as he buries his face, his lips and mouth working me over, sucking me, tasting me, as his fingers grab my flesh, keeping me close.

"You are so good at that." I don't recognize my own voice. I moan and pant, my hands white-knuckled as they wrap around the edge of the kitchen counter. Ironic, really, since the kitchen sink was how we first met, and now it is where we have our first sexual experience together.

He moans again, the vibrations running through me,

and my legs automatically widen, giving him more access. I am naked, spread out with Eddie firmly between my legs. I should feel vulnerable. Uncomfortable. Self-conscious. Every other man who has taken me made me feel worthless. Merely a tool for their pleasure. Gave no consideration for me. Barely waited for consent, and some didn't even get that. That's what I thought sex was. That's what I was taught. But this is entirely different. I feel like he is worshipping me. He is on his knees, with the power mine to give. I keep one hand gripped to the counter tight so I don't collapse, while with the other, I reach down and run my fingers through his hair. He growls, obviously liking me touching him as the pressure of his mouth increases. He is so good at this. My breath quickens, as I pant and moan and whimper, the noises coming from me entirely foreign, but I can't help it. My fingers tangle through his hair. It is soft, well kept. I love it. It isn't shaved, colored, or roughened. It is silky, long enough for me to get a good handful, and I do as my hips start moving of their own accord. I knew Eddie was different. I knew it the minute I met him.

"Hold on to the counter, baby," he says, his voice deepening, and I move my hand back to the counter just as he lifts me off the floor entirely, placing my other leg over his other shoulder. I am now firmly sitting on him. My elbows anchor my upper body onto the counter, my legs draped around his neck.

"Oh my..." is all I get out before he dives back in. His tongue licks me as his lips suck on my clit, his hands gripping me tight, pulling my hips to his face. He buries himself deeper, and I feel sparks crawling up my body.

"Yesssss, yesss," I pant out, the feeling already overwhelming.

"Eddie... Eddie... Eddie..." I moan his name, calling for him to help me, needing him to give me this release. It's overwhelming. I feel emotional as my whole body starts to shake. He growls against me, and my hands squeeze the counter edge as he holds all of me, acting like I weigh nothing. His tongue swirls before he sucks hard, and I still. The air has completely left my body as I quiver all over.

"Oh, my... Eddie!" I half scream, half cry, tears rushing to my eyes rapidly as my orgasm rips through me. He holds me tight, licking me as I work through it. His hands splay out, cupping me, keeping me close. My heart races, thumping hard in my chest as a light sweat covers my brow and my tears fall rapidly down my cheeks in pure joy and ecstasy and relief. It is like I had a tension tap, tightly turned, and Eddie has just undone it. I have never felt like this before. Completely open, giving myself to a man, not just my body but a little more of me each and every day.

He pulls back slightly and lowers my feet to the floor, but my body continues to shake, and the tears continue to fall. His hands remain on me, running up my legs and body as he stands, looking at me with concern.

"You okay?" he asks as his hands cup my face, his thumbs wiping the tears. I swallow roughly, trying to pull it together. I haven't cried in a long time, and now I can barely stop.

"I didn't hurt you, did I?" Looking like he is in pain

himself, I almost scoff at his ridiculous statement. He is the softest, most caring man I have ever met.

"No, Eddie. You didn't. I'm not sure why I'm crying," I tell him as more tears stream uncontrollably down my cheeks, and he leans over, kissing them, catching every tear that falls onto his lips. This man. Where the hell did he come from?

"It's okay. As long as you are enjoying yourself." He pulls back to search my eyes.

"You are so good at that. I don't think I have ever orgasmed so hard before." I laugh, and he smiles, relief evident as his face relaxes.

"Oh, Pinkie, I plan on making you come at least another few times tonight. You think you can handle that?" I feel him hot and heavy through his swim shorts against my belly, anticipation building inside of me. My body feels electric. Like I have woken from a deep sleep. I wanted to climb his body before, but now I am aching for him. I wipe my cheek one last time, the tears now drying up as pure arousal skirts over my skin.

"Bring it on, pretty boy," I say, smiling, and he doesn't hesitate. He moves quickly to his bag and fishes out a condom from his wallet, then he picks me up and throws me over his shoulder, stalking to the bedroom.

16

EDDIE

"Ahhhh!" She screams and laughs at the sudden movement, and I slap her bare ass, which is fast becoming one of my favorite things, as I walk her toward the bedroom. She is tiny, much smaller than me, and I have wanted to throw her around playfully ever since I met her. Now is my chance, and I am taking full advantage of it.

I still taste her on my lips. Fucking ecstasy is what she tastes like, and I am already addicted. I loved having my mouth on her, feeling her quiver against my face, knowing that I make her knees weak. I am hot and ready. The urge I have to thrust into her and take her hard and fast is almost overwhelming. But I wasn't lying earlier. I want to take my time with her. Now, after her tears, I am almost certain that this woman hasn't experienced the pleasures of a man taking care of her and that is exactly my plan with her tonight.

As she giggles on my shoulder, I turn my head and

bite her ass. It is fucking perky and perfect, and right there next to my face; it would be a crime to ignore it.

She gasps. "Did you just bite me?" she asks in shock.

"Yep," I say, laughing before I kiss the same spot, not wanting my lips away from her. I hear her giggle again, so I think she approves of it.

As I reach the bed, I throw her onto it, looking at her. She is beaming. Naked, flushed, her eyes lust drunk, her lips pink and perfect. I gaze at her pussy, where I was just moments ago, and bite my lower lip so I don't groan. Hairless, wet, her skin tinted pink from where I was sucking on her. I could die happy with my head buried against her. She is breathless, and for the first time, seemingly lost for words.

"You okay, Pinkie?" I ask again, wanting her to communicate with me. I want to know she is into this as much as I am. I want to ensure she is having a good time, because I sure as fuck am. "Did I fuck the sassy out of you already?" I ask her, my smirk on full display, and she laughs.

"No, I'm just waiting to see what you have next in that toolbox of yours," she says, raising her eyebrows in a challenge. I grab hold of the waist of my swim shorts, shoving them down my body, showing her exactly what I'm packing. I love it when her mouth drops open.

"Hmm, it seems like your mouth knows exactly what to do with my tool?" I ask, stepping closer to the bed. She sits up on her knees then, lifting her hands to her hair, and takes out the top knot. She runs her fingers through it and shakes it up, her body curving, and I have never seen a woman look so feminine in my life. Her pink hair falls like a waterfall down her shoulders, the ends touching her nipples, the waves soft. She looks like a goddess. Licking her lips, she slowly gets on all fours and fucking crawls to me. Her body sways, her ass pert as she makes her way across the bed, her hips moving, back dipping slightly, perfect tits swinging. I groan as I feel like all my dreams are coming true with this sexy, independent woman crawling to me like I am her everything.

"You are beautiful," I murmur, barely able to speak. I feel like I am in a movie. No man is ever this lucky. I see her eyes flash with uncertainty for the briefest moment before they fill with lust again. It is something I have noticed before, like she isn't used to getting compliments or she just doesn't have a clue about how fucking amazing she really is. But I plan on giving her all the compliments I can, because there is no way this woman doesn't deserve every single one of them.

"You like me crawling to you?" she asks, looking up at me with her big blue eyes, and I struggle not to grab myself and jerk off right here right now. Fuck, I am right on the edge.

"I fucking love everything about you." The honesty comes out quickly, and her eyes sparkle in delight. Eye level with my cock now, I am thick, red, and throbbing as she stares at me. I bite the inside of my cheek, praying I don't come as soon as her mouth is on me. She leans forward, and I watch, holding my breath as her tongue licks up my length. I slowly release the breath I was holding, coming out like a hiss. She twirls her tongue around my tip, and I clench my fists at my sides, biting my bottom lip.

"You look good down there, Pinkie," I grit out, barely hanging on.

"Mmmm... and you taste good," she moans, just before her tongue twirls again and she takes me into her mouth. She is warm, wet, and fucking perfect, and I watch as she takes me in. Little by little, she works me over, her head bobbing, ass high in the air. I reach out and run my hand down her back, squeezing her ass cheek as she continues to bob up and down on me.

"You are so fucking perfect," I say, my mind whirling. I bring my hands up and grab her hair. I pull it up off her face so I can get a visual of her, and I see her lower, taking me in. I feel it when I touch the back of her throat, and I let out a groan of restraint. She pulls back and moans in response, her nipples pebbling.

"Touch yourself, Pinkie. I want you to make yourself come." She maneuvers herself, doing exactly what I ask. I feel the moment her fingers touch her clit because she gasps around my cock, and her eyes close briefly.

"That's my girl." My hips start to move a little as I bring my other hand forward and hold her head, keeping her with me.

"That's it, baby. I want you to come. With your fingers on your perfect pussy, I want you to come while my cock is in your mouth," I say, watching her as she whimpers around me. I grit my teeth, trying not to come. God, there are so many ways I want to take her. So many ways I want her screaming my name.

I feel her throat relax as a loud moan falls from her, vibrating up my length, and her hips buck a little as she comes, moaning and whimpering while I continue to thrust into her mouth.

Watching her orgasm pushes me over, and I come. Hard. I let go, releasing myself in her warm, wet mouth, and she swallows every drop. That act alone leaves me breathless. I see stars, feeling lightheaded, and as she pulls away, I fall forward onto her bed, needing to lie down, almost disbelieving how perfect that all was. I take a few breaths and steady myself, looking down at her shy smile.

"Come here," I murmur to her, and she leans down, lying next to me as we both catch our breath. I pull her naked body close, not finished with her yet, but needing to gather myself.

"That was..." she says quietly as I strum my hand up and down her back.

"Yeah... it was..." The two of us are in shock and awe at how perfect our bodies are with each other. She cuddles in, and my hand continues to strum. Despite our height difference, we fit perfectly.

Just like I knew we would.

17

KATIE

My eyes blink open, my mind tired, my body sore. Yawning, I wish I could stay curled up in bed, but I know I have to get moving. As my eyes adjust, I look around my room before I see the space next to me. The bed is empty. He didn't stay. Disappointment runs through me instantly. I'm not sure what I was expecting. It has been almost a year since I slept with anyone, and even then, that was just sex. But this felt a little more. It felt different. I thought he was different. We get along so well, and I think I may really like him. No, scratch that, I know I really like him. My eyes threaten to sting. It was amazing. Our night. I have never felt more cared for, more alive, more feminine.

"Morning! Coffee?" I sit up with a start as Eddie comes through the bedroom door, wearing nothing but a pair of jeans hanging off his hips, not unlike the first time I met him. His hair is ruffled as he steps in with two coffees.

"You're here?" I ask, my eyes now wide open, not able to stop the smile dancing on my lips.

He balks. "Of course, I'm here. Did you not want me here?" He stalls midway to the bed, looking unsure, balancing the two coffees and watching me carefully. We haven't discussed what this is, where we are going. We only just connected, but I have no idea how these things go, having never been in a healthy relationship before.

"Yes. I just woke up alone, so I just thought..." I trail off, giving him a shrug, feeling vulnerable.

"I want to be here. I thought last night was amazing..." He looks at me in question, like I might not feel the same.

"It was. You are. Thank you," I'm quick to reassure, and his body relaxes as he continues as he comes closer. I sit up and bunch the blankets around my naked frame before he leans over, kissing me on the lips softly, slowly, like he has all the time in the world.

"I didn't know I had coffee," I say, surprised that he is handy in the kitchen as well.

"It was in one of the baskets. I also made you lunch," he says, sitting on the bed next to me.

"You made me lunch?" I ask as my eyebrows shoot to my hairline. Is this man real? Is this normal? No one has ever made me lunch. I was always the girl who went hungry at school, as no one even made my school lunch when I was little.

"Well, you work long shifts, so you have to stay well fed. I plan to keep you busy when you get home," he teases, wiggling his eyebrows.

I laugh. "Are you working today?" I ask, taking a sip of the hot brew, the coffee waking me up a little more.

"I work every day. But today, I do have a game of golf scheduled with my brothers."

"Golf?" I snort. I have never met anyone who plays golf, and it is not something that I ever thought Eddie would play. Football or basketball, maybe. But golf, no way.

"What's that snort for?" he asks, smiling.

"Golf sounds so boring," I admit. "I mean, I have never played it, but it is an old man's game, isn't it?"

"I like to spend time with my brothers. We are all pretty close."

"What do your brothers do?" I ask, and I see his body still. He hasn't said much about his life. And while I have kept most of mine hidden as well, I feel like there is something he is not telling me.

"One is in construction, one is in law..." he says, acting like it is no big deal.

"Wow, a lawyer? He must be super smart," I say, sipping my coffee. I have met a few lawyers in my time, all of them slimy, but I have a feeling Eddie's brother would be the real deal.

"He is a smart-ass, is what he is." He laughs, then promptly changes the subject. "You better get up so you aren't late for work. Lunch is packed and on the kitchen counter, and Tony is waiting downstairs." I look at the clock, seeing I have about thirty minutes to get ready and get out of here.

"Will you be here when I get back tonight?" I already sound needy, but I like having him around, and it's not like he hasn't been in this apartment without me before. I swallow as I wait for him to make an excuse. No man has ever hung around before, so I shouldn't be surprised. But I hold my breath, waiting for his response.

"Sure, can I cook you dinner?" he asks, and my eyes widen in surprise for the third time this morning. *What did he just say?*

"You cook?" I know he mentioned expanding his repertoire the other night, but clearly, he already has a dish or two in his arsenal.

"Well, *cook* is maybe a little bit of a stretch, but I make a mean pasta. It's nothing special, but I know you will be hungry and tired, so it will fill you up." He shrugs like it is no big deal.

"Sure, sounds great!" I can barely contain my excitement. I already can't wait to get back home.

There is something about Baltimore. Ever since I arrived, everything I ever wanted has turned up. I feel equal parts unsure and relieved. I am not into woo-woo stuff, but I feel like I have a fairy godmother and she is waving her wand. Aside from Steve's arrival, everything has been magical. But I am trying to be the *new me,* and the *new me* is free and easy, with new friends and a man who makes me dinner.

"Come on, let's get in the shower," he says, pulling at my legs, and I have just enough time to put down my coffee on the bedside table before he slides me along the mattress. I noticed last night he loves to throw me around a little. He is so big, and I am tiny in comparison. It was bound to happen, and I feel safe and content in his arms so I don't mind one bit. He pulls me up onto him, my legs automatically wrapping around his waist.

"Mmmm... you feel good in my arms," he murmurs, his lips connecting with mine. He tastes of coffee as my tongue tangles with his. His hand cups my bare ass as he walks me to the shower. I run my hands up his broad shoulders and secure them behind his head, my fingers finding the familiar hair at the nape of his neck.

"I like your hair," I say as he holds me with one hand, while reaching in to turn the shower in with the other.

"I like you," he says, kissing me again as the bathroom fills with steam. I love this shower. It is large, the water is hot, and there isn't any mold or mildew. I couldn't count the number of times I had to endure a cold shower in my lifetime. It was often. Now, instant warm showers are a luxury that I get to indulge in daily. I love it. He lowers me to my feet, and I step in, the water encasing me in a warm hug before he makes quick work of his jeans and steps in with me.

"How do you feel today?" he asks, and I look up at him as the water hits his shoulders, running down his amazing body.

"Good. A little sore, but good," I say honestly, because I had more activity with him last night than I have ever had in one night. Now I feel muscles in my body that I have never felt before.

"Turn around," he says, and I give him my back. He grabs the soap, lathering it up, and starts running his lathered hands over my body. His hands massage my shoulders and neck, any tension leaving immediately.

"Eddie," I groan. This is yet another new experience

for me. His hands feel like they are everywhere as they move down my back.

"God, every time you say my name, I get hard," he growls in my ear, his lips kissing my neck from behind. I know he is telling the truth because I can feel him on my back.

"You are so good with your hands." I lean my head back on his chest, and his hands move to my front, cupping and massaging my breasts.

"You are so fucking beautiful," he growls again as his hands lower down my belly, the warm water spraying above us, keeping us cocooned. I go to talk, but then his fingers hit my clit, and all I can do is moan.

"Eddie," I moan, my teeth digging into my bottom lip, and I take a step wider, giving him access.

"Just lean back on me, baby. Let me take care of you." So I do. I give him all my weight. My back arches slightly as he wraps one hand around my hips, pulling me to him tight while the other hand circles me below, my arousal so instant it is almost embarrassing.

"Oh God, don't stop," I pant out, my hands grabbing on to his shoulders. My fingers dig in so I don't fall.

"Are you going to come for me, Katie?" I nearly come undone as his fingers work a little faster. My hands release from his shoulders, and I slap them on the glass in front of me.

"Eddie..." My teeth grind together as my legs start to shake. I have no idea how he does it. Every time he touches me, it is electric, like nothing I have ever experienced before.

"That's my girl. I've got you." I look up at him, and he

seals my moans with a kiss. His tongue delves into my mouth as my orgasm ricochets through me. My legs shake, and he growls his praise in my mouth.

When he pulls back and looks at me, my eyes are half-lidded as I give him a grin. "Good morning," I say again, my smile now wide.

"A great fucking morning," he says, smiling as his hands spread wide and run up my torso.

"You are a morning person, aren't you? Up early, making coffee, making girls moan your name," I say jokingly as I spin in his arms.

"Not girls. You," he corrects me. "Just you."

"Just me?" I ask, swallowing roughly.

"Exclusive. Me and you. I am not interested in sleeping around with multiple women. Never have been. If that is what you want, then we are not on the same page, and this is not something I can continue." My heart stutters in my chest. I like his honesty, and I can see in his eyes, he means every word.

"I don't want that... I mean, I don't do that either..." I stutter, this conversation going from lighthearted to reasonably serious in a breath. I feel like I must be on one of those candid camera shows and any minute a TV host is going to jump out and say *gotcha!* He's too perfect.

"Good," he says thoughtfully as his eyes look over my arms at the scattering of small tattoos.

"Is there anything wrong with you?" I ask, my eyes thinning.

"What do you mean?" he asks, confused.

"Do you snore? Burp at the dinner table? Do you steal, cheat, lie?" I am joking, but I see it in his eyes that there is something. Something he is not telling me. Call it a woman's intuition. Call it my history telling me nothing is ever perfect. But I saw his eyes just now as they lost a little shine.

"I don't think I snore. I mean, you would have heard it last night if I did?" he says, not really answering the question as his hands caress up and down my arms. "Tell me about your tattoos?" He has done that a few times, switching the subject, as have I. Maybe we are both hiding our pasts.

"What do you want to know?" I ask as I let the water run down my hair, and I see him grab the shampoo.

"When did you start getting tattoos?" His fingers dig into my scalp, and my eyes close as I relax into him again. It feels amazing.

"Hmm, I got my first one when I was fourteen, I think..." I say, and I feel his hands stop.

"Fourteen?" he asks.

"Yep, this one." I don't even open my eyes to point to the small outline of a heart tattooed on the inside of my wrist.

"Does it signify anything?" His hands get back to work on my scalp.

"That I was too young to get a tattoo," I murmur with a light laugh. "There is no meaning behind that one. Just pure rebellion."

"Which one does have meaning?" he asks, rinsing out my hair, the water mixed with his hands making me feel like I am at a day spa, not in my morning shower on a normal weekday.

I think for a moment before I point to a small script

on the inside of my forearm. "This one reminds me to be strong," I say as I look down at the words *Still I Rise*.

"I don't think you need a tattoo for that. You are one of the strongest, borderline stubborn, women I have ever met." My eyes flick up to see his sexy smirk on full display as he looks down at me.

"Are you teasing me?" I quirk a brow.

"Maybe, but right now, we need to get you out of this shower and changed; otherwise, you will be late for work," he says, slapping me on the bottom and turning off the shower. It isn't until he steps out of the shower and wraps a towel around me that I realize I didn't return the favor. He is still hard, and I pause for a moment as he wraps a towel around himself.

He made me come but didn't ask for anything in return. My eyes flick around the room, because surely that TV host will jump out at any minute, or maybe pigs with wings will fly past the window. This is all too good to be true. There is no doubt I must be dreaming.

AS THE CAR moves through the morning traffic, I sip on the fresh coffee Eddie made for me as I got ready for work. He left with me, his car parked in the basement of the building, telling me he had to go to another building he manages to sort out a few things.

"Tony, do you know Eddie from the building very well?" I ask my driver, who seems like a trustworthy man. His eyes flick to mine in his mirror.

"You could say that, yes," he says, giving me a small smile.

"Is he a nice guy?" I ask, wanting to know what other people think of him.

"One of the best men I have the pleasure of knowing," he says without hesitation, smiling widely,

"Does he date a lot of women?" The minute the question falls from my lips, I regret it. But Eddie is handsome. After this morning, I am also acutely aware that he is genuinely a nice guy, one who is cooking me dinner tonight after a long day at work. He said he wants to be exclusive, but sometimes men say all the right things, then do the opposite.

"No, hardly ever. I have never known him to have a long-term girlfriend. Maybe a few dates here and there, but nothing too serious." I think about it for a moment, then he continues. "He would do anything for anyone. Very generous with both his time and money." I can't help thinking I am missing something.

"He is a good guy, Miss Taylor. You have nothing to worry about," Tony reiterates as the car pulls up to the hospital. I look out the window at the massive building and steel myself for the day.

"Thanks, Tony," I say as he opens the door, and I climb out. The sunshine hits me first as I take a few steps toward the building. I feel good. Happy. Confident in myself. All a first for me.

"Excuse me?" a young woman asks from the side, and I stop to help.

"Yes?" I look at her. She is familiar, but I can't place her.

"I'm sorry, but I am lost. I'm trying to find Dr. Wilson's office?" she asks, and I see a file in her hand. It hits me then that this is the same woman who was trying to find Dr. Wilson last week.

"Oh, sure. Just through the door and down the hallway to the right. You will see the signs for the professional offices," I say cheerily. I feel like a new person. I have a new spring in my step. And while I still look around for Steve, that dark cloud not yet erased, I can't help but feel a little lighter.

"Thank you so much," she says genuinely as she pushes her glasses up her nose and turns and walks in the direction I told her. I watch her go, before looking up at the sun, letting the warmth skirt on my face.

Can this be my life?

18

EDDIE

I have had a shit round. The sun is warm, the course in great condition, but my mind is racing with the fact that I need to finish up here, shower and change, get to the supermarket to grab the ingredients for my pasta carbonara, and make it in time for when Katie gets home.

Our cart pulls up, and my brothers and I jump out. As I grab my putter from the back of the cart and walk to the green, all three of my brothers stand next to each other, shoulder to shoulder, with their arms crossed over their chests, looking at me.

"What?" I bark, probably a little too harshly, but their stare is putting me off.

"What's up with you?" my older brother Ben asks, eyeing me suspiciously.

"Nothing, what's up with you?" I shrug it off, but none of them are budging as they stand side by side, assessing me like three thugs in a dark alleyway.

"Something's off," Harrison, the eldest of us boys and current governor, says, rubbing his chin in thought.

"Nothing's off." I shake my head and brush them off.

"You look different," Harrison says.

"I look the same." I feign boredom, but I do *feel* different. Jumpy. Light. Excited. Happy.

"No, your hair, it's longer. You need a cut?" Harrison questions, trying to work out what is different about me.

"I'm not cutting it," I say sharply. The way Pinkie loves my hair, I am not touching it at all.

"Touchy?" Tennyson joins in. He is the biggest asshole of all of us.

"I'm not touchy," I sneer.

"You need to get laid," Tennyson says, and I huff a laugh and shake my head.

"Shit, I forgot about that woman at Harborside you were meeting. So you *are* getting laid?" Tennyson asks, wide-eyed, a smirk on his face, clearly happy that he has caught me out.

"What is so shocking about that?" I say, mildly offended.

"You have been so quiet lately, that's all. Who is she?" He continues to push me for information.

"No one you know," I offer, grabbing a golf glove from my bag, ready to take my putt.

"Bullshit, we know everyone," Harrison says, and he does. *He* knows everyone. It is so annoying.

"You don't know Pinkie," I say, not able to stop the shit-eating grin on my face.

"Pinkie?" they all say in unison, looking at me in shock.

"Yeah, she has pink hair," I say, shrugging and acting nonchalant. Even though I am itching to be with her.

"Pink hair?" Ben clarifies.

"And tattoos," I say, grinning. I fucking love her artwork, and I can't wait to delve into them more.

"Mom is going to fucking flip!" Tennyson says, laughing.

"Speaking of Mom..." Harrison says, and we all stall and look at him.

"What now?' Tennyson moans, running his hand down his face.

I look at Harrison, trying to determine the look on his face. It isn't good.

"I can confirm what we all thought," Harrison says, looking at us all.

"She had an affair?" Ben asks, and I look at Harrison, waiting for his response. It isn't exactly news. We always thought something was going on.

"With the doctor, right?" Tennyson asks, and Harrison nods. I shouldn't be shocked. We have spoken about this before, and this cements it.

"How did you figure it out?" I ask, wondering what proof he has. Not that we really need any, since the dots already connected for us all over the past few months as we started to piece things together.

"Had some people follow him. Looked at what they have been up to," Harrison says before he swallows.

"Wait. They are still together? What the fuck?" I ask in shock.

"Looks that way. They are keeping it extremely private, obviously not wanting anyone to know. We won't know for sure until we confront her, but from everything I have found, it seems like they got together years ago and have been friendly on and off ever since," he confirms. We all stand quiet. We knew. Deep down, we all knew. It doesn't make the sting any less, though.

"Well. Fuck that. I don't want to think about that today. Eddie, tell me more about this girl," Tennyson says, quickly changing the subject, and I take a deep breath.

"Who is she?" Harrison adds, his suspicion now rising.

"She just moved here. Lives at Harborside. She thinks I am the maintenance man." I come clean with it all. If anyone can help me get out of this web of lies I have told, it will be them.

"What the fuck?" Ben asks, looking at me like I am crazy.

"I fixed her leaking sink; she patched me up after an accident, then I saw her in the swimming pool the other night, and..." I take a big breath, knowing the rest is self-explanatory.

"Fuck, you really like her?" Tennyson says. He is observant like that.

"It's early days," I say, not denying it. Because I do. I fucking like her a lot. I pretty much demanded that we go exclusive this morning, which is so not me, but I couldn't cope if she said no and had needed to know we were on the same page. I don't want to fumble along with her with anything casual. I want to dive right in and never come back up.

"What are you doing tonight? Come over. Tell me all about her," Tennyson teases.

"Can't," I say sharply.

"Why not?" He is quick.

"I'm making her dinner," I say, and the three of them look at me, their mouths agape. I sigh and just come out with it.

"She is a nurse, so she is working all day. She works with fucking Colin Wilson," I grit out, still not liking that, and by the looks on their faces, neither do my brothers. The fact that it is now confirmed that my mother is having an affair with him makes the whole thing extremely hard to swallow.

"Cardiac ward?" Harrison clarifies.

"Yeah."

"Shit. Well, we need to meet her," Harrison says. He is the eldest brother, so he is protective of all of us, but he also needs to know who is coming into the fold and who we spend time with. He is planning to run for president in the coming years. He and Beth are already strategizing and moving chess pieces. I wonder what Katie will think when I tell her that my brother will be the leader of the free world one day. I swallow, knowing she will be shocked.

"No can do." I shake my head.

"Why?" all three of them ask, mildly offended.

"Because, like I said earlier, you fuckwits, she thinks I am the maintenance man," I say, hating that I dug this hole for myself.

"Wait. What?" Harrison growls, his brows furrowed.

"She doesn't know I am a Langford. She thinks I am just Eddie, the maintenance man." I feel sick to my stomach.

"This is the funniest shit I have ever heard," Tennyson says as he bends over and slaps his leg, laughter spilling out from him. But he is the only one.

"You lied?" Ben questions, the lawyer coming out in him.

"I didn't lie... I just didn't tell her everything."

"This is not going to be good..." Harrison huffs a breath, shaking his head.

"I tried. I tried to tell her." I sound pathetic.

"Try harder. We don't need this to come out in the media. A Langford playing trick games with a young woman new to the city just to bed her." Harrison scowls.

"I am not just bedding her." I step forward, my finger in his face. He looks at me, glances down at my finger, and back at me.

"Make it right, Eddie. She deserves the truth. If she likes you, it shouldn't matter if you come from money. You're a good guy. Better than most. She will like you for you, I'm sure of it," he says softly, slapping my shoulder and giving it a squeeze.

"Now take your shot, fuck boy. I need to get back to Willow's," Tennyson says, making mention of his woman, the one who didn't care too much about his last name either.

"Mom presented me with a list," I say to them as I take my putt. The ball overshoots, missing the hole completely. My game is going from bad to worse.

"What kind of list?" Harrison asks. He steps up to me. He is my father figure, has been ever since Dad died years ago.

"A list of potential women to make my bride." I hear

Tennyson curse, causing him to overshoot the hole as well. He slams the club down on the ground like a child, his jaw tight. He hates our mother.

"Did you tell her that you are not interested?" Harrison presses, as Ben takes his shot.

"Yeah, did you tell her that you are too busy being balls deep in a pink delight to worry about marrying anyone from high society?" Tennyson says, walking past and throwing his club into the bag as he sits back in the cart.

"Shut up," I murmur to him.

"Seriously, Eddie, you need to tell her to butt out or she can be dangerous," Ben says. He hasn't seen our mother in months. Even before then, it was only for business meetings. He has shut her out completely.

"I know. I told her." My brothers all look at me with concern.

"Sounds like you got some things to sort out. Between telling your new girl that you are a Langford, and then telling Mom to back off, you are stuck deep in women's problems this week, brother," Tennyson says, his tone serious.

I nod. I agree with him. "I will tell Pinkie tonight. I will tell her everything," I say, trying to push down the rising nerves. I haven't been nervous of that fact before. Probably because most people know exactly who I am, and I usually don't care enough to be bothered by what they think of me. But Pinkie is different.

So, I know I need to tell her. I need to come clean. She needs to know the real me.

19

KATIE

I open my apartment door and am immediately greeted by the most amazing smell.

"That smells delicious," I say, my smile instant, my heart skipping a beat as I walk on autopilot toward Eddie, where he stands in the kitchen. He is in his jeans and a tight top. His sleeves are pushed up his forearms, and I can see his strong arms as they stir the contents of the pan.

"Just in time. It is all ready," he says, looking at me, openly devouring me with his eyes as one of his hands reaches out for me, pulling me close and sealing my lips with his.

We kiss like we haven't seen each other for weeks, not merely the day. He pulls me close, tucks me into him, and I do what I have wanted to do since I met him. I sink into him. His large arms circle my body, and he pulls me tight. Our chests are meshed, our hips connected, and I feel the stress of the day leave me immediately.

I pull back and look at him. "This feels oddly domesticated," I say as I look around. He has the wine open and the table set, including fresh flowers in a vase in the middle.

"It does, doesn't it? I kinda like it." His hands run up and down my body, making butterflies swirl below. His hands, like him, are large and cover my back with ease.

"I kinda like you," I say, smiling. He has melted me like butter.

"That's good, 'cause I kinda like you too," he says sweetly, and I laugh as he pulls me in, taking my lips in his again.

"Go wash up. Dinner is ready," he says, slapping my butt as I quickly walk out of the kitchen to go change and freshen up. I select a dress to put on, sick of wearing my scrubs all day. As I go through the motions, I hear him serving, and I wonder if this could be life. A buzz of excitement fills me. For the first time ever, I allow myself to just sit in it. I don't push it away, don't tamp it down. I relish it. I want to feel loved, and if this is the beginning of that, I don't ever want it to leave me.

I smile at everything as I walk back out. The table set, wine, fresh bread, nice napkins.

"Bon appétit," he says in a perfect French accent as he pulls out my chair for me. I'm impressed. He watches me as I take a seat at the table, and I don't hesitate to grab my fork and swirl it in the creamy pasta, my stomach growling in anticipation. I didn't have a full lunch break today, but I did manage to eat the lunch Eddie prepared, and it was delicious.

"Okay, be honest. I can put in an order at the pizza place around the corner if it is shit." The pasta hits my tongue, and the creamy, cheesy goodness delivers the most amazing flavors ever. I chew eagerly, loving every bite.

"This is amazing," I say to him, trying not to moan out loud. I can't remember eating anything this good.

"Seriously?" He doesn't seem convinced.

"Seriously. This is so good. Like, perhaps the best thing I have ever tasted." I laugh when he looks at me, cocking a brow. "Okayyyy, maybe the second-best thing I have ever tasted." That makes him laugh. I can't remember the last time I laughed so much. Maybe never?

"How was Dr. Wilson today?" he asks as he pours a small glass of wine for us both and starts to dig in.

"His usual asshole self. But we had our new volunteers today. They are always a mixture of fun and frustration, but it helps the day to go quickly," I offer. "So how was golf?" I ask, shoveling the pasta into my mouth, already almost finished, the serving just the right size.

"I had a shit game," he grumbles, then takes a sip of his wine.

"Oh, why's that?" I ask, pushing my plate away and settling in.

"I kept thinking about you. My mind wasn't on the game at all." His honesty is one of his best qualities. He reaches out to grab my hand, and I squeeze his. Taking a sip of my wine, I look at him over the rim, admiring his sexy smirk as his thumb strums over my hand. He is very swoony. His hands are soft. Not at all like the hands you would expect a man who frequently uses tools to have.

"So what thoughts did you have about me?" I ask cheekily, intrigued.

He barks a laugh. "What thoughts didn't I have of you?" he says as we both smile at each other.

"Hmm, well, I thought about you too." I stand up from my chair and walk to him. He sits back, and I straddle him. We are chest to chest as he slides his chair back from the table a little, his hands cradling my hips.

"What thoughts did you have about me?" He throws my question back at me as his hands find the hem of my dress, and he caresses my bare thighs.

"Dirty ones…" I say as my hands run from his shoulders down his chest, landing on his belt buckle. He takes a deep breath, and my eyes flick to his.

"There is something that we need to talk about." My hands freeze because he looks a little nervous. He has tried to talk to me about something a few times now, and I always dismiss it. I have no idea why. I am scared of what he is going to say. It is like my mind already knows it is going to be bad and I don't want to know. I hold my secrets, and he can hold his. It may not be the best plan, but it works for now. So, I say the first thing that comes to mind.

"Do you have an STD?" I ask, not sure why my mind goes there, since it probably should have been something we discussed before we had sex, but it does. I blame my work.

"What!? No!" He pulls back slightly, looking at me like I am crazy.

"Do you suffer from some other contagious disease?" I ask, as my hands get back to work unbuckling his belt before I start to open the button on his jeans. Trying to get us back on track.

"No." His eyes squint in confusion. I pop his button open and lower his zipper.

"Then talking is for later. I have had a long day, and now I just want to do wicked things to you, and then fall asleep in your arms," I say as my hand dives into his pants, and I hear him suck in a breath. His length is hot and heavy in my hand as his hands skirt up my thighs and cup my bare ass.

"Are you not wearing any underwear?" he asks, shocked.

"No, pretty boy. I am not." He groans before leaning forward, slamming his lips to mine. I push his jeans and underwear down as best I can and stroke him, feeling him harden even more under my touch.

"You are killing me," he mutters as his lips leave my mouth and trail down my jaw. I sit up a little, positioning myself closer to him.

"Condom is in my wallet." I reach around to his back pocket and pry his wallet loose, grabbing out a condom and ripping it open with my teeth.

"I like your hands on me," he moans as I sheath him. His hands move and open the few buttons on my dress before he whips the flimsy material off my body, leaving me completely naked. In contrast to him, who is still fully dressed, with just his pants undone.

"You were naked underneath this dress this whole time?" He bites his lip with a groan, leaning forward and taking a nipple into his mouth.

"Mm-hmm," I hum as my hands run up his torso and delve into the back of his hair. Shimmying up his lap, he grabs my ass and pulls me up, and I position myself, ready to take him. I slide down, feeling him stretch me, the pleasure instant as I take him deep.

"You feel so good, Katie... like you were made just for me..." We both share a moan, and my breath gets caught in my chest at his words. Said so simply, yet it means so much. He lifts me back off him before I sink down again. I move then. His hands rest on my hips as I move up and down, bouncing on his lap, feeling like a stripper giving a lap dance. I grip on to the back of his chair as his hands run up my spine, holding my upper back.

"If this is the thanks I get for cooking you dinner, I'm fucking making it a three-course meal tomorrow night." His hand slaps my ass cheek and grabs on to me, pulling my flesh as he grits his teeth.

"You like me bouncing on you, pretty boy?" I tease, my breathing becoming rapid. I have never been this sexually liberated before. Ever. I like making him come undone, making him moan for me.

"Only you," he pants as the two of us get into our rhythm.

"This feels so good," I say through a whimper, enjoying every moment. I feel alive. When I am with him, I don't think about anything else. I feel his hand move from my back and trail around my hip before his fingers land on my clit and start to circle.

"Fuck, your tits are perfect, your ass is perfect, your fucking pussy is perfect."

"Oh. Oh my," I cry out, not prepared. The rush is almost instant. Just like it was this morning in the shower.

"You like that?" he asks, always making sure I am okay.

"I love it," I say, panting, his fingers playing me perfectly as I continue to take him over and over.

My head falls back as our bodies mesh, and I start to whimper all over again.

"Eddie..." I whisper, not understanding how it feels so good and so different with him.

"I've got you, Katie," he says quietly, looking at me as my eyes come back to meet his. A silent assurance runs between us. I feel it then. My orgasm rushes through me, and I clench into the back of his neck, my fingers delving into my favorite spot, the hair at his nape.

"Oh my... Eddie..." I groan out as I grind onto him. My orgasm is long, and I feel him coming right after me.

"Katie," he groans in my neck, where his head falls as he thrusts up into me and chases his release, the two of us now breathless as I hold his head to my chest. I think about what is building between us. It happened so naturally yet took us both by surprise. I spot the heart diagram on the wall behind him. Then I realize why it is different.

I trust him. I trust him with everything, maybe including my heart.

20

EDDIE

As she sleeps next to me, I try not to wake her as my hand strums up and down her naked back. The secret I keep slowly eats away at me and my insides. I should have told her as soon as I kissed her. Now, we are practically joined at the hip, and she still doesn't know.

I am such an asshole.

Her skin is soft under my touch. She is lying half on me, her legs tangled with mine. Her lips puff out, and I feel her warm breath skirt across my bare chest. She does this little half-snore thing, which sounds like a mix of a moan, a hiss, and a hiccup. I have never heard anything like it, and it is cute as hell.

I stare at the ceiling, deep in thought, as I realize I am completely fucked. She is a seductress, and I am totally in her web, and I have no plans to leave. She has captured my attention, and there is no way I can give that to anyone else. I don't want to, even if I could.

It is early, the sun is barely up, but I need to move. I

have to be across town for a meeting at eight this morning, and my day just gets busier after that. I have no idea where my clothes landed, but I know I need to get home, shower, and change into Edward Langford before I can even start my day.

I move silently, wanting her to keep sleeping, and as I escape the bed, I hear her continue to snore, so I know that I have succeeded. Once I've put on my clothes and grabbed my things, I close the bedroom door and clean up the kitchen and living room from last night, not wanting her to wake up to a messy house. As I look at the dining chair, the memories of her moaning body sneak up on me, and I have a sudden desire to crawl back into bed with her.

Ignoring the thought, I make her a coffee and pull together a quick lunch of leftovers and put it on the kitchen counter before I sneak back into her room with the hot brew. I place the coffee on her side table, and I bend down to kiss her cheek before I whisper to her.

"Bye, Pinkie. I need to go and make a few million today." I smile a little before I pull back and start to turn.

"Okay, good luck with that," she murmurs, and I still before I smile.

"Bye, baby. See you tonight," I say, coming back and giving her another peck on her cheek.

"Bye, pretty boy," she says, still sleepy, and I leave her to rest as I quietly exit the apartment, then run to the elevator, already late for my busy day.

∽

I READ the contract in front of me as I pace my office. My cell phone sits in my hand. I just sent a text to Katie, asking her favorite dessert, secretly hoping it is chocolate, because I have already ordered supreme chocolate sundaes from Softies, the local ice creamery—they are old school, make the best sundaes, and are not too far away. I will pick them up after work so we can eat them in the apartment, the two of us not eager to get out into the world yet. I know the minute we do, her life will change, and I am not yet sure if it is something she wants.

My cell vibrates.

> Pinkie: Um, chocolate. It is seriously
> God's work.

Laughing, I send her a laugh and heart emoji, knowing that she can't be on her cell at work, yet not able to stay away from her for long periods. I'm a goner for her. Hook, line, and sinker.

"Here's your coffee, sir," Miranda, my assistant, says, walking into my office and placing the steamy cup in front of me.

"Thank you, Miranda," I say as she slowly retreats. "Oh, Miranda?" I question, a thought suddenly coming to me.

"The baskets that the marketing team prepare for all our tenants..." I start, my mind racing to Katie's kitchen and at the fact that out of the two baskets I gave her since she moved in, only the artisan biscuits were gone from both of them. Even the wine sat untouched until I opened a bottle with dinner last night.

"Yes, sir?" Miranda asks, bringing me back to reality.

"They have these cookies in them. A passionfruit and white chocolate?" I rub my head. This is such an odd request.

"Oh yes, they are delicious. My favorite." My eyebrows shoot up. Okay, clearly, they are good. I must try them.

"Can you bring me a carton?" I ask her, and she pauses.

"A box?" she clarifies.

"No, a carton," I clarify. I grabbed the other box from Brian's office, and the rate in which Pinkie consumes an entire box, I know I need a good supply handy.

"Sure. I will have them bring it up today," she says with a smile. "Also, your mother is due to arrive any minute." At the mere mention of my mother, my smile drops.

"Shit. I forgot she was coming in. What is she in for again?" I ask, her visit totally slipping my mind.

"She only said it was to go through a list?" Miranda replies, confused, and I sigh, already feeling the weight of her and she isn't even here yet. It is a month, almost to the day, since she told me of her desire to set me up with one of Baltimore's socialites. Giving me her deadline to find a suitable woman, one which I have no intention of sticking to. I run my hand through my hair, thinking of Katie. I can't believe I met her almost the same day and have fallen so hard so quickly for her. Two totally different outcomes, none of which was expected.

"Shit," I say, scrubbing a hand down my face. This is absolutely the last thing I need.

"Oh, not at your desk again, I see." My mother walks

straight into my office and immediately berates my assistant.

"Thank you, Miranda," I say, nodding to her as she leaves, closing the door on what will no doubt be a highly sensitive discussion, at best.

"Mom. Good to see you," I lie through my teeth, but still feeling upbeat. I have found a woman. It just isn't a woman Mom is going to like.

"Edward," she says, her tone clipped, as she takes a seat, smoothing out her unwrinkled clothing.

"So what's happening?" I ask her as I take a seat at my desk, opposite her. Needing the desk between us. Needing the authority of my position in this discussion.

"It has been a month, Edward. Now I know you haven't found anyone on the list, so I have taken the privilege of organizing dinner for you tonight with Valerie Van Cleef." My teeth grind instantly. The Van Cleefs are nice. One of the nicer families in the city. I know Valerie too. She just turned twenty-one, and I am pretty sure I saw her at a club a few months ago, dancing with her friends. She is nice, just not the woman I want.

"Well, you can cancel it," I tell her, trying to keep composed.

"The Van Cleefs are one of the wealthiest families in the state. Valerie is a nice young girl, who shows great potential in society circles, and with her model-esque looks, she will be sure to produce good-looking babies for you, Edward." She says this like we are discussing an arranged marriage business deal, not my love life.

"I mean, you can cancel it, because I have found someone," I state, pulling off the Band-Aid.

My mother looks at me like she is trying to see in my soul. The hairs on the back of my neck stand up. The very same spot that Pinkie loves on me is also now my danger radar. I can see my mother about to combust.

"Who is she?" she asks with a swallow, trying to remain composed.

"No one you know," I offer, not planning on telling her anything.

She scoffs. "Stop playing, Edward. I know everyone," she says, rolling her eyes at me for dramatic effect.

"Her name is Katie. I met her a few weeks ago. It is new, and she is from out of town." I adjust myself in my chair, already feeling like I have said too much.

"What does her family do?" my mother asks, eyeing me with suspicion. I balk because I actually don't know. While I have been focused on keeping my own family identity under wraps, I also haven't delved into Katie's. Although I do have my suspicions they aren't close.

"I don't know." Her father could be anything, and it would make no difference to me. I don't need a woman from society. I also don't need a woman with money. I have enough of that as it stands.

"You don't know? What do you mean, you don't know? She can't be that important if you don't know anything about her family." Her voice rises, and I see her vein start to pop at her temple. I am amazed for a moment at why she hasn't cosmetically fixed that, since the rest of her face is almost frozen solid. My shoulders feel stiff as frustration builds in my body.

"I don't care what her parents do or what her family owns or what part of society she is from." My mother's face contorts. We are black and white, always have been. The words I say are the truth because I don't care. I understand what it is like having parents who give you more pain than love. Hell, my mother wins the award for crazy. The fact that she can even sit here and ask me these questions at all without a hint of self-reflection just shows her lack of awareness, and it is pissing me off.

"Edward, you cannot be serious. You hardly know this girl. You have been brainwashed by your brothers, haven't you?" she says, a small snarl coming to her lips. She is about to go crazy. I can feel it.

"Mom, I am not marrying anyone because of social status. I am planning to marry for love," I grit out, and that lights the flame inside of her.

"Love? *Love?* What do you know about *love,* Edward. Life is not *made* of love. It is not *enhanced* by love. You need status. You need financial growth. You need a woman who will stand by your side and smile for the fucking cameras, even when she doesn't want to. You need to approach your marriage like a business arrangement. The woman you choose needs to be up to Langford standards. Being a Langford is more than just having the name, Edward. We are a strong, wealthy family. We have history, a name to uphold, and that is a lot of pressure for a woman who isn't already from our world. She will only bring you down. Just like your brothers."

She sounds like she is speaking from experience. I feel my cell vibrate and look at it quickly. I see Katie has sent me the kissing face, and I try to stop the smile, but I can't.

"*Edward!*" My mother screams my name so loud, I

jump in my seat. Fuck, she is really not happy. I look at her, the scowl already forming on my face. "For God's sake, get your head out of that phone and show me some respect. You will go on that date with Valerie tonight, and you will do it with a smile. Do I make myself clear?" She says it like her word is final, speaking to me as though I am eight. A mere boy. Not the man I am. Her angry outbursts are in complete contrast to the sweet, flirty nature of Katie's text messages. So much so, it is startling.

"No, Mom. I will not. So, you can call Valerie and tell her I can't make it, or she will turn up to the restaurant and be eating alone. Either way, I am busy with my *girl-friend*," I say, liking the sound of that. That is what Katie is. My girlfriend.

"You will not—" she starts but stops suddenly mid-sentence as she takes a breath. Her face looks a little red, and I stare at her sharply.

"You alright, Mom?" I ask, sitting forward in my seat. She looks okay, although her expression is a little more pinched than normal. I start to become concerned when she doesn't speak right away.

She looks at me, takes another breath, and scoffs again. "I am fine. But I can see that I am not getting through to you today. I will reschedule Valerie for next week," she says, standing, offering a sudden end to this heated discussion.

"I won't change my mind, Mom. I am seeing someone. Someone I really like. I won't be dating Valerie, or any other woman you put in front of me."

"We'll see, Edward. We will see." She doesn't look

back as she opens the door and walks out, and I wonder what the hell has gotten into her.

I slump in my office chair and think about our interaction. The whole ordeal left me feeling heavy and out of sorts. The secret I keep sits heavier in my chest, now more than before. I rarely listen to anything my mother says these days, but something she mentioned rings true. It is hard being a Langford, and when you are not from our world, there is a lot of pressure. While I don't know Katie's family or too much about her history, I already know she is not society. Me, and everything I bring with me, is going to be a lot for her.

We are going along so good together, fitting together so well, I don't want to rock the boat yet. This is the first time I have felt real happiness with a woman, and I just want to feel it for a little longer. I will tell her... I just need more time with her. More time to connect, so that whatever we have can't be severed by my mother, by my name, by anyone.

21

KATIE

"What about this one?" Eddie asks as we both lie in bed, snuggling, him pointing to another tattoo, wanting to know the meaning. We have been doing this every night since we got together. We work, he meets me at home, we either cook or we get food delivered, and we talk, have sex, cuddle, sleep, and repeat it all the next day. It has been a tonic for my soul because I don't want to be outside, knowing Steve is still around, and Eddie doesn't appear to want to go out either. This situation is perfect for both of us.

"I got that when I was seventeen," I say, looking at the small butterfly on the inside of my bicep. I think briefly about that traumatic time in my life.

"Does it signify anything?" he asks, extremely curious about my artwork. He asks about each piece before kissing it and then moving to the next.

"A rebirth, I guess. A caterpillar has a second life

coming out as a beautiful butterfly," I tell him, knowing even back then, I was full of hope that there would be something more for me.

"A rebirth at seventeen is pretty heavy stuff," he says as his lips touch the tattoo, lingering there a little longer than the rest. He is right. Most seventeen-year-olds were partying, hanging with friends, shopping, or getting their first boyfriend. I was couch surfing, trying to find food, keeping my head down in school, and wondering if there was a point to it all.

"I think if I could tell my teenage self anything, it would be that there is light at the end of the tunnel. The tunnel is dark and long, but there is light." It feels like he understands what I am saying, and he looks at me with intense adoration. "What about you? What would you tell your seventeen-year-old self?" I ask, interested to get a glimpse into his upbringing. We still haven't delved into that part of our lives.

"Don't listen to my mother..." he mutters as he looks up to the ceiling. He has mentioned her a few times, and none of it in a positive light.

"She was trying to find you a wife, wasn't she?" I ask, the memory sitting in my gut, a little like lead. Would he introduce me to his mother one day?

"Still is. But I told her that I have a girlfriend, and I am not interested in any woman she tries to set me up with," he says, looking at me. *Girlfriend? He's told his mother about me?* There are so many feelings running through my body at once. I look at him as I smile, not able to hide the happiness I feel in this moment. I really like the new me I have found. My past is still there but buried a little deeper than it has ever been.

"What did she say?" I ask, my heart beating faster.

He laughs. "Well, she wasn't too happy that she didn't get to pick you." I am not sure if that is a good or bad thing.

"Do you think she will like me?" I ask, looking at him seriously, all of a sudden feeling extremely vulnerable. He stares at me as the question runs through his mind.

"My mother is not a nice woman. She doesn't talk to any of my brothers' partners. They don't have a relationship with her at all. I am the only son who still talks to her." My chest hurts as I see pain in his eyes. I have never had a mother, so I don't really know any difference, but I have had some wicked foster moms, and I couldn't wait to get away from them.

"I take that as a no, then," I say, smiling, trying to lighten the mood, but feeling a little deflated.

"My brothers are all dying to meet you, though," he says, grinning.

"Really?" I ask, surprised and delighted. "You've told them about me?"

"Pfftt. I told them about you ages ago. I was a goner the moment I met you, I told you that." His fingers push back the hair at the side of my face before they cup my cheek. "My dad would have liked you too..." he says, his voice drifting a bit.

"You know I am just keeping you around for your amazing skills in the kitchen," I joke, leaning into him.

"And my amazing skills in the bedroom." His hands sneak around my back, starting to tickle me.

"Eddie. Stop!" I say, my laughter already bouncing around the room. I have never felt this light, this carefree. It is almost like the stormy clouds of my life have finally parted and all I see is the bright-yellow sun. Eddie is drenching me in sunlight, which is overwhelmingly welcome after so many storms.

"Stop what? I'm not doing anything." He feigns innocence as his fingers continue to tickle me, and I squirm underneath him.

"Eddie!!!" I scream and giggle, my legs kicking out. My laughter bounces around the room. I have laughed so much since I met him, I feel like a new person. He is quick as he flips me onto my back and hovers over me, his hands gripping mine, our fingers intertwined at the sides of my head. I pant to catch my breath, and he looks at me, intensity burning in his gaze. I swallow at that look. We went from playful to erotic in under a minute. This man is a magician.

Our eyes remain locked on each other as he lowers his head, and his tongue swipes across my nipple.

"Eddie..." I breathe out a moan as I relax under him. He maneuvers his body and uses his legs to spread my own, positioning himself on top of me. His hands are still tight in mine.

He sucks then, his lips and tongue playing with my breasts as he takes his time teasing me, moving from one to the other, getting me all hot and flustered. I try to move a hand, wanting to touch him, sink my fingers into his hair, but he holds me tight. Instead, I move my hips to feel more of him, needing the friction.

"Mmmmm, I want you... I like you doing that..." I moan. When I am with him, I think of nothing else. Not work, not Steve, not my bank balance. When I am with him, nothing else matters.

"Making you mine," he says as he lifts his head and his eyes meet mine. I melt a little more at his words, just as he moves his hips and pushes into me. My mouth opens on a gasp as I feel him, my hips automatically lifting to take him deep.

He pulls back and then pushes again, his movements slow, almost erotic as his head lowers and he continues sucking on my breasts.

"Eddie... Oh ..." He thrusts so slowly it is hard to take. I feel like I am about to explode yet tiptoe the edge so often it is almost frustrating.

"Yes, baby?" he asks, knowing exactly what he is doing. His lips trail up my chest, and he kisses my neck.

"Eddie, I need... I need..." I pant out, not sure what I need, but needing something.

"What do you need, Katie? Tell me what you want," he whispers teasingly as he kisses my jaw. His thrusts are sensual, pushing me closer and closer to heaven before pulling me back again. I try to move my hand again, needing to touch him, but his grip is tight.

"I need..." I whimper, moving my hips, trying to get more from him, but his movements stay on pace, his slow thrusts almost killing me.

"Does this feel good? You like me taking you like this?" he asks, and I can hear his voice wavering, so I know he isn't immune either.

"I want... please..." I have resorted to begging. I am panting. I don't know how much longer I can take it.

"Tell me. Tell me what you want," he grits out, his head buried in my neck. My body arches into him, pushing me right to the brink, but his pace doesn't quicken. He is steady, his discipline astounding. My chest hits his, our bodies touching from the tips of our toes to our hands joined at my side.

"I want you. Eddie, I want you." I get it out, and that is all he needs to hear before his hands leave mine, and he grabs my wrists instead, throwing my hands up and pinning them to the bed above my head.

"Are you mine, Katie? I want you all to myself, every inch, every thought, every fucking moan and quiver and feeling. Tell me you are mine." The claim is whispered against my skin as his nose traces my cheek.

"Yours. I am all yours," I pant out, barely hanging on, but meaning every word.

He doesn't wait before he slams into me. His thrusts now fast and furious.

"Say it again," he demands, his head hovering above mine as his hips thrust powerfully.

"I'm yours. I'm all yours, Eddie," I say again, and it feels like a promise. Like they cement something between us. That we are no longer just hanging out and getting to know each other, but we have moved to another stage. A more serious stage.

"Fuck, I want you, Katie. I have been waiting for someone like you my whole fucking life." I feel it then, my orgasm as it crests. I stare into his eyes, and I know the words he is saying are true.

"Eddie," I breathe, knowing I am about to lose control. About to give it all to him.

"I've got you. I've got you," he repeats, and I let go. Giving him another little piece of my heart.

22

KATIE

Walking into the cardiac ward, I see Shelley sitting at the nurses' station. I begin to wonder if she lives here, given that whenever I am here, she is too.

"Morning!" I singsong to her as I check that I have my pen and a fresh pair of gloves in my pocket, ready to start my shift.

"Good morning. You seem happy today," she comments, and I can't help the grin that lands on my face.

"The sun is shining. It is a great day outside," I say, sounding not like myself at all and she stares at me.

"Is that all that has you walking on cloud nine today?" Her eyes narrow as she quizzes me. We have only known each other a short time, but we get along so well.

"I'm seeing someone," I say sneakily. After our declarations to each other, Eddie and I have become more serious. I am itching to tell someone, and Shelley is the closest to a friend I have here.

"Ohhh, do tell," she says, swiveling her chair around and grabbing her coffee, her full attention now on me.

"Well, his name is Eddie. He is a few years older than me. He manages the maintenance in the apartment building I live in," I say, giving her a quick rundown, skipping the parts about his panty-melting kisses.

"You're down in Harborside, aren't you?" Shelley clarifies.

"Yeah, right on the water. A doctor friend from Philly offered me her place."

"Not that big skyrise?" Shelley's eyes widen a little as realization crosses her face.

"Yeah, I'm not right up at the top, but it is pretty amazing," I say, still dumbfounded that I live there.

"I think that one is owned by the Langfords," Shelley says, her eyes crumpling as she thinks.

"Langfords?" I ask, having no idea who she is talking about.

"Yeah, the richest family in Baltimore. One of them is the governor of Maryland." None of that is familiar to me. I am not really into politics.

"Well, they are generous with their welcome baskets. I got two welcome gifts when I first moved in, both full to the brim with food and whatnot," I say to her with a nod, one that she returns.

"So Eddie? Tell me more about him," she prompts.

"He cooks me dinner, makes me lunch, organizes a car to drop me off and pick me up. He is funny, caring, thoughtful, and sweet..." I say, drifting off a little as I think about him.

"Clearly, he is alright in the bedroom department too,

because you are looking like a totally different person than when you first arrived here. You have a fresh glow to you," Shelley comments with a laugh as she looks me over.

"Hmmm, a lady never tells," I say, smiling, feeling too happy. This is all still very new. Not just in terms of a relationship, but for me in general. Having never really had a boyfriend before, and certainly never a man who treats me this way, I have no idea if this is normal, over the top, how things progress, any of it. I am just going with my gut and trying to live life to the fullest.

"Well, Baltimore, or perhaps *Eddie*, is looking good on you. Glad that you are settling in so well."

"Um, excuse me?" a voice sounds from the nurses' desk behind us as we both turn quickly. "Sorry, I don't mean to interrupt," the woman says, and the familiar long brown hair and thick glasses hit my mind immediately.

"Not at all, how can we help you?" Shelley says, smiling.

"I am just looking for Dr. Wilson. His office said he might be down here?" she says, looking at us both with hope.

"You have been here before, right? Looking for him?" I say, taking in the thick file in her hands, and I watch as she pushes her thick glasses up her nose. If I had to guess, I would say she works in a library.

"Yes. Sorry. I can't seem to catch the doctor. He isn't taking appointments and so his office said I am best to try to catch him here." She obviously doesn't know Dr.

Wilson at all, because he would totally railroad her if she was to approach him here.

"Well, I think he is in surgery at the moment and probably won't be available for a few hours," Shelley explains, and the women's shoulders visibly slump.

"Ohh," she says, clear disappointment on her face.

"We can pass on a message. Or can another doctor assist you?" I offer, because this is the third time I have seen her here over these past few weeks. It is obviously important.

"Thank you, but no. I just need to speak with him directly about my parents' medical file. I have some questions," she says with a small smile. "I will pop back tomorrow. Perhaps I might catch him then. Thank you." Giving Shelley and me a warm smile, she turns and walks out the door.

"She is such a pretty girl. Even with those thick glasses on," Shelley murmurs to me quietly.

"I've seen her a few times trying to find Dr. Wilson. It must be important," I say as I grab my things, ready to do my rounds.

"Maybe it is malpractice. Maybe she is trying to serve him papers?" Shelley murmurs, rolling her eyes. No one likes Dr. Wilson. Not one person.

"Who knows. But right now, I need to get to work," I say with a smile, one which she returns, and I leave her to it as I walk down the hall to see my patients.

23

KATIE

I feel a little nervous in the back seat of the car. Tony is driving, but the car is different than what he usually picks me up in. This one is bigger, seems fancier, and the windows are fully tinted. Eddie sits next to me, his hands holding mine.

He asked me out on a date. Chuckling, he said that for weeks we have been together and yet haven't left the apartment. I lied and said I didn't really like crowds. Then he offered to take us somewhere private, and I lied and told him I was exhausted from work and needed to sleep. But I couldn't hold him off forever. It isn't his fault that I am scared to step out of the apartment. You would think I would be used to living in fear, but I am not. The constant looking over my shoulder when I leave the hospital is hurting my neck. The swirl of anxiety as I step out of the apartment to meet Tony is almost suffocating. But like always, I push it down. I know that in order to have some semblance of a life, I need to push through it. So when Eddie broached the subject of a date outside of the apartment again, I didn't decline. Although now that we are driving down the street, I can't say my nerves are steady.

I look out the window at everyone and everything. I should be looking at the sights of Baltimore, since I haven't had a chance to play tourist in my new city yet. However, my eyes are peeled at everyone walking about. The traffic is a little congested, our car moving, but slowly.

Eddie feels a little on edge too, but I have no idea why. Maybe he is picking up on my anxiety, and that thought alone makes me feel guilty. I don't want to ruin his day. I take a breath and try to relax. The windows are so dark that no one can see in unless they plaster their face right against the glass.

"How far away is it?" I ask, looking at Eddie. He senses my nervousness, I am sure, because he grabs my hand and gives it a squeeze. That small action helps me lower my shoulders a little, and I smile at him.

"Only another fifteen minutes," he says softly as he strums my hand with his thumb in soothing motions. My heart thuds at his sweetness.

"Are you sure you don't want to tell me where we are going? "I ask, trying to get it out of him. He has been awfully secretive.

"Nope. It is a surprise," he says, grinning. It is a beautiful day. The sky is blue, there's a light breeze, and I start to relax a little in the back seat, enjoying the soft leather while biting my lower lip in anticipation.

"I don't think I have ever had a surprise date before..." I say out loud, thinking about it.

"Impossible. Never?" Eddie asks in disbelief.

"Hmmmm, not one I can remember anyway. What about you? What was the biggest surprise you have had?" I ask him, keen to know what makes a man like Eddie surprised.

"The biggest and best surprise I have had was this one time, I was working on the maintenance in the building, and I got a call that there was a leaking tap in one of the apartments. I went to investigate, found this gorgeous woman, wet from head to toe, with amazing pink hair and fantastic breasts..." My smile widens, and I feel my cheeks heat.

"That is not what I meant." I pout, even though I love how playful he's being.

"I know, but it is the truth. You were a total surprise that day, one of the best ones I have had." Eddie is teasing me as he gives me a wink, and I laugh as I look back out the window, taking in the view.

We pull up at the lights, still in the city, and I jump, startled when a male face suddenly appears at the window, slamming the side of the car with his hands. *Steve*. His face is squished against the glass, his eyes finding mine immediately. I physically feel all the air in my lungs leave my body, and I freeze. He is following me. His eyes thin, and I can't move.

"Jesus. *Tony*," Eddie barks out as he grabs me around the waist and pulls me across the seat to him. Away from Steve and away from the door.

"He can't get through. The doors are locked, the glass bullet proof," Eddie says to me. But Steve isn't even trying to open the door. He is looking directly at me with a sick smile on his face. He is just reminding me that he is still around. These are the types of games he plays. He continues to stalk, remind me that he is there, keep me scared, my anxiety high and my fears warranted.

"Shit, Katie." Eddie pulls me onto his lap, taking my attention away from the window. "It's okay, baby. Look at me." I bring my gaze to his, but I can't hide the fear on my face.

"He is just a homeless guy. You are safe. I'm here," Eddie murmurs, and he is saying the right things, but he doesn't know it is Steve. He doesn't know that the home-less guy is my stalker foster brother. The one who likes to taunt me, blackmail me, and keep me fearful. I swallow roughly as Tony starts to drive away, and I nod in under-standing.

"Are you okay?" he asks, cupping my face in his hands, clearly concerned, which melts my heart. I sink into his body and let him hold me.

"I am. Just got a fright, that is all," I say, again a lie falling from my mouth as I try to stop my hands from shaking, not wanting to spoil this amazing date Eddie has arranged.

"We can go back to the apartment. I can get Tony to go around?" he asks me, his brows furrowed as his eyes search my face.

"No. Let's keep going. I'm fine." I give him a small smile. While I am scared, there is no way that Steve will follow us. He has done his job. Scared me half to death and reminded me that he is still around. I am so sick of him always turning up and ruining my life. I am so sick of being constantly scared. Walking on eggshells, not being able to progress my life the way I want, all because I know he won't leave me alone. He is always one step ahead of me, and I just can't escape.

But for right now, for today, I know I won't see him again. He has had his fun. He has made his point. *I hope.* I sit on Eddie's knee for the remainder of the journey, taking deep breaths, him strumming my back as I get my heart rate back under control.

"We're here," he says softly as we pull up to large iron gates fencing off one of the biggest and most luxurious mansions I have ever seen.

"Where are we?" I ask, sitting up in awe, looking around out the windows as Tony drives us through, the gates closing behind us. We pull up the long driveway and slowly past the large white stone mansion.

"Just outside of the city. Come on, let's explore," he says as the car stops in front of the large garden, where I can see a full picnic setup, with champagne and food and a large rug.

"Eddie..." I whisper, unsure. "Are we meant to be here? We are not trespassing, are we?" I ask, squinting at him, and he gives me his sexy-ass smirk in return that immediately defrosts any and all fear I have.

"No, baby. I know the real estate owner. The place is empty, and he said I can have it for a few hours to wine and dine my girl in the sunshine." I smile. I like being his girl.

"Wow... it is so beautiful..." I look around at the large oak trees that line the perimeter, the manicured boxed hedges, the roses in bloom decorating the lawn that looks and feels like carpet that travels for miles, with our little picnic oasis sitting right in the middle.

Tony drives the car down the side, parking away and giving us some privacy for a few hours as Eddie takes my hand and leads us over to our lunch.

"Eddie... this is amazing," I say, smiling, my shoulders lowering instantly as I hear nothing but the birds chirping and the light breeze flowing through the trees. It is like a garden oasis. Private, secure, large enough so I don't feel claustrophobic. I will admit, when Eddie said he was taking me for a date, I just assumed it was going to be a café or restaurant for lunch, but this... this is so much better than I was expecting.

"No. You're amazing. Come on." I giggle as we walk together, taking it all in.

"I can't believe your real estate friend sells these kinds of houses. It is a mansion." We take a seat, and Eddie opens the bottle of champagne that sits in the ice bucket.

"It's beautiful, isn't it? One of the best houses in Baltimore," he says, popping the champagne and handing me a glass.

"A toast?" I ask, looking at him.

"To beautiful things..." Eddie murmurs, his eyes on mine, and I swoon.

"To beautiful things." We clink our glasses and sip our champagne.

The fear that rattled my body earlier is now either all gone or buried deep. My thoughts are only on this man in front of me and how just his smile and his touch can settle me, alleviate my fears, and help me rise above them. But how can I tell him about the danger that follows me? How can I lead him into this life?

The answer is easy. I can't. As I sip the champagne, I swallow my heartache, knowing that this fairy tale is going to end soon. Because while Prince Charming sits in front of me, I can't take him into hell with me. That is a fight I need to continue on my own.

24

EDDIE

We finish our lunch and champagne, and I pull her close to me, wanting to touch her all the time.

"Hmmmm, you had enough to eat?" I ask, because she barely ate a thing. She usually doesn't eat a lot, but after the scare in the car, I think she lost her appetite.

Fury builds in my body, even now as I think about it. I have driven around Baltimore all my life and never once had an incident such as that. Now, the one time I take her out, a homeless man slams his face against the window and scared the living shit out of her. It was unusual and had me on high alert. Given that she just moved here, and that is the second fright she has had since she arrived, it is not doing anything to show her that Baltimore and I are safe choices for her.

"I'm completely satisfied." She sighs, leaning into me as I hold her, her back to my front.

"Completely?" I whisper, my lips running down her neck. I can't get enough of this woman.

"Eddie…" she half moans, half growls with caution.

"There is no one here, baby. Just me and you," I say, running my hands up her front and cupping her breasts.

I have had my eye on this place for months. This is what I want for my forever home. The fact that it's neighbors with my brother Ben's residence is also a bonus. This place is currently for sale, and I have expressed an interest. Although the owners are currently overseas and not looking at offers until they return in a few months' time, it is only a matter of formalities until they sell it to me. It isn't cheap, in excess of fifteen million, but it is private, secure, has all the mod cons. It's exactly what I want.

"Cameras?" she asks tentatively.

"No one is going to see you, I made sure of that," I tell her as my lips find her ear, and I kiss her jaw, getting hard in the process. This place has a state-of-the-art security system. One I turned off this morning and will reactivate when we leave, thanks to a healthy fee I paid the current owners. They know I am here. Everything is aboveboard. They are old friends with my dad, so they know all about my need for security and privacy. They are currently on their yacht in Europe, so they don't really care. This house is merely one in their portfolio of many.

"Eddie," she breathes my name again, and I notice her eyes close as I tweak her nipples in my hands, her back arching, telling me she is very much enjoying my mouth and hands on her.

With one hand, I start undoing her dress, opening the buttons to get better access to her breast. My other hand runs up her chest, and I cup her jaw, turning her face to me, wanting my lips on hers.

"Let me kiss you, baby," I say, my dick throbbing against my zipper as I pull her back to my chest, taking her weight. Her hand comes up to cup my head, keeping my lips on hers as small moans fall from her pretty mouth.

I run my hand down her throat, across her breasts, and straight down. Her sundress is floating around her thighs, and I strum my fingers up her legs, under her dress, to the tops of her thighs.

"Touch me," she begs, her voice wavering, and even though I haven't touched her, I know she is already on the edge. I will come the minute she touches my cock. I put it down to not only our insatiable appetite for one another, but also being in the outdoors where anyone could see us.

"You want me to touch you out here? What if a gardener comes, a pool boy?" I tease, knowing full well no one will turn up because I ensured our privacy. I drag my fingers across her skin, up her inner thigh, and back down again, aching to touch her, already knowing that she will be warm, wet, and ready for me. She spreads her legs then, opening for me as my lips continue to kiss hers, panting in between kisses.

"Touch me, Eddie. Please, touch me," she whimpers, and although I class myself as a gentleman, there is nothing that will stop me from finger-fucking her right here in the garden of my dreams.

"Anything for you. I will do anything for you," I murmur as I tighten my hold on her jaw and pull her head back, leaning her against my shoulder and kissing her neck. My other hand travels up her thigh again, and I can feel the desire swirling, her breasts peeking out of her dress that is now open at her chest. I drag the material of her hem up her legs as my hand finds her underwear.

My breath hitches as I skirt my fingers over her lace. She is wet and warm, just as I predicted. I rub her clit on the outside of her underwear, and she moans right in my ear.

"You're so wet for me already, baby," I moan back, biting her neck a little, the urge I have for her almost overpowering.

"Please... please..." Little moans fall from her lips as my fingers slide under her lace, and I circle her clit a few times. Her hips immediately rock against my hand.

"Is that what you want, baby?" I ask her, holding back a groan.

"More... Oh, Eddie, I need more," she pants, her breathing rapid, her back fully arched against me. She looks fucking fantastic.

I run my fingers up and down her a few more times before I push inside of her, and she moans low and deep into my ear. I keep up the pace, the heel of my palm pressing on her clit as my fingers move in and out of her center. Her body starts to quiver, and I need to grit my teeth with how much this is turning me on right now.

"Eddie... don't stop, don't stop..." she whimpers as both her hands come up and round my neck, gripping on to my shoulders. I keep my lips on her skin at that special junction, where her neck meets her shoulders.

"You want to come for me, come on my fingers. Let go,

baby. Let go just for me," I grit out, and she does. I feel her clench around my fingers as her hips jerk, and her voice cries out loudly as she comes. I hold her through it all, kissing and biting her neck, her fingers digging into my skin at my nape, the two of us no doubt leaving marks on each other. I remove my fingers from her, circling her clit a few times as I continue to kiss her neck.

"Ohhhh, Eddie..." she says, sinking into me a little, keeping her legs wide, liking me stroking her. I cup her breast with my other hand, squeezing her nipples as she starts to squirm again. My girl is strung tight, and while I just relieved a little tension, there is still more. After spending so much time together, I am starting to know what she needs, what she likes, and if there is anything that will remove her fears and tension she carries, it is an orgasm. Multiple ones.

I am painfully hard, yet I can't move my hands from her amazing body to do anything about it. She shuffles then, sitting up, but still close as she edges away from me slightly, turning around with hurried passion.

"What..." My words get stuck in my chest as she unbuckles my belt and lowers my zipper quickly.

"Baby?" I ask her.

"I want more... I *need* more..." she says, leaning in and capturing my lips, and I am not complaining. My cock springs out of my pants, rock-hard, and she wraps her hand around it, giving it a few pumps.

"Take it easy, baby. That is a bomb literally about to explode," I grit out with a smirk on my face, because if she gives it any more attention, I will come all over her.

Her eyes flick to mine, hers with deep desire swirling and a hint of cheekiness as she sits up on her knees and pulls off her underwear. I remain quiet, letting her lead, and watch with keen interest as I pump my cock, wondering what she is going to do.

She sits on me then, reverse cowgirl style, and I groan in pleasure as understanding washes over me. Up on her knees again, she grabs my dick and positions it at her entrance before she takes me in.

"Jesus..." I growl, low and deep, the pleasure almost too much, the feeling of her taking control, showing me what she wants, that she wants me, almost makes me come on the first thrust.

I lift my hands up and grab her waist, letting her jump up and down on me, her hips grinding and swirling.

"Eddieee." She says my name just how I like it, and all I can do is groan. I grab her around the neck and pull her to me, kissing her mouth as her movements stop momentarily so our tongues can tangle.

"Permission to throw you on the ground and fuck you from behind like a goddamn animal?" I growl on her lips. I am barely hanging on. This woman is merciless as she teases me a little more by moving her hips and grinding on me.

"Permission granted," she whispers against my lips, and I don't hesitate.

I hold her around the waist, flip her over on all fours, and I push her upper back, getting her chest lower to the ground.

Lifting her dress over her bare ass, I watch as it pools

around her waist, and look at where we are still connected, feeling almost feral. I squeeze her ass in my hands, massaging it hard in my fingers, and she moans and pushes back onto me.

"Fuck, what are you doing to me, woman?" I say before I thrust, pushing into her over and over, sweat beading on my forehead, small moans and pants falling from her lips, and I see her white-knuckled hands pulling at the picnic rug.

"More... more... Eddie... more." I hold her waist tight, leaving bruises with my fingers and fuck her harder. I can't get enough, can't get close enough. I want her more than I have ever wanted anything before in my entire life.

I give her my everything. All of me, I transfer to her, every feeling, every piece of my being, every inch of my soul until I feel her quiver, and then I let go too.

My orgasm rushes through my body at an unfamiliar pace, and we scream in unison as our releases overtake us. I didn't expect this to occur at a sunny afternoon picnic. But I am starting to realize that, as far as Pinkie is concerned, nothing is off-limits. I can't fucking help myself.

"Oh my God..." She sighs, now lying underneath me on the blanket. I lean over and pull her shoulder, turning her to face me. She is now sprawled out on her back, looking up at me with her pink hair sticking out everywhere, her face and body entirely relaxed. I hover over her, taking her lips again. We kiss silently for a moment, slowly, seductively, secure in each other's embrace.

I lean back a little and look at her, completely lost for

words as I feel as though the two of us have just pushed through another layer, creating a deeper connection.

"Now I am completely satisfied," she says with a grin, and I bark out a laugh before I pull her close and kiss her like my life depends on it. Because my heart sure does.

25

EDDIE

"Are you going to eat that?" Tennyson asks me from across the table. My brothers all seem ravenous as they shove their burgers into their mouths. We are at our usual haunt for lunch. We try to do this every week at the bar around the corner from our office. We all work in the same building, but none of us come up for air too often to see each other during work hours unless it is scheduled, which this regular lunch is.

I push my plate of half-eaten fries toward him and watch him hoover them up.

"Not hungry?" Ben asks, looking at me suspiciously. Probably because, like all us boys, I have a healthy appetite. It is a rare day if one of us is not eating.

"Just a lot on my mind." I sigh, feeling equal parts amazing and frustrated.

"Can we meet this Pinkie yet?" Harrison asks, looking at me intently while he bites into his burger. His team only allows him an hour, so he is on a strict schedule, and

I look over his shoulder at them all hunched over their laptops at a nearby table. He has a few security team members nearby as well, doing a terrible job of looking inconspicuous. Glancing back at Harrison, I remain silent.

"Shit. You still haven't told her?" Tennyson says, leaning back and looking at me.

"I've tried. I have tried almost every day. But it is like she knows what I am going to tell her is big and she keeps dodging the conversation. Usually, with foreplay." I murmur the last bit. Whenever I get close to telling her about my life, she amps up the sexual tension to a point that I can't ignore it. I don't want to ignore it. I know she is happy in the little bubble we have created, but I want to take her out, date her in public, and to do that, she needs to know who I am.

"It is not going to end well. The longer you take to tell her, the harder the fall. Just tell her and get it over with," Ben says, and he is right. I know that.

"Surely, she will be okay with you being a billionaire versus a maintenance man?" Tennyson adds. I have rolled that theory over and over in my mind for the past few weeks. Everything I have given her is the truth. My personality, my cooking, my intimacy. People close to me call me Eddie. I *do* run the maintenance in the building. The only things she doesn't know about me are my full name, my family history, and the number of zeros in my bank account.

"I don't know. I hope so," I say, pondering it some more. *It's just a name, right?*

"Harrison." One of his staff members comes to the

table, cell phone in hand. Us four boys sit up straight. I see another one of his team members jump off the stool and run outside, hailing a taxi while the others all grab their cells. Something is going on, and we already know by the look on her face, it isn't good.

"What is it?" he asks, his eyes thinning, and his assistant looks at him before she looks around the table at all of us.

"It's your mother."

"Jesus, what has she done now?" Tennyson asks, throwing his napkin on the table in frustration.

"She had a heart attack. The housekeeper found her in her office at home and called 9-1-1. The paramedics are taking her to the hospital now," she says, and all us boys still.

"Shit," Ben mutters, standing and grabbing his jacket.

"Get the cars," Harrison says to his team in a tone that has them all scrambling. He's already off his seat, gathering his things.

"I'll call Willow," Tennyson says as he grabs his cell and calls his girlfriend, who is an expert in reputational management and will no doubt be needed, alongside Harrison's girlfriend Beth, to manage the media.

I sit in shock. Not able to move. *Mom had a heart attack?* A memory surfaces of her rubbing her arm last time I saw her.

"Eddie," Harrison says. "*Eddie!*" he says, a bark in his tone that knocks me into action. I jump up and follow my brothers out the door to Harrison's waiting car. His staff's now scattering into different taxis to get to different places. This is going to be front-page news in a matter of minutes.

"Willow is calling the girls, and they will meet us at the hospital," Tennyson relays, pocketing his phone.

"Which hospital?" I ask, already knowing that if she has had a heart attack, there is only one place in Baltimore she will go. My three brothers look at me as the car drives quickly through the streets to get us there.

"Shit," Tennyson says. "Well, looks like we all get to meet Pinkie today."

My hands delve into my hair, digesting this situation. "Mom had a heart attack?" I ask in disbelief. "Pinkie will know?" Dread creeps up my chest.

"I didn't even know she had a heart," Tennyson says, and his joke falls flat as Harrison thumps him in the arm.

"Is it bad?" I ask, looking at Harrison like he has all the answers. None of us get along with our mother, but a heart attack isn't really wanted either.

"No idea. I sent some people over to the house to sit with the housekeeper, to make sure she is okay. I have a team member arriving at the hospital now. We will know more once we get there," Harrison says just as his cell phone pings.

"What is it?" Ben asks, his teeth grinding. It is clear that none of us know how to take this news, and it is evident we are all operating in a state of shock.

"Ambulance just got to the hospital. She has been wheeled straight into cardiac emergency," Harrison says, frowning as he looks at his phone.

Within moments, our car pulls up and us boys jump out. I am a mixture of emotions as I follow my brothers in through the double glass doors. We all come to a halt once inside, looking around. The disinfectant smell of the hospital stretches up my nose, and my eyes dart around at everyone in the immediate vicinity. The four of us stand there with no idea where to go. All dressed alike in our suits, we must look a sight because everyone stops and stares.

"I think I spot Pinkie," Tennyson murmurs, and we all look in the direction he is looking, and sure enough, I see Katie. Standing in shock at the nurses' desk, she looks beautiful in her scrubs. Her hair is on top of her head, a few stands curling down around her face. Her mouth is open, and I can see a hundred questions running through her mind. I watch her as the lady next to her says something to her, and I see it the moment that she learns who I am. Her smile at seeing me drops. Her eyes house the heart I just broke, and then all hell breaks loose.

26

KATIE

A s I stand next to Shelley at the nurses' station, I feel like I may be dreaming.

"Eddie?" I say in a whisper, my eyes crumpling, confused.

"That's Eddie?" Shelley says, her eyes wide, as the four men stand just inside the door. They are a sight to behold, all tall, extremely good-looking, wearing business suits as if they just walked off a catwalk.

"But he looks different..." I say, confused, squinting at him as I try to pinpoint what it is, knowing that the deep-seated feeling in my gut right now is trying to tell me something. My forearm itches, a telltale sign something is not right. His eyes are on me and only me, searching for my reaction.

"That's Edward Langford and his brothers. Richest family in the state. Hell, the richest family in the country, probably. His brother is the *governor*," Shelley whispers at me just before they walk toward us and approach the desk.

I feel dizzy, my heart pounding as disappointment fills my veins.

"Hey, you must be Pinkie. My brother Eddie here has a serious thing for you, but right now, we need to know where our mother is," a tall, rather good-looking guy says, and Eddie smacks him in the arm. There is a rising hum to the hospital, as nurses, cleaning staff, other patients, and visitors stop and steal glances. Then there are people buzzing about them. Staff, security people, our own hospital security all here already at the door. *What is going on?*

I remain quiet, still not sure what to say, so Shelley jumps in. "Yes, sorry," she says, fumbling over her words, completely flustered, her cheeks tinted a bright shade of red. *What the hell is going on?* "Governor... sir," Shelley says, looking at a man on the other side of Eddie. *Governor?* "I am just getting the information." She taps on her computer before looking at the four men in front of us. Meanwhile, my eyes remain locked on only one. "Your mother has just arrived. Looks like she went straight into surgery, and Dr. Wilson has been alerted." She addresses the other man. *He is our governor?*

"Thank you, Shelley. Where can we wait?" the governor asks with an air of authority, and I feel like I am going to faint.

"We have a private lounge. Katie, can you show the Langfords to the private lounge down the hall?" Shelley asks me, and if I could, I would kick her under the desk. I remain still, not sure if I can actually breathe until Shelley elbows me in the arm, and I try to pull it together.

"Sure," I say, pushing off the desk where I was holding

myself up and walking around to meet them, praying I don't faint or start yelling at him. Either option's highly likely at this point.

"Pinkie, I can explain," Eddie says, panicked as he rushes to me. His hand grabs my elbow softly, but I pull it away.

"This way." I ignore his words, because I have no idea what is happening right now. I need to get my bearings, and I don't want to be doing that with the audience that is now building.

"Pinkie, look at me. It is just me. Just Eddie." His steps match my quick pace as I stalk down the hall, the other three men following us. I remain silent, my teeth biting the inside of my mouth. *It isn't just Eddie, though, is it? It's Edward fucking Langford!*

"Just in here," I say, finding my voice suddenly as I open the door and walk in, holding it open for all four men, who take up the entire space in this small lounge. A few other people follow and sit down straightaway as they start tapping on their cells and laptops, with two security men standing by the door on the outside.

"Pinkie, can we talk? Can we just go somewhere and talk privately?" Eddie presses, his hand reaching for mine. I swallow as I let him hold my hand in his. The familiar strum of his thumb on my palm relaxes me, and I almost melt. Almost. *Who even is Edward Langford? What else has he lied about?*

"I need to go and sort out a few things. I will get an update and come back with further information. Hold tight," I say to all of them, and I see Eddie look at me, hopeful, as his brothers nod. I walk out of the lounge and shut the door, heading quickly back to Shelley before I completely lose it.

"What the hell is going on?" I hiss quietly at Shelley, who looks at me, concerned. "That is Eddie, but it isn't Eddie." I'm trying to grasp the situation. I wring my hands together to stop them from shaking, in nerves, in uncertainty, in anger.

"That, my dear, was the four Langford brothers. Their mother just had a heart attack and is currently in surgery," Shelley says, less flustered, but still on high alert.

"But Eddie is a maintenance man?" I say in disbelief.

"Well, Eddie owns the building, so I guess he can maintain it, if and when he wants to," Shelley says with a shrug. "I can't believe you are dating Edward Langford. He is one of the most sought-after men in this entire city. You are going to have so many women upset. Apparently, he hasn't been seen with a woman for months." She points at her computer screen, showing images of Eddie, all dressed up attending balls and dinners. It didn't take her long to bring up the social media, since Eddie has his own hashtag.

I lean over, looking at everything. I see Eddie, his dazzling smile, appearing every inch a billionaire and nothing at all like a maintenance man. He hasn't been seen with a woman for months because he has been with me. Do I embarrass him? Is that why he didn't tell me who he really was?

"He lied to me..." I straighten my shoulders and grind my teeth. I knew he had something to tell me, yet I didn't let him. Was this it? Was he going to tell me about his true identity? I am not sure if I should have let him or not. Truth is important, but he is a *billionaire*? I am so confused. I look at his photo on the screen again. I am such a fucking fool. I should have known it was all too good to be true. So, he is a billionaire playing house with the poor girl. It is a tale as old as time. I'm the poor girl only used for a good time. Never the girl who is taken seriously. Never the girl you introduce to your family. My mind is a mess.

"Lied, omitted the truth, but the way he was looking at you just now tells me that he certainly has feelings for you," Shelley says, and I snort.

"I doubt that. Look at him!" I wave at the screen. My feelings are all over the place. He looks good. Smart. Like he is from a fancy magazine. That alone makes me feel extremely self-conscious. What the hell is someone like him doing with someone like me? Me. He doesn't even know the real me either. This is such a mess.

"His brothers all knew who you were..."

"Maybe they are all liars too," I spit out, not making any real sense as my own stupidity swirls with anger. She is right, though. They seemed to know exactly who I was.

"Listen. Your shift is nearly over. Why don't you go? I will take care of them. You have cuddle duty today anyway, right?" I do have cuddle duty, and after what just happened here, I need it. I look up the hallway to the room where Eddie and his brothers are, and the door is still shut. The two burly security men stand tall and menacing on the outside. I need to push it all behind me. I have secrets too, but they can never come out.

So, I need to remain strong. I have to keep my head

down and work hard. I should never have gotten mixed up with him in the first place. All this talk about the new me. The new, stupid me. There is no new me. There's the same silly girl there always was. Not anymore. I feel my walls rebuilding slowly the longer I stand here. I swallow down the feelings that arose from seeing him. It is the only way I know how to deal with this. Block it out. Block it all out.

My eyes flick to the glass double doors that lead outside, and I see cameras and reporters starting to appear. I then look back at Shelley's computer screen at the dapper man in a tuxedo with a sexy smirk and glistening eyes.

Eddie. Edward. A billionaire. A Langford. A liar.

27

EDDIE

"She's cute," Tennyson quips, and Ben rolls his eyes.

"I've completely fucked it up, haven't I?" I look at them all in question, hoping one of them tells me I am wrong.

"Probably got a lot of groveling to do, that is for sure," Tennyson replies with a shrug, slapping me on the back and taking a seat.

"We will have to just leave your love life to the side for a while, Eddie. Mom is in surgery. I will have to make a media statement at some point later today. Cameras have turned up outside, and social media already has the news," Harrison says, holding up his cell, and we see an image of the front of the hospital, the door we just walked through now almost covered in news crews and cameras.

"Is there nothing she does that doesn't create attention?" Ben asks, running his hands through his hair before taking a seat next to Tennyson.

"Did any of you know she wasn't well?" Harrison asks, looking at us all.

"I remember she rubbed her arm last we met. Said she hurt it playing tennis," I mention.

"She hasn't played a game of tennis in her life!" Ben balks, shaking his head.

"I should have picked that up. I should have said something to her. Maybe if she went to see a doctor before..." I start, frustration at my lack of empathy for my mother now creeping in. She is a handful, but she is still our mother.

"Don't," Tennyson barks at me. "Don't blame yourself for any of this."

"I don't think you could have said anything anyway. It's not like she listens to anything we say," Ben offers as he loosens his tie.

"Ironic, really..." Tennyson mutters, and we all look at him and wait.

"What?" Harrison questions, as he starts to pace the small lounge.

"That it is her heart that is not working properly. Just goes to show. You've got to use the muscle; otherwise, it just wastes away."

"How long do you think we will be waiting here?" I ask them all as Tennyson and Ben sit back and go through emails on their cell phones. Harrison looks at me and sighs.

"Go find her, Eddie, but be discreet. There are people everywhere who are more than happy to make a quick buck from the media for just a photo of us," Harrison warns, looking at me with concern.

"Call me if you have any updates. I will stay in the hospital. I will try and find her," I say with conviction, stepping out the door. As I close the door behind me, I almost fall straight into the nurse who was with Katie earlier.

"Excuse me?" I say, stopping her in her tracks.

"Yes, Mr. Langford?" she asks, looking a little less flustered than before.

"I am looking for Katie?" I say tentatively, and her lips thin.

"Her shift has ended. She left for the day." My eyes flick to her name tag. Shelley. Her name sounds familiar. I am sure she is friends with Katie.

"Can you tell me where the neonatal ward is?" I ask, having my suspicions of where she might be. A small smile plays on Shelley's lips, and she looks at me knowingly.

"You will find her in room 204, down the hallway and to the left. Tell the nursing manager that Shelley sent you down to find Katie," she says in a small voice, like she is telling me a secret.

"Thank you," I offer, feeling a little more at ease.

I hear a small but distinct click over my shoulder, and I turn and see a paparazzi edging around the corner.

"Security!" Nurse Shelley says loudly, making the pap jump, and the hospital security staff follow him quickly. *There are people everywhere who are happy to make a quick buck from the media.* Harrison's statement rings in my mind so I fix my collar and nod to Shelley, walking briskly past her, following the directions she gave me.

It is quiet down at this end of the hospital, a far cry

from the bustling cardiac center. The nursing manager at the front is surprised to see me. It is probably not often that men in suits come to this part of the hospital. I swallow as I walk down the peaceful hallway. All the doors are shut except for one. My shoes clicking on the tiled floor is the only sound. My heart is racing, as nervous energy strums in my limbs. I lied. I lied to her face. I slept with her, knowing she didn't have the whole truth about the man she was sleeping with. Maybe she will like rich me just as much as she likes poor me? It is still just me. I'm still just Eddie.

I slow my walk as I come to room 204. The door is open, and I stand in the doorway and look inside. She is like an angel. The lights are low, the room quiet. She is sitting in a large armchair, holding a baby in her arms, patting its bottom in slow, soft movements that I am sure anyone would find relaxing.

"I was born to a drug-addicted mother in Boston. My mother was a sixteen-year-old girl from the wrong side of the tracks. She left me to die on a park bench. I'm told an early morning garbage collector found me just in time; otherwise, I would have died. I would like to think that back then, I had a cuddler too," she says, not looking at me, and if I thought my heart was already in pain, it has just split completely in two. This is not what I was expecting.

I pause as I take in the information. Now is the time. I need to spill it all as well.

"My name is Edward Langford. One of four boys born into the Langford family dynasty. I got top grades at school, and I went to Stanford. My brother is Harrison

Langford, governor of Maryland. I am not a building maintenance man... I actually own the building. I enjoy learning the trades on the weekend, though. It is a hobby of mine, I guess you could say. I am personally worth over ten billion dollars. I have a penthouse not far from your building. Tony is my driver; Brian is my staff member, and I have never wanted for anything in my life until now," I say as the air leaves my lungs.

Her eyes flick to me, but she remains silent.

"I want you. I lied about my job, about my position in society, but I didn't lie when cooking you dinner, helping your foot cramps, or getting you your morning coffee. It was me who held you when you were sleeping; it was me who made you lunch; it was me when we were in bed together. All of that was one hundred percent me," I say, my voice already pleading with her. Her facial expression is one of sadness, yet she is calm.

"Was it? How will I ever know? Are you ashamed to be seen with me? Are you just with the poor girl to get your kicks? Is that it?" she questions, her hands continuing to pat the baby's bottom, but I see steel in her eyes. She is mad.

"No! Fuck, I want to parade you in front of the world. I want everyone to know you are mine. I want them to see how amazing and beautiful you are. It's just, my life is complicated. I was selfish and wanted to keep you just for myself for a little while. While we got to know each other and built something solid. Women usually only like me for my money and my name. I wanted to see if you would be with me just for me. It sounds stupid, but once we come out as a couple, once the world knows, life changes dramatically. Media follows you; you start trending on social media; paps take your photos. Your whole history will be dragged through the newspaper. Everyone will know who you are," I explain, feeling a pain in my chest.

"Worried I will tarnish your reputation? I probably will, let's be honest. I grew up in a trailer park. I bounced from home to home. When I was younger, I had days when I didn't eat. I was an outcast at school, bullied. I wore the same clothes for an entire year when I was twelve. Even now, my life is less than perfect. I worked hard to get myself out of the situation I grew up in, but I still survive paycheck to paycheck. Those baskets the building..." She pauses, taking a breath. "Those baskets that *you* got me, I knew exactly how to ration so that they fed me for an entire week. The food you filled my cupboards with, it felt like I won the lottery."

"I am not ashamed or embarrassed about you at all. If I had one ounce of the grit and determination you do, I would be such a better man. All of what you saw was all me. I want the chance to make it up to you. I want us to date in the real world and not holed up in your apartment. I want to take you places, show you off to everyone," I say, my words rushing out before I really have a chance to think them through.

"I am not a handbag, Eddie. I am not someone you can splash around. The alternative girl with the pink hair and tattoos. Is that why you like me? Because I am not some rich, posh, stuck-up bimbo? Maybe you are rebelling? You did say your mother was trying to marry you off. How do I know I am not just a phase?" she asks, and I can see her breathing become more labored, the anger simmering at the surface.

"You want to know why I like you?" I ask, my eyes creasing in confusion that she doesn't already know. "I like you because you are genuine. You say what's on your mind. You are strong and independent. You are sassy, smart, and fucking sexy as hell. I like laughing with you. I like sleeping with you and watching you snore. You do this little half snore when you are really tired. That is cute as hell," I say, a small smile dancing on my lips as I remember her in bed this morning, with that very snore on repeat.

I watch her sigh as she offers me a resigned, small smile.

"I think some things are just not meant to be. I'm too broken and you're too perfect." She lowers her head, looking at the baby, putting an end to this conversation that is going nowhere fast. I watch her in silence for a minute before I step away. I need to figure out how I can keep her, because there is no doubt in my mind that Pinkie is the girl for me.

28

KATIE

I don't look at him, but I hear him step back, and I listen for his steps as they retreat down the hall. I feel stupid. He is a liar. My heart hurts. I am used to being let down. By people who I thought were friends, by people who legally had to raise me, but for some reason, I didn't think Eddie would make me feel this way. I have no idea what it is like not to live on the poverty line, and he is a man who has never had to worry about it at all. Not even once. I bet he has never eaten packet ramen in his life.

I look at the baby in my arms, who is now sleeping soundly. He fussed a bit as I spoke, so I kept my voice low and calm so as not to startle him. He has already been through so much in his few weeks on earth; he doesn't need my shitstorm of a life impacting him further.

I feel sick. The heaviness in my gut almost has me rushing to the bathroom. The anxiety swirls, familiar but not welcome. Boys have never treated me right. Ever since I started to develop, men have shown an interest. The problem with being the poor kid at school was that the popular boys always thought they could just do what they wanted because they never got in trouble. I remember being ten and Jimmy Dennison pushing me against a wall and shoving his tongue down my throat while all his friends laughed and lined up for their turn.

That was my first kiss.

Then I remember when I was sixteen, walking home late after staying in the school library until it closed. It was the warmest place I had. The cold apartment where my foster parents lived offered nothing but nightmares. Steve stopped his car when he saw me walking on the side of the road. He picked me up. I was excited because I hadn't seen him in a long time, him being a few years older. He had aged out of foster care and didn't really keep in touch. When he offered to take me to a party, I said yes because I was cold and hungry, and at a party, there is normally food. I was happy because I was with Steve, and I was about to eat.

That was the worst night of my life.

I breathe out, trying to steady my nerves. I thought Eddie was different. I thought I was really getting my chance at a normal relationship. I wonder what else he has lied about. Eddie. Edward Langford. I struggle reconciling them both. Of course, it is the same man, but *is* it the same man? Is the Eddie I get the real Eddie, or is he just some rich dude trying to get his kicks?

I wonder if the media have caught on. I don't really spend time watching the news, and I steer clear of social media. It fucks with my mind, but I have a suspicion after seeing Shelley's reaction that the fact that his mother is in hospital may already be a trending topic.

His mother.

I forgot about her in all of this. His head must be a mess of emotions. I personally have no idea what it would be like to have a loved one in the hospital, but I see it every day. My heart clenches, but I squeeze my eyes shut. He has softened me, and I need to build my walls back up. I need to keep him out. There is no future for us. While it may take me a while to erase the imprint he made on me, I am merely a blip on his radar. As Shelley says, he will have women lining up for him. That thought alone makes me vomit a little in my mouth.

As I sit in silence, the minutes pass, and looking through the window, I see it is getting dark outside. It is time for me to go. I have hidden in here long enough, and I now need to go home and not think about a certain billionaire every time I look at my kitchen sink. *Or my kitchen counter.* Or any other spot in my apartment, for that matter. I sit up from the armchair slowly, my body stiff from sitting here for so long. I am surprised that Tracey didn't come and check on me, as I must have been here for a few hours. Slowly, I place the baby in his bassinet and wheel him into the nursery room, where a team of nurses will look over him and feed him through the night. I stroke my finger against his tiny hand, feeling his soft skin underneath, and give him silent prayers for a warm, comforting night and a long happy future.

I shuffle to the door and a yawn breaks through as I grab my bag and walk out to the hallway. I look up as I shut the door and abruptly stop. Eddie is sitting on the floor at the door. His jacket is off, his tie undone, and his shirt sleeves rolled up. He's looking more like the Eddie I know in a crumpled shirt. He should be with his mother, but he is here. Along with the three other men who look exactly like him.

"Hey..." he says, scrambling up from the floor and looking a little sheepish.

I swallow down my surprise, but don't say anything. What else is there to say?

"This is my brother, Ben. He is the lawyer," Eddie says, making an introduction.

"Nice to meet you, Pinkie. We have heard lots about you," he says, extending his hand. I take it automatically, feeling skeptical, but not wanting to be a total bitch.

"This is my oldest brother, Harrison, governor of Maryland." Eddie introduces his other brother, who gives me a tired, but big grin, which is oddly charming.

"Katie, Eddie here has obviously not done the right thing, but he means well. It is a pleasure to finally meet you," Harrison says very diplomatically, and I shake his hand and nod.

"This is Tennyson..."

"I'm the good-looking one," Tennyson interrupts, stepping forward and putting out his hand. "Eddie is a dickhead for not telling you the truth straightaway. Make him work for it," he says, giving me a wink, not unlike the way his brother does, and I bite the inside of my cheek to dampen the smile that threatens to surface.

His brothers clearly have his back. Eddie rolls his eyes before stepping toward me.

"I swear, the only thing you didn't know about me was

my last name and my bank balance. Everything else you got was me. I'm just Eddie. I'm Eddie to those who love me the most. My brothers. I'm just Eddie with you," he says and each of his brothers nods in solidarity. I know he is trying, but I'm bone-tired, still confused, and I just don't see how we can even work anymore. We are too different. Polar opposites.

"I'm tired. I need to go home. You should be with your mother," I say to him quietly, almost on autopilot. The uncomfortable feeling of locking down my emotions rests heavy on my shoulders. Eddie looks heartbroken. He steps forward and wraps his familiar hands around my waist, brushing his head to my cheek before whispering, "I am still the same man, just with a few zeros at the end of my name. That's it, baby."

"That's the problem. I don't even have a number..." I whisper back, hoping he can understand. We are not on an equal playing field. We are not even in the same universe anymore. I grew up without food most days. He grew up with a silver spoon and a fucking driver. How could we ever be together? I can't keep up with his lifestyle. What could a girl like me ever offer a man like him?

Stepping back, I look at his crestfallen face and swallow. I was so close to being happy. I really thought I may have found it. But as usual, happiness isn't for a girl like me. It is just not meant to be. I walk past Eddie and his brothers as they all look at me with concern etched on their faces, and I take a different turn than usual to head out the side entrance of the hospital, away from the busy emergency and cardiac wing.

I make it only a few steps before I hear him following

me. I keep my head forward and walk steady, making my way out of the hallway and toward the exit.

"Pinkie," he says, his voice low, but sounding urgent. I keep walking. I can't falter now. I need to remain strong, be the girl I always was, no longer the new me I tried to be.

"Pinkie!" he repeats, a little louder. His determination has my steps faltering, and I stop. Swallowing, I wait for him to catch up, which he does in two strides.

"Pinkie, listen I..." is all he gets out.

"You made me believe," I say, tears stinging my eyes. My body swirls with confusion, anger, embarrassment. "You made me believe, Eddie. You made me believe that..." I stop before I say the words. *That I could be loved.* I'm still in shock at the internal revelation. The pain in my heart blooms across my chest and almost feels debilitating. I tried to be strong, but now I feel weak. Pathetic.

"Baby, I believe. I believe we have something. I believe we both feel this connection we have, and I am sorry for lying. I am sorry for not telling you sooner," he says, his tone growing more desperate, gripping my hand like he is going to lose me. And he is. I lift my watery eyes and look up at him. His breath in is sharp, sudden.

"So am I. We both lied. Who does that with someone who is special? We are just not meant to be, Eddie," I say, pulling my hand from his and turning to walk out the door.

As I step out into the cool evening air, I pull my backpack a little tighter over my shoulder and keep my head down as I protect myself from anyone approaching me.

Back into the darkness, where I belong.

29

EDDIE

I sit in the quiet of my mother's room, a break from the ICU ward where she has been. The only sound is her heart monitor beeping as she sleeps. It has been a few days since she was brought in and my life exploded. I haven't really slept, not really eating much. I've been sitting at my mother's bedside each day, whether it is from the guilt for not picking up on her symptoms or the fact that I want to try to see Pinkie, I'm not sure.

Probably both.

"How is she?" Harrison asks quietly, opening the door. He comes once a day, playing the role of diligent son. Governor carrying the weight of a family health crisis. Tennyson and Ben call but have only been in the day she was admitted.

"She's the same. Resting. Showing small signs of improvement. Dr. Wilson has indicated she isn't entirely out of the woods yet, though." Dr Wilson offered the news to Mom and me this morning. His brow furrowed, doing nothing to make either of us feel better about the situation.

"Has she said much?" Harrison asks, coming to stand next to me, the two of us looking down at her resting frame.

"Not really," I murmur.

"Stop talking about me like I am going to die. For goodness' sake, it will take more than a blocked artery to keep me down." The sound of her voice startles us both. She has been so quiet, it is like she is rising from the dead. Harrison and I look at each other, questions in our eyes. It is clear she has been awake this entire time. Probably listening in to all kinds of quiet conversations that have been happening at her bedside.

"How are you feeling?" Harrison asks her, his stance firm. It's not like we don't care, but there isn't the loving hand-holding atmosphere in here. We check on her, ensure she is comfortable, and leave the rest to the professionals. I see her eyes flick to me, and she looks at me suspiciously as I sit slumped on the chair.

I feel half the man I was a week ago. That's how long it has been since I heard *her* voice. I text her every day with no reply. I call her every day, but she doesn't answer. I get coffee delivered to her every morning, that I am pretty sure she doesn't drink. Tony is at the building every morning, and here at the hospital every night, but she never gets in the car. So instead, he follows her home slowly, like a stalker, but ensuring her safety. She is ignoring Brian, not even offering him a smile. And here at the hospital, she walks in the other direction as soon as she sees me.

"For God's sake, get that sad look off your face. I will be fine. Stop being so worried about me," my mother says groggily from where she lies in the bed. I sigh. I should be worried about her. She had a stent put in when she first arrived and seemed to be okay for a few days, but then she had to be rushed to the operating room again for another stent. Her arteries are apparently not very healthy. Probably because she gets drunk every day instead of playing tennis.

"How are you feeling?" I repeat Harrison's question to her as the door to her room opens. I look up and see Pinkie entering, and a rush of hope fills my chest. As she checks my mother's chart, her eyes flick around the room, taking in all the flowers. It looks and smells like a fucking florist. Every flat surface is covered. Every day more bouquets come, but my mother won't let anyone touch them. She doesn't want any of them moved. My brothers and I know it is because she wants to show everyone who comes to visit exactly how loved and adored she is. I watch Pinkie as she writes a few notes on the clipboard, glancing at the monitors and scribbling some more.

"Hey..." I say quietly, not bothering to listen to my mother's answer, instead fully focused on her nurse instead.

"How are you feeling, Mrs. Langford?" Katie asks my mother, completely disregarding me. My mom is on heavy medication, but I see her eyes move from Katie to me and back again, and it's more than obvious before she even opens her mouth that she now realizes something is going on.

"*Her*? This is who you chose?" Mom barks at me, and

Katie stills. Without a word, my girl stares at me, her eyes wide like a deer caught in headlights. Harrison watches on as I stand, walking toward Katie, the two of us wanting to take control of the situation.

"Yes, Mom, this is Katie," I say, pushing my shoulders back. "My girlfriend," I add with full confidence. I need to show Katie the real me, and she is about to get it. My mother and all.

"Do you want me to die, Edward? Because I will have another heart attack if you are serious!" Her voice rises, and I cringe. Not words I really wanted my mother to say to my girlfriend, but this is my life. This is the real deal.

"Mrs. Langford, I need you to stay calm," Katie says, remaining professional as she stalks to Mom's heart monitor and looks at her spiking heart rate.

"A nurse? Someone who gives sponge baths and empties bedpans! Edward Langford, you will not do this to me!"

"Mother, calm down." Harrison's voice filters into the conversation as he steps forward, eyeing our mother suspiciously.

"Mrs. Langford, I really need you to calm down for me and take some deep breaths," Katie says. The way she's acting, you'd never know she was being insulted.

"Calm down? *Calm down*? Seriously, how much money do you want? You have my son wrapped around your little finger. Every time he is here, he looks at you. Every time he is here, I see him waiting for you, yearning for you. He is like a lost puppy waiting for his owner to return. I don't know what kind of magical vagina you have, but you will not get a cent. Do you hear me?!" My mother is yelling at his point, so much so, Shelley rushes into the room, and I run my hands through my hair, pulling it at the ends as Harrison walks over to me, giving my shoulder a squeeze in support.

Now Katie sees all of me.

"Nurse Katie, you are needed in room 423. I will take over here," Shelley says, and Katie steps back. I see her hands shaking, and she doesn't look at me as she stalks out the door. Harrison looks concerned, and I don't hesitate to follow her, my steps quick, the energy in my body electric.

"Edward! Edward!" I hear my mother shriek before Shelley tells her to calm down again, their voices becoming mere murmurs once the door closes behind me. I see Katie up ahead, stalking down the hallway, so I stride to catch her. When she ducks into a room, I follow right behind her.

"Katie!" I reach out to grab her shoulder to turn her to me, but that is all I get out before she turns sharply without my help and her hand slaps my face.

"How dare you!" she seethes, her hands now fisted by her sides. While my cheek stings, I leave my hands down, hurt, but happy that at least she is talking to me. "You lied to me. But if that is not bad enough, you bring our private situation and make it a public scene at my place of employment. Now your mother will have a major setback in her recovery because of me." Her breathing labors as I watch her chest rise and fall. I run my hand through my hair again, taking a breath, feeling shittier than I already did. I didn't think before I acted. I just wanted to tell my mom who I was with, not taking into consideration that

Pinkie was not ready and her workplace is not the right setting.

"My mother won't die. She has too much misery to instill upon everyone for that," I grit out as I rub my stinging cheek.

"You need to leave me alone," she says, her voice now calm but filled with sadness as her shoulders slump a little.

"Not going to happen." I'm just going to go for it. I have nothing to lose at this point.

"We are over. Whatever we had can't continue." Her eyes plead with me, anger leaving her body, and I feel her presence softening. Her words are lackluster at best. She doesn't mean them, not one bit.

"No, we are not. I want you. I want you in my life. My crazy fucking life, with my crazy-ass mother, but my life just the same." I need her to understand. I'm desperate for her to.

"We are too different," she says with a small shrug, like it is gospel.

"I don't care. Different is good," I banter back just as quickly.

"It is never going to work." Swallowing roughly, she looks unsure.

"It will work if we both want it to."

"Eddie..." she breathes out, shaking her head, and I *feel* it. She is almost back to me. I reach out and take her hand, and she lets me. I squeeze it in mine, wanting to feel her a little more as I step closer to her. She looks up at me, her blue eyes glistening under the overhead lights.

"I want to be with you. I want to make you bad pasta

carbonara; I want to fix your sink; I want you to bandage me up when I hurt myself. I also want to take you to nice restaurants, hang out with my brothers and my niece, maybe take trips to faraway places and eat goat balls..." I say, my heart in my mouth. I watch her suppress a laugh, smiling ever so slightly up at me.

"We... We are not doing this here, okay? You should go back to your mother." My first instinct is to shake my head and disagree, but I understand. She deserves all my respect, and I need to save this conversation for when she's not at work. I want to circle her waist with my hands, pull her close, keep her with me, but that will have to wait until we're truly alone.

"Promise me we can talk later. Promise me you won't shut the door on us entirely," I basically plead with her, my eyes searching hers.

"Yes. I promise," she says softly, and it is the sweetest surrender I have ever heard. She doesn't let me get another word in before she walks around me and back out the door. I take a moment and pull in a deep breath before I follow her out and walk back to my mother's room. It's progress, and I will take anything she gives me.

Harrison is standing outside Mom's room and looks up as I approach.

"She is being assessed by the doctor," he says, concern lining his expression. He's trying to gauge how things went with Pinkie.

"It's fine. I think it's going to be, anyway," I say, answering his unasked question. She may not have budged much, but she smiled a little, and I am taking that as a win. The noise of the busy hospital hits my ears, the hum of chatter, machines, a phone ringing, all bringing me back to reality. My eyes immediately seek out the nurses' station, where they rest on pink hair and the sparkling blues I miss more than anything.

"Eddie," a soft feminine voice says from the side, and Harrison and I both look up.

"Governor," she says a little more formally as Valerie Van Cleef walks down the hallway toward us, carrying a large vase of white flowers, almost bigger than her head.

"Valerie," I say as Harrison offers to take the flowers, putting them on a nearby chair as we wait outside Mom's room.

"I was so upset to hear of your mother's health worries," she says in a soft, sincere tone. *Out of all the women that my mother could set me up with, Valerie is the nicest.* She is young and beautiful and is currently dressed and acting like a woman of high society. High heels, perfect curled hair, full face of makeup, and a dress that does everything it should. She is just not the woman I want.

"Thanks for coming. Beautiful flowers," Harrison says, giving her a small smile, always trying to win the votes.

"Of course. How are you doing, Eddie?" she asks, her hand coming to rest on my shoulder. To anyone on the outside, it would appear we know each other well. She is a friend, here to lend her shoulder for me to cry on. But I hardly know her.

How am I? That's the million-dollar question. Mom's health is one thing. Obviously, we are worried, but from what I saw of her earlier, she is going to be totally fine.

But my eyes flick over Valerie's shoulder to the nurses' station, and if looks could kill, Valerie would already be in the morgue. Pinkie's eyes are glued to where Valerie's hand rests on my shoulder.

"Fine, under the circumstances. Nice of you to drop by." I offer her a small smile, keeping my hands firmly in my trouser pockets. In the moment of silence that follows, I hear the familiar click of a camera. Harrison hears it too, because both our heads whip around, and we see a familiar paparazzo leaning around a corner.

"Security," Harrison grits out to his nearby team, and they spring into action. My shoulders stiffen even more as I look to the ceiling. Exhaustion and frustration seep into my bones. This was a setup. A total setup. Even from her hospital bed, my mother has concocted a scene in order to get society talking. I can see the headline now.

Edward Langford is comforted by Valerie Van Cleef at his mother's bedside.

"Oh, Eddie," Valerie says, obviously coming to the same conclusion and dropping her hand immediately. I step away just as quickly. The two of us completely set up.

"Go for a walk, Eddie. I will deal with it," Harrison says, grabbing my other shoulder and pushing me along, separating her from me. He knows. He knows as well as I do that this is a setup, and I give him a forced smile and walk down the hall. I have no idea where I am going, but I let my legs carry me away, wishing I could just walk straight to Pinkie, yet knowing she doesn't want me. Not anymore.

30

KATIE

I watch him walk away, defeated.

"Who is that?" I ask Shelley, the two of us are trying to look busy at the nurses' station, but looking over the computer screen at one situation only.

"Valerie Van Cleef. A society princess. Her family owns the other half of Baltimore," she whispers as we watch the governor now talking to the beautiful woman. She is everything I am not. Shiny chestnut hair, untarnished skin, glossy lips, big brown eyes. Her outfit immaculate, her nails long and polished. I am pretty sure the bag she is carrying is designer and probably worth what I get paid a year.

"Are she and Eddie...?" I let the question linger, not sure exactly what I am asking.

"Apparently, Eddie hasn't been seen with a woman for months. Obviously, we both know why, because he has been with you," Shelley says, clearly on team Eddie, although I know she isn't happy he lied to me.

"She looked a little *familiar* with him," I say, jealousy

coiling in my body. When I saw her touch his shoulder, I wanted to walk over there and scratch out her perfect eyes. I wanted to rip her hands from his body and jump into his arms instead.

"Of course, she did. That's what women do with the Langford boys. They throw themselves at them. I kinda feel sorry for them," Shelley says, and I squint at her.

"What do you mean?"

"Well, it is easy to look at them and think they are good-looking and wealthy and own half the state, but what do you think it would be like for them to meet someone, only to understand that ninety-nine percent of the people they meet only like them because of their name or their money?" It sounds similar to something Eddie mentioned to me, but now that the stubborn fire in me has had a chance to calm down, and the shock of it all has worn off a little, the words penetrate more than they did before.

"I think it would be much easier to fend off the advances of beautiful women than it would be to wonder where your next meal is coming from," I huff out.

"Now don't go putting your own trauma onto others who had nothing to do with putting it there. Seems to me that you and Eddie both have feelings for each other, and while I don't condone lying, I think he needs you now more than ever if Valerie Van Cleef is on the scene. Just wait. I will put money on the fact that at least three other society women rock up today with flowers, all trying to outdo the others." I don't reply as I think about what she has said.

As I gather up the paperwork for my rounds and dig

around trying to find a new pen, I think about the lunch in my bag today. My favorite sandwich that Eddie makes. It was left at my door this morning, along with the hot morning coffee. Today was the first day I drank it. My stomach already grumbles for his lunch offering.

"And what do you know... I was right," Shelley says, and I look up, just in time to see a stunning blonde walking through the door in a sleek white suit, high heels clicking on the tiles, and a large bouquet of flowers in her hand. My fingers grip around the pen so tight, I am surprised it doesn't break. I watch for a brief moment as Harrison greets her, and I hear her ask about Eddie before I huff and turn, not wanting to see any more and needing to get to my rounds before I finish for the day.

TRACEY LOOKS at me funny as I walk into the neonatal ward this afternoon.

"Hi. Which room am I in today?" I ask with a smile, although I feel it falls flat. I'm just relieved that my shift is over, and I can sit in the peaceful nursery and cuddle a baby to sleep.

"Room 206. You can take over from the new volunteer who is in there," she says, giving me a soft smile.

"No problem." Smiling, I push off her desk and start walking down the hall. Sometimes, I hold the same baby, and other times I can come in and have a different one each week. I look forward to meeting who I have today and hope that if it is one I have cuddled before that I can see progress. Those are the best days; when you come in after a few days away and see the baby calm, feeding well, sleeping well. Doing all the things little babies are supposed to do.

As I find the room, I walk into the door and stop.

"Eddie?" I suck in a breath, shocked, as I look at the man sitting in the armchair, cuddling the same little boy I had when we spoke a few days ago. The baby is sleeping, peaceful in his arms, Eddie looking tired as well.

"Hey, Pinkie," he says quietly, looking up at me, and I watch as this large man, jacket off, shirt sleeves rolled up, holds a baby and ever so gently pats his bottom as he sleeps. He is doing everything right.

"How many babies have you held before?" I'm intrigued as I lean against the door, unable to tear my eyes away from him.

"This is the first," he says, appearing to be a natural. "Tracey sat with me for a bit to make sure I held him just right. She told me a bit of his history." He looks from me down to the baby and back again. "Apparently, they are looking for a foster family for him now." I knew they would be, and immediately my skin crawls. Not all foster families are bad. Some are the most beautiful, caring people in the world. But that just wasn't my experience.

"I miss you," he says, and the air lodges in my throat.

"I miss you," I admit. Honestly, because I do. I am just not sure how we can move past this. How can I let my walls down? How can I let him in? He has now revealed everything about himself, but I am too scared to do the same. The guilt of my situation weighs heavily. The horrible tentacles of my past continue to wrap around me and drag me back under. That is not something that Eddie can be a part of.

"Can we start over? Maybe we can just start spending some time together?" he asks, and I want to. I do. Everything in my body is pulling me toward him. But he lied. He lied so easily to my face.

"I don't think..." I start, trying to find the words, because all I want to say is yes. But it is safer if my answer is no. I swallow the bile rising in my throat. I shouldn't have gotten this close to him. I should have just kept my head down and laid low.

"I understand. I do. You see me as a liar. How can you trust anything I say now, right?" The baby stirs in his arms as he speaks. On instinct, his pats on the baby continue, tapping a little firmer, ensuring the baby knows that he is still there.

"Eddie..." My heart races, knowing everything he's about to say will only make me want him more.

"It's just, I know I hid things from you. I shouldn't have, and I am sorry. I really wanted to know if you liked me for me. I don't often meet people who don't know who I am or what I bring to the relationship. But you were a breath of fresh air. You were a total surprise. Then the fact that you actually wanted to spend time with me. Not because you knew my name, not because you wanted my money, but because you enjoyed just being with me. That is something I haven't ever experienced before. I am sorry I wasn't honest. I should have been. I know that. But you also weren't open about your family history either. We were just happy with each other. Taking it day by day, not wanting our history or our families to play a part in us just yet." He is right. I wasn't entirely honest with him about my family. Shit, he still doesn't know about Steve.

"Your volunteer shift is over. You are free to go now," I say, keeping things as they are. I walk inside and place my bag against the wall, standing in front of him.

"Pinkie. Please." I can't look at him. I hear his voice breaking a little, and I don't want to see the pain in his eyes.

"Just hold him out, and I can scoop him up from you." I say what I would say to any volunteer I take over from. He stands and lifts his hands out a little, passing the baby over. I scoop my arms under, our skin touching and sparks flying, but I ignore it. I grab the baby, pulling him tight to my chest as Eddie shuffles around, vacating the armchair completely. I take his spot and sit, looking down at the baby and making sure he is alright and tightly wrapped in his blanket. Eddie walks to the door and stops to look back at me.

"Bye, Pinkie. Take care of yourself." At the sound of his voice, I know this is goodbye.

My eyes remain glued to the baby, and I remain quiet. I feel the pain in my heart as it breaks, the water in my eyes as it gathers. I hold my breath and feel like I am drowning as he turns away from me and walks out the door. When I look up and see the empty doorway, panic rises in my throat. I want to scream his name. Yell for him to come back. I want to jump up and run down the hall. But my body won't move. My heart feels like it is pushing out of my chest, trying to get to him, yet my body is frozen. Instead, I put my head back and take a deep breath, smelling him all around me as I sink into the soft armchair. I close my eyes, imagining him holding me, and as I sit there with the little boy in my arms, for the first time since I met Edward Langford, I cry, without him there to catch my tears.

31

EDDIE

"Coffee?" Tennyson asks, stepping to my side and thrusting a cup toward me. I take it, grateful. The hot black liquid makes me feel right at home. Dark, desolate, depressing. Dr. Wilson called all us boys into the hospital today. Apparently, Mom had to go back to surgery, and he wanted us all to be here when she was wheeled back around.

"Thanks," I say, not looking at him. My chest hurts. My body feels heavy. It has only been a few days since I last saw and spoke to Katie. I have apologized. I have laid out all my cards. I have ensured she has coffee and lunch every day. Tony still follows her home every night and to the hospital every morning. I have sent flowers. I have tried to make her see how much she means to me. But she isn't budging. She trusted me, and I broke that trust, and I have no idea how to get it back.

"Still no Pinkie?" Ben asks, coming up to stand next to Tennyson, the two of them looking down at me where I sit. I see the concern etched into their brows. The room is hot with so many of us in it, but we prefer to be in the private waiting area. None of us wanted to wait in Mom's room. The place looks like a florist. The number of young women who have paraded through this ward in the last week has been overwhelming. They are beautiful women. They mean well. But I am immune to them. I only want one, and she won't even look at me.

"Nope," I say, sipping the awful coffee, telling myself I deserve the bitter taste. After what I did, this hospital coffee is the least of my problems.

"You look like shit," Tennyson says, looking me over. He is right. I have barely slept. I am not really eating. I am not sure what is wrong with me, but there is just too much on my mind for it to rest. My bed is empty, and I don't like it.

"She'll come around. Have you groveled?" Harrison asks from where he sits opposite me, going through his schedule for the rest of the week.

"That's what I'm trying to do every day," I say to him.

"Have you begged?" Tennyson asks, and I look up at him. "Like actually told her what a fucking idiot you are."

"I am a fucking idiot," I say on a sigh, running my hands through my hair. The Langford name opens doors, never hearts. Maybe Mom is right. Maybe I do need to marry for convenience, not for love. Maybe love is all just a hoax.

"I think you need to do something that means something to her," Emily says, looking at me from where she sits, Beth on one side and Willow on the other. I look at the three of them, and I know love will always find a way.

Because my brothers are in love, and it all worked out for them.

"I agree. You need to think about the things that matter to her. And even though I don't know her, from what you have said about her, materialistic things are not it. As thoughtful as they might be, I think you need to try another way," Willow says, looking up at me from her cell, her workload now increased as she manages our family reputation, trying to stave off the intense media interest.

"I just have no idea what that is," I mumble as the three women all stare at me, mouths agape.

"What the hell have you been doing with her for all this time?" Beth asks, her eyes narrowing. "Actually, don't answer that. I don't need to know," she says quickly, lowering her head back to her cell.

"And here I was, thinking I was the only brother who thought with his dick," Tennyson quips from beside me and ducks just in time as Willow throws a pen at his face.

"Media are having a fucking field day," Harrison grumbles, scrolling through his phone.

"They have developed a fashion column each morning in the Society News," Willows says as she taps on her laptop.

"A what?" I glance up at her, my brow crumpled.

"The who's who of Baltimore and surrounds have been showing up here. Obviously keen to capture which woman Edward Langford leans on during this *time of crisis*. There is actually a trending hashtag featuring all the women and what they are wearing each day as they come to visit," she says, looking just as tired of it all as the rest of us.

"Shit," Ben murmurs, rubbing his chin.

"They have a leaderboard and everything," Willow adds.

"A leaderboard?" Em snorts, shaking her head. I think she would get along well with Pinkie.

"Yes, and Valerie Van Cleef is in the lead, her class and sense of style putting her front and center. She is a walking billboard for the high-fashion brands. They are probably all scrambling to dress her at this point. Not to mention, the photo making the rounds of her touching your shoulder, it almost makes me blush," Willow says sarcastically, her eyes flicking to mine, waving her hand to her face, pretending to be flustered. I roll my eyes at her.

"Jesus. Even from her hospital bed, Mom is orchestrating your love life," Tennyson says, rubbing his eyes. It has been bedlam here, the constant women coming through more of a hindrance than a help. There is a knock at the door that interrupts our conversation as we all look at it as it opens. *Pinkie.*

"Sorry to disturb you, but Dr. Wilson wanted me to let you all know that Mrs. Langford is out of surgery. Everything with the additional stent went well, and she is currently in recovery and will be back in her room within the next hour or so. He will come around to see you all shortly," she says, looking at everyone but me. My hand wraps around the cup. She looks beautiful today. Like every day.

"Thank you, Pinkie," Harrison says before he gets an

elbow to the side. "Ow, what was that for?" His head whips to Beth, who is glaring at him.

"Her name is Katie. Not Pinkie," Beth corrects him with a quirk of her brow.

"He just told me her name was Pinkie." Harrison points to me.

"She's Pinkie to me," I say with a shrug. Katie looks at me then, and the spark between us is still there. I feel it as bright as day.

"Hi, Pinkie, I'm Emily, so nice to meet you." Em stands and walks over to where Katie is standing just inside the door.

"Oh, ahh. Hi," she says, shaking Em's hand, a light-pink tint coming to her face. My girl is cute when she blushes.

"Hi, I'm Willow. Glad to finally meet you. This one has talked about you nonstop all week," Willow says, waving her hand at me.

"Nice to meet you too," Katie says, and I think I see a hint of a smile as she looks back at me. I can't stop the goofy smile from spreading on my face at seeing them all getting along.

"Please excuse the governor. He and his brothers have a lot on their plate at the moment. I'm Beth," Beth says diplomatically, stepping forward, giving me a sly look, and I wonder what she is up to.

"Oh, nice to meet you." Katie now appears to be overwhelmed by the women in my family who are all circling her like sharks.

"Anyway, make sure he grovels," Beth says in a faux whisper, and my eyebrows shoot to my hairline.

"Yes, make him really pay for that stunt he pulled," Willow says, and I sit up. *Are they ganging up on me?*

"I would go so far as to say I would make him massage your feet for a week," Em says, nodding dramatically.

"Pfft, an entire month!" Willow agrees with way too much excitement.

"Maybe he should cook you dinner every night?" Beth suggests, comically tapping her finger to her chin like she is thinking.

"Alright, enough. I don't think she needs all the Langford women wisdom you want to share," I say, standing up, trying to give Katie a break from them. Although, the way she is smiling now, I have a feeling she is enjoying the girl time. I know she said she didn't have any siblings. Blood-related ones, anyway, which is still something I need to uncover, so maybe she is missing this type of interaction.

"Us girls have to stick together," Beth says, curving her arm into Pinkie.

"Yeah, girl power and all that," Willow says, taking Pinkie's other arm.

"Someone has to keep all you boys in line," Em adds as she crosses her arms over her chest. And all four women look at us boys.

"What did we do?" Ben asks, all my brothers now standing.

I look at Pinkie, and her eyes are alight with humor. I think I hear her laugh a little.

"It was nice to meet you all, but I really need to go. I need to sign off on my patients before the next shift starts," Pinkie says, smiling at the girls. She looks good in my inner circle. Too damn good.

"Well, don't be a stranger. We will have dinner sometime," Beth says, smiling warmly.

"Oh yes, a girls' night!" Willow says, her smile wide.

"Oh, that would be so much fun," Em joins in as they all step back and give Katie room.

"I'll see you around?" Katie says, looking at me, and I can't stop the grin from spreading wider across my face.

"You will," I say, and I feel instant relief when I see her smile at me before she walks out the door.

After a week of feeling like shit, I finally feel that I may have a breakthrough.

"You're welcome," Beth says as the door closes and she takes her seat.

"You owe us," Willow says, looking at me pointedly.

"Big-time," Em adds.

"What are you talking about?" I ask, still not able to erase the smile on my lips. Because things between Katie and I just shifted. I know it.

"She needs to know there are people in her corner. From what you have told us, she has grown up in hard circumstances, with not many people to rely on, and the one person she started to rely on lied to her," Beth says, and I can tell the way she is saying this to me that she knows from experience.

"She needs you to not give up on her, Eddie. The way to prove your love for her is to be there, even when she pushes you away," Em reiterates, and it all makes sense.

"Now thank us for the girl power and go and get your

girl already," Willow says as they all look at me
expectantly.

"Thank you. I owe you," I say quickly before I dump
my disgusting coffee in the trash and rush out the door in
search of Katie.

32

KATIE

As I walk out of the hospital, the cool air hits me, and I feel a little lighter than I have in days. I have seen the women in the Langfords' private waiting room before. Shelley has given me a thorough debriefing on who they all are. From a distance, they look as untouchable as all the other women who have paraded around the hospital this week. It is not that they are fancy or wearing head-to-toe designer clothes, but they are polished. Well put together. Almost graceful and oozing confidence. But in the five minutes I spent with them, I can tell that they are friendly and genuine. The way they gathered around me, making me feel like I was part of something. Like they were welcoming me in their friendship circle. The way they joked with the brothers, and everyone had a laugh at themselves. It made me feel good. Connected. Like I had people who supported me. Who would have thought that the richest men in the state live life like that?

I can't believe they actually invited me out for a girls'

night. I haven't really had that before. I never had a lot of friends growing up and have been too busy trying to keep my head down, avoiding my history as an adult, to contemplate making friends. It makes me think. Maybe people can look a certain way but be the complete opposite. Stunning, beautiful, wealthy women to the outside, but get to know them and they are just like me. Normal. I think of Eddie, seeing him all week in his suit, his hair slicked to perfection. Yet in the private moments I have seen him, he is without his jacket, sleeves pushed up, hair crumpled. He is just Eddie.

"I need money." My body jolts, and I come to a stop. I was daydreaming, but now I am wide awake. Looking around, I see a few people walking away, and although I am not far from the main hospital entrance, this side entrance I have used tonight is quieter and out of the way, so no one else is here. Even though I have been ignoring him, my eyes now dart around for Tony and the car before I internally curse. He usually meets me at the other main entrance.

"I don't have any," I say, waiting for Steve to appear. My eyes widen as I see him emerge from the bushes at the side. The familiar silhouette of the woman who was with him last time lingers farther away. She looks at me with what seems to be blame, and certainly her face portrays more venom toward me than last I saw her. Her eyes thin, yet she doesn't come closer, preferring to let Steve handle me, her merely observing in the distance.

Steve looks even worse. Our eyes lock as he slowly stalks toward me wearing dirty black jeans, a ripped black t-shirt, and his hair messy like it hasn't been brushed in weeks. He is in complete contrast to Eddie, who is inside in his polished business suit attire that I have grown accustomed to over this past week or so. I look back over my shoulder, through the glass doors and inside, but see no one, just the vacant hallway. The polished floor tiles reflect the bright fluorescent lights, the few chairs that are scattered along the hallway sitting empty. I swallow as I look back around.

It's just me. It is always just me.

"You have been hard to get to, with that bodyguard of yours following you every night," he growls as he positions himself right in front of me. I take a deep breath to settle myself and get ready for his onslaught. As I do, I breathe him in, smelling stale alcohol and cigarettes. Up close, I can see his face is filthy, and his inner elbows are bruised. The smell makes my mind whirl back to when I was a kid. It's something that is hard to forget.

"I did some digging. Apparently, that bodyguard is from Edward Langford's private team. Seems like that pussy of yours is made with gold," he says, a sly smirk on his face. The woman behind him huffs a laugh. She is a few feet away, but already on my nerves. *Can't she see that he is trouble? Doesn't she want to get away?*

"I think you need to leave," I state, trying to be firm, not wanting him to see how rattled he makes me. But he knows. He always knows.

"Fuck, you aim high and always get there, don't you? Got out of foster care by getting a college housing scholarship, got your nursing degree at community college, thanks to that special foster kid funding you applied for, and now you're a fancy nurse at a top-notch hospital, living in a high-rise and fucking billion-dollar dick." He spits out the last word, his saliva hitting my cheek. He is mad. I have seen him mad before, but not like this.

"Does he know who you are, Kitty Cat? Does he know that he is fucking filth? A dirty whore? Does he know that you should be on your knees, cleaning his house, not sucking his dick?"

"It is none of your business." My voice hitches as he grabs my upper arm.

"You are my fucking business," he seethes.

"I am nobody's fucking business," I bite out at him. If he is taking me down, then I am not going without a fight. I feel the familiar survivor mode of my past creeping into me. My body stiffens, my muscles tight. My nails dig into my palms, yet I don't feel the pain. The fear he brings is constant. Everlasting. Like a dark cloud that always shrouds me, it never disappears.

"Maybe your new boyfriend would like to see the video I have of you, huh? I actually think he would pay me a lot of money for that video." Stepping forward slightly, he gets right into my face, smiling like he has won the lottery. Meanwhile, I feel like I will vomit. It is the only thing he has on me. That vile video.

"He isn't my boyfriend. We are not even friends. He won't care. Why don't you and your girlfriend just move on. Find a new beginning," I offer, lying through my teeth, trying to get Eddie off his radar. I'm not sure what I have of value to trade, but Eddie cannot see that video.

"Hmm, then maybe the hospital board will be interested? Maybe your new boss would like to see it," he threatens, ignoring my earlier plea, a new plan coming to his mind. I see paparazzi stationed a few yards away, waiting for Eddie and his family to leave the main entrance of the hospital. My lips are dry, and I try to swallow. I don't like either option.

"What would the hospital like?" I hear Eddie's voice from behind me and feel instant relief before complete mortification.

"Ahh, well, if it isn't the billionaire of the hour," Steve says, looking up at Eddie, who is slowly walking out of the hospital toward us. Eddie seems confused, probably wondering who Steve is and why I am talking with him.

"Steve, we are not together. Mr. Langford is just here for his mother," I hiss, my teeth grinding as my worst nightmare is starting to eventuate. I see the moment what's happening clicks in Eddie's brain. That he knows something is very wrong. His eyes home in on where Steve has a tight grip on my upper arm, and his posture changes.

"You need to remove your hand from her before I break your fucking arm," Eddie seethes, walking toward us quicker, and my eyes almost bug out of my head. *Angry Eddie is hot*.

My natural instincts kick in immediately, and my other hand flies out and connects with Eddie's chest, halting him. I start pushing him back into the hospital. This is bad. This is really, really bad. I want him to hold me. I want to fall into his arms, be protected, loved, and secure. It is in this moment I realize I trust him. I wholeheartedly trust everything about Eddie, regardless of his identity. It was always him. His name and status are irrelevant.

"Eddie, it's fine. You need to go," I say to him, pleading with my eyes. He grabs my hand then, pulling it from his chest and enveloping it in his by his side. The familiar strum of his thumb on my hand provides almost instant relief. But I can't lean on him. I have to handle my own shit and not get him involved.

"Not without you," Eddie says, looking at me intensely. Steve's grip on my arm tightens, and I wince.

"I said, get your fucking hands off her," Eddie says again, his tone lethal, moving forward faster than I can blink and grabbing Steve's arm, shoving him away from me. Pulling me against him, I feel his body heat as he steps in front of me slightly, his chest full and high. I nearly lose my breath when I realize he is putting his body in front of mine for protection. His body is tight, his already tall posture now looking even taller. I grit my teeth harder, surprised they don't crack under the pressure. I can't get him involved, but my body won't move as Eddie still holds my hand. I lean into him a little. I need him. I need Eddie to be safe and to be with me. Steve takes a few steps back and starts to laugh.

"I have a tape," Steve taunts with a grin on his face like this is the best day ever, and my body shivers.

"What tape?" Eddie asks, moving forward again, not at all intimidated by Steve. The first person in my entire life not to be. My breath stops in preparation for Steve's words. I can't move. My body is in complete shock and my muscles are locked in place. Eddie is going to find out exactly who I am, and he will drop my hand quicker than touching a hot poker. As if a billionaire wants to be involved with a girl like me.

"It's Katie here, flat on her back. Enjoying my dick," Steve spits out, and I feel like I'm going to be sick, my eyes stinging with renewed tears. I hate him. I always hated him, but at this moment, I absolutely despise him. My heart hurts. I didn't think it was possible for it to hurt any more, but it does. The sting of shame coats my skin as bile rises in my throat.

"Stop, Steve. I will get you the money. Eddie, just go inside," I say, not sure how I am even standing upright. I feel dizzy. Eddie's body is still stiff beside me, and I feel his hand begin to move. I start to let go of him, and my heart shatters all over again. He isn't here for me. He would never have loved me, anyway. But I really, really want him to.

But he doesn't let go. He regrips my hand and holds me tighter.

"Go inside? This fucker is blackmailing you?" Eddie says, looking at me, his eyes molten fire. I see him clenching his jaw. His body is wired. He is not happy. Not at all.

"No. I'm blackmailing you," Steve says, walking toward Eddie slowly, cocky, with a bit of swagger like he holds all the cards in this situation. Because he does. "You're a Langford, aren't you? Worth billions, and you probably fund this entire hospital. Kitty Cat, is this who you fucked to get this job?" Steve is toying with us and enjoying it.

"Fuck you," I spit out.

"You got trouble out here, brother?" I hear a man's voice from behind me, and I turn quickly, looking over my shoulder to see Tennyson standing there, just behind us, arms crossed over his chest like a security guard. Harrison and Ben are just behind him. But Eddie still doesn't move. His eyes are firmly on Steve. It is all my fault. I am going to take down all these men. My eyes flick across to the media, and I see the three Langford women over there, grabbing the journalists' attention and moving the cameras farther away from us and around the corner. *What is happening?*

"Well, now we have a billionaire-dollar audience. Let me cut to the chase. I want a million dollars, in cash, or else I will put your girlfriend all over the internet for the world to see just how perfect her little pussy is," Steve says, and in that moment, I realize that my life is never going to be the same again.

33

EDDIE

The guy harassing Katie barely finishes his sentence before my fist flies out and connects with his face. I hear the crunch of his cheekbone before he falls over, lying flat on his back on the sidewalk like the piece of shit that he is. If he has a video, no one will be seeing it.

"Shit!" I hear Harrison curse from behind us.

"Go, baby bro," Tennyson says, stepping up to us, grabbing my shoulders just as I lunge forward to punch this fucker again. Not even a second later, I hear yelling as security comes running. They hold him on the pavement, but he is barely lucid.

"Get up, you fucking piece of shit," I seethe. I have never been this furious. My body hums with adrenaline as I try to get out of Tennyson's grasp just so I can punch this fucker again. How dare he touch her. How dare he threaten her. How dare he blackmail any of us. I look down at Katie, who I can feel is shaking by my side, and I try to rein in my anger. Her eyes water as she looks up at me.

"I'm sorry. I'm so sorry," she says over and over, like this is her fault, and she starts to step away from me. Pulling her back to me, my hand still holds hers tightly. I reach out for her with my other hand, cupping it around her middle and tugging her close. She isn't going anywhere.

"It's okay. I've got you." I hug her tight, wrapping one arm completely around her, the other cupping her head, keeping her with me. I breathe the words into her hair as I tuck her into me. She takes a deep breath, and then I feel her let go, her body relaxing into mine as she lets me hold her. She gives herself to me, and I am never fucking letting her go. Her arms circle around my torso, and she buries her head in my chest. I don't need to look at her to know that she is crying. Her body is shaking almost uncontrollably, my shirt already wet.

My knuckles hurt, but my heart hurts more. I have a million fucking questions running through my brain, including who is he, and why is he calling her fucking Kitty Cat? It took me a while to find her tonight. After searching half the hospital, Shelley pointed in this direction while she was on the phone, clearly knowing who I was searching for. When I looked through the doors and saw her speaking to this guy outside the hospital, my stomach churned, and I almost walked away. But there was something about the way she was standing, and one look at him and I knew he was trouble, whoever he is.

"You guys should go," Harrison murmurs, coming up to my side, looking down at the piece of shit before us.

My eyes are glued to him as he rolls around and moans on the pavement, his hand grabbing his cheek. The more I look at him, the more I realize he is obviously drug addicted. His eyes are black, his appearance disheveled, and he stinks. I glance at his hand, his skin scattered with random tattoos, reminding me of the way he had a hold on her arm just moments ago. I want him in pain. I want him hurt and on the pavement, but my immediate concern is her.

"Sir," Tony says, grabbing my elbow, and I look back at my brothers.

"Go. We got it." Ben nods, and I know that they do so I don't hesitate. I lift Katie into my arms, her barely weighing a thing, and her arms wrap around my neck, her fingers instantly digging into her familiar place at my nape. As Tony and I walk to the car, I see movement to the side and look up, noticing a young girl who looks just as disheveled, her blond hair matted, her face dirty, and her eyes lock with mine. I watch her as I walk. She doesn't have a camera or cell phone, so she's not taking photos of what's happening. She is just watching everything before she steps away and ducks back into the shadows.

"You fucking asshole. I will sue you for that," the guy says from where he lies on the sidewalk as he is pulled to his feet by Harrison's security team. His hands are secured behind his back, and I notice his face is already starting to swell. I want to step forward and hit him again. I am not a violent person. Never have been. But I swear if I ever see him again, I will end him.

"My place, Tony," I instruct him as he opens the door

of the car, and I sink into the back seat, keeping Katie on my lap, my hold on her unwavering. She hasn't seen my place before. All the time we spent with each other has been in her apartment. Even though both places are secure, mine is bigger, and I know my brothers will come around later. There is a lot to unpack from this.

"I'm sorry," she says again quietly, her face leaning on my chest, now looking out the window as we drive down the street. Her body is still shivering, her nervous system almost completely out of control.

"You have nothing to be sorry for," I say, my hand rubbing up and down her back, trying to soothe her, the other curled around her legs.

"I have probably just ruined your life. He will sue you. He is an asshole like that." Shaking my head, I lean down to place my lips on her head.

"As long as you are with me, I don't care what he does," I tell her honestly.

"You still want me?" she asks, rearing her head back, looking at me like I am crazy.

"Why the fuck wouldn't I want you?" She is everything I want and more. Why would this change anything?

"Because I'm a mess that comes with a cargo ship of baggage. I have no family. I grew up in trailers. I have no friends. I have a stalker who will continue to blackmail me until I die. Most likely at his hand..." she says, and I growl.

"How long has he been holding this over you? How long has this fucker been blackmailing you?" I spit out, angry not at her, but at that vile piece of shit that I left on the pavement.

"For years..." she admits. My hand continues to rub her back, keeping her warm, her body still shaking.

"Is he the person who was following you? The one who has you scared? Shit, he was the guy who planted his face in the car window when we went for our picnic, isn't he?" I ask her, the puzzle pieces slowly starting to fall into place.

"Yes. He follows me everywhere. He followed me to Baltimore. He is everywhere I go." I feel the fear rolling off her.

"He is not fucking coming anywhere near you ever again."

"But he has the tape..." she whispers, her wet eyes searching mine.

"No one is going to see that tape," I promise her as we approach our building, and the car drives down to my basement.

"How do you know? He will do anything for money." Her eyes plead with me, and I hold her even tighter.

"Who is he? How do you know him?" I ask what has been on my mind since I saw them together.

"He is my foster brother." She swallows, waiting for my reaction. *She slept with her foster brother?* Her answer leaves me with even more questions.

"Do you trust me?" I ask, gritting my teeth together. Now is the time. I will help her with this situation, regardless of what she says, but this is my last attempt. If she really doesn't want me, then she will let me know, and I will walk away after I help her. I watch her swallow, but her eyes don't waver from mine.

"Yes. Yes, Eddie, I trust you," she says with such

conviction, there is no doubt. I release the breath I didn't realize I was holding, and my hand runs up her body. Cupping her face, I look into her eyes. I lean forward a little, rubbing my nose against her nose, taking a moment to just be with her. Reveling in our closeness, I take a deep breath and smell her familiar floral scent. Her hand comes to my neck, her fingers tangling in the hair at my nape.

"I fucking missed you." I feel like I can breathe again.

"I fucking missed you." She smiles a little, and I huff a small laugh.

"Good. Now let's get inside. We need to talk." Tony opens the car door, and I step out with her still in my arms, carrying her to my private elevator, then up to my penthouse where she will see the real me, and I will hear about the real her.

34

KATIE

As the elevator opens and he steps into his space, I am not sure what to look at first. The apartment I am staying in is luxe. This one... I have no words.

"Here, sit. I will get us some drinks." He puts me on his soft white sofa, and I still.

"What's wrong?" he asks, concern laced in his face. "Are you hurt?"

"No," I say quickly, not sure what to do. I feel vulnerable right now. Raw. Not sure what I should or shouldn't do. Reality starts to seep in that I now have to tell him everything. I look up at him, wondering if he can handle it. Keeping my hands in my lap, I sit on the edge of the sofa, too scared to move.

"What is it?" he says, looking down at me, trying to figure out what is wrong.

"You have a white sofa," I say almost in a whisper, my body trembling.

"Yeah..." he questions, his brows furrowed. "And?"

"What if I get it dirty?" I ask, confused as to why he doesn't understand this. I had a foster family that had a white sofa. I remember I sat on it and made it dirty, and they were not happy.

"I don't care. It is just a sofa," he says, his face softening as he continues to watch me. I remain quiet, trying to get my body to relax. I feel like I have been bared wide open, my past filling my body again, everything I usually push down now floating to the surface as memories rear their ugly heads. "Pinkie," he says as he squats in front of me. "I don't care about a dirty sofa. I just care about you." Leaning forward, he kisses my lips. I forgot how soft his lips are, how tender his touches. I feel my body relax instantly, and he pulls back, the kiss over too soon. "Relax. Let me get us a drink, then we can talk," he says, his hands rubbing up and down my arm, soothing me.

"Okay," I whisper and watch him stand again to walk over to his kitchen. I inhale a deep breath and take it all in. I feel guilty again. Guilt for bringing this mess into his life. Guilt for not being honest with him when I demanded it from him. Guilt for not being stronger, not handling my own shit. The guilt continues to swirl, mixed with adrenaline and nerves, making a sickening concoction in the pit of my stomach.

The white sofa I am on is massive and so soft. I count the spaces, wondering how many could sit here, and I stop at around nine. It faces a couple of matching white armchairs. There is a large gas fireplace and just beyond the room are floor-to-ceiling windows, taking in the entire city below.

"Here," he says, passing me a bottle of water, which I

take eagerly, not realizing until now how parched I am. I take a quick sip as I watch him move around and sit next to me. He has an ice bucket and a small towel, and I look at his bruised and bloodied knuckles.

"Let me," I say, putting the water bottle down and grabbing the towel, placing some ice in it as he sits next to me. Our legs are touching, and I lean over to grab his hand. His knuckles are red, one of them split open a little. There is a small amount of blood, but he is ignoring it. I wrap his hand quickly to remove it from his sight completely. His hand comes up and cups my face, stopping my action.

"You are safe here. I want you more now than I ever have. When I saw that asshole had his hands on you, I wanted to rip his arms completely from his body." His words make me swallow. They both calm me and make me want to vomit. I lean my face into his palm, preparing myself for what I'm about to tell him.

"I met Steve when I was around ten. We were put into the same foster family. He is a few years older than me, so I idolized him. I would follow him and his friends around everywhere. He stood up to the bullies at school for me. Used to give me some of his lunch when I had none. We were both outcasts, and he was my big brother. Protective. Helpful. Consistent," I say, starting this story, yet knowing that over time, I will share many others. I pause to ensure my voice is steady, a lone tear running down my face. I go to wipe it, but Eddie beats me to it. Cradling my face in his hands, I look him in the eye and continue.

"We were in that family together for a few years. The foster father was violent. A bit of a drinker. He hit me once, and Steve was angry. That night was the first of many beatings that Steve took from him for me. It was like Steve declared a war, but because he was just a teenager, he could never fight back. He was never strong enough. He got beat almost weekly for a while. He couldn't compete with the man who was supposed to look after us." I think back to that man who was the one that changed Steve's life. It was because of that foster father that Steve's personality changed. I see Eddie's nostrils flare, but he remains quiet, letting me speak.

"Steve was sent away after a while, and I didn't see him again until years later when I was sixteen. I used to stay in the school library until it closed at around eight at night. It was warm and they had free coffee. I used to fill up on coffee because I was hungry. My foster family at the time wasn't generous with food and the heating bill was always too high so they never put the heater on. The library became my haven for a while," I say, shrugging. I can see Eddie not liking any of this, but I push through. He needs to know.

"They didn't feed you or welcome you?" he asks, and I just shake my head. That's another story for another time.

"Anyway, I was walking home, and a car pulled up. It was Steve. He was much older, but I recognized him straightaway. He offered to take me to a party, and I didn't hesitate. It was Steve. My big brother. I had missed him, and he was cool, you know. He had a car, and he was taking me to a party, where I knew it would be warm and they would have food. Plus, he had some friends in the car and they all seemed happy to have me along, so..." I shrug again, the worst part coming.

"We got to the party, and I lost Steve almost immediately. He was in the corner, kissing some girl. One of his friends got me a drink. I remember the house being nice and warm, because I took off my jacket and drank that drink fast. After a while, I felt a little funny and started looking for Steve. Two of his friends escorted me down the hallway, telling me Steve was in one of the rooms. I wanted to go home. I felt sick and just wanted to let him know I was leaving."

"Jesus, fuck." Eddie removes his hands from my face and rubs his palms up and down his thighs. He sits forward a little, almost bracing himself, obviously aware that what I'm about to say is going to be upsetting. I curl my hands in my lap, take another breath, and continue, but before I do, his hand grips mine, giving me the strength I need. I hold his hand tight, not wanting to let go.

"They opened a bedroom door, and I walked in. Steve was there. I remember him sitting on the edge of the bed, looking up at me and smiling. I started to tell him I wasn't feeling good, then the door shut behind me, and his two friends stood between me and the door. I don't remember too much after that. I remember feeling panicked as they grabbed me and put me on the bed. I remember looking up at one who was holding a cell phone and filming. The light on the phone was bright, and I remember trying to lift my arm to my face to block it. They took it in turns. But Steve was first. He wanted to be the one who took my virginity. He wanted to take as much as he could from me," I say, silent tears now rapidly falling. Eddie's hand holds mine so tight, it is almost painful.

"They raped you and recorded it?" Eddie grits out, his body still, his jaw clenched. I can hear his teeth grind from where I am sitting.

"He said it was for safekeeping. Because he knew that, out of all the kids in the home, I was the one who was going to make something of myself, and he wanted a backup plan in case he didn't make it." The words Steve said to me that night still ring clear in mind, even though the actions don't.

"Let me guess, he didn't make it?" Eddie snarls.

"He has been an addict most of his life. He blackmails me so he can feed his habit. That is why I moved to Baltimore. To get away. To try to break free," I say, my body and mind nearly totally exhausted now.

Eddie looks at me with deep concern. He leans closer and kisses my cheek, one and then the other, and I realize he is kissing my tears away.

"I don't remember it, Eddie. But I have seen the tape. I know it happened." I'm kind of glad I don't remember.

"Did you go to the police?" he asks, and I huff a laugh.

"They didn't care. No one cares about the kids who are from the wrong side of town. The ones who look scruffy, act up, roam the streets at night. The police think we are looking for trouble, but in reality, many of us are just looking for a safe place to sleep."

"But he was your brother. He protected you. He was supposed to protect you," Eddie says, like he is in pain and trying to understand the situation.

"He did. But he took all those beatings. After a while,

the protectiveness turned into blame, which turned into the need to get revenge. He was also high on drugs, and he is now so dependent on them that he visits me every few weeks or months for money. That's why he turned up here. He wants money."

"You are the most amazing woman I have ever met," Eddie says, looking at me in awe.

"Doubt it. Did you see any of those women who are parading around the hospital looking for you this week?" I say, rolling my eyes. He drops the ice, and his hand reaches out for mine.

"They have nothing on you. You are a fucking warrior, a survivor, and I am so incredibly lucky to have met you. You are safe with me. We will work all this out together," he says, making me feel at ease. Like what he says is true.

His cell rings, and he grabs it quickly. "It's Ben," he says, showing me his brother's name on the screen.

"Answer it." Nodding, he jumps off the sofa and starts pacing the room, intently listening to whatever his brother is telling him, before he stops and looks directly at me.

"Ben says the police need to interview us both." My head automatically shakes, and I can feel the panic rise. "Are you okay to go to the station tomorrow?" he asks me, and my brain doesn't function.

"No..." I whisper, the fright running through my body visceral. "Not a police station." I saw many of them growing up and none of the outcomes were good.

"No police station. They can come here," Eddie says to his brother, and I look at him, wide-eyed. *They do that?*

"I want a female officer as well," Eddie says automatically, and my eyes nearly bug out of my head. *You can request who interviews you?*

"Fine. See you then," Eddie says before ending the call and tossing his cell onto the coffee table.

"They will come here tomorrow. They will interview us both, and Ben will be here as our lawyer. Ben and his team are currently building a case against Steve. They will work throughout the night so he can put that forward to the police tomorrow to ensure Steve remains behind bars for the immediate future as the case continues to build," Eddie says, giving me the rundown.

"Okay. I can do that," I say, nodding, because that will be much easier. If I ever see the inside of a police station again, it will be too soon. I have spent many a night at a station, waiting for whatever available carer to come to take me somewhere to spend the night. While the officers were generally friendly, the inside of a police station only conjures bad memories. Eddie looks at me with concern on his face, the type of look I want gone.

"I think there is a lot to take in, and we have had a big day. Let me run you a bath, and I will organize some dinner for us." I let him pull me up off the sofa. I can't really grasp what I am feeling. Fear a little, relief even more. A strange new feeling of giving up control of the situation and passing it over to Eddie. I'm exhausted, like the flight response I have lived with for the past years has finally eased, and I am almost happy to let Eddie help me. Even though I don't want this to tarnish him at all, because I am wary.

"Eddie..." I say, but pause, trying to find the right words.

"It will be alright, Pinkie. I got you." I know that he does. He gives me his smirk, my smile mirroring his as he puts his lips on mine, and I sink into him.

"Come on." He holds my hand as he walks me down his hallway, and I take the opportunity to look around and discover something new. There is a lot to look at. Large, high ceilings, luxurious decor, artwork, mirrors, soft furnishing. The lights are low and moody, and his place is almost silent. I can't hear any car horns or people's voices. We pass bedrooms, an office, bathrooms, until we reach the end, and he pushes open the door to what I assume is his bedroom.

"Wow," I say too loudly as I stop short, causing Eddie to stop and look back at me.

"You okay?" Eddie asks, his brow crumpling.

"This is your room?" It is big—bigger than any bedroom I've ever been in. The carpet is lush, and his bed looks extremely inviting. I see a large walk-in wardrobe off to one side, but the star of the room is the fireplace. It's a large fireplace, the flames flicking, bringing immediate warmth into the space. He walks into the bathroom, and I hear him run the bath as I remain where I am, looking around the room.

He has floor-to-ceiling windows in here as well, with a small terrace just outside. As my feet automatically move and follow his steps, I realize the fireplace is double-sided. The flames and heat emanate into both the bedroom and the bathroom. I have never seen a fireplace in a bathroom before.

The bathroom is full marble, oversized and lavish. The water rushes into the large tub, and soft, thick gray towels are hanging nearby. My feet are warm from the underfloor heating, and I almost moan from the feeling.

"Let's get you naked," he says again, smirking, and I huff a laugh. My body is exhausted from everything, so I let him undress me. He pulls my scrubs over my head, and I help him with the bottoms. As I unclip my bra, he turns, and I see him grab a small bottle of bath oil and put a few drips into the steaming water. I smell it immediately, the floral aroma hitting my nose. It smells almost like the cheap perfume I wear, yet I can tell that the oil is the real deal. Probably pressed from the flowers directly, not synthetic like mine.

"That smells nice," I say to him as he takes my hand and helps me into the tub. The warmth hits my skin, and I basically melt. I can't remember the last time I had a bath. But it wasn't anything like this. I lower and sink into the water, my head resting back and my eyes closing immediately. This feels like the most decadent thing I have ever done, and my body is aching for it.

"I bought it because it reminds me of you," Eddie says, and I open my eyes and look at him. He sits on the edge of the tub, looking at me like I am his most prized possession. Unspoken words pass between us. Words I am not ready to say out loud and haven't yet processed. His hand reaches out, and he touches my cheek, his fingers gently trailing my cheekbones.

"How are you feeling?" he asks me, and this is the Eddie I know. Always checking in with me, ensuring I am alright. At least today warrants it.

"I'm... I don't know." I sigh, trying to gather my thoughts. "I'm worried. I'm relieved. I'm hopeful but scared to be too hopeful. I am tired, so tired..." I say, shaking my head, trying to ensure the tears don't fall. My adrenaline is well and truly wearing off. "I am just sick of running. Always running. Looking over my shoulder. I just want to stop. Plant roots, you know?" I ask Eddie, and as I look back at him, his eyes gaze into mine with so much concern and compassion.

"You won't ever have to see him again. You stop running as of now. The only place you will run to is to me. Into my arms, because I meant what I said. I will always catch you," Eddie says, his tone washing over me like a balm, and my heart thumps. I nod to him silently, scared that my voice will crack if I respond and really not wanting any more tears.

"Sit forward," he says, and he gets up, still fully clothed outside of the bath, then kneels on the floor as he grabs a washcloth.

"Are you not getting in?" I ask, because this bath is huge. You can probably fit four people in this.

"No. I want to take care of you. Let me wash your hair." He cradles my neck in his hands, and I lay my head back into his hold. As he runs the water down my scalp, the sensation relaxes me, my eyes fluttering closed. I take in another deep breath as he shampoos my hair and then gives me the best head massage ever.

I am not sure I can get used to a billionaire treating me as though I am his everything.

"Mmmmm. You are too good at that," I murmur, as he rinses the conditioner, my body fully submerged. When I open my eyes, I'm feeling tired and a little bit drunk on the feeling in the air.

"You relax here," he says as he lowers the lights, leaving a warm glow to the room, enhanced by the fire that is still illuminating us. "I'm just going to call my brothers and will organize us some food." All I can do is nod. Because I do need time. I need time to sit with my thoughts and figure out what is happening. It is like Eddie can read me like a book. He knows exactly what I need and when.

He kisses my forehead and steps away, and I release a big breath and sink lower into the water. Tonight will be a night I remember for the rest of my life. But for the first time, it won't all be because of trauma or negativity, even though I have that in spades. It will be because it was the night I fell in love with a billionaire.

35

EDDIE

I pull the bathroom door closed and let her have some time. I can barely keep it together. My hands clench, my teeth grind, and my shoulders haven't left my ears since we got home. When she told me what those boys did to her, I saw red. I strut out of my bedroom and retrieve my cell from my living room before texting my brothers. We need to talk, because after what happened today, I know tomorrow is going to be a shitstorm.

Within ten minutes, my brothers are sitting in my living room, on the white sofa Katie was too fucking scared to sit on earlier. Yet another thing I need to get to the bottom of.

"What the fuck happened?" Harrison asks as he runs his hands through his hair.

"He is Katie's foster brother, who is currently blackmailing her and me. Apparently, he has a video. From when she was a kid, a sex video. He is threatening to go public with it unless I give him a million dollars," I say, looking at all my brothers. Tennyson rubs his eyes, and Ben is deep in thought.

"Like fuck he is getting any money. He spat at my guys, resisted arrest. The police want to interview you and Katie because he is charging you with assault," Harrison says, and I nod. I already spoke to Ben earlier, so I knew that was the case.

"You will be charged. They have it on camera, but it will be self-defense and a small fine at best," Ben says, and I am glad that it won't tarnish our family and make an issue for my brothers. Especially Harrison.

"What about him?" I ask, because I want to bury him. Literally and figuratively.

"In possession of drugs, assault on Katie, blackmail... How old was Katie in the video?" Ben asks. My body stills. I haven't had time to digest everything I have learned the past few hours, but I remember her age clearly.

"She was sixteen. It was nonconsensual. It was a group of men, and they drugged her, and her foster brother was the ringleader," I grit out, the bitter taste on my tongue feeling like it is saturating my mouth.

"Fuck," Tennyson bites out, leaning back in his seat in shock.

"Sixteen?" Harrison asks, his eyes wide, eyebrows shooting to his hairline.

"Sex with a minor. Video proof of gang rape, administering drugs without her knowledge. Fuck, this case keeps building on this guy," Ben says, and I can see his mind ticking over.

"He is a fucking piece a shit." Tennyson shakes his head, now sitting forward and cracking his knuckles.

"How long has he been blackmailing her?" Ben asks, and I see Harrison's eyes narrow at me. It hits me then that he has probably been holding this over her since it happened. Close to ten years of her life. As she has tried to move forward, he keeps pulling her back. My shoulders stiffen even more, and I crack my neck.

"Since it happened, I think."

"Shit," Ben says.

"How was she ever going to get herself out of this situation?" Tennyson asks, and I rub my eyes.

"I don't think she thought she ever would," I say quietly, shaking my head in disbelief as I realize that Katie has probably lived a life in full flight-or-fight mode. My stomach feels heavy, my body tense, my mind racing, and I have no fucking idea what is going to happen. All I know is that she has me in her corner now.

"My team is calling," Ben says as he stands and answers his phone. I watch him, trying to decipher his facial expressions, but he is a good lawyer, never letting anything show.

"I will be addressing the media tomorrow, first thing," Harrison says, looking at me from under his brow.

"Thought as much," I say, stretching my hand, trying to get my fingers working normally, even though they are swollen from my punch earlier.

"The fact that you assaulted a man outside the hospital has already been picked up online. We can't let it go too long before I address it. Beth, Willow, and I are currently building a plan."

"A plan?" I ask. I have no idea what he is talking about.

"As governor, I need to reiterate that Baltimore is a safe place, but my brother just hit someone. So, I also need to support you while ensuring I reiterate that violence is not the answer," Harrison explains, and under normal circumstances, I would feel bad for putting him in this position, but I don't. I would hit that asshole in front of the entire nation on prime-time TV if I had my time again.

"Willow already has things in motion," Tennyson says, clearly proud of his woman.

"Like what?" I ask, wondering what he is talking about, my eyes flicking to Ben, who is walking a path in my living room floor while talking on his cell.

"Willow has seeded the media. She already has stories up about the drug issues in Baltimore, revenge porn, and sexual assault issues. Harrison will be addressing those in the morning, so in a roundabout way, he will be supporting you and Katie while reminding his constituents that, as governor, he will be putting new policies in place to support the citizens of Maryland with these issues. Everyone—man, woman, and child—has the right to feel safe, and he will reiterate that," Tennyson says.

"Especially a child," I spit out, knowing that no one was there for Katie when she needed them the most. Ben ends his call and walks back over to us. I look at him in question.

"As I said to you earlier, the police will be here tomorrow morning to interview you both. They have footage from the hospital security cameras. The audio isn't too clear, but it is evident what happened. But..." Ben says, and I look at him sharply, waiting for him to continue.

"But what?" My eyes narrow.

"But that is just for the assault issue today. Given the history she has with her foster brother, she will need to sit with them for another session in order to bring charges against him for the earlier assaults on her," Ben says as diplomatically as he can.

I let go of a breath as I think about how Katie will manage reliving the trauma she has endured. I know there is more, and none of it is probably anything she wants to repeat.

"There is one other thing we have forgotten that may cause issues..." Tennyson says, looking at all of us.

"Mom," I state, because she would have already heard about it all by now. No doubt the media have even tried to call her to interview her on the matter. It is a wonder my cell isn't blowing up, although given she is just fresh out of surgery, she is probably in no state to call.

"Well, there isn't too much she can do from her hospital bed," Ben says, and Tennyson rolls his eyes.

"Any word on when she will be released?" Tennyson asks, and it is a good question. She was meant to stay just for the one stent to be put in and should be home already, but she had a second one put in today, and now she is under observation again.

"I'll speak with Dr. Wilson. See if we can get an update," Harrison says, his teething gritting.

My doorbell rings, and I know that is the food I

ordered. Us boys have been here talking for the better part of a half hour, and I need to get back to Katie, who I am hoping is now a little more relaxed.

"Let's go. We will regroup tomorrow," Harrison says, standing, and my brothers grab their things.

"I haven't said this yet, but I am proud of you, brother. I've never known you to punch anyone, but that right-hand jab today was one of the best ones I have seen," Harrison says, grabbing my shoulder and giving me a squeeze before pulling me in for a full hug. I huff a laugh and squeeze him back, knowing my brothers all have my back, and I will always have theirs.

I see them out and rub my eyes. It is bedlam. The police are involved, and Harrison is making a statement. This whole thing is going to blow up into a media shit-storm. But I got the girl, and I will protect her at all costs.

36

KATIE

I lie in his arms, feeling warm, safe, and secure.

"I didn't mean to bring you and your family into trouble, Eddie," I say honestly, because this is the last thing I wanted. We have been talking all night. After the long soak and some warm soup for dinner, we climbed into his bed and have been talking while staring at the flickering flames of the fire ever since.

"You didn't. Steve did when he decided he could put a hand on you and demand money from me," Eddie says as my head rests on his naked chest. I can hear his heart thump a little faster as he talks.

His family is rallying. But it isn't just money. It isn't even just his name—although those things help. It is the contacts, the professionalism, the research and time and effort his family is putting in. Yes, they are protecting their name. Yes, they are protecting Eddie. But they are also protecting me.

"Why were you so concerned with my white sofa

today?" he asks me, and I sigh, not sure I have the energy to dig up yet another ugly story from my past.

"Long story short, I stayed in a short-term foster home for a few weeks. The couple was childless, and they had a nice place with a white sofa. I was the first child they had ever fostered and the first child who ever set foot inside their home. Needless to say, they weren't equipped for children. I was about eight, full of energy and spunk, and so I was always into things. I was messy," I say, a small smile on my face as I remember the younger me. I had fire in my belly, even back then.

"You weren't messy, you were a kid," Eddie says, and I strum his bare chest again, soothing this new wild beast who is now my protector.

"Well, as I said they had no real experience with kids. They had me for about two weeks, I think, and every time I went to sit down, the wife would scream at me not to touch the sofa because I was dirty and she didn't want me to ruin it. I guess it is kind of burned into my brain. Now, whenever I see a white seat, I hardly ever sit on it. Even though I am no longer that messy, vibrant child."

"You can sit on our sofa and paint your nails while eating chocolate ice cream. I don't care," he says, and my strumming stops. Did he say *our* sofa?

"I am not as messy as I was back then, so I think we are all good," I reply, continuing my strumming again. His small spread of hair across his chest is fast becoming my second favorite part of his body. He is broad and strong, and my head and hands both fit across his torso perfectly, his skin soft to the touch, his muscles contoured and perfect. But my favorite place is still the nape of his neck. I love playing with his hair. It is soft, with a bit of a curl. Even when he slicks it back when in Edward Langford mode, I still want to rake my hands through it and mess it up a bit.

"So what is it about police stations that make you so uneasy?" he asks, and I am usually not this open about my life, having buried it so deep over the years and trusting no one with any information about myself or my past. But Eddie has firmly unlocked that security door I had shut tight, and now the words and memories flow out. It feels cathartic. I have seen a few counselors over the years. All have been helpful in some small way. But talking to Eddie like this feels like we are baring ourselves to each other. There will be nothing he doesn't know, and I am not afraid to tell him everything.

"I have spent many nights in police stations..." I murmur, thinking of my past.

"Behind bars?" he asks, and I snort a laugh.

"No. I have no record, Eddie. But when you're a kid in and out of foster care, there are not many places open to manage relocations in the evenings or on weekends. Nine to five is managed via the foster care agency, but outside of that, I would be dropped off at police stations, sit on the hard wooden bench or in a quiet small back office for hours until they found someone who could take care of me for the night. Sometimes, I would spend the night there. I often wondered if the police officers just forgot I was there. I heard and saw things in those stations that no child should ever really see. Mostly on busy Friday and Saturday nights. The police officers themselves were mostly nice, especially when I was young, but I really never want to set foot in another police station in my life. Because if I ever saw a child like me in there, waiting for a person to come so I had somewhere to sleep that night, I would probably adopt them myself."

"The system really needs to change. There has to be a better way for kids in this country," Eddie says, and I can hear his brain ticking over, thinking about it all. "But I am glad you are here with me now. I am glad that you were strong enough to endure it all and be here now." Not for the first time, his honest words take my breath away.

"I don't know what to say..." It all sounds heavy, and it is hard to wrap my head around it all even now, but I trust Eddie. His fingers caress my bare back in a soft rhythm, his touch soothing. We are both naked, nothing between us, our legs tangled in what could be best described as a postcoital snuggle, but we haven't had sex. Just talked all night.

"I want you to stay here with me for the foreseeable future," he states, his voice solid, confident, and certain. I stay quiet, wanting to give the question the due diligence it requires. I know he needs me close, just as much as I need him. I have no hesitation. There is no question, no doubt that being with Eddie is exactly where I want to be. It surprises me a little that I don't feel more scared, that I have been on my own and independent for so long and it only takes me mere seconds to decide. But Eddie is my future, I always hoped to meet a man like him, but now I have, and I know this is where I need to be.

"Okay," I say, my eyes glazing over as I stare at the flames that continue to dance. I breathe out my fear. My fear of letting someone else take care of me. After years of not having that as a kid, I never wanted to feel let down again. But I know Eddie has got me, and I want to fall into him and never leave. I like it here. It feels like what I always thought a home would. Warm, soft, welcoming. We felt together and cocooned at my apartment, but this is different. The level of security I feel here is new. My apartment is secure, I know that, but here, we are so high up, accessed by a private elevator only, and it's so well soundproofed that I can't hear anything from outside. Just the crackling of the warm fire.

"You will have a few days off work. I have already called Dr. Wilson and explained," Eddie says, taking care of so much while I soaked in the bath earlier. That time was much-needed.

"But I just started." I am a little panicked. I need my job. How the hell will I pay my bills if I don't have a job?

"I made sure he understood," Eddie grits out, and I remain silent, knowing that he has taken care of it all.

"When you do go back to work, Tony will take you, and I will join you most days. I don't know how I can ever let you leave my sight again." Eddie's honesty is one of his best qualities. Even though he lied to me about exactly who he is, he wears his heart on his sleeve. "But he is in police hands, and he won't be coming out."

"But he might?" Steve is like Teflon. Nothing sticks to him. He has been picked up by police before, and within a few hours is out walking the streets again without a care in the world.

"He won't. You will never see him again," Eddie reiterates with so much confidence, I almost believe it.

Almost.

37

EDDIE

I lay awake all night, staring at the ceiling, grateful at some point for hearing her quirky snore so I knew that at least she got some rest. Now as she sits on the sofa, I look at her with concern. She holds her head high, but her vibrant personality is not back in full force yet. That bright light that always shines from her is still a little dull. Exhaustion sits in her shoulders, and if I could take away everything she is going through, I would. But I can't. Anger still vibrates around my body. I thought about her foster brother all night. The things I wanted to do to him. But my thoughts all ended on one thing. *Her*. Her strength and resilience are now some of my favorite things about her. She gives me a small smile from where she sits on the sofa, and love thumps in my veins.

"It is going to be a big day," I say, like she doesn't already know. She is fresh-faced, her hair falling long around her shoulders. I sit next to her, the two of us drinking coffee, waiting for this hellish day to begin.

"I know," she says, sucking in a deep breath in preparation. I hear the doorbell and steel myself, wanting to have more time together this morning before the barrage of my life barrels through the door, but knowing that this is me. And my family. She gets to see it all.

"Are you ready?" I ask her as I stand.

"Ready for what?" she asks, looking around, wondering what is going on. It is still early, but I couldn't hold them off any longer.

"My family. My brothers and their girls are about to walk out of that elevator at any moment. They have been itching to make sure you are alright," I say, pinning her with my eyes. I see shock flash across her face, then slight confusion, before a small smile emerges. Barely there, but it is. Before she can answer, the elevator arrives, and I see her take another breath and settle herself. I wish I could tell her what is about to happen, but I have no idea what to expect.

"How are you feeling?" Beth is first out of the elevator, and not even looking at me, she makes a beeline straight to Katie, who is now sitting almost in shock as my family all barrel out of the elevator toward her.

"That would have been so frightening. What can we do?" Em says, a little more soothingly as she sits next to Katie, and her arm instantly cuddles around her shoulders. I step away slightly, making room for the women to sit with her. Katie looks up at me, unsure, and I give her a warm smile, one I know doesn't quite meet my eyes.

"I brought cupcakes," Willow says, putting a large container on the coffee table before sitting next to the girls as my brothers all come and stand by my side, looking down at them all.

"You okay?" Ben asks me, and I release a breath. *Am I?* I have no idea how bad this situation is—for Katie, for us.

"I think so," I say, my eyes remaining on Katie, watching her interact with the girls as they all hug her and dote on her. It is one hundred percent overbearing, but she seems to like it, if her soft smile is anything to go by. I clear my throat as my brothers stand next to me and we get everyone's attention.

"So, what is the latest?" I ask, knowing there would have been developments overnight and needing to get on the same page.

"He was charged last night with possession, resisting arrest, intimidation, and blackmail. All of it was caught on security cameras, and we have all written our statements already from what we witnessed," Ben starts, and I already know there is more, so I look at him and wait for him to continue. "It is also not his first offense. He is wanted in Massachusetts as well for similar crimes."

"Okay, what else?" I ask, looking at Katie, and she nods at me. She is still vulnerable, but I can see her gaining confidence, getting her strength back.

"I put in a protection order last night. He is to stay away from Katie, you, all of us, our residences, and places of employment, including the hospital," Ben says, ensuring she knows that she is safe. I watch her swallow.

"What about Eddie?" Tennyson asks, and Ben and I swallow. I don't care what happens to me. As long as he rots in jail for his crimes, I will be happy.

"The police are coming here in a few hours to take your statements. However, I spoke with them this morning. You punched him in what we positioned as justifiable self-defense since he wouldn't let her go. You can't be punished criminally, nor held responsible for damages in a civil action, as long as we can show that you used no more force than what was reasonable. Which you did by only punching him once," Ben says in his legal jargon.

"So I saved you, baby bro?" Tennyson asks, raising an eyebrow at me in a mock question, and I roll my eyes. He is right, though. Had Tennyson not grabbed my shoulders, I would have pounded that asshole into the pavement. So he did, in fact, save me.

"That is all for today. But, Katie, there are other charges we can talk about in regard to your history with him. At any point, you can speak to a police officer with me or one of my team present, and further charges can be laid against him," Ben says to her, and I watch as Em rubs her back.

"I want that. I want to do that," she says, looking up at me, steel determination in her features, and I grit my teeth together. She is a warrior, no doubt about it.

"Okay, I can arrange that to happen here at home as well," Ben offers, and she nods.

"All that combined means that he will go away for a very long time, Katie. Add on his other outstanding crimes, he will be looking at anywhere from ten to over twenty years," Harrison says, looking extremely dapper as he will be fronting the media soon.

"Thank you. I appreciate everything that you have done," Katie says to Ben. "All of you," she reiterates, looking at my family as we all gather around her.

"No thanks needed," Harrison tells her. "Our family comes with lots of baggage, stress, and media attention.

But we look after each other. We have each other's backs and that now includes you." I still at his words before my eyes flick to Katie.

"Well, I have a lot of baggage as well, so it looks like I am in good company," she says with a small smile, breaking any tension or unease in the room, and I huff a laugh. We have a lot to get through, but knowing she is feeling safe and is happy here in my space, with my family, puts my mind at ease.

Today is going to be long, demanding, and emotional, and I have the feeling that it is just the beginning.

38

KATIE

I t's been a week, and I haven't slept or eaten as much in my life as I have at Eddie's. Coffee and breakfast are ready for me each morning. Lunch is fully organized by a chef who comes in to prepare healthy meals. We have a warm dinner, glass of wine, and long talks well into the evening. I am still exhausted, but it has been extremely healing.

"How are you doing?" Shelley asks me for what feels like the hundredth time today.

"I feel like an animal in a zoo," I tell her honestly. It is my first day back at work, and it is as bad as I thought it would be. People are staring at me everywhere I go. They whisper as I walk past. Media are milling around the hospital because Mrs. Langford is still here—not that I have seen her. I am giving her a wide berth, as per Eddie's instructions. After my previous introduction to her, I am happy to follow Eddie's advice.

"Hmmm, do you need security up here?" Shelley asks me, looking at me with concern. My smile is thin. Security following me around is just totally ludicrous, but Eddie and the hospital staff all still think it is a good idea, one I keep refuting.

"No." I sigh. "I just feel like I am back in school and am the outcast. I even caught a patient trying to take my photo earlier. I have no idea what for," I say, scrunching my nose up because it all feels just too weird. Like an invasion of my privacy.

"To sell to the media," Shelley says, tapping on her computer.

"What?" I ask, looking at her in surprise.

"You are a hot topic at the moment. Everyone wants to know who the local nurse is who bagged the last billionaire *and* who he loves so much that he hit a guy outside of this hospital protecting you, *all while* his poor mother is on her deathbed inside. That is what the media are saying, anyway," Shelley says, almost without taking a breath.

"Oh God," I say, my hand wiping down my face, wondering when it will all just end. *Will I ever have a quiet, non-eventful life?*

"Excuse me?" I turn at the voice and see the familiar face of a woman standing behind us, no doubt hearing our entire conversation.

"Ohhh, hi. You're back?" I ask with a half smile.

"Sorry, you must be getting sick of me. I was just hoping I might catch Dr. Wilson today?" she asks, cringing in hope. I hear Shelley sigh next to me and already know that this poor woman will be turned away again.

"I'm sorry, love, he is not available right now. You

could wait on the seats over there, but you could be waiting a while," Shelley offers, giving me a side-eye. We both know that Dr. Wilson will probably walk straight past this woman, but this is the fourth time she has been in over these past few weeks and clearly, she really needs to see him.

"Thank you. It may be a waste of time, but I might just wait for a little while."

"No problem. We can let you know when he is coming through," I offer, feeling sorry for this woman. I put her at about my age. Extremely polite, quiet. I am not sure why she needs Dr. Wilson, but it is obviously important as she is very persistent.

"Oh, that would be great, Thank you so much." Flashing me a small smile, she retreats over to the chairs next to the elevator bank.

"What do you think she needs to see Dr. Wilson so badly for?" I murmur to Shelley as we watch her pull a book out from her bag and sit down, quietly reading.

"I don't know. If it was anything to do with a patient or medical matter, then I assume his office would have helped her out already. If I had to put money on it, I would say it is personal," Shelley says, and I have come to realize that Shelley loves a bit of work gossip.

"She brings that thick file in with her every time. It looks decades' old," I say, my eyes flicking to her tote bag that sits on the floor at her feet, the thick file full of paperwork sticking out.

"Maybe it is a malpractice waiting to happen," Shelley murmurs before turning back to her computer and tapping on the keys. The woman looks up at me then, like she knows we are talking about her, and gives me another smile. Her cheeks are pink, looking a little awkward. There is something about her smile that is eerily familiar, but I return her smile and gather my paperwork, knowing that this week has been a lot, and I am probably imagining things. Or slowly going crazy. Either option is likely.

That makes me think of the past few days. I have spent hours with Ben and the police, recounting almost every interaction I have ever had with Steve. It has been tough. Tougher than I ever expected. I had to try to remember dates and times and situations. By the end of it all, once I had gone through everything, Ben and the police had pages and pages of notes. They looked astonished, and I felt instant relief. In those sessions, I just let everything out, and boy, it felt good to get it all off my chest. The heaviness that usually sits on my shoulders is almost nonexistent, and with plans to start regularly weekly counseling, I feel positive.

I know Eddie has a lot on his plate with his mother, along my issues arriving on his doorstep, and now the legal ramifications of that. My heart feels heavy, knowing that if it wasn't for me, he wouldn't have to deal with all the issues.

Then I spot a tall, stunning, blond woman walking through the door, strutting like she is on a catwalk. Yet another society princess trying to stake her claim. My shoulders tense, and I bite my tongue as jealousy nips at my shoulders. As she walks past the chairs, the woman from earlier stands up for a moment, fixing her long skirt, and doesn't seem to notice the society princess strutting past, and accidentally trips her. Shock covers her face as the woman stumbles, her designer handbag flying from her hands, landing on the polished tiled floor before she grabs a passing nurse and prevents herself from falling.

"Oh, I am so sorry!" the woman exclaims, looking horrified as she attempts to help the princess become steady on her heels.

"Ehhh, don't touch me. I am wearing Chanel." She scoffs, throwing her hands away as she straightens herself and I roll my eyes.

"Ohhh." The young woman stands still, almost in shock, looking at her. She glances at me, and I roll my eyes, which enlists a small smile and a whole lot of relief from her, and we both watch as the polished woman starts limping away. I look down at her body, wondering if she is injured, but I soon smirk when I realize that she has broken the heel on what is no doubt a very expensive pair of shoes. She clearly does not want to meet Eddie or the Langford men without her shoes intact.

"One down, about twenty others to go..." Shelley murmurs, and I snort a laugh.

"Maybe we should keep our new friend around a little longer," I say, looking at the pink-cheeked woman who again sits on the plastic chairs, waiting.

"An unlikely bodyguard, but one that will totally throw them off their game..." Shelley conspires before we both have a laugh at the ridiculousness of it all. The life of a billionaire is nothing that I can even comprehend.

39

EDDIE

I sit in this room, wondering how much longer we all need to be here. Pinkie is back at work today, and like we are magnetized, I can feel her, knowing she is probably right on the other side of the door. No doubt sitting at the nurses' desk with Shelley, who is now under strict instructions to look after her. I rub my hands together, trying to will my body to stay where I am. Let her have space. I have been hovering over her all week. Feeding her, running her baths, listening to her, then holding her tight. Whatever she needed, I got for her. She had a few sessions with the police, and Ben told me she did really well. The information she gave was not only descriptive, but also accurate in terms of dates and times and names of witnesses. It will take the officers a while to chase down all the leads and information, but Katie's part is now done. We can slowly start to move on.

But the media have been a minefield to deal with, and it took us a while to get through them when we arrived at the hospital this morning. Harrison has already spoken with the hospital management, and as of today, our family can use the basement parking lot; security has been placed on all the entrances, and we can now miss the flashing cameras and the shouts of questions.

"Well, you are all quiet," my mother says from where she lies in her bed. She isn't looking too good today. Her skin is almost as white as the bed linen, her hair not as tidy. With no makeup on, she looks older than her years, and I know if anyone saw her like this, she would not be happy. The thought alone makes me want to take a selfie with her, just to have it on file in case I need it.

"We are just waiting for Dr. Wilson," Harrison says, clearing his throat, and I don't miss the slight hitch of his shoulders. He is tense. I can feel it. All us boys are. We are all here because the doctor called us all in. News of more surgery that needs all our approval, apparently. Ben and Tennyson would prefer to be extracting their eyeballs out with a pair of tweezers, but they are here to support Harrison and me, if nothing else. Harrison is here because, as governor, he can't be seen as a heartless asshole. I am here because I get to see Pinkie. If only our mother comprehended that she is not our sole purpose anymore.

"Edward." She watches me, her eyes narrowing, and I feel the air around me evaporate just from her look.

"What the hell have you been doing? The media are having a field day over you hitting someone. Please don't tell me it had anything to do with that pink-haired nurse, because if it did, I will likely have another heart attack..." she huffs out, her tone still spiteful, despite her obvious lack of energy that she usually displays. She closes her eyes, like blinking takes all her energy.

"No, Mom. It is all true. I still have the pink-haired nurse girlfriend, and yes, I hit someone," I tell her. She looks at me sharply, her jaw now tight, her eyes bright with fire.

"Here we go," Tennyson mutters from where he stands behind me, scrolling through his phone, obviously wishing he was somewhere else entirely. My eyes flick to Ben then, running his hands through his hair like he will make a run for it at any moment.

"For goodness' sake. I told you Valerie Van Cleef is who I chose. You must rectify this all immediately. I will call Valerie to come over this afternoon. The two of you must go out for lunch. Be seen around town," she says before she takes a breath, like the sudden movement of aggression pains her. Harrison raises an eyebrow, and I notice Tennyson stops his scrolling.

It is silent for a moment as the four of us watch our mother, her face contorting in pain before she breathes again, better than she had been.

"Are you alright?" I ask her, standing as I move closer to her. "Shall I ring for a nurse?" My hand goes to the call button, not wanting her to die on my watch. That is the last visual I need, her taking her last breath in front of me. That would haunt me for decades.

"Don't be stupid," she hisses, slapping my hand away.

"Jesus..." Tennyson mumbles, and the door flies open.

"Hello, everyone." Dr. Wilson says, and I walk back to my seat as he struts into the room like he owns it.

"Doctor." I nod at him, and I am the only one. My

three brothers are currently shooting laser beams from their eyes.

"How are you feeling, Diane?" Dr. Wilson asks, grabbing her chart from the bed and looking over it before walking to her bedside and grabbing her hand. Harrison shoots up immediately.

"Why did you call us in today?" Harrison asks, grabbing the doctor's attention.

"We need to prepare your mother for another operation," he says, and I sit back.

"Another one? She has already had two," I ask, wondering what exactly is going on.

"She has had two minor procedures, where we put in the two stents, but unfortunately, they are not doing the job. Her risk of another heart attack is high," he says, looking at us all.

I can vaguely remember Dr. Wilson from when I was a kid. He was around the house a lot. But when I moved away for school, then went traveling, I didn't see much of him until now. The fact that he and my mother have been together gives me a disgusting taste in my mouth.

"How did her arteries get so blocked?" Tennyson asks, stepping closer, and I stand, all four of us now shoulder to shoulder, looking right at the doctor.

"Stress, most likely. You four and your antics over the years haven't helped, I am sure," he says offhandedly, still gripping my mother's hand. *What the hell did he just say?*

"I suggest you watch your words, Doctor Wilson," Harrison seethes. He is not happy. Not at all.

"What is the next operation and when will it be?" Ben asks the factual questions as he stands firm, the cell in his hand recording this entire conversation. His tone remains professional, even though I see the whites of his knuckles.

"Open heart surgery. She requires a triple bypass." He may be an asshole, but he is an excellent surgeon, and we know he will take good care of her.

"I am in good hands, boys. No need to worry. Although, Eddie, once I am out of surgery, please rectify your current situation. I hope to wake up and see both you and Valerie at my bedside. That would alleviate some of the stress I have been having this week," she says, and a few years ago, I would have felt guilty. Perhaps done exactly what she asks for fear that I may actually cause her death. But not anymore. Now I just feel a burning frustration. She still doesn't get it. She ruined her other three sons and still doesn't get it. I wonder if she needs a brain surgery instead of heart surgery, although I am not sure any would help her at this point.

I run my hand down my face. When is life going to get a little easier?

"Now I just need to run some small tests to ensure you are well enough to go through the operation. Boys, please give us a moment," Dr. Wilson says, effectively dismissing us like we are twelve and no longer required for the adult conversation. Harrison clenches his hands and Ben cracks his neck.

"Let's go to the waiting room," Tennyson growls, and we walk out of her room, one after the other, and strut down the hall. You can see our frustration in the way we're carrying ourselves. People give us a wide berth as we make our way farther down the hallway into the familiar room that has been our haven since we arrived. I can't see Pinkie, but I follow my brothers quickly before the door closes behind us.

"I want to punch that asshole in the face," Harrison says as he walks back and forth in the tiny room.

"You and me both," Tennyson says.

"How long do you think it has been going on for?" I ask, knowing that Mom and Dr. Wilson had an affair, but my mind too consumed these past few weeks with Pinkie to really think about it.

"Hard to say, but I would guess maybe thirty years," Ben says, slumping on a chair.

"Thirty years?" That would mean they were sleeping together before I was born.

"Makes sense. He was around all the time growing up. He was there with her when Nanny Helen died," Tennyson says, the accusation hanging in the air, and I see his jaw clench. I know that cuts him deep.

"I remember being home on vacation and always seeing him around, especially when Dad wasn't home," Ben says, running his hand through his hair.

"Remember when Mom went away for a few months traveling with Grandma?" Harrison looks at Ben.

"She missed my sixth birthday and didn't even call. Maybe they went away together then," Ben spits out, the memory still raw.

"Have either of them admitted it?" I remember Dr. Wilson being around too, but I was too young to really think anything of it.

"No. But it is pretty fucking obvious now. The way he dotes on her, holds her hand. Fuck, Mom blushes every time he walks into the room. She never blushes. Ever," Tennyson snarls.

"To think that all these years, Dad was painted as the villain. The one who had a woman in every city. Multiple women, multiple affairs," Harrison says, shaking his head.

Our parents are less than stellar in their loyalty and love for each other. Not anyone we wish to aspire to be in that regard.

"Yet Mom was doing the same thing. Or even worse, because it wasn't just a fling. She has been with the same man for years. Clearly, she and Dad were just not meant to be together," Ben says.

"An arranged marriage?" I ask. It would makes sense. My grandparents were wealthy and had a special way of doing business. I remember what Mom told me a few weeks ago when talking about marrying Valerie Van Cleef. Not marrying for love.

"Who fucking knows. But I swear, if he talks down to me or any of us again, I will lose it. He is not my dad and doesn't get to berate us," Harrison snarls, and I can tell he is really upset by this. Probably because when Dad died, he was the one who took on the head of the household role, stepping into my father's shoes.

"They both hid what happened to Nanny Helen. They can both rot in hell," Tennyson says, his voice harsh, but there is a lot of pain that sits within him. "How soon can I get the fuck out of here?" he asks, looking at Harrison. At this point, he is only here to support him. The future of his political campaign can't have any of us boys stepping out of line. We must remain the caring sons of Diane Langford in the eyes of the outside world. Even though I know both Tennyson and Ben don't give a shit about her anymore.

"Let's just get through this hospital visit. Once she is out of the hospital, and she has a clean bill of health, and things calm down with Pinkie, we can get to the bottom of everything," Ben says, the voice of reason.

"Fuck, our lives are hectic. Are you sure you want to run for president one day?" Tennyson asks Harrison, and he looks up and smiles.

"All of this is my training. Do you have any idea how many different policies and ideas and communities there will be in this country for me to try to support and represent if I become president?" He huffs out a laugh, and I see it then. His stature, his confidence, the air of integrity and surety. He will be president. I know it. I smile then. Feeling proud of him.

"Well, you get my vote," I say, grinning at him.

"Mine too." Ben nods.

"I'm voting for the other guy..." Tennyson teases.

"What other guy?" Harrison's eyes thin, as he no doubt runs through the mental list of potential opponents. We all laugh. There is only one man suitable for the job and that is the one sitting opposite me.

40

KATIE

Brian and I sit on Eddie's sofa, looking at the mountain of shopping bags around us.

"That was such a full day," I say to him as we both lie back, exhausted. I toe off my shoes, needing a foot rub, and Brian sucks on some champagne Eddie handed him.

"Looks like you two had fun," Eddie says, his smile wide and his eyes sparkling. When he told me that he had arranged for Brian to come over and take me shopping for the afternoon, I wasn't sure what to think. Then Brian arrived and practically dragged me out the door, and I didn't look back. Armed with Eddie's black credit card and Tony as our chauffeur, Brian had me giggling all day, and it was just what I needed. To feel normal for a day. Like a girl would feel shopping with friends.

"You looked hot in everything you tried on, so we just had to buy it all." Brian waves his hand over the shopping bags. He is right; I did buy almost everything I tried on. I didn't want to, but he is a good shopper and practically made me. New shoes, a handbag, clothes, skincare, and makeup.

"Here, take your card back. Clearly, it is not safe with us," I say, giggling, handing the card back to Eddie. He looks at me with a glint in his eye but doesn't move to take it from me.

"Keep it. It's yours. Use it for anything, whenever you want." I still in surprise.

"If you are giving them out, I will take one," Brian says, downing the remainder of his drink, giving Eddie a grin.

"I can't take this." *I can't, can I?*

"Why not?" Eddie asks, seemingly affronted.

"And... Mom and Dad are going to start fighting, so that's my cue to leave," Brian says, jumping up from the sofa and grabbing his things. "Call me later and we can debrief." Brian kisses me on the cheek before he walks over and hits the elevator button.

"Thanks, Brian. Glad to see you both had a good time." Eddie stands and shakes his hand, ignoring the elephant in the room.

"Ohh, anytime, bossman. You know shopping is my favorite hobby, especially when it is done on your dime," Brian says with a grin before stepping into the elevator and waving goodbye.

"What do you mean you can't take the card?" Eddie asks, turning swiftly around to look at me as soon as the elevator doors close.

"It's your money. One shopping trip to get me out of the house is nice, but I don't need your money, Eddie," I say, not sure if I make sense or not.

"I'm not taking it back. Keep it and use it if you want, or don't if you don't. But I would feel better knowing you have it and can use it if needed. I want you to go shopping with Brian, have girls' nights with the girls, maybe a day spa afternoon or hair appointments. Whatever you need or want to do, I want you to do it and not think about the money side of things. Baby, I am being totally honest with you now when I say, money is not an issue, and I won't even look at the statement. My people will just pay it," he says, smiling, and I put the card down on the table, not yet sure exactly what to do with it. "Also... I moved you out of Harborside..." Looking at me with a hesitant expression, he starts to gather up all the shopping bags.

"Moved me out?" I raise my eyebrows as his warm hand envelops mine, and he pulls me off the sofa, walking me down to the bedroom. I rest my head on his shoulder and breathe him in. I love his smell. He always smells fresh, like he stepped out of a rainforest.

"I want you here with me. Every day," he says as he opens the walk-in wardrobe and places my shopping bags down, and I see a whole side now designated to me. I see my familiar clothes—jeans, tops, a few shoes—but now they are all supplemented with additional things. Pants, sweaters, jewelry, accessories, shoes, dresses, a variety of things. I walk in silently, taking it all in. *He has moved me in? In with him, permanently?* My fingers skim over the fabrics as I walk the length of the hanging space. He has bought me an entirely new wardrobe, way more than the few bags I purchased today, and I grab a few things out to take a look, loving every single thing. They are all exactly what I would buy myself.

"Eddie…" Overwhelmed, I am still in shock at what I am looking at. We have only been together for a few months, at most—with those months being interrupted by bedlam and blackmail. But this place already feels more like home than any other place I have lived in. I know that is because Eddie is here.

"I had the girls go shopping for you today as well. If you don't like anything, we can take it back, exchange it. I told them what I thought you would like, so I hope it all fits," he explains quickly, and I see him swallow, clearly nervous.

"It's too much. You don't have to spend your money on me like this." I frown.

"I want to. I want to give you everything. I want you here. That may make me selfish, but I want you to be comfortable here. With me." His voice rises at the end, like it is a question not a statement.

"I am. I am happy with you. But are we moving too fast?" I ask because I don't know. I have never had a relationship like this. It doesn't feel fast. It feels right, but should we?

"I would have moved you in within the first week had I not been such a fucking idiot and let you believe I was the maintenance man. Do you have any idea how badly I want you? I want us." I can hear the vulnerability in his voice.

"Hmmm, well, I think we are both guilty of hiding the truth. Are you sure?" I ask again, looking up at him.

"I want you here. Do you want to be here?" I see his breathing speed up as his eyes lock on mine.

"I don't want to be anywhere else but where you are."

The honesty feels like it comes from so deep within, my chest hurts as the words float out of my mouth. It is like slow motion, and I see the moment he understands. His lips part and widen in a large smile.

"I got you a few other things..." Eddie says sheepishly.

My brow furrows. *What else could there possibly be?*

He walks back to the bedroom, and following him, I notice some boxes on the bed.

"I got you a new cell phone. With a new number. It is private, so no one will have this number without you giving it to them," he says, and my heart stutters. Steve or anyone from my former life will never be able to reach me again. It will cut all ties. It is something I should have done years ago, yet never could. I never had a safety net that gave me the confidence to let go of it all. Until now.

"I also put in a call to Dr. Catherine Wakeford," he states and I freeze.

"What did she say?" I ask, as she was my other lifeline. The one who helped me make this move, the one who made it possible.

"She was fully supportive of whatever made you happy. She is writing you another letter of recommendation, so you can move away from Dr. Wilson. Maybe into the nursery ward to do more cuddling?" he offers, his smile small but loving.

"I would love that," I whisper to him, scared to use my voice. My eyes are welling, even though I have shed thousands of tears this week.

"I know," he says, smiling. "I also told her that I was moving you in with me. She told me to tell you that if you need anything to call her. If I am not the man you need me to be, she will always be there to support you. I programmed her number into your phone so you can call her whenever you want to. She also suggested we make a trip back out to Philly for dinner with her and her family soon." I need to take a slow breath in.

This is a new life for me. A new opportunity. Slowly, I am cutting ties with my old life. Now all I need to do is step into the new one and embrace it all. In my new home, with my new wardrobe, but most of all, with my new man.

"I also got you these... Actually, I stocked the kitchen with them," Eddie says, almost laughing at himself. I take a step closer to the bed and grab the box. It is a box of the delicious cookies from the baskets at Harborside.

"Oh I love these!" I have been dreaming of these cookies for weeks, having devoured the three boxes I got almost immediately.

"Yeah, I thought so. I noticed the other boxes were the first to go in your apartment, so I ordered a heap of them. Now they are all in the kitchen for you whenever you want them," he says, smiling at my reaction.

"I am going to put on so much weight. These are seriously so addictive." I open the box and put my nose to it, wanting to eat one.

His eyes twinkle, and I think I swoon a little. Putting the box back down on the bed, I take a few steps closer to him and run my hands up his arms.

"Thank you, Eddie. For the clothes, for the phone, for the cookies... but really, for everything." He has done so much for me, it feels like my words are not enough. I can't begin to express my gratitude. He looks at me, and I feel his arms warm on my body as they circle around my waist. My hands sink into the familiar place at his neck as we lean on each other.

"You know, I am pretty sure I fell in love with you the minute you opened that door with wet hair and a wet t-shirt. Then, when you patched me up when I almost died fixing that cupboard at Harborside, I knew you were someone special..." he says, giving me a cheeky grin.

"Oh my God, you were not dying, Eddie," I grumble playfully, rolling my eyes at his dramatics.

"Then when you turned up at the swimming pool, wearing that sexy one piece, your hair piled on your head, with those sexy tattoos showing, I knew I was utterly and totally yours," he says, and my grin falters at his sincerity.

"Eddie..." I whisper. God, why does this man make me want to cry all the time? Just when I thought my heart couldn't get any fuller, he keeps giving me more.

"I am utterly and totally in love with you, Katie Taylor." I stop breathing. My lungs don't move. They are frozen, as is my body, and I still in his arms. No one has ever said those words to me.

"What?" I whisper, my eyes searching his. I feel like I am in an alternative life at the moment.

"I said, I am utterly and totally in love with you," he says, smiling, like a kid in a candy store. His hand rubs up and down my back, soothing me, and I feel my head and heart reconnecting.

"I didn't think I was made for love, Eddie. I didn't think that I would be so lucky to experience it. In any way. The life I have lived is not one that comes with that kind of emotion. But you... you make me feel like I am worthy. Like I am deserving. Like I matter..." I say, trying hard not to cry.

"You do matter. You matter a lot," he says.

"I know that. I know my worth. I know that I am strong and capable. I have had to be. But I didn't think anyone else did... until you," I say honestly, because deep down, I always believed that I mattered. I always believed there was more for me, but I always felt invisible until Eddie came along. "I love you, Eddie. From the tips of my toes to the top of my head. I give all of me to you, including my heart. It is yours," I whisper.

"I will protect it with everything I am and everything I have." He is committing himself to me. Engraving his words on my chest. I feel it scorch into my skin, never being this sure of anything or anyone before in my life.

I push up on my tiptoes and kiss him. My hands run up his arms, around his neck, and I pull him to me. I put everything in my kiss, every emotion, every word I want to say, every feeling I have. His hands circle my waist, holding me tight as our lips part and our tongues tangle, his touch moving up my body, and I completely melt into him.

"I want you naked..." he grumbles against my lips, and I huff a laugh as his lips trail down my jaw. My head falls to the side as his hands run up my body on the inside of my scrubs. I shiver then, the feeling of his hands on my skin sending waves of arousal through me, my body aching for his. The need I have is almost overwhelming.

"I want you naked too," I say, just as his hands slide

up, taking my top with them, straight over my head, and he throws it across the room.

"No problem," he says, throwing his jacket off his shoulders and across the room to join my top, then making quick work of his shirt. As he does, I scoop my bra off my body, and we both take a moment to look at the other.

"You are so fucking beautiful." His voice almost croaks, and I swallow, his words carrying meaning. I feel every one of them. His hand gently touches my shoulder, then he traces his fingers down my chest, his eyes watching intently. My nipple pebbles and my breathing quickens as his fingers trace my breast, and then coast down my stomach. His hand flattens, landing around my middle.

"Come here," he says, almost growling, and he doesn't even have to ask, because I move toward him naturally. Our naked torsos touch, heat running across my bare skin as his hands move down my lower back, underneath my scrubs and over my ass, taking the pants down with them.

"Bossy much?" I tease as he pushes the pants down my legs. I step out of them, standing in nothing but my very basic cotton underwear.

"Yes. Now come here." Cupping my head, he pulls me toward him again, and we ignite.

41

EDDIE

I smash my lips to hers, barely containing my desire. I meant every word I said. My love for her, how fucking beautiful she is. Everything. This woman had me from the moment we met, and after everything we have endured since, there is nothing I want more than to make her mine.

"Eddie," she says my name in that familiar breathy moan that makes me harder than a teenage boy, and I growl into her mouth.

"God, I need you now, right the fuck now..." I say, undoing my belt and pushing down my pants, kicking them off as my hands go back to her, tracing her curves, feeling her skin under my touch. I push down her underwear until they fall at her feet, then I pick her up, her legs circling my waist. I like us like this. Naked. Together. Nothing between us, our bodies meshed tight. There is no hiding from each other. We are completely open, physically and mentally.

The urgency I have for her is intense, but I pause.

"What's wrong?" she asks, looking at me.

"I don't have a condom." I meant to pick up a box today, and I totally forgot about it.

"It's okay. I'm clean. I had a medical exam before I took on the new job," she says, looking at me expectantly.

"I'm clean, baby. Always have been." I watch as a small smile comes to her lips.

"I trust you," she says, and those three words hit me square in the chest. After everything we've been through, after the things I omitted telling her, she says the words with such certainty that there is no doubt she is mine.

"I have no idea how I got so lucky to find you, but I am sure glad I did. Are you ready, beautiful?" I murmur, kissing her, feeling her body mold to mine.

"So ready..." she moans as I start to push into her. Grabbing her ass, I hear her breath hitch a little and watch her face as she bites her bottom lip. Her head arches back, her long pink hair falling to my hands at her lower back.

"Eddie," she moans, and I grin at the sound, her hips already starting to move, wanting the friction.

"That's it, baby. Fuck, you look good grinding on me. So fucking beautiful," I grit out, barely able to contain myself. My muscles work overtime, holding her up like this, but this is exactly how I imagined taking her. Me standing here, pulling her on and off me. My moves are quick, and her hands dig into my shoulders, hanging on for the ride.

"This feels so good," she moans, her movements getting quicker.

"So good. You feel so fucking good." Taking her bare like this feels fucking amazing.

"Don't stop. Please don't stop," she pants, and I can feel our bodies heat, sweat starting to shimmer on our skin.

"Fuck me, Pinkie, you feel so fucking good," I groan, thrusting into her harder and harder, not able to get enough. My fingers dig into her flesh. I must be bruising her skin, but I can't get enough.

"Eddie, oh God, Eddie," she whimpers, my hips slamming into her clit with every thrust. Her hips push back into me, jumping on top of my body. Our movements are animalistic, the two of us chasing the massive wave of ecstasy approaching. It has never felt like this. I have never felt like this with anyone else. The deep desire, the carnal need, the urgency I have to bury myself inside her. She is mauling me, holding me close, her hands delving back into my hair, and I lower my lips to her bouncing breasts.

"I love your perfect breasts, your amazing ass, your fucking fantastic pussy," I stammer as she holds my mouth to her breast, where I lick and bite as her body slaps against mine. I have fucked a lot of ways, but I have never fucked standing up like this. There is no wall, nothing near us, just us standing in our room, me lifting her hips and slamming them into mine. I think it might be my new favorite position.

"I'm coming... I'm coming!" she screams, and I clench my jaw.

"Such a good girl. Fuck, you are perfect. Come on my

cock. Come for me, Katie," I grit out, wanting her to orgasm before I explode, knowing my rush is imminent.

"Eddieeeeee!" she cries out as her body quivers in my grasp, lowering her head and biting my shoulder as her body jolts, thrusting on me. As she lets go, I feel her muscles spasm and clench, and I help her through it, watching her face as she comes.

"Such a good girl," I groan, grabbing her ass, our skin sweaty, and I slowly lower us to the floor. I am still rock-hard as I lay her down, looking at her dreamy face. Her pink hair splays out around her, her cheeks tinted a matching pink. Her perfect breasts rise and fall quickly, her lips a ruby red and the kind I really want wrapped around my cock, but that is for another time. Because I am not finished with her yet.

I kiss her. I lick and suck on those slightly swollen lips and run my hands up her bare torso to her breasts, molding them before I tweak her nipples. Her back arches as she responds to me instantly.

"God, you look incredible naked. I want you walking around our home naked all the time," I say, moving my mouth from hers and trailing kisses down her jaw and neck before I settle on her chest. I take a nipple in my mouth, sucking it slowly, teasing her with my tongue.

"Mmmmm... Eddie..." she hums as her body starts to squirm underneath me.

"Yes, Pinkie?" I ask her, playing dumb. I know exactly what I am doing, teasing her as I move to the other breast, licking and nipping. I run a hand down her curves to find her wet, warm center before I circle her clit slowly.

"I can't," she moans, her body already reacting. Her

legs spread a little more, her hands lifting out to her sides, grabbing the soft rug underneath her, her whole body now wide open for me.

"You can, baby," I whisper, lifting my head to watch her face as my fingers play with her clit. She bites her lower lip, her hands gripping and regripping the rug.

"No, I can't... Eddieee. Oh... I want you..." she pants, her breaths heavy.

"Tell me what you want, baby. Tell me what you need," I say to her, watching her build up. Watching her slowly lose control. I move my fingers then, dipping them inside, and she moans.

"Eddie... More..." She moans my name, and my balls feel tight and heavy, and I am astounded at my own stamina. I feel so close to the edge, but I need her to come again. I bring my fingers back to her clit, and then repeat the move, over and over, starting a new rhythm.

Her hands reach out, wrapping around my back, pulling me closer, her nails biting into my skin.

"God, Eddie, fuck me... please, fuck me..." she begs, the look on her face ravenous, and I don't hesitate.

I position myself over her and sink into her in one swift move, causing us both to moan.

"Fuck, you feel good. You feel so fucking good," I breathe out as I start to move.

"Yes, God, yes..." she says, her nails scratching up my back as her hands delve into the back of my neck, pulling my lips to hers. I kiss her hard, swallowing our moans, as I thrust into her, over and over. She pulls my hair tighter, and I move my hips faster, my orgasm so close I can taste it.

"Eddie? Eddie...?" she pants, saying my name as if in question.

"Come, baby. Come again for me, beautiful," I grit out, and she does exactly what I tell her, her second orgasm stronger than the first. Rolling through her, her legs wrap around my hips and her fingers scrape into my scalp. I push my forehead against hers as she lets go, her mouth opening on high-pitched moans as they sing out to the room. And I am right there along with her.

"Fuck, fuck, fuck..." I chant as I push in again and explode, my release barreling through me, and I grind into her, wanting to sink deep, to burn myself into her, make a mark, combine our love together right here on the bedroom floor, our love for each other so eager, we didn't even make it to the bed. I grip her muscles, and I hardly feel her bite on my shoulder as my hands press into her flesh, sticking her to me, keeping her in my arms, wrapping her up until our bodies are almost one.

My body is exhausted as I breathe in deeply, my head on her chest, listening to her heart beating rapidly. Her fingers sink into my hair, combing through it, running her nails across my scalp in a massage as we both catch our breath.

"I think I have carpet burn on my ass," she says quietly, and I smile.

"Wait until you get it on your knees." I smirk, already wanting round two.

"I guess at least then I will match." I huff out a laugh.

She is perfect. Pinkie is perfect.

42

KATIE

I sit cuddling the little boy who has been here for weeks already. No longer a tiny scrunched-up newborn, he is starting to grow, has put on weight, and is becoming a little more alert. Aside from him, all the other babies have been discharged. Most of them are now with foster families, and I say an internal prayer for each of them, hoping their experience is better than my own.

"Thought I would find you here," Eddie says from where he now stands in the doorway. He leans against the frame, hands in his trouser pockets, sexy smirk on his face, looking every inch the billionaire people see him as.

"This is my lunchtime hiding spot," I say with a smile.

"Buddy has been here for a while," he says, stepping toward us where we sit on the large armchair.

"Buddy?" I ask, grinning. It is cute that he is giving him a name.

"Yeah, my little buddy." His fingers trace across the

baby's small head delicately, playing with the small tuft of hair. He still has the newborn smell.

"Hmmm. Well, he is taking a little longer to get stabilized, and because he has some ongoing medical issues, he isn't a baby who many people want to foster," I explain the sad reality.

"How old he is?" Eddie asks as he sits on the arm of the chair, and I lean back into him a little.

"He was born at thirty-four weeks, and he has been here for a few weeks now. They probably won't release him until he reaches full term at forty weeks, and even then, it also depends on his health." Each baby is different, but that is usually how it goes. "He also has special needs. He was without oxygen for a little while after birth. He isn't hitting his milestones, so they will continue to monitor him and conduct tests."

"I told him all about you the other day," Eddie says, and I look up at him and see his smile.

"What do you mean?" I ask, intrigued.

"I was here, having a cuddle. I just needed some space from my mother and her situation, and I told him all about how we met, how stupid I was about my keeping my identity a secret, how amazing my carbonara pasta is. You know, the important bits." I huff out a laugh.

"Well, you are a natural." she says, as I hear the soft snores of Buddy as he lies in my arms. Eddie *is* a natural. The babies I have seen him hold have all slept soundly in his arms as he is caring and nurturing.

"We should invest in this," Eddie says, his face serious now.

"What do you mean?" I ask, confused.

"We have a new foundation my brothers and I started a little while ago. We invest in charitable causes to help people," he explains, shrugging like it is no big deal.

"A foundation? What do you mean, a foundation?" I ask, wanting more information, having no real idea what he is talking about.

"My brothers and I own a lot of different businesses. Harrison is governor, as you know. Ben runs our law firm; Tennyson manages our construction business, and I run our property division. We also have investments in other industries and a lot of real estate all over the country and overseas." He runs his hand to my shoulder, giving me a squeeze, and I realize I am gaping at him.

"I guess the point I am trying to make is we have a lot of money and we recently set up The Langford Foundation, where we can start giving some of it to people and causes that need financial support," he says, sighing, looking at Buddy.

"That is amazing." I am genuine with my words, yet I still have no real idea how it all works or what it must be like to have so much money.

"I think we should invest in the cuddle program and look at doing more for the foster care system. Maybe build a twenty-four seven center so kids don't have to wait all night in police stations or something like that." It is clear he has thought about this. He is smart and empathetic and so kind. I smile, feeling like he is talking to me as his equal, like this is a choice we both get to make, even though it is clearly his money. He is asking for my thoughts and input, and I feel even more connected to him. Like I am part of it all. I am beginning to understand that this is what building a life together feels like, and it gives me so much joy already.

"That would be amazing. I mean, there is a lot that needs to be done. A lot of work needs to happen to support children in this country."

"We can make a start. If we start it, maybe others will get on board and help too. I can't take away the hard times you had, Pinkie, but I sure as hell don't want any other kid to experience it. Every child should have a decent start in life, and if we have the means to help make that happen, then I think we should." I wonder if it is possible to fall more in love with him than I already am.

"Oh sorry, I didn't mean to interrupt," a female voice says from the door, and we look up.

"Hey. No problem," I say, smiling to the familiar woman. "Still trying to find Dr. Wilson?" I ask, and I feel Eddie stiffen beside me.

"Yes and no. Apparently, he is in surgery again today, but the nurse at the desk said I could sit down here somewhere for some quiet space. The hospital main foyer gets a little loud and busy sometimes."

"Sure. I'm Katie, by the way. This is Eddie." I feel like it is time, as I have seen her so many times now.

"Oh, I'm Lucy," she says, and I look down, seeing the file in her tote bag.

"I feel like you are almost a local here," I joke, giving her a smile.

"I feel like it. He is a hard guy to catch," she says with a sigh, as if exhausted.

"Are you sure there is no other doctor who can help you?"

"No. I don't think so. Dr. Wilson signed off on some medical forms years ago that I found in my parents' files, and I just wanted to ask him some questions."

"Well, feel free to grab any of the armchairs out the back. There is a small lounge there that no one uses, so it is quiet. Plus, they have the heating up a little more in this ward so it is super cozy," I say to her with a small smile.

"Thanks. I have a book I am in the middle of, and this offers me the perfect chance to finish it," she says, pushing her glasses up her nose. There is something about her eyes, but behind her Coke-bottle glasses, I can't really see them clearly.

"Enjoy," I say softly, patting Buddy as he stirs a little. I watch her retreat and hear her quiet steps as she walks down the hall.

"Know her?" Eddie asks, his hand massaging my shoulders, making my body melt.

"She has been in regularly, trying to see Dr. Wilson. He won't take her appointments and won't take her calls. It is super weird."

"I think we both know that Dr. Wilson is a bit of an asshole," Eddie grits out, and I laugh.

Just as I am about to say something else, Buddy snorts in his sleep. It is small and sounds like a laugh.

"Did he just laugh with us?" Eddie asks, wide-eyed.

"No, I think he is just dreaming or had some wind," I say, smiling at Eddie getting so excited.

"No, seriously, I think he just laughed with us," Eddie

says again. "He is a smart boy, my buddy." Leaning down, he kisses me on the top of my head.

We both gaze at this beautiful little boy, Buddy, who apparently now laughs, just like we do.

43

EDDIE

With my mother now out of surgery and comfortable recovering, I didn't hesitate to jump in the car and head to the office today. Pinkie has now been back at work for a few days, and with everything that has been going on, I have been absent from the office. I have so much paperwork to get through, Miranda's stress is at an all-time high. I should feel on edge. Overwhelmed, but I am not. I have a lot on my mind, as there is a lot resting on my shoulders, but I haven't felt this happy in my life in... forever. All I need to do is think of the pink-haired beauty and everything is alright in the world.

"Okay, so I have everything in order of importance. At the top is the contract for the new Singapore build, those amendments that needed your final sign-off. Then working down, we have new tenancy paperwork for the new building in DC. In this pile are more personal affairs, so invitations to the Heart Start Gala that happens every year." Miranda is going through things that make my mind a blur.

"That's a no, but send a donation," I tell her, passing the invitation back to her, feeling good to tick something off my list immediately.

"No problem. This next one is an exclusive invitation from Whiteman's Whiskey, releasing their new product at their distillery," she says as I lift the invitation. We have known the Whiteman family for years. Tanner Whiteman started the distillery when he was young, after becoming a teenage father, his girlfriend leaving him to raise the kids on his own. Turns out, he made it a huge success, and they are now one of the wealthiest families in the country. I went to school with Connor, Tanner's son. There is no way I would miss catching up with them and flying out to their distillery in Tennessee. Pinkie would love it too.

"Add that to the schedule. RSVP for me and Katie. Also, call my brothers' offices and see if they are going. I know Tennyson and Willow will probably go, so we can take the jet together," I tell her and watch as she scribbles things down.

"Great. Another thing, this third pile is internal employee issues," she says, looking at me.

"What issues?" I ask, because we run a tight ship and reward our people well.

"Nothing bad. Just to update you that Mary in finance is leaving this week to have her baby; Tom over in the mailroom has morning tea next week for his ten-year anniversary, and reminding you it is my birthday this week," she says, smiling.

"I remember it is your birthday. Gucci or Louis?" I ask her. Every year, I tell her to go shopping and get herself a new bag. After all the shit she has to deal with for me, it is the least I can do.

"This year... Louis."

"Done. Put it on my card and enjoy yourself. For Mary, get her a baby bonus organized, and for Tom, talk to HR and see if we can give him a little something for his loyalty too. I will try to make it to see them this week, but things are pretty hectic at the moment," I say, looking back at the pile of paperwork that sits in front of me.

"Will do, thank you." I know she appreciates it. I like rewarding my team. It is important for morale, of course, but the people who work for me make a choice to come in every day and give their all. Now that Pinkie is in my life, I appreciate it even more. All the late hours, the working on the weekends. I never really understood it before. Being single with no one at home, work was really front and center for me. But now, I just want to be with Pinkie all the time, so the ability to leave her and come into the office to work is an effort.

I feel the tickets in my pocket. A surprise date tonight is something that I thought would bring a smile to her face. Tickets to Broadway. Tenn is going to fly us up in his helicopter, and I am planning for us to spend the night. Tony will get us in the morning. Just something to get us out of the apartment, get our minds off all the police interviews, and give us a little break, even just for the night. But before then, I need to get things in motion here at work.

"Before you go, can you get a memo organized for our

next foundation meeting? I want to raise the issue of funding a baby cuddling program and twenty-four seven foster care solution," I ask her, and she takes some notes. "Do a bit of research, see what is out there and where we could have some impact."

"Done and done. Anything else?" she asks, but before I can answer, Ben rushes into my office.

"Have you heard?" Ben asks, panting like he ran here. I am on alert straightaway and stand quickly, pushing my chair back suddenly, it hitting the wall behind me.

"What? What happened?" My heart is already racing, and I see Miranda standing, wide-eyed, clearly as surprised as I am.

"There's a fire at the hospital. It's in the cardiac ward. Just heard it on the breaking news," he says, just as Tennyson flies into the room behind him.

"There's a fire at the hospital. We gotta go," he says, just as out of breath as he stands, gripping my office door.

"Oh my God," Miranda whispers in shock, looking between us all. I see the fear in her eyes as the air leaves my lungs. The hospital? On fire?

"Pinkie is there," I say quietly as the news penetrates my brain. My heart starts beating harder and faster in my chest. "*Pinkie is there!*" I yell as panic sets in, and the three of us bolt out of my office quicker than we have ever run before.

I think of nothing else as I run through my office and grab the elevator just before it closes, my two brothers hot on my tail.

"Fuck, fuck, fuck," I yell and pull out my phone, the Broadway tickets falling to the floor, and I leave them there. Our date is no longer top of my mind. Why does this keep happening to us? Pinkie and I have had nothing but hurdle after hurdle. Just as we are starting to see the light together, it all gets ripped away again.

I dial Katie's number and wait as it rings.

"Is she answering?" Tennyson asks while Ben is trying to get a hold of Harrison on his cell.

I shake my head, only hearing the ringing and my own heart pounding. This can't be happening.

"Eddie!" I hear the panic in her voice as soon as she answers.

"Katie! Are you alright? Where are you?" I almost scream into the phone. I hear loud alarms ringing in the background, and then she starts coughing.

"I'm helping get the patients out. I'm nearly done. The fire department has just arrived. I'm just going to your mother's room now. She is the last one." I can hear the fear in her voice. I just want her to leave. I just want her out of danger.

"Get out of there. You need to get out now," I say, because if there is a fire in the hospital, with so many medicines and cleaning products, it is full of fuel for a fire. But I know my pleas fall on deaf ears, as she would never leave anyone behind. I hear her cough some more, and anxiety crawls up my chest.

"Katie? Katie?" I'm panicked as the elevator door opens, and we run out to Tennyson's car.

"I need to go. I love you," she says before the line goes dead.

"Fuck!" I scream into the empty basement, my voice echoing around the walls as my brothers and I run to the car. I'm scared. I need her out of there. I need her safe. I need her with me.

We waste little time. Tennyson has the car out of the basement, just as I hear Ben talking with Harrison. He meets my eye, and we share a look of foreboding. I clench my fists and swallow the lump in my throat.

This is not happening. This cannot be fucking happening. I look out the window, praying that everything will be okay.

44

KATIE

"How was the man in 204 today?" Shelley asks as I meet her at the nurses' desk after my afternoon rounds. I feel good today. Eddie and I having some quiet time in the neonatal ward helped, and I am excited to see what he can do with the extra funding requirement for the babies.

"He was okay. Grouchy and a little angry, but nothing out of the ordinary," I tell her. He has dementia and came in for a stent, but since he keeps forgetting, his recovery time is a little longer.

"Did he keep his IV in this morning?" Shelley asks me, already knowing the answer.

"Nope. Saw it, got a bit scared, and ripped it out again." I sigh. I put that IV into his arm almost every day because he forgets where he is and what is happening. His hand is now a little bruised from all the activity.

"Hey, watch it!" We hear a man yell, and we both look over to see a young blond girl walking swiftly down the hallway, pushing her way among the people. She turns to look at me on the way past, and my breath catches in my throat as I see her unkempt bleach-blond hair and dirty attire, but this time, she gives me a smile. Showing me her blackened teeth. My heart starts racing, and I quickly look around for Steve, even though I know he is still in custody and can't possibly be here. My eyes find hers again, and I realize her smile is not one of warmth, but more sinister than that. The look is fleeting as she begins to run, again pushing her way past people and out the door.

"That was weird," Shelley mumbles. "Do you know her?"

"No. But I have seen her before," I murmur, still looking at the doors, wondering what she was doing here. I should ring Eddie or Ben. Maybe security or someone. There is no reason for her to be here unless she was visiting someone, and I have a feeling she doesn't know anyone on this ward.

"Do you smell that?" Shelley asks, and I look at her.

"What?" I ask automatically, sniffing the air.

"Smoke?" she says, and I take another big sniff and I do.

"Oh my God, I can smell it." We both frantically look around. The desk phone rings then, and Shelley grabs it, listening, then looking at me wide-eyed.

"We need to evacuate everyone immediately. A fire has started on both the east and south sides. Fire department is on their way, but not here yet," she says as we throw down our paperwork and start to move quickly out from the desk, just as the alarm sounds and everyone begins to panic.

"We need to evacuate!" Shelley yells to staff, patients, and visitors, some running, others walking, and others just standing around, looking at everyone, wondering if this is just a drill or serious. Then people start coming from everywhere else, security, patients, visitors, nurses, doctors. It is complete bedlam as everyone runs in every direction. The panic is further enhanced when the automatic sprinklers come on.

"Katie, clear rooms 200 to 205. I will clear 206 through to 210. Then we meet here and walk out together once we know the ward is clear," Shelley shouts at me to get over the noise, and I nod, trying to rub the water out of my eyes, my hair and face now completely drenched from the sprinklers.

"Got it," I yell back as I get a push from behind, almost slipping on the floor tiles before we rush off in opposite directions. I check rooms 200 and 201, both having older male patients in them, and both have their family here visiting. So together, I help put them in wheelchairs, clip their paperwork to them, and send them all out with an orderly to the evacuation location outside.

Rooms 202, 203, and 204 are all completely vacant already, so I leave the door open, and the curtains around the bed pulled back to help the fire department see that the room is empty. I learned emergency procedures early on in my career and have kept up with annual training since. Who knew it would come in so handy this early on in my career.

My cell phone buzzes in my pocket from where I kept it since my lunch break. Eddie.

"Eddie!" I yell, hoping he can hear me above the noise.

"Katie! Are you alright? Where are you?" he screams through the phone, but I can barely hear him over the alarm and yelling. I cough then, the smoke starting to linger around me, my throat dry and scratchy, despite the amount of water coating my frame.

"I'm helping get the patients out. I'm nearly done. The fire department has just arrived. I'm just going to your mother's room now. She is the last one." I walk down the hallway, covering my mouth and nose with my elbow. I see a few people running, but not many. I feel like we are nearly all evacuated.

"Get out of there. You need to get out now!" Eddie says, but I can't. I can't leave any patient behind. I don't answer him, because I can't lie to him, especially as the smoke thickens as I run to his mother's room, this end of the hallway obviously closer to the main fire.

"Katie? Katie?" Eddie says, and I need to concentrate. My eyes are stinging, and the noise is too loud.

"I need to go. I love you," I yell to him before I end the call, pocket my cell, and run to his mother's room.

Pushing open the door, I am surprised to see her still here.

"Mrs. Langford, we need to evacuate the hospital," I say calmly as I walk around her bed. Having just come out of surgery earlier, she still has a range of monitors and IVs connected to her. Since I haven't been managing her at all, it is all unfamiliar to me, and I try to quickly work out what it all is and what she needs. I can't wheel her bed out and maneuver all these machines at the same time; it would take at least three people at best.

"What is all the commotion?" she asks, and I can see that she is still a little dazed due to the heavy drugs she is on to recover from open heart surgery. She is in no state to be moved or rushed, but it is a full evacuation.

"I need to move you, Mrs. Langford," I say, coughing as the smoke begins to fill her room. Whatever started the fire must be water resistant because it is not letting up, even though the sprinklers are practically turning the floor into a swimming pool. I pause for a moment. If the fire is electrical or is near the hospital gas or oxygen lines, then the water spraying from above is going to do very little to stop it. If anything, it could make it worse. I start moving quicker as panic starts to set in because I can't hear any sirens or the fire department yet at all.

"You have some nerve coming back in here," she seethes as I try to unhook all the tubes and monitors to get her ready to evacuate.

"Some nerve, ma'am?" I ask, not paying too much attention to her words as they still slur from her mouth. She coughs a little then, making me move faster.

"You need to leave my son alone," she says angrily, and I look at her. Her eyes narrow at me, and I can't believe this is what I need to deal with while trying to evacuate her.

"We can discuss that later, Mrs. Langford. Right now, I need to wheel you out of this hospital." I hook machines to her bed and unlink others, trying to determine what is most important and what I can leave behind.

"Katie?" Shelley screams from the hallway.

"On my way, last one, you go!" I see her out in the hallway, wheeling a man in a wheelchair.

"Be fast!" she yells. "The smoke is really thick now!" I see her push the man quickly, almost running, him gripping the arms of the wheelchair tight before another body rushes into the room.

"Diane, we need to move you now," Dr. Wilson says as he rushes into the room and straight to her bedside. He starts unplugging things without a care in the world. He throws monitors away and puts the IV bags on the bed.

"Nurse Taylor, she is still recovering. Her heart can't take too much right now," he says to me like I don't already know.

"Yes, Doctor," I say as I lift the brakes from the bed and we start pushing her slowly.

"Colin?" I hear her ask him, a little fright in her voice.

"It will be okay, Diane." I don't miss him grabbing her hand and holding it in his.

"Okay, let's open the door wider and get out of here," Dr. Wilson says, looking at me, and I open the double doors to her room, pushing them back to create enough space for us to move through. As I do, smoke bellows into the room, so thick, I close my eyes immediately, the stinging making my eyes water instantly.

"Shit," Dr. Wilson says.

"Oh my." Mrs. Langford starts to cry as I run around her bed, feeling my way, and I start to pull her through the doors.

"Let's go, Nurse Taylor!" Dr. Wilson snarls at me as I rush, meanwhile he stands watching me do everything. The bed starts moving, and I feel the momentum as we get to the door, but before we can make it through, the bed stops suddenly. Dr. Wilson and I continue to push, but it is not working.

"It's caught on something!" I yell, my hair splattered against my face. Dr. Wilson seemingly waits for me to do something. I dive under the bed, looking at each of the wheels.

"Hurry up!" Dr. Wilson berates me, and I move to the last wheel, underneath where he stands, so close I can make out the color of his socks, and I see it. The IV cords that he haphazardly threw onto her bed earlier are now all caught in the wheel because he didn't move them properly.

"It's her IV. The cords are stuck!" I yell to him as I get busy, trying to unhook the mess.

"Well, get them unstuck for Christ's sake!" he yells at me again, but I can't. Panic fills my chest as I pull on the plastic tubes and then push them in the other direction, moving them every way I can to try to get them out of the wheel, but there are about three cords all squished together, none of them coming loose. I could cut them, but the way they are all mushed together, I still don't think they would come unstuck, they are wound tight. My chest hurts as my cough becomes consistent, so much so, I can't really stop. Panic continues to rise, and my heart thumps in my chest. The alarms are deafening, smoke even thicker, and my throat is on fire.

"We need to move her into a wheelchair," I splutter to Dr. Wilson as I stand back up and look around the room, my eyes stinging. There is no wheelchair; someone must have moved it.

"I am not getting in a wheelchair! I am not an invalid," Mrs. Langford says as Dr. Wilson bends over to take a look down at the wheel on the bed. Standing up quickly, he looks at me, obviously coming to the same conclusion about our predicament.

"There is no wheelchair. Pick her up, Nurse Taylor." He is kidding, right? She is dead weight, completely out of it on her medication after her surgery. He looks at me seriously, so not wanting to waste any time, I start to pull her toward me. Maybe I can put her over my shoulder, although that would hurt her chest immensely. She starts slapping my hands away, not wanting me to touch her. The smoke is getting thicker, so now I can barely see either of them. Then I hear a hiss. Oxygen.

"Where are the oxygen lines?" I scream to Dr. Wilson.

"What?" he yells.

"Which way do the oxygen lines run?" I ask as I look around. I have never seen the plans for the hospital, and as I look to where the flames are coming, I get a deep-seated feeling that the wall the flames are running up are right near the oxygen storage.

"We need to go now!" I start pulling her off the bed. She screams in pain, and my heart lurches.

"Stop, don't touch her!" Dr. Wilson says, slapping my hands away, and I can see the panic now on his face. He knows what is going to happen.

"We need to go! It is going to blow up!" I scream. I can hear yelling in the distance, but the flames are not calming. If anything, they are flaming brighter, moving faster. In our direction. The fire department won't come inside if the place is not secure. I run to the door of her room and look around. The hospital is empty. Smoke covers the ceiling and is filling the entire space.

"Help! Someone! Help!" I scream but hear nothing besides the alarms. I see no one. I told Shelley I was right behind her, so she probably thinks I am on the way out.

"We need to go now!" I say, turning back to the doctor and Mrs. Langford.

"Shut up, you stupid girl! Stop acting like a baby," she says, and I balk. Baby. Oh my God, the babies. Did someone get Buddy?

"Just leave, Nurse Taylor," Dr. Wilson says to me, and I can see it in his face. He knows what is going to happen.

"I can't leave you," I say, my chest pained, my eyes watering. I can't. I'm not wired that way. They will die. If we can't move her, then she is stuck. "Can't you pick her up?" I ask him, although he is a thin wiry man and probably can't move her dead weight either.

"I am your boss, and I demand you leave. Now!" he screams at me. I jump a little at his anger and look at them both. He is holding her hand, and she is leaning into him. They look like a couple in love. I am so confused. I have no idea what is going on. I stand, looking at them both for a moment. Mrs. Langford is so relaxed on her medication, I don't think she really understands what is happening. Dr. Wilson is looking older and less in control now that he is saturated in water.

"I can't just leave you both here. I need to help you. I am a nurse, that is what I do. *That is my job*," I say, but the doctor cuts me off.

"Go!" Dr. Wilson yells again, and I jump at his angry tone.

"Go. Tell my boys I love them. Tell them I am sorry... for everything. Tell them..." She chokes as the reality of what is happening starts to infiltrate her medicated mind. "Ohhhh, Colin," she says, looking up at him with her forehead creased in question, her eyes pleading with him. Her hand holds his, and my heart is almost thumping out of my chest.

"I won't leave you. I love you. I have loved you for over thirty years, darling. *Where you go. I go.*" he says to her in a tone that doesn't allow for questions. My eyes, although stinging from the thick smoke, are almost bugging out of my face. *They are in love?* He is a horrible boss, but the words he just spoke were some of the most romantic I have ever heard.

I feel like I am intruding on their moment, but I can't leave them. There has to be something I can do. I look around frantically again, trying to find something, anything. Someone. I dive back under the bed, pulling at the IV lines, pushing at the wheel. It is still not budging. By the time I get back on my feet, the smoke is so thick I can barely stand it.

"Go. Just leave. Leave now before it is too late," Dr. Wilson barks out. Tears run down my cheeks, my heart breaking. I run to the door, taking another look around.

"Shelley!" I scream before I start to cough. "Shelley!" I try again, but my throat is too dry.

"Go. Go to my boys. Tell them I didn't suffer. Tell them... tell them..." she says as her eyes start to water, and I look at her in slight shock. This woman is the matriarch of their family. The one who has a sharp tongue, one that she lashes at everyone who doesn't meet her expectations. I have learned from Eddie a little of her history. Yet now she is soft, looks remorseful, and dare I think it, committed to the outcome that is about to take place for her.

"I'll tell them," I say, nodding, trying to give her a little peace in these final moments. You would think that I would be used to it. I have had to do it a few times now in my career. Give comfort at the end. The difference in this is I am about to leave, not sitting at her bedside and holding her hand.

I hear a loud bang down the hallway and jump out of my skin, the movement enough to get my feet moving. I give them both a final look as the doctor steps up onto the bed with her, lying by her side and taking her into his arms. I turn and run out, not able to watch anymore.

I sprint for the exit and make it almost halfway when I stop. *Buddy.* I need to make sure he is evacuated. I need to make sure he is okay. I turn sharply, coughing and spluttering as I feel against the wall and start running down to the neonatal ward. I can't leave Buddy. What if no one got him? I push through the door, the smoke a little less in here.

"Hello!" I yell out, wanting to ensure that it is empty, and I run down the hall, looking in each room as I stumble. All the doors are open, all curtains open. I know there is only one baby in here at the moment, and that is Buddy, so I run to his room and feel relief as I see it empty.

"I'm here!" I jolt as I hear a female voice, and I run back out to the hallway. The smoke is covering my vision, making it impossible to even see a few inches in front of me.

"Who is it? Where are you?" I scream, the alarms so loud I feel like my eardrums will burst.

"Katie?" the voice says, and I run down the hall to the small lounge at the end.

"Lucy?" I say, surprised, as I round the corner and see her there. I run to her and grab her hand. She is in a state of shock by the look of her. "Is anyone else here?" I yell my question, even though we are standing side by side.

"I don't know. I went to the bathroom, and then when I came out, the alarms were on and water was every-where. Then the smoke came, and I got disorientated. I couldn't remember which way the exits were."

"Let's go, we need to hurry." I grab her hand and we run. Together, we sprint down the wet hall and through the sprinklers, back out to the main hallway. Both cough-ing, we pull each other along. When one of us falters or slips, the other pulls to keep us going. Our steps are slow as the smoke gets to us, but through it, I can see the exit door at the end. I point to it, and we make our final big push, slamming ourselves into the door and falling out, our legs pumping fast and hard.

"Katie!" I hear Eddie and run toward his voice. It is dark outside, nighttime coming while we were evacuat-ing. Bright, beaming lights illuminate the ground, and I push my legs to go faster, pulling Lucy along with me.

"Katie!" I hear Eddie scream again and look up, where I see people gathered and flashing blue and red lights. I see Eddie then, as he jumps over the police barricade and ducks under the police tape, running toward me. His brothers start yelling at him. Tennyson jumps the barricade too, and I hear Willow scream. I run so fast, I can't even feel my legs as Lucy keeps up with me. We are nearly together, only a few yards apart, when I hear it. A *boom* hits my ears just as I am knocked off my feet and thrown into the air, and I hit the ground hard, still holding Lucy's hand, my eyes firmly on Eddie before everything goes black.

45

EDDIE

The hospital is in complete lockdown, and I pace the police barricade, wondering how on earth that is possible when we know people are still inside.

"I need to get in there. I know exactly where they are!" I grit out to the fire chief in charge of this shitshow.

"No one is going in. It is unsafe. We are fighting it from above and evacuating as fast as we can," he says to me as all his people remain outside at the doors, pulling people out as quickly as they can.

"It is not fucking fast enough!" I yell as I pull my hair, stress eating my insides.

"Harrison is here," Ben says as I see a small motorcade pull up, and my brother steps out before the car even stops.

"Eddie." He rushes over to where Ben, Tennyson, and I stand. He was down in DC today, so it has taken him forever to get here.

"Mom and Pinkie are still inside," Ben tells him, and he swallows before looking up at the hospital. Flames are now starting to glow out from the roof, and I see a steady stream of patients and nurses all flowing out the doors. I watch closely for Katie, but she isn't coming.

"She said she was going to get Mom out when I last spoke to her. That was about twenty minutes ago," I say, feeling useless as the police stand nearby, knowing that I am going to jump this barricade the minute they turn their backs.

"She should just leave her there. I wouldn't be saving her," Tennyson mumbles, doing nothing to help the situation.

There are people everywhere. Paramedics, patients, families, even the media have started pulling up. Their large white vans and cameras are on, and they are doing a livestream to their respective news stations. Dusk has fallen already, and large spotlights have been put in place. We are all just standing here, waiting to see our loved ones, while watching the whole place burn.

"Governor Langford, any news on your mother?" A young woman comes up to us and sticks a microphone into his face. He frowns and doesn't answer the question as police come over to her immediately and escort her back over to where the media are congregating. Harrison looks concerned. Mostly for our mother and Pinkie, because they are both still inside, but also for Baltimore, because this is a terrible day for the city.

"Harrison. We have our name, we have money, but that still can't get me my girl. I need to get in there. I need to get her," I grit out, and he looks down at me before looking back at the hospital. The bright-orange flames are now bigger and brighter than before.

"Oh my God." I hear a woman's voice and see Willow, Beth, and Emily rushing toward us, and they stand, all looking at the hospital in awe.

"Chief, give me an update," Harrison snaps at Chief Warden as Harrison's people mill around, some on phones, taking notes, all looking busy.

"We are securing the grounds, as it is too dangerous for our guys to enter. We are controlling it from the air now," he says just as a chopper flies over.

"Don't you understand? Can't you see that people are still inside? We need to get them out," I seethe. Harrison's brow crumples even more.

"As I said before, we are doing everything we can. There are still people coming out. Our guys are at the emergency exits and helping, but we can't go in too deep. The risk is too high," he says, and on paper, it makes sense. Why send in hundreds of men to potentially risk their lives for a few people. But doesn't he understand that my whole heart is in that building?

I see a few other nurses making their way out, and I squint, trying to see if it is her. I see Tracey from the neonatal ward, a baby in her arms, and I immediately know it is Buddy. She runs past me, looking at me, wide-eyed and terrified.

"Are you okay?" I yell out to her.

"Fine. The baby is fine too," she says as she lowers her arm a little, and I see him sleeping peacefully through it all. I watch as the nurses rush around her, and she walks over to the far end of the crowd, where all nurses and patients are congregating. I look back to the hospital doors and see more people rushing out. I'm frantically looking for the pink hair I love, but I can't see it. I do see Shelley pushing a man in a wheelchair, though, and I rush over to where she is going.

"Shelley. Shelley!" I'm panicked as I grab her, spinning her toward me. She looks frazzled, wet, and is coughing up a storm. Tennyson takes the man in the wheelchair and pushes him toward the paramedics before coming to my side. "Where is she? Where's Katie?" I ask, fear spiking my veins.

"She was in your mother's room, just unhooking her from the monitors before pushing her out. She said she was right behind me," she says as we both look toward the doors, and new hope flames in my chest.

"She is still alive. She is okay. She will be out in a minute," Tennyson says, grabbing my shoulders and pulling me back toward where Harrison and Ben stand. My eyes don't leave the door, and I stand and wait with my brothers as one minute turns into two, then two turns into three.

"Come on, Pinkie. Come out. Come out to me," I murmur under my breath as me and my whole family wait, watching the door, waiting for the sight of the woman who has ingrained herself into me, my heart, and my life.

Then I see her.

"Pinkie!" I yell the minute I see her frame push

through the door. She is with another woman who looks a little familiar, the two holding hands and stumbling out, coughing and falling into each other. I don't hesitate then, my body already moving.

"Eddie!" I hear Harrison yell behind me as I jump the police barricade to shouts and curses from my brothers and surrounding emergency services. But nothing will stop me from running to her.

The lights are bright, people are screaming, and the flames are hot against my face the closer I run to them, but I can't stop. It is complete bedlam. The flashes of cameras and the movement of the crowd behind me feels like a pulsating wave.

"Jesus Christ!" Tennyson grits out behind me, followed by Willow screaming his name, and I know he has jumped the barricade too. I don't look at them, though, my eyes firmly on one person and one person only.

"Eddie!" Harrison yells again, this time more panicked, and I know he is right behind me too. Red and blue lights flash, the spotlights bright above us, and I hear a small rumble and a gasp from the crowd.

"Watch out!" Ben warns, his voice close, so I know he is also hot on my tail. I look up briefly and see smoke plume into the dark sky and immediately know part of the roof has collapsed.

"Eddie!" Katie screams, running straight for me, only a few yards separating us. I recognize the other woman with her then. It's Lucy, who I met with Pinkie in the baby ward.

I grit my teeth and will my feet to move faster, and

then everything changes. My feet are no longer on the ground, and I get pushed back like I am merely a kite in the wind. When my eyes meet Katie's, I watch both the women as they fly toward me in the air, still holding hands, complete fear and shock on their faces. I land hard on my back, my ears ringing so loud it is deafening. People run everywhere, and then the noise comes back loudly—sirens, screaming, someone yelling my name.

"Eddie!" Harrison is on his knees in front of me, his right in front of mine.

"You're a heavy fucker," I hear Tennyson groan from underneath me, and I look around, seeing that my brothers caught me, and I lean back into their embrace.

"Eddie?" Harrison says again.

"Here. I'm here," I groan, my body sore, my ears thumping. "Pinkie? *Pinkie!*" I am alert again as I sit up, Harrison helping to lift me slowly. Then I see her, right in front of us. Looking around, it is what I would imagine a war zone to be. People are running everywhere. Medics and the fire departments, water being sprayed, smoke clouding the entire scene. The media are all talking over the top of each other, the general public behind us all, watching from a safe distance.

"Pinkie!" I say again, stumbling over to her, crawling to her on my hands and knees. I nearly had her. She is only a few feet away from me, lying on her stomach on the grass. Lucy is the same, both unconscious, face down.

"Pinkie." I reach out my hand and brush it across her face gently. "Pinkie!" I yell, but she doesn't answer.

"She won't wake up," I say, panicked, looking at my

brothers who all gather around us. "*She won't wake up!*" I yell louder.

"Give us room, sir," a paramedic says as a group of them rush to her side, and they gently roll her over. There is blood, so much blood. It drips down her face, along her arms, in between her tapestry of art.

"Pinkie..." I croak out, feeling nauseous, but my eyes remain glued on her.

"Is she breathing?" Harrison barks at them.

"Yes, sir. She is breathing, and her pulse is still strong," they say, and I sag in relief, with Tennyson still holding on to me.

Lucy looks in worse condition. Her leg is bleeding profusely as a piece of building material sticks out from her thigh, and I grit my teeth as my world starts to spin a little.

"Where are you taking her?" I force out, now standing, the adrenaline kicking in as I watch them lift Pinkie onto a gurney.

"The University Trauma Center, sir," the paramedic tells me without looking at me as he continues to bandage and monitor Katie.

"You need medical attention, sir," a young female medic comes up to me, pushing a bandage onto my forehead.

"I'm fine." I swat her away. As I do, her hand pulls away, and I see the familiar bright red on the bandage, and my fingers immediately go to my head. I feel the warm liquid and pull my fingers away, seeing them coated. Bright red runs down my fingers, and I start to sway.

"Eddie..." Ben says, watching me. I swallow roughly, my mouth dry as my stomach curdles. But I shake my head and grit my teeth. I need to be awake. I need to follow Katie and not leave her side. She is all that matters. She is everything.

46

KATIE

As I open my eyes and look around, I wonder what the hell is going on. Rubbing my eyes because they sting, they water immediately, and I squint and blink, trying to get them to clear. The room is quiet but extremely hot. My ears are ringing and feel full, like I am underwater. I swallow roughly, my throat dry, and the familiar dull beep of a monitor repeats next to me. I see bandages on my arms, my head feels heavy, and I slowly lift one hand and touch my face, feeling another bandage there too.

I try to take a deep breath, and I smell smoke, panic filling my body instantly, even though I am not near a fire. I try to calm myself, taking smaller breaths, and I realize the smell is in my hair and up my nostrils, and my memories come back to me. The hospital, the fire, Lucy. My eyes well with water as I think about Eddie's mom and Dr. Wilson. Did they get out? Are they safe?

Tears run down my cheeks as I try to process everything,

my heart rate increasing, letting the room know as the beeps become faster. I take a breath and look at everyone. Harrison and Beth are lying asleep over on an armchair. Ben and Emily are similar next to them. Tennyson and Willow are sitting asleep uncomfortably on a few separate chairs. It must be the middle of the night, but it is hard to tell because the curtains are drawn across the window.

I look down at my bed. Eddie's head rests on the mattress near my side. He is sitting on a hard plastic chair, which he has brought right next to my bed, his hand wrapped in mine. His eyes are closed, but I see the gash on his head and frown. I remember him. I remember him running toward me. There was so much yelling and screaming and panic, but I remember him. Putting his own life on the line to get to me. Jumping that police barricade, the screams of his brothers who panicked and chased him.

I lift my finger and trace his jaw softly, and his eyes ping open immediately.

"Pinkie?" he says groggily, lifting his head, his eyes now open wide.

"Hey..." I say, my voice rough.

"Oh my God." He releases a breath. "You're okay? You're okay?" Moving up the bed, he cups my head in his hands. "Fuck, you scared me," he whispers as he peppers small kisses to the parts of my face that are free from bandages.

"I'm okay, Eddie. A little sore, but I am okay." Tears now flow freely from both of us.

"Oh my God, you're awake!" I hear Willow say from

the side, before she and Tennyson stand and walk over behind Eddie.

"Hi..." I say, not really sure how to greet them. It's not like I can just say *Hey I'm fine, you guys totally saved my life for a second time.*

"I'll get the doctor." Harrison stands to attention immediately and walks out the door, Beth coming to my bedside and giving my other hand a squeeze.

"Hey, you gave us all a bit of a scare," Ben says as he slaps Eddie on the shoulder, giving him a squeeze, and I see Eddie wipe his tears with the back of his hand. Em joins Beth and passes me a tissue so I can wipe my own.

"What happened?" I ask, looking at each of them, and Eddie takes a deep breath.

"There was a fire in the hospital. It is still early days, though. They are not sure how it started," he says, and I nod, more memories coming back.

"Your mother?" I ask him, and he remains silent, his lips pursed as he just shakes his head.

"Oh..." My voice catches in my throat as the tears start again.

"There are still a few people unaccounted for, and Mrs. Langford is one of them," Em says, looking sad but not emotional.

"Shelley?" I ask quickly, panic rising all over again.

"Fine. Home resting. She will come and see you tomorrow," Eddie says, and I relax into the bed in relief. "Buddy too. He was moved to this hospital and is sleeping well," he adds, a small, sad smile on his lips. With that news, my heart finally slows back to normal.

"Miss Taylor, it's great to see you awake. How is your

pain level?" a doctor I have never met asks as he walks into the room, with Harrison behind him, followed by a nurse who comes to my side immediately, fixing up my bed and refilling the jug with fresh water.

"Fine. A little sore, but nothing too much," I say as he tests a few things and marks them off on my chart.

"Good. Good. You are a little battered and bruised, with stitches in your leg here, and a slight concussion. Your ears will be ringing for a while, and I suggest a hearing test in a couple of weeks to ensure no permanent damage, but your eardrum is all intact and there have been no other issues from the blast that we can see. All in all, you are made of tough stuff, and as long as you take it easy, you should be able to go home in a few days," he says, smiling, and I sigh in relief, as does everyone else in the room.

"Great, thank you," I say, feeling my body relax little by little.

"Thank you, Doctor," Eddie says, stepping forward and shaking his hand. As he does, I notice a bandage on his inner elbow. In fact, as I look around, I notice all their sleeves are pushed up with the same kind of bandage.

"Why do you all have bandages on your elbows?" I ask.

"We gave blood. We wanted to keep busy while you were being treated. We don't know if they need it, but it was all we could think to do so we didn't all go mad waiting to see you," Beth says. I look at Eddie with admiration, wondering how he got through it all with his aversion to blood. Like he knows what I am thinking, he gives me a small smile and shrugs.

"Actually, about that, I do need to speak with you boys, please," the doctor says seriously, looking at all the Langford men.

"Anything you need to say, you can say here. We are all family," Harrison says, stepping forward. The doctor looks around the room at each of us, and we all look at each other, just as confused.

"We have a patient who needed a blood transfusion, but her blood type is AB negative, which is extremely uncommon," he relays.

"That's us. We are all AB negative, so we are happy to donate more," Ben says, stepping forward just like Harrison.

"Perfect, that would be great. She had a severe leg injury and has lost a lot of blood. She will require another blood transfusion and, well, since it is such an uncommon blood type, if you have the ability, we sure could use your donations."

"We will follow you down to the blood bank now. We are all happy to donate," Harrison says, and everyone nods, standing and gathering their things. Eddie remains by my side, holding my hand.

"We will let you guys have some time. Good to see you looking better, Pinkie. You had us all worried there for a moment," Harrison says, smiling, his wide grin oddly charming. I only just now see the appeal. There is no doubt he is a leader.

"Thank you," I say quietly, still in awe of this family and what it all means to be a part of it.

"Thanks, brother," Eddie says, giving Harrison, then

Ben and Tennyson a hug and a backslap, before they all say their goodbyes and walk out the door.

I sigh. My mind feels heavy, like a jumbled mess.

"I have so many questions..." I look at Eddie, knowing he is the one to give me the answers. "I tried to get your mom, Eddie, I really did," I say, choking up.

"I know. I know you would have. I also know she would have given you a hard time, probably called you a name or shouted at you." I can't talk, so I just nod. "Was Dr. Wilson with her?" he asks, his expression pinched, like he is still processing everything too.

"Yes. He came, and we both tried to get her wheeled out, but the wheel on the bed got caught, and the smoke, the alarms..." I say shakily, reliving the memory.

"He stayed with her, then? She wasn't alone?" My heart breaks at that question, and I cry, nodding.

"He yelled at me to go. The last time I saw them, they were together," I'm barely able to say through my tears. "I tried to find Buddy too," I say, letting him know that I wanted to try to get everyone. I feel like I failed.

"I know you would have. Like I said earlier, he is fine. He is all fine. You did the best you could, baby," Eddie says, his fingers brushing my wet cheeks and wiping my tears away.

"What now?" I ask, melting into his touch. This month has been a month to forget. Just when I think life can't throw anything more at me, this happens. Eddie leans in and gives me a soft smile.

"Now we make a life. We both now know how quickly life can change, so we are going to continue our relationship how it started."

"How's that?" I ask, holding my breath, feeling over-whelmed and even more grateful.

"We are going to dive headfirst into it. You and me, Pinkie. The two of us. Together," Eddie says, kissing my chapped lips with a light brush of his.

"Always," I say, the confirmation of commitment in my bones.

"Always and forever," he says, taking a seat and leaning forward on the bed. He stays with me all night and into the morning as we start to rebuild our life together. Not once leaving my side. Not once letting me down.

47

EDDIE

I adjust myself on the hard timber pew. The priest talks about life, love, legacy. Us boys sit tall and straight in the front row, looking directly at our mother's casket. Black. Shiny. Overflowing with white roses.

I feel heavy. In my chest, in my legs, in my mind. My saving grace is the beautiful pink-haired woman sitting next to me. She squeezes my hand, our palms sweating together since I haven't let go of her for even a second today. She has not only been going through her own traumatic experience, but has also been there for me, every minute of every day as I wade through this loss.

The loss of a matriarch. A woman who, despite all her hate, venom, and pure black soul, actually did donate many dollars and many hours to charities around the state. Who raised four boys who turned into men. A woman who died, knowing exactly what was coming for her, like they were the flames licking up at her from the depths of hell. The devil himself was probably at the gates waiting for her.

I swallow at that thought. I now know that smoke inhalation would have taken her and Dr. Wilson before the flames had even arrived. Their bodies were removed from the damaged hospital twenty-four hours after the whole place erupted. They were still holding each other.

The sermon ends and we stand. I move on autopilot. Buttoning up my jacket, I keep Pinkie close and follow my brothers and their girls down the aisle of the large cathedral past the people who knew her, of which there are many. There must be hundreds of people in attendance today, and as we shake hands with the priest and walk down the front stairs to our waiting cars, I see many more outside, with media flanking the walkways and the roads congested. I grab Pinkie's hand tightly, the two of us remaining quiet until Tony opens our door, and I get her inside and follow her quickly, happy for the small amount of privacy it affords us.

"That was a lovely service," Pinkie says, my hand finding hers again immediately.

"It was." I release a large breath and try to get myself under control.

Grief is a funny thing. For the most part of the service, all I could think of was that this was nearly Pinkie. My heart was in my throat the entire time, and I fought tears, yet not for my mother. But for how grateful I felt that it wasn't Pinkie in that casket that sat before us. I feel guilty for that. She was my mother, and I have grieved for her in my own way. She wasn't a nice woman, and over the past days and weeks, my brothers and I have all spoken and pieced together her history, which has brought new light to who she was and explained why she was so evil.

"She would have been happy with it, I am sure," Pinkie says, looking at me with concern as Tony follows all my brothers' cars, us traveling in a convoy to the private crematorium to say our final private goodbyes.

We now know that the fires were deliberately set. CCTV footage from inside and around the hospital shows us the moment the young blond woman, who is friends with Pinkie's foster brother Steve, walked inside, deliberately lit small fires using alcohol as an accelerant around the hospital, particularly targeting the cardiac ward, before running out and down the street. If it was only one fire, then it would have been easy to contain, causing a small amount of damage and that would be it. But she lit five individual fires, in different areas all in under a few minutes. She had a plan. She was strategic. It was deliberate. That weight sits heavy on Katie. I see the pain in her eyes every time someone talks about the fire, which they often do. It has been a hot topic in the city. In the news, on social media, in general conversation at the coffee shop. She carries it all because she thinks if she hadn't moved here, then none of this would have happened. But Steve was so unhinged that it undoubtably would have been something similar some-where else. She can't carry the weight of other people's actions.

The young blond girl hasn't been seen since. I suspect she has probably moved states, because the results of her actions have been catastrophic for Baltimore.

Baltimore is not the same, and it won't be for a very long time.

I squeeze Pinkie's hand as Tony stops our car behind the gates of the crematorium, and we step out.

The media at the gate looks to be about five lines deep, lights from the cameras flashing almost incessantly. They shout questions, accompanied by low murmurs from the surrounding crowd. I secure my hand around hers and join my brothers, stepping inside the small room. The floor is made of marble with white walls. It is all very clinical and cold apart from the abundance of flowers that adorn the two coffins now sitting at the front.

"How is everyone holding up?" Harrison asks, standing tall as we group together before we take our seats.

"I feel guilty for feeling free of her. I'm happy, yet I can't smile," Tennyson says, not upset by our mother's death. He calls it karma. Willow runs her hand up and down his arm, remaining quiet.

"I'm not sure what I feel. Maybe relief?" Ben says, looking at us all, his girl Em standing close to his side.

"I almost feel grateful, but guilty for feeling grateful," I murmur as we try to keep our voices low.

"What do you mean?" Katie asks, looking up at me from my side as my brothers all look at me in quiet question.

"Grateful that it is her in that box and not you," I say to her, my eyes growing glassy. She leans her head against my arm, hugging me closer, and I pull her in, kissing her hair and smelling her scent, reminding me that she is here.

"What about you?" I ask my eldest brother. He is carrying a lot. Addressing the media, trying to also help the city through it all. His plans for a presidential run have been derailed a little by this activity. He now needs to regroup and reassess, but there is no doubt in my mind that he will run, just not right now.

"I feel..." He trails off, looking around at each of us as the eight of us stand together in a small circle, almost like a football team at halftime, listening to our head coach. "I feel like we are now a solid family. We have each other's backs. We are strong. United. We love and care. We support, we help, we are one." All us brothers nod as the girls remain quiet, and Pinkie tears up. Harrison clears his throat. "Mrs. Wilson and her family are here." He looks briefly behind us. They are all together, sitting on the other side of the room, talking quietly and looking at us.

We have all spoken at length with Dr. Wilson's wife. Apparently, she was the only one well aware of his affair with our mother. It was an agreement in their relationship, she herself having other suitors throughout their married life as well. Although she said the doctor only ever had Mom. Mom was his real love. His first love. Through discussions and looking over our mother's personal belongings, we have uncovered that our mother and father had an arranged marriage as our grandparents wanted to ensure the family business was well looked after. They wanted someone to look the part, and as a kid in medical school, Dr. Wilson was never going to fit the bill. So she married our dad, a successful businessman in his own right. They were

married, businesses were joined, and extreme wealth
followed.

In hindsight, all the dots connecting start to make
sense. Mom and Dad were somewhat respectful of each
other in public, but behind closed doors, they didn't
really spend any time together. Dr. Wilson was her one
true love, my dad merely a chess piece. While never okay,
Mom's behavior is explained a little more. She took
arranged marriages seriously. It was something that ran
in her family. But with our grandparents and Dad gone,
there was no one to help her to manage that kind of tran-
sition for us four boys.

So along with Dr. Wilson's wife, we decided that Mom
and Dr. Wilson would be jointly laid to rest. Finally
giving them the peace together that they always wanted. I
look at Dr. Wilson's wife, sitting quietly at the front. That
woman is as strong as steel. She has four daughters, all
young and beautiful yet completely heartbroken and
dismayed. None of them had any idea their father was in
love with another woman.

Harrison has offered support should they need it. Not
that money will ever be an issue for them, but our door
will always be open to her and her girls, now that their
father is gone.

We follow Harrison down the small aisle and take our
seats on the opposite side of the Wilsons. Small smiles
are exchanged, as well as a few handshakes and cheek
kisses, before a small private ceremony begins, and we
can finally say goodbye.

I look at Katie beside me, feeling an overwhelming
sense of contentment. After this, we plan to go back to

Ben's and talk some more, and afterward, the two of us will visit the hospital, where Katie can sit with Lucy for a while. Poor Lucy has had extensive operations due to her severe leg injury. The stray building material wedged itself into the flesh of her thigh, creating chaos with her femoral artery and ligaments. She has a long and slow road to recovery, and I know Pinkie plans to be by her side for all of it. The two of them have become close, united in the grief and terror that they both endured. I still don't know too much about the girl. Katie tells me she went to the hospital regularly to find Dr. Wilson, and apparently, he was a signatory on her adoption almost thirty years ago. She wanted more information. Information that she now won't get, her history now all erased after losing all her paperwork in the fire and Dr. Wilson being gone. She probably could get some support from an adoption agency, as maybe they have all the information on some type of digital file. But her adoption was close to thirty years ago, and given her current medical issues, I doubt that is something she is really looking at working on for the moment. She doesn't have any family anymore, so Pinkie is helping to fill that gap for her, and I know it helps Pinkie too.

My eyes lock with this pink-haired angel who infiltrated my life, turned it upside down, and then put me right again.

"I love you," I whisper to her, and she looks up at me sharply.

"I love you," she says, and I squeeze her hand and turn back to the front, knowing after today, life will be very different.

EPILOGUE - KATIE

"Okay, keep your eyes closed a little longer..." Eddie says, and when I hear his carefree voice, I smile. It has been about six weeks since the accident, and to say life has completely changed is an understatement. We live together, finding our new normal, and I have been going to counseling regularly to help me move through not only my past trauma, but my recent trauma from the hospital fire as well.

We had a funeral for Mrs. Langford. It was big, elaborate, and a media circus, telling me everything I needed to know about how much these Langford men deal with day in and day out. Eddie has shielded me from a lot. The two of us are still a hot commodity, cameras following us wherever we go. But Willow has been amazing in coaching me and talking me through the various media processes, what to do and say if I am ever caught out.

"Eddie, I have no idea where we are!" I say, giggling, because after spending a lot of time in the apartment together, I know I am now outside. I can feel the fresh air on my face and hear birds chirping. It is so peaceful.

"Okay, two more steps... There. Right, are you ready?" Eddie asks.

"I have no idea. But okay. Let's see the surprise." I'm grinning like a fool. Eddie has been spoiling me so much since I was released from hospital. His promise of diving headfirst into things hasn't wavered. We have already booked a vacation together, talked about what we both want out of the future, and even started the process of becoming foster parents, wanting to make our time with Buddy more formal. He ensures I am eating, resting, and has invited Shelley over a few times, the two of them getting along surprisingly well. He also comes with me every day to the hospital. Taking me to visit Lucy, my new friend, who is still healing from her injuries and is now hopefully on the mend.

"Okay, three, two, one," he says before pulling off my blindfold.

I squint into the bright sun for a moment and shield my eyes.

"Wow. Oh my God!" I look around quickly. "This is where we had our picnic!" My heart explodes as I think about that day, remembering what a good time we had in this very garden. Perfectly manicured grass, gorgeous red roses bordering a path that leads to what I can only describe as a mansion. Taking everything in, the grass goes for as far as my eyes can see, shielded by tall green trees. It is private, tranquil, expensive, and breathtaking. Just like I remember. "What are we doing here?" I ask him with a wide smile, wondering if he has a picnic basket in the car.

"It's home," Eddie says, looking at me expectantly.

"Home? What do you mean?" I step toward a rose-bush and take a sniff. They are beautiful.

"Our new home," he says simply, and I still.

"What?" I ask, looking at him with a furrowed brow. This house is amazing. The kind a girl dreams about. The kind of house I always dreamed about. The kind of dream I always tried to hide, bury deep, knowing my fantasies would never come true.

"I've had my eye on this place for a while. I have always wanted a big house with lots of space. Room to grow. I was already in negotiations when we came here for the picnic. I kind of wanted to show you it then, see what your reaction was. Given you screamed my name in the garden just here, that cemented for me that this was the place for us," he says, looking at me with a hopeful gleam in his eyes. I would like us to grow here together too.

"This is our house? This?" My eyes are almost bugging from my head as I try to wrap my mind around this situation.

"Yes, but if you don't like it—"

I cut him off. "Don't like it? It is freaking amazing!" I say on a breath, still in shock.

"We have talked about starting our life over. Your counselor mentioned a fresh start like this could be good for you, for both of us. There is lots of land to walk around without the media pestering us. If we get Buddy with us, he will have a lot of space to explore. We are neighbors with Ben and Em. Their place is just over the tree line, and we have a little gate we can use to go over and hang out. There is a pool so we can both swim..." Eddie trails off.

"It's perfect. It's beautiful. I'm in shock," I say, my eyes still glued to the beautiful garden. His cell phone chimes then, and he pulls it out and looks at it. I watch his face as he does, and I see it morph into confusion. "What's wrong?" I ask immediately, my heart already thumping in my chest.

"Harrison just texted 911. We need to go to Ben's." He quickly grabs my hand and leads me across the luscious grass. With his fast strut, I run a little to keep up.

"What is this 911?" I ask, a little worried.

"Whenever there is something serious happening in the family, we text each other 911. It is basically code for drop everything you are doing and run immediately to the advised location. We started it a few years ago when Dad died and things got a little hectic. Unfortunately, we have used it a few times since then, mostly because of our mother," he explains, his brow crumpled.

"So there's an emergency?" An all too familiar panic and anxiety fills my chest as we rush through the garden gate, and I am enveloped into a new garden wonderland that I can't admire because my mind is racing.

"Must be," Eddie says, a little unsure. Just then, we spot two cars heading up the picture-perfect driveway and watch as Harrison and Beth rush out of one, and Tennyson and Willow jump out of the other, walking just as quickly as Eddie and I.

"Let's get inside. Ben's waiting," Harrison says, looking serious as he walks straight in. I feel sick.

"Hey, come in." Em hugs me as we walk inside, through to their living room.

"What's going on?" Eddie asks as he stays standing, and I sit with the girls on the sofa and hold my breath. Harrison paces, the other brothers looking totally confused.

"I got a call from the hospital blood bank," Harrison says, looking a little pale.

"What happened?" Ben asks, stepping forward.

"They called about the donation we made back at the time of the hospital fire," Harrison says, his eyes quickly flicking to me. My chest feels heavy, and I can barely breathe.

"What about it? Are you sick? Was there something wrong with your blood?" Tennyson asks, stepping forward, and all the boys frown.

"No. We are all healthy." He looks like he is gathering his thoughts.

"Well, spit it out," Eddie says as we all wait on tenterhooks.

"It appears that our blood type is a match for one of the severely injured." We all look at him, confused.

"Of course it was. We are AB negative, so that means we are super rare. That is why we gave extra, for that other patient who needed it," Tennyson says, none of us sure of where this is headed.

"No, I mean, genetically. They did a genetic test. Apparently, it is a research procedure, and when we signed up to donate, we all ticked that box. The injured patient from the fire is a complete match. Genetically," Harrison explains.

"I don't understand," Tennyson says, looking at everyone in confusion.

"What he is trying to say is..." Beth says, standing, taking over for Harrison, who appears to be struggling with the information. "Your blood is a thirty-two percent match with the patient, which means you have a half-sibling."

"Excuse me?" Ben says, gaping at Beth like she is crazy.

"We have a half-sibling, so one of our parents had a baby without the other," Harrison says. "I got notified, looked over some paperwork, and it appears to be correct." He releases a heavy sigh, appearing exhausted as he takes a seat.

"There are more of you?" I ask, bewildered.

"Wow, if this gets out, it is going to explode," Willow says, her eyes wide, obviously thinking of the media impact.

"So we have another brother?" Tennyson asks, still confused.

"Or sister," Beth says, a small smile on her face.

"Wow, a sister..." Eddie says, looking at me, as his face relaxes slightly, his eyes widening in awe.

"I mean, it is a shock, but wow, another Langford?" Em says, her smile passive but supportive.

"Well, who is it? Was it Mom or Dad?" Ben asks, and we all look at Harrison for the answers.

"I don't know anything about the patient. They can't tell us because of patient confidentiality. But we can put paperwork through to request information, and if the patient agrees, we can meet up and talk and figure out how this all came about," he says, and I lean back.

"Can I ask a question?" I ask, looking at everyone in the room.

"Of course," Eddie encourages.

"Is there ever a dull moment in this family?" I ask, a small smile dancing on my lips, because I already know the answer. This family is larger than life; their hearts are massive, and their bank balances are huge. This is their normal.

"No, never." Beth huffs a laugh, and I laugh with her. Soon, we are all smiling and laughing as the boys start discussing how to move forward, all of them keen to meet their new sibling and find out who it is.

Over all the commotion, Eddie looks at me, and I smile. The panic I felt earlier is now all gone, the joys of being around everyone soothing for my soul.

"So how about it? Want to move next door? Start our new life?" he asks, sliding up to me, as his family all start talking over one another in shock and excitement.

"Let's do it."

WANT to know what Eddie and Pinkie are up to now? Download a bonus epilogue to get a glimpse into their future here.

. . .

To READ the next instalment of the Langford family, and learn about the new sibling and get their story, download The Bossy Billionaire here!

ALSO BY SAMANTHA SKYE

My Fight

My Chance

Boston Billionaires

ABOUT THE AUTHOR

Samantha Skye is an international bestselling author. A country kid turned city slicker, she writes spicy and suspenseful contemporary romance novels that leave you hot under the collar and on the edge of your seat.

Samantha lives in Melbourne, Australia and when she's not plotting her next novel, she can be found travelling, drinking margaritas and enjoying a sunset or a stargaze somewhere.

To join in the conversation join Skye's The Limit Facebook group here;
https://www.facebook.com/groups/skyesthelimit books

www.ingramcontent.com/pod-product-compliance
Lightning Source LLC
Chambersburg PA
CBHW070205120726
47909CB00001B/257